I0738089

THE GHOST REVOLVER

THE GHOST REVOLVER

A Mick Priest novel

WYATT HARVEY

terebinth tree publications

The Ghost Revolver

Copyright © 2021 by Wyatt Harvey. All rights reserved.

No part of this publication may be reproduced, stored in a retrieval system or transmitted in any way by any means, electronic, mechanical, photocopy, recording or otherwise without the prior permission of the author, except as provided by USA copyright law.
This novel is a work of fiction. Any similarity to persons living or dead is purely coincidental and probably very entertaining, delightful and stimulating. Enjoy.

Published by Terebinth Tree Publications
"A place of true inspiration."
Terebinth Tree is committed to publishing truly inspired, uplifting works of literature. It draws its name and fundamental belief from the Scriptures,
Genesis 18:1
"Then the LORD appeared to him by the terebinth trees of Mamre..."
It was near those trees that God appeared to Abraham and it was there Abraham would be given great promise and inspiration.
Book Design Copyright © 2021 Interior, Layout, Cover by Wyatt Harvey

---

Published in the United States of America

The New Testament Book of

Matthew, a Gospel of Jesus Christ

Chapter 23 Verse 37

O Jerusalem, Jerusalem,
thou that killest the prophets,
and stonest them which are sent unto thee,
how often would I have gathered thy children
together,
even as a hen gathereth
her chickens under her wings,
and ye would not!

Despite the things the Hebrew children did to violate their relationship with God, Jesus reminds them how God had been hoping for their return to His love. How often He would have gathered them together to love and protect them.

Jesus sends that message to us today. No matter what we have done, it is God's desire that none should perish, none should die a spiritual death. He invites all to receive His forgiveness, mercy and love. He sees us as His children and He wants all of us to come home to Him.

Come home today. You will never regret it.

to my family
my friends
my acquaintances
my confidants

If you see a name that resembles yours or a character with your
characteristics…
…it is a coincidence, he says, with a wicked grin...

for Tara

my best friend
my lover
my counsel
my partner
my romantic heart
my longing

my wife

No matter the name you wear on the page…
…you inspire the best of them.

"Fire's goin' out. Gonna get cold. Better get up some wood."

The little man fidgeted nervously. He stepped from one dusty boot to another, wringing gloved hands. In the flickering light of the campfire, his eyes were hard to see though he turned them skyward. The agitated individual watched the full moon as if he were watching a clock.

"Clinton, that's the third time you done said that," another man said.

Flat on his back on a wool bedroll, head propped up on a downed limb and covered by his hat, he gestured for the first man, Clinton, to go away.

"You wanna go pick up sticks, go. But quit yer yammerin' 'bout it."

"Yeah, yeah, I guess," Clinton said. "I just...ya know, we got that posse ridin' after us...it's got me all worried. My hair's standin' up like an ornery ol' cat's."

"Oh, no foolin'?" the resting cowboy said. His sarcasm was as disdainful as his expression beneath the dusty hat. "Never woulda knowed it."

"Easy, Kent," a third man warned. "A little worry keeps ya livin'. Go on, get that wood, Clinton. An' you get first watch. Stay awake with your fire."

He sat with his back to a rocky formation, hat pulled down to shade his eyes. The man was difficult to see, even in the firelight, dressed in all black. His bone handled, silver revolvers glinted brightly enough, however, as he cleaned them, readying them for reloading.

Clinton rubbed at the scruff of his gaunt, unshaven face then nodded. Hesitantly, he finally decided to leave the firelight, a last glance thrown to the moon. His short, wiry frame skittered away into the underbrush and the nightshade as if dangled by a puppeteer's strings.

The man in black stared after him for a long moment.

Even for Otis Clinton, the behavior was extreme. The small man was always nervous but he seemed downright afraid of something, staring at the moon the whole night.

In the distance, something bayed wildly at that moon, proving Clinton was not the only one watching it. The horses shifted about, side to side, tugging at their tethers, testing them.

The man on the bedroll, Ben Kent, the gray in his stubble proven tracks of a lot of years, snorted. That was his usual prelude to a deep snore. The other man finished reloading his revolvers then slowly pushed his hat up with a single thumb. There was a change in the air, in the night itself, and he could feel it. The hair on his neck rose like the hair Clinton had been chattering on about. He eased the hammer back on one of his silver hand cannons, the clicks inside the Colt Navy the only sounds around them besides the steady snore of his partner.

Suddenly, the night came alive with voices and shouting. Into the ring of firelight charged a handful of men, guns already in their hands. The booms of black powder bellowed to life and sparks flared from the rocky landscape, bullets singing the mournful whine of ricochets.

The raiders were more concerned with the element of surprise than the discipline of aim, disciples of their quantity of shots rather than apostles of accuracy.

The horses tore their tethers from the light undergrowth to which they were tied and bolted.

The man in black never even stood. He fanned the hammer on his pistol and dropped the first three men to appear. Turning to his right, he thumbed the hammer and fired twice more and put two more men flat on the ground. Five men lay deathly still just that fast; the only thing on them still moving was the campfire's reflection on their shiny badges.

The man from the bedroll whipped up to his feet with a shotgun in hand. He fired, unloading both barrels at a newcomer, nearly blowing the man in two. He then tore his revolver free of his leg holster and got off a shot at another man. He never got the hammer levered back for a second time, however, and was shot down.

The man in black rose to his feet and popped off his last shot, killing the last invader. His partner shot dead, his associate, Clinton, vanished before the fight and all of the men in the posse dead, the gunman in black was alone. Only the taste and smell of black powder, swirling about the camp like a gray ghost, remained with him.

"Clinton!" shouted the man with silver revolvers. "Clinton, I know what you did! Run, little man! Run as far and as fast as you can! Even when I'm a ghost I'll be huntin' you and one day you'll see these revolvers and you'll know it's your time!"

The man wiped spittle from his rock hard jaw and swore bitterly.

"An' my work won't never stop, Clinton! As long as I got breath and as long as I can pass these *judges* on to other men..."

He stared at the silver revolvers. The etching down their forms, the bone handles and his own, shaking hands spoke to him. They spoke of vengeance...and killing.

The night air caressed me, a sensation both cool and crisp. It evoked an image in the mind, a thing gentle but sharp, dragging its fingernails across everything over which it breezed. It was the time of night that defied clarity. The hour whispered in my ear with descriptions not quite right, discrepancies on which I could not quite put a finger. Intangible, in a word...like the hour itself.

The starlight and moonlight radiated with an odd glow. They streamed in through the french doors that led to the balcony but had none of its natural, silvery white shine. The room flooded with a cold, bluish radiance new to me. My body shivered more from the look of it than the cool of the night.

She sashayed into view as if a creature purely nocturnal, as if born of the bluish glow of the heavens. Her flowing, lithe shape materialized slowly as she approached. A thin, gossamer dress, spun from thigh length, ivory dream webbing, added to her weightless look as she drifted, perhaps floated, toward me. It was as if the room were some underwater kingdom, as if she were a siren from the deep.

"Mr. Priest," her voice drew me. "Trouble sleeping?"

Full, plum lips pulled at the corners, a playful tug at work on them. Her pixie face, as beautiful as an angel, angled slightly, high cheeks and pointed chin building the classic heart shape. Bright, glowing green eyes boldly sought my own, pushing, pressing into them, trying to see inside me. I could not look away, caught in them. It was not until her flame red, ethereal hair floated about her and a lock of wavy crimson came between us, that our stare was broken.

"What are you doing in here?" I asked, my thoughts finally free.

I knew the woman by sight. She did not belong in my bedroom. A famed actress I had never met, she did not even belong in my house. Of course, my bedroom, my house, seemed foreign to in and of themselves. Nevertheless, Johanna Crimson was in what I perceived to be my room and I had neither heard nor seen a door open.

Her sly smile curled thick lips as she tamed her mask of hair.

"In here...out there...what really is the difference? There isn't one...if I'm neither in here nor out there..."

She ran a fingernail horizontally across her chin. The faintest hint of a beauty mark was there.

My wife will be able to explain the difference if she finds you in here, I thought to myself.

At least, I had thought I was only musing to myself. It was odd because she giggled and nibbled at her fingernail, staring into me, as if reacting to my thoughts. It seemed as thought she had heard my silence.

"Not to worry, Mr. Priest," she answered my thoughts. "I won't be here very long...if I'm here at all..."

I tried to comment but it was hard to think, harder to form cohesive conversation.

"Ms. Crimson-"

Thunder crashed violently and shook the foundations of the house. She threw both arms out to her sides with the ominous boom and, as if she controlled them, the two doors to the balcony blew open. A raging wind ripped through them and into the room, overturning tables and blowing away bed covers. The sound, a deafening rush, almost hid her words.

"Am I here at all?" she called, barely audible to me.

She arched her neck backward as her blood red hair masked her completely.

The nocturnal glow darkened from a soft, faint blue to a deeper, more threatening violet. The new hue seemed to envelope her and, incredibly, it lifted her up from the floor. She shook where she hovered, suspended in the storm.

"Am I here? Where am I?" she howled, the voice of a whirlwind.

I had both hands up before my face, trying to see into the gale, trying to peer beyond the the rage of a tempest.

"Who...am...I?" she roared and the thunder shook the earth.

I toppled backward in the storm.

My eyes popped open with a start where I was alone in my bed. I wore very little, not even intertwined with the gray, silken sheets. Regardless, a cold, anxious sweat adorned my bare skin in a glistening sheen.

"Mick, can you get the door?" Sarah shouted from our master bath.

The sound of the shower and its rhythmic, pulsating water spoke in a voice not unlike that of the rainstorm from the manic dream. Thick, rolling and insistent. Demanding. Foreboding.

The doorbell sounded again and Sarah shouted for a second time. "Mick, baby, the door!"

Uneasiness rode the air itself. Electricity arced invisibly along my senses. Warm, summer wind blew heat in from the open balcony doors and lush drapes of velvet blew to life in the room, puffed like a ship's sails. They lifted ethereally like those from the dream.

I pushed out of the bed, blinking a lot and rubbing my eyes. I was caught somewhere in between the sleep from which I had been roused and the dream I worried was closer to reality. Sarah and I had slept late, taking advantage of the start of our three day weekend. Nothing was on our scopes other than a getaway to the Outer Banks. Just sun and sand, shaking out the old beach blanket...

...then figuring out the odd, singular nightmare...

I managed to slide into my pants without the knee brace for my left knee. I had never had its injuries properly addressed. Once I limped to the front door of the apartment, however, I already regretted my haste. The knee pain bit into me, piercing me.

I reached the door while fussing at myself for the bad move. A voice outside argued with someone else. The voice was very familiar, distinctive and easily recognizable. I jerked open the door without even looking through the peep hole.

"Whoa, hey," James Wyatt said.

"What?"

Looking me up and down, his phone in his hand, he asked, "You can't put on clothes before you open a door?"

"I have on pants," I said and limped away from him.

"Congratulations," he said, following me inside and shutting the door. He spoke back into his cell phone. "What? No, he's got on pants. Well, I don't know. Why? Nope. You need to keep your mind outta the gutter. He's married. And you are, too, by the way. To me."

I plopped onto the mocha leather couch and pulled a Colt 10mm out of my waistband holster. The small of my back appreciated the relief.

"First, a nightmare. Now, this," I said quietly.

"Look, I gotta go. Yeah, love you, too."

He stuffed the telephone into his pocket and looked around. Finding a nearby chair in matching materials, my long time friend felt it was too far away from me, apparently. He pulled it out of place, sliding it several feet closer to my end of the couch. After dropping into it and looking around again, he sat down and leaned forward, arms propped over his legs.

"So, you coming and opening the door without looking to see who's there? That's not like you."

I replied, "I knew who it was, James. I heard your voice before I ever reached the door. Who was asking what I was wearing, anyway?"

"Who else? My old lady. She sends her love."

"Back at her," I said.

"You ever think of answering your phone?" he blitzed me.

"About to enjoy a getaway, alone with Sarah, nothing but quiet and privacy for a few days? What about that says 'cell phone' to you?" I asked with a wink.

Then I pointed at the suitcases I knew he had noticed by the door.

He let his hands dangle loosely after a quick nod toward the luggage.

"I hear ya," he allowed, though regretfully.

I asked, "What does that mean? The tone, not the words. I know what the words mean. I also know the tone doesn't match."

The worry in his nearly black eyes finally impressed me. His sober concern gave me pause. James Wyatt was rarely serious and his lack of banter and nonsense left me guarded.

"I know you got plans, Mick, but I need a hand with-"

"Nope."

"Just hear me out," he pressured. "It's a case-"

"James, I'm not working a case, right now. I'm about to go for a long weekend retreat, just me and Sarah-"

"What's going on?" Sarah questioned, walking into the living room.

Her brown and blonde hair stuck to her bronze skin. The long, wavy tresses still dripped, a thick towel still in her hand. Sarah had dressed for the outside heat of the summer day. Thin spaghetti straps held up a bright teal top and a sarong offered brilliant greens below it.

James winked, saying, "Mornin', Sarah. You goin' out?"

"Well, James, I am. I suppose my 'going out' bag gave me away," she teased, wagging her small clutch about. "That's not exactly an answer, though. Since you live hours away from here, you didn't tell us you were coming and you have that teenage paranoia look in those black eyes of yours, I ask again; what's going on?"

James Wyatt cut his eyes to me.

"Yeah, she's a detective, too," I said with a shrug.

"I got this serious case-" he began.

"Nope."

"Sarah, hear me out-"

"I tried to tell him," I said to my wife, rolling James under the bus.

"No, James," she reiterated.

Her tone was not unkind. It did, however, leave no room for uncertainty. She bore no hesitation and no shadow of compromise. Sarah and I wanted our little getaway. There was little that could change that.

"I'm up against a big wall and I-" James said urgently.

"It's a 'no' from me," she answered while he was still talking.

"-really, really need a partner I can trust-"

"And a 'no' on my end," I added, knowing there was terribly little he could say that would change it.

"-cause I'm bodyguardin' a celebrity right now, a big time, 'A list' level star, and she's got a contract out on her just as big," he muttered.

The breath caught in my throat. My chest tightened. My ears rang. There was so little he could say to change my mind...

"Johanna *Velvet Edge* Crimson," he breathed out softly, then leaned his head back.

There it was. Exactly what he would have had to say. The dream was so much more than a dream, after all.

Sarah and I locked eyes. She knew something weighed on me.

"She's big time," Sarah admitted, still looking at me. "A contract out on her life? Just as major as her fame? That would have to be serious..."

"Deathly serious," he said. "She gets crackpot stuff all the time, like most celebrities, but not like this."

"Like this?" I asked, still looking into Sarah's eyes.

I swallowed but my mouth and throat were so dry it felt as if I were choking down cotton.

"She got some pretty convincing hate mail, followed by a detailed account of her contacts, movements, habits, properties-"

"We get it," my wife interrupted him.

"Each one from the source has a tag line. *Your destiny lies with the Ghost Revolver*," he said slyly. "That's code for something, ya'll."

"That's a term I've heard before, a term for assassins," I said, finally turning my eyes back to my friend.

"Yep. But that ain't all, bud. Ghost Revolver isn't just a typical, blanket code for a hitman anymore. There's a serious specialist out there, one of the deadliest exterminators to ever work. Calls himself *the* Ghost Revolver. Claims to be a real ghost, the same revolver who's been workin' under that name since back in the old west. Layin' claim to a history hundreds of years long, tryin' to be all spooky and ghosty, that don't impress me. The recent record? That's a different story."

Getting riled, Sarah's Spanish lilt was heavy.

"I've heard this *asesino's* name on the wind! Like, officially, through the Agency! This could be trouble!"

"James, Sarah," I calmed, my voice an even tone.

"James can't sit and wait for that *payaso* to move!" Sarah shouted.

"She gets it," he said to me, pointing to Sarah.

"Believe me, I get it, too," I said.

"What do you know?" Sarah asked him.

"Turns out, her in house pisto laro says-"

"*Pistolero,*" Sarah corrected my buddy's terrible Spanish.

"Tomato, tobacco," he said with a shrug. "Either way, he says she's been havin' death threats since *Velvet Edge 3*, her last movie done in Wilmington. The film and her return scheduling for local guest shots and whatnot seems to have set off this Revolver thing. He thinks this is real trouble, not a prank or a fake or-"

"I'm afraid he's right," I said. "I'm convinced he's right."

"Have you had *un sueño*?" Sarah abruptly asked, spinning on me.

"What's a zwennyo?" James Wyatt asked in the worst Spanish mimicry believable.

"A dream," I said, once again only looking into Sarah's eyes.

"I knew it," Sarah snapped, folding her arms just under her bosom.

"Oh, you mean like one of 'the dreams', I get it," James nodded.

A light of recollection went off in his eyes. He was one of a very select few who knew of the dreams and visions given me by God. Dreams where I saw the dead, visions where they communicated with me and pointed me toward truths too elusive for the living. I was never really sure he believed me about any of it but he respected me and kept it confidential, unwilling to brand me crazy.

"Did the dream have an animal in it?" James asked.

"What?" I answered hesitantly.

"My grandfather believed the animal in a dream could identify what the dream was really about. Went a long way toward understanding or deciphering a dream."

"Well?" Sarah interrogated. "Animal or not?"

"Just relax," I eased. "No animal."

"My grandfather used to say monsters in our dreams were a part of us, some unconscious part of us speaking to our consciousness. Was there any kind of monster that-"

"James, your grandfather also used to say he had an albino grizzly bear in his house," I said.

"In his defense-" James started.

"It was a Pomeranian, James," I interrupted. "A very little, tan Pomeranian."

"Like I was saying," James retorted, "that thing was vicious. Grizzly vicious."

Sarah could not help grinning and even breaking into a light giggle.

"I hated that dog," James said finally, staring off into space.

"What did you dream?" Sarah asked me.

I took her extended hand and led her around to sit beside me.

"About the dream...I think she was dead, James."

Then I explained the dream to both of them. James wiped sweating palms on his jeans and excused himself to make a call, his face pale.

I took that time to consider things, listening to Sarah as she encouraged me. I touched my cross and prayed thanks to the Lord Jesus, knowing I was never without God's love and presence. No matter the case at hand or the lack of one, I knew Jesus Christ walked with me.

James Wyatt nodded furtively when he came back into the room.

"Prayin' is good. We need to do a lot of that."

"Is she..." Sarah started.

"She's alive," James said. "I talked to Gibson, her security lead. He says she's fine. For now. She won't turn down her next appearance at that writers' gala, though. She refuses to be intimidated."

"I'm involved," I said. "The dream decided it; God decided this. Looks like our vacation will be a working one."

"I'm ready," Sarah assured. "When you're called, you answer. That's who you are. The man I love."

"Where's this gala?" I asked James.

"Right here in North Carolina," he said. "Shadow Mountain. And look at it this way; this killer ain't got a chance against all of us, Mick."

"I sure hope not," Sarah said.

"And, hey, what's the chances, right?" James continued. "You get drug into a case an' it's at a writers' gala. You, a writer, yourself."

"Yeah, but don't remind me," I said with a sigh. "I may love the written word but it means I have to spend my vacation with you, too."

Sarah popped my shoulder playfully.

James, however, had a very thoughtful look on his face.

"James?" Sarah asked, concerned. "What is it? Mick's only playing."

He took a long moment of introspection and sighed.

"Nah, it ain't Mick. I was just thinkin'. That Pomeranian sure was vicious."

The brass bands around the old wooden chest were antique, like the rest of the large container. It spoke of a time long gone, when travelers kept clothing and traveling materials in those old steamer trunks, as they were called, instead of soft shelled luggage. The brass was plain, bearing no engraving, no etching in its surface. It contrasted the ornately carved, though thin, wood of the chest. The carrier was old and beautiful, just not as beautiful as the item atop everything else within it.

Black gloved hands lifted a very aged, delicate wooden box from the old trunk. Elaborately carved, the darkened cherry tones of the wood held time at bay but it showed the passage and the weathering. Small points had split. Spots had faded, while others had dulled, losing the luster it once held. Intricate, silver filigree bound the corners of the rectangular base and the lid, as well, and the designs matched the engraving on the hinges and the tiny clasp holding it closed.

Gentle fingers unfastened the clasp and lifted the lid.

Inside the case rested two 1800s black powder revolvers, cast with lovely, graven silver bodies and white bone handles that had yellowed somewhat with time. With them were lead molds, paper casings and powder for making antiquated bullets, all placed on a bed of blue silk.

The gloved fingers traced part of the design adorned, metal curves of the revolvers. The touch was intimate, almost sensual. At the very least, it was intent.

*"I should be very much obliged if you would slip your revolver into your pocket...*Sir Arthur Conan Doyle, your masterful Sherlock Holmes never had a better thought than that one..."

The whisper faded as the lid to the pistol case slowly closed.

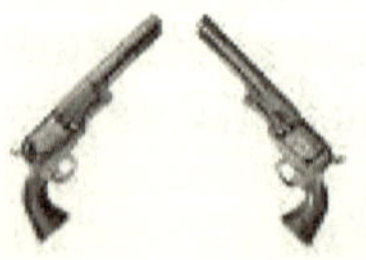

CHAPTER ONE

"They will come by air, yes," a distinguished, mature man announced in exasperation. "We have a dual helipad and a helicopter of our own for a reason. I have told you all multiple times that the roadways on this mountain are more dirt trails than anything. Still, vehicular limitations aside, our helicopter will be delivering guests and the travel helicopters will, no doubt, be doing the same, likely at the same time. Please pay attention at all times and be ready and available to porter the guests from the landing pads, the loading areas and so on. I do not want them wandering. They are to get the five star treatment here with no mistakes."

He clasped white gloved hands behind his back.

"We're not runnin' on a real big staff right now, Jenkins. Wanna share how we can cover all the guests, the arrival locations and the baggage?"

The tall, graying gentleman in the suit and tails lifted his nose even higher and stared at the very distant, cathedral ceiling. He clenched his jaw before responding to the much younger man's query.

"Mr. Kent, as you know, there is much to be done. I suggest you wait, listen until you are told what to do then go and do that and only that and let decision makers make the decisions."

He then locked his dark eyes on the younger man, tilted his face downward and blinked. Once. He waited until the other man was about to reply and spoke again, his voice lower, rumbling.

"And never call me Jenkins again."

For whatever reason, the older man suddenly seemed far more imposing, almost intimidating. The low voice seemed to vibrate the very marble of the flooring. That, in turn, somehow managed to draw attention to his broad shoulders and the build beneath his formal attire.

The younger man, his bright shock of red hair unkempt, fell silent.

"It is *Mr.* Jenkins to all of you, offered with the same respect I extend to each of you. Now," he continued, not waiting for a response, "gentlemen, you will act as escorts, guides and porters, taking guest arrivals in turn. Ladies, you will be handling initial registration, tablets in hand, while guests wait."

The six young men and three young women waited, saying nothing.

"Mr. Pool, you will team with Mr. Barr. Ms. Prince, you will act in tandem, registering and entertaining arrivals as they wait. In like fashion, Mr. Grey and Mr. Raynor will work with Ms. Singleton. Mr. Ayers and Mr. Kent," he said, his voice somewhat disdainful, "you will work with Ms. Griffin. Let's begin and remember: five star service."

No one moved, eyes fixed on the distinguished gentleman.

"Now," he growled lowly.

In a nervous clump the little band departed, a young Mr. Kent casting wary glances over his shoulder. Gesturing at him with an open palm, Jenkins gave a last, exacerbated directive.

"Do you not have a comb, Mr. Kent? Tame your hair, young man."

Kent was the last to exit, all the while raking fingers through his hair.

"Summer hirelings," the formal man muttered, hands clasped behind his back again. "Khakis and polo shirts will be the death of me."

"You've already deployed the soldiers?" a lofty voice asked.

Jenkins turned to see a shapely silhouette strut across the marble threshold, coming in from the dining hall. The shape became clear quickly and he recognized the lovely lady in her stride.

"Ms. Clark," he greeted and nodded, almost providing a bow in gesture. "I have, indeed."

The vivid scarlet wrapping her from neck to knee set the observing eye afire. Thick chocolate tresses crowned her.

"You weren't too hard on them?" she asked, big eyes concerned, a hint of a smile on her lips. "They're just college kids, you know. Not all of them are even interns in the industry."

"What industry might that be, Ms. Clark? The 'greed and weed' movement?" he asked.

She could not resist laughing but shook her head.

"You're bad. They're all just young-"

"No, ma'am. You are young, not much older than most of them. I'm afraid age is no excuse."

She sighed and put a long nailed hand on his arm.

"They're temporary," she comforted, her smile telling.

"Words bringing life to my very heart," he said, his handsome face a mask of disdain.

"Other than our young temps, are we ready to meet the guests?"

"Professional pens and their scribbling? Inking the future on the pages of their careers?" Jenkins asked in grandiose nature then gestured upstairs. "The writers' rooms are in final preparation now."

"What about Grip? Mr. Bridger? Is his security ready?" she asked.

"He is making the final rounds and has already sent the rest of his team home. He plans to stay this weekend himself and watch over his department, as he is the Director of Security. With the celebrity attendance, he thought it best to remain. So he says, mind you. I believe the real truth is that our security supervisor plans to personally keep watch over young Ms. Clayborne, not our guests," the man said, speaking of their staff helicopter pilot.

"What about Tye? Mr. Richter?" she cooed, leaning onto his arm, locking eyes with him. To do so, she was looking upward at a sharp angle. His significant height dwarfed her.

"Our Director of Engineering sent his crew home and is staying to watch over all the facility operations himself; electrical, mechanical, digital, what have you."

"He's dedicated."

Jenkins huffed. A tug of a grin at his lips, the first crack in his rigid veneer, belied his stone demeanor.

"I suspect Mr. Richter, like Mr. Bridger, is staying to watch over some*one*, not a department."

"Jenkins, that's enough of that," she said, blushing.

"Indeed, Ms. Clark," he allowed, stifling his grin.

"Jenkins, you always insist I call you by name, no prefix, no title."

"You are the director, ma'am," he retorted.

"The least you can do is call me Cassie."

"Absolutely not-" he began, his face surprised.

"At the very least, call me Cassandra!" she chimed.

"No, that would be too-"

"Cassandra, or I go back to calling you Mr. Jenkins like the temps," she warned.

He locked his jaw, his face pained.

"I could just call you Reggie, or Bard," she said airily, calling out the names from his employment file.

"Cassandra it is," he added almost instantly.

The man bore no love for his given names. Reginald Bard Jenkins he gladly exchanged for just Jenkins on any given day.

"Remember that!" she ordered. "Now, I have to go upstairs and check behind housekeeping. It's time to send the rest of them off. I don't understand some of these 'exclusive privacy' bookings we get. Wanting an almost invisible, bare bones staff? That's not luxury service."

"Nor in my opinion," he said with raised eyebrows. "I do hope we will be spared another event such as last month's 'Escape Room Extravaganza' and the illustrious 'Motel Murder' weekend..." he trailed, shivering from the word motel.

"I'm sure we won't have a lot of those," she said. "And this one, except for the request of having as little staff as possible, should be a normal convention."

"Blessings from on High."

"Let's cross our fingers, though...just in case."

With that, she spun her high heels on a dime and strolled away from the older man. She took one of two elaborate, plushly carpeted staircases curling up the far walls at both ends of the room.

He watched her go affectionately, a soft smile on his face.

"Yes, ma'am," he said.

One hundred acres of manicured, tended landscape sprawled out in the middle of a literal wilderness. On the side of Shadow Mountain, sitting in distant view of Mount Pisgah, the Horse and Heraldry Resort dared to defy nature. Dense forestry and rocky formations, all part of some of the wildest span of the Blue Ridge Mountains, framed in the high powered, luxury getaway but did not encroach upon it. Nature was kindly asked to stay back, beyond the ten foot cedar fencing encompassing the properties, beyond the one hundred acre boundaries.

Neighbors near and far were amazing elements of natural beauty. The Mount Pisgah National Forest, Looking Glass Falls and famed Table Rock made up just a handful. Further out were the wilds of the Shining Rock Wilderness and well known Cold Mountain. Mount Mitchell peaked in the north and far, far to the west were even more mountains, the Great Smoky Mountains. The wild surrounded the Horse and Heraldry Resort on all sides.

At least a major thoroughfare wound up Shadow Mountain and brought travel to the sights, even if from a distance. Smaller roads, trails, ruts and lanes broke from it to creep closer to attractions and locations of interest. The major highway was more than forty miles from Asheville, North Carolina, and the Asheville Regional Airport.

The closest a major passage came to Horse and Heraldry Resort was the exit that broke from the highway for Shadow Walker Bridge. That bridge spanned a gap called Nightshade Pass. A few miles of privately paved passage would then find the resort's gated entrances.

In the dead center of the somewhat square shaped property stood a truly massive structure. It was designed purposely to resemble a tremendous, four story horse barn. Stark white covered the exterior with its black window shutters and vivid red gutters and drains. Decks, forming long, connected balconies on the east and west sides of the resort, perched outside the second, third and fourth stories, formed with black planks for the decking and white for the banisters and railings.

French double doors dotted the walls along the top three floors at regular intervals, marking the placement of lavish rooms. Five stars had been given by critics and fans alike, honoring the extravagance of the rooms. The bottom floor had stable doors facing outward instead of French doors and the residents were horses.

The outside mask may have been *HGTV* chic but the interior leaped right out of *Popular Science* meets *Modern Castles and Chateaus*. High tech gothic had been born in the mountains of North Carolina.

Reginald Bard Jenkins stood on one of the balcony outcroppings, regarding a silver pocket watch. Abruptly, he clicked it closed and gestured at the brilliant sky.

"Now...let the weekend begin."

The timing was perfect. For a moment, he could have been a wizard calling a dragon to his fortress.

On cue, a nigh silent, sleek helicopter swept right into view. It soared out of obscured sight, clearing the forest and whipping over the locale, then buzzed low over four major paved areas. It passed by them all and slowed for a landing pad lit on all sides with marker lights. Dusk was approaching and the timed, fire red lights kept a watchful vigil on the hour, resembling the torches of a bygone era. The landing gear dropped like talons beneath a great, whispering predator and it sat down, claws grabbing concrete.

Polo shirts and khakis rushed from the nearby hangar and its lobby to meet the AirShip ACH170, heads bowed against the wind shear. A wooden facade covered the metal and concrete building so that the functionality of the building remained beneath the rustic, ship lap planks on its exterior. The people milling about had something besides decor on their minds, of course, as they bolted from the huge hangar structure to meet guests as they arrived.

One man walked along behind them in a perfect calm, hand at his earpiece, eyes hidden behind coal black Costa sunglasses. He was pale, probably in need of protection from the sun for his skin as much as his eyes. Even in a black suit coat his build was obvious. Short, blonde hair spiked upward over his head and popped back into place as quickly as he wiped over it.

"Okay, everybody on deck," he spoke, holding the earpiece. "I'm on our resort bird, like always, personally. You know who it's bringing. Ayers, Kent, Ms. Griffin, ya'll work with me. The rest of you, get ready for the others. We know more guests are coming in on those two airport birds that are still airborne. Stay ready."

He had hardly released his earpiece when he met the first guest. That man stepped clear of the chopper's passenger cargo door with an outstretched hand.

The security specialist took his hand with a smile.

"Welcome to Horse and Heraldry Resort. My name is-"

"Nice boots," the guest interjected. "Ariats?"

"Durangos," the much younger man replied quizzically.

The other man, a full head of white hair above laser blue eyes, wore around sixty years of life under his soft, gray sports jacket, black polo shirt and gray cargo pants. He hefted one leg and tugged at the pants, showing the Director of Security his boots.

"Carhartt," he said, nodding sharply. "Don't get any better. I mean, company's been around since 1889. You gotta figure they got stuff right by now."

Kent went around them, pushing a baggage cart, with Ayers close behind, doing the same. A a silver briefcase was on top of the second load. The Carhartt man's eyes followed them, squinting.

"Like I was saying, I'm Grip-" the resort man began one more time.

"Falgrip 'Grip' Bridger, Director of Security. Red haired kid with our bags is Jeffery Kent, a summer temporary you guys hired for the rush, and his partner is Beau Ayers," the older man said, eyes narrowed into a keen, razor sharp awareness. Noting the younger man's surprise, he thumbed over his shoulder and added, "Pretty young lady with the electronic clipboard is Shaye Griffin. Yeah, I know everybody with feet on these grounds this week. Employees, guests, temps, all of 'em. It's my job, Grip, and I might just be the very best at what I do. I'm not as old as Carhartt but I'm just as reliable."

"Wow," Bridger said, allowing an impressed smile etch his face. "What do you do, Mr..."

"His name is Mark Gibson. He is, among other things, my protector."

The voice was velvet. Just inside the passenger bay, sitting with shapely, bare legs protruding through the open door, a woman extended one gloved hand while brushing back thick, red hair with the other.

Her vibrant, violet dress, split at the outside of both legs from ankle to hip, clung to her curves like a second skin. Deep purple heels, at least four inches high, matched the small clutch that hung over her shoulder and her satin gloves. The dress rose all the way up around her neck but had no sleeves.

"My name is-"

"Wow," Bridger breathed out unintentionally. "I mean...wow..."

Mark Gibson took the woman's hand and led her to her feet.

"No, that would be a silly name," she said playfully.

She tilted her head to one side, smiled coyly and pulled off her sunglasses. Brilliant green eyes smoldered with a fire like a jade dragon's. Pink lips pursed a bit then returned to the smile.

"My name is-" she began again, taking a deep breath, her figure straining against the dress.

"You're Johanna Crimson," Bridger spat. "I mean, *the* Johanna Crimson. I've seen all your movies...Deepest Winter, Hearts in Flames, Red Means Go, Shadowstar, Blind Journey-"

She allowed herself a giggle then reigned it in, replacing the sweetness with a sultry stare. She bit at her lower lip and hummed softly.

"So, you're a fan," she concluded in a tease.

"Who isn't a fan?" Gibson interrupted with a chuckle. "Everywhere you go people like young Grip go brain-dead and start short circuiting. Poor guy would burst into flames if you kissed him."

"W-what? I didn't...what?" Bridger stammered.

She giggled again and angled her head downward, her grin mischievous. She stared provocatively at him through the top of her eyes.

"Even just a friendly kiss on the cheek? I don't know, he might be okay..."

Gibson sighed and rolled his eyes. He turned to the young lady with the tablet and began to answer questions.

"Grip!" the helicopter pilot shouted as she stepped down from the controller's door. "Get a move on!"

"What? Oh, yeah, yeah! This way, Ms. Crimson," he spat quickly, backing away from the starlet. "We should get going."

Johanna Crimson popped her eyes open wide, her mouth agape, as she feigned hurt and disappointment. She pressed an open hand to her chest in a mock wound as a sly grin then began to tug at her lips.

As the embarrassed, reddening Bridger looked at the cute pilot and then looked away for the resort, Crimson looked over her shoulder at the chopper pilot for herself. She gave a slight shrug that was anything but innocent before walking away.

Gibson was soon following in the flesh. The shadowblack haired chopper pilot only followed with her eyes, incinerating Crimson with them and her every thought. She called her boyfriend, Falgrip Bridger, a few choice names then slipped under the belly of the bird.

A newcomer to the landing pad ducked under the chopper with her and the two began the landing checklist. He was a handsome young man in a black jumpsuit.

The other guests from the resort helicopter engaged with Shaye Griffin in turn then also made their way toward the main resort structure, referred to by Griffin as Stable Manor. Each stared at the massive, two tiered fountain in the center of the cobblestone pathway, halfway between the manor and the landing pad. Out of white granite rose four larger than life horses, one facing each main compass bearing. They were forged of copper and bore the expected patina as they spewed water from mouths and nostrils.

When the other staffers had abandoned the streamlined machine to its pilot and her newly arrived partner, two other birds began a descent toward the other landing zones. The pilot of the sleek air dagger, Gretchen Clayborne, closed up the panel before her and pointed, squinting behind her sunglasses.

"At least we don't have to tend the airport's whirlybirds," she said, running both hands through flowing, shadowblack hair.

"Yeah. Still, though, let's make sure those rent-a-pilots do their checklists before they lift off again," the young man said. He smoothed the brown mustache and goatee he wore, adding, "None of those blade riders hold a candle to you, Gretchen."

The sudden kindness softened Gretchen Clayborne. Big, brown eyes wide, she froze perfectly still and said, "You're sweet, Tye. Thanks."

He took off his sunglasses and tucked them into the pocket of his jumpsuit, chuckling. His hair stood upright in spikes like Grip Bridger's but his was brown, not blonde. Still, he swept a hand through it and let it snap back to attention like the security specialist.

"It ain't sweet, it's the truth," he sighed.

"Yeah, well, it's a nice truth. You could've said something true that wasn't so nice. Like, I need to lose a few pounds or I-"

"Oh, stop," he groaned. "You look great."

"I'm no Johanna Crimson!" she snapped sharply. "Just ask Grip!"

"What? Is he going all fanboy or something?"

"Wouldn't you?" she countered.

"Nah. She's not my type," he quipped. "I don't even like her movies."

CHAPTER TWO

Sarah handed away her last bag and just stood there, the light wind blowing her hair. Her thick, wavy locks fell below her shoulders once freed from the confines of a navy blue hat Sarah had employed to maintain her hair in travel. NC SBI rose in stitched, white lettering on the face of the hat, above its bill, a reminder that she was always on the job and always prepared, even off duty. Nevertheless, she folded it and put it away into a hip pocket.

I caught myself staring, watching her every move, reading her every curve, studying her beauty anew. How many years had it been since we met in Wilmington? And she still made my breath catch in my throat. Not with just her physical beauty but with the beauty of who she was.

She smiled at me as the hostess moved away from us, tablet in hand. The young lady had registered us as the staff escaped with our luggage.

"What?" Sarah asked.

"You know."

"Know what?" she asked, a coy lilt in her voice.

I gave her my trademarked sideways grin and said, "Oh, you know. And I know you know."

"You're babbling again," she teased and turned away.

Sarah led away for the main building but I paused. I glanced across the pavement to the resort's private helicopter, emblazoned with H and H on the fuselage. Its pilot and a young man had been going over it as it wound down but something had interrupted them. They were examining something just off the pavement, in the grass.

"Priest, you gonna make me take this vacation alone?" Sarah called.

I looked back and saw that she never slowed.

"Go on ahead, babe," I suggested, turning again to the resort aircraft.

James Wyatt joined me as I found myself wandering for the mystery.

"I thought you'd still be with Ms. Crimson," I noted, gesturing with my head. "She's long since gone to the resort."

"She's got her full time watch dog close to her and resort security met us at the bird. She's good, for now. What're you doin' is the question," James said.

"I suppose," I huffed.

It was true enough. My interested distraction was yet to be determined as pertinent, important or nothing at all. There was a certain something about the scene that stuck out to me, however, a question in need of answers.

"Mick?" James asked, his eyes already on the destination. "You got your hackles up like when we got somethin' goin' sideways. We goin' sideways, Priest?"

"I'm not sure, James."

"Mind if I go along with you?"

"More the merrier," I muttered.

The black jumpsuit looked our way. He said something discreetly to the woman, the curvy pilot, then picked something up from the grass. Both of them straightened up to greet us.

"Gentlemen," the man acknowledged. "Can we help you?"

"We were just curious if we might need to help you," I replied.

"We have everything in hand. This is our Director of Facility Operations, Tydas Richter," the pilot said, a slight aggression evident in her raspy voice. "I'm Gretchen Clayborne, resort pilot."

"Relax, Gretchen," Richter eased.

"Yeah," James Wyatt retorted, head leaned to one side. "Relax, G. You weren't nearly this uptight during the flight up."

"This is James Wyatt," I interjected, "and I'm Mick Priest. We're working with Johanna Crimson's security detail."

We shook hands with Richter and Clayborne even as the woman offered her rebuttal.

"Sorry. I'm more comfortable in the air. And when I'm not being crowded."

"They're guests," the man insisted, nudging his resort partner. "They've already been logged in. It's all good."

"We just wanted to see if we could help," I calmed and cut a sharp look at James. "The two of you seemed...preoccupied."

Gretchen said nothing.

Richter, to our surprise, opened right up to us.

"Only if you saw who dropped this," the young man said.

He revealed both hands. Previously, he had been keeping one at the time concealed behind himself. A white skull mask stared up at us from his grasp, a hard shelled mask, forged in fiberglass or impact resistant plastic, from the look of it.

James and I looked at each other.

"This...item," said Richter, "was lying here, underneath the helicopter. Nobody noticed it being dropped, I don't guess."

"Or where he or she went," the pilot said.

Richter shrugged with, "I'm not really the type who gets easily spooked but this thing is weird. We're not on a masquerade weekend and I can't think of a single reason anyone would've brought this thing. Well, no good reasons, anyway. Someone has to know how it got here. One or maybe even more of our guests. We probably need to ask around."

"Only answer. Either that or a ghost dropped it," my buddy said and gave me a sidelong stare.

Don't even start with me, my eyes warned him.

"Is there anything we can do?" I asked.

"I don't think so," Richter answered. "We'll tell the Resort Director, get a little direction. Thanks, though."

"No problem," James answered. "Do us a favor though, okay? Share your find with your head honcho and with your security lead but nobody else. Tell 'em to play it close to the vest, too. If this is bad news, I don't want whoever dropped it to know we know, you know?"

Clayborne narrowed her pretty eyes at my friend's clumsy speech but Tydas Richter nodded.

"Will do," he said.

"Come on," I muttered at James. As we walked away, I added, "I trust you can recall everyone on that resort 'copter with you and Crimson."

"Can trees leave?"

I rolled my eyes, adding, "Good. That might be-"

"Won't help."

"What?" I asked. "Why not?"

"Simple. 'Cause none o' them dropped it, threw it, flung it, tossed it-"

"Okay, okay," I said with a sigh. "You sure?"

"I was on the job, Mick. I can tell you without a doubt, ol' buddy. It didn't come from that chopper."

"So much for easy."

"You know what that is, though, right?"

"Yeah, James. According to Sarah, that's our hitman's calling card; a discarded mask, always left behind, just like the killer's real one. Always used in the hits. It's part of the Ghost Revolver identity..."

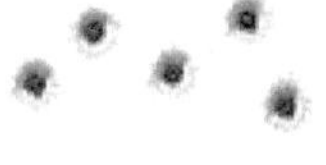

"Grip needs to see this," Tye Richter started. "He's security. It's what he does. Let him stress it."

"If it just got dropped here, during unloading, someone would've noticed it," Gretchen Clayborne mumbled.

Tye Richter just stared at her for a long moment.

Then, "Gretchen, we kinda know that much."

"Okay, okay," she allowed irritably.

He touched his earpiece and called for Falgrip Bridger. When the security specialist answered, Richter addressed the situation.

Afterward, Bridger came back with, "Just don't touch anything else. One of you stay there until I get to you. Don't move around too much. You'll contaminate any evidence on the scene. Bridger out."

"Evidence? Of what? Never mind. Confirmed," Richter said and chuckled. To Clayborne he chirped, "That guy. I love 'im but ridiculously officious should be his code name."

Clayborne was clearly more put off by the find than Richter. She peered into the empty eye sockets of the skull where the duo had placed it back on the ground. She shivered and looked all around again, an odd sensation washing over her.

"Some guy could just be sitting somewhere, staring at us with the eyes that were behind that skull," she mumbled.

Richter huffed with, "Nice thought."

In the distance, a loud boom sounded and resounded, the concussive bellow echoing down the mountain and through the valley. A sharp crack followed it with echoes all its own.

Tydas Richter took off his shades and stared out into the amassing clouds. A very long way off, the sky played host to a mass of angry looking cloud formations but none of them looked to be importing rain.

"Heat lightning," Richter mused. "Summer rage..."

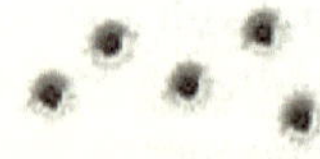

There was a strange creature, indeed, on the side of Shadow Mountain. Out of place in its alien, albeit chosen, habitat. Out of place with and within itself. So perched the chimera known as Horse and Heraldry Resort, a place so much a conglomeration of faceted ideas that it could not resemble any other, for it did not even resemble itself.

'Five star plus' accommodations waited within a manor built into the shape of an equestrian stable. Marble flooring and velvet draperies adorned a backdrop of dark stone walls and iron sconces on its insides. Ship lap wood planks and old fashioned shutters decorated the exterior.

Highly technological touch screens stood at the ready in halls, the main lobby, every table in the convention center spaces and in every single guest room. They provided internet, teleconferencing, research and even digital room service ordering. However, writing desks reared antiquated inkwells and quill pens, parchment paper and rotary style, royal telephones, all in the same locations.

Electronic key cards to every room dangled on a ring with an old world, iron skeleton key. Rooms were soundproofed for privacy but digital video cameras watched every public space, every hall, every entrance and exit. Every electronic and digital accommodation that could be offered would be, while the entire complex looked like the equestrian getaway it also genuinely offered.

Both long sides of the main building, called Stable Manor, horses waited in their stables twelve to a side. All the English and Western tack a rider could desire was available, too. Please the customer. Impress the guest. The location seemed to be an equestrian dreamland.

However, throughout much of the rest of the compound, art and displays centered on ancient shields and coats of arms, medieval weapons, armor and archaic weaving. The duality was striking, if not a little schizophrenic. All the while, technology was still the word of the day.

Guest rooms lined the walks above both stable sides on the third and fourth floors, where modern niceties and accouterments befitting only the richest hotels in the world would be found.

Modern lighting. Infrared and thermal camera imaging.

Candles on sconces and iron chandeliers.

Some marble flooring, some blackened slate, some planked hardwood and some plush carpeting, all fitted together somehow.

Lassos and chaps spoke of their place in time while, on a wall opposite them, a battle ax and a broadsword crossed below a round shield. Other shields bridged the connection; they wore horsemen as their crests. Near some of them, saddles on display with embossed leather work depicted knights in battle. Not just the English saddles on ceremonial stands but Western ones on log tripods, as well.

Even in the kitchen and dining areas there was a war of style. Stone bread ovens and great, iron wood stoves competed with gas and electric burners and ovens, while classic, full sized pizza ovens warred with all the tiniest microwave advancements. Vat fryers and air fryers competed or complemented each other, depending on the personal opinion. Timers, clocks, and digital alarms stood hand in second hand, at the ready.

Horseback riding and hiking trails without, virtual reality video gaming rooms within. Rustic blacksmith displays promised a chance to participate and learn in the artisan trade. They glowed, red hot, in small outbuildings not far away from air conditioned, luxury spas and a gymnasium.

In short, H and H Resort offered all... in abundance.

There was a monster, a chimera, prowling on Shadow Mountain.

"And the prices are vulgar," a handsome, mature man said from the group, ruffling his snowy white hair.

Several gasps, sprinkled with a few chuckles, broke from the crowd.

"But you're more than worth the cost, I'm sure!" he added quickly, Eastern Carolina charm oozing from him. "If not, you wouldn't be here!"

The gentleman had already introduced himself to the congregation as Victor Jackson, Chief Financial Officer for a major, East Coast publishing company. That company had organized the writers' retreat, attempting to woo a few more scribes into their fold, covering every cost. Considering the cost to get some of them there, like Johanna Crimson, it was impressive. The publishing house dispatched their very best head hunter, too, a lovely, lithe woman with night black hair and one of the sharpest minds in the business.

Maureen Li, pulling that silky, black hair into a ponytail, shook her head vehemently. She shook a warning finger at Jackson, as well.

"There is no doubt," she informed. "They are worth it all."

"Besides, I don't think I would say vulgar, Mr. Jackson," the resort director, Cassandra Clark, corrected. "I would think it only equal to the quality of exclusive stays H and H can offer."

"I'm sure," Jackson allowed with a big, endearing grin. "And I can only add that I'm glad I'm not covering the bill with any checkbook other than the company one."

Again, amiable laughter spread through the ranks.

All of the attending writers and guests had enjoyed an orientation tour upon settling into their accommodations. All the guests were happy to have their first glimpse of grandeur. The hour had grown dark, however, the introduction a long one. The outside lights ignited to stay the approach of night by the time they had all reached the flower gardens. They lay at the south end of the main building, not far from the main, circle court in the forefront of the structure. The gardens were lit by softly flickering lanterns and smokeless braziers. There, with the mountain's cool, night air stirring the sweet smell of the flora, the gathering drank in the moment.

"It's lovely here with night falling on the roses. I could definitely write a whole novel here," a tall, elegant young woman said cheerfully.

"Who couldn't, girl?" another woman asked, though a hint of lewdness played within her grin. "I just need the right inspiration."

She was shorter and paler than her tanned, amazonian counterpart. Her sandy blonde hair contrasted the other woman's caramel tresses.

Not too far from them, an ebony titan of a man stared their way. He smiled and nodded at them both. The tall, reserved woman returned the smile with a nod while her less ladylike counterpart returned a carnivorous smile, a wink and a nibble at her lower lip.

"In about a half hour we'll have a candlelight dinner in the main dining hall," the director told them all.

"Twenty-three minutes, ma'am," the formal Jenkins pinpointed. "And remember the staffing points," he muttered, leaning down to her.

"Oh, yes, thank you, Jenkins," she gushed. "Ladies and gentlemen, we've released the majority of the staff so you can have the most exclusive, private retreat possible. Housekeeping prepped your rooms and all of them have gone. The dining staff prepared the necessities for Jenkins to provide you top notch service and dining and they've gone, with the exception of our head chef and his best assistant. The stable hands and trainers have gone but I'm a lifelong equestrian, should you need or want to take advantage of the riding options. In short-"

"Too late," someone muttered, incurring a few more chuckles.

"-you are in very capable hands. We have Jenkins and myself, our head chef, one lead server, our operations director and our security chief still on site. Other than that, you're here for a 'guests only' experience. Anything you need we will happily handle, even if it takes a little time. "

"So, the people who checked us in and the baggage handlers are all gone?" the short, sultry blonde asked.

"Yes..." Cassandra Clark answered, wondering to herself how that had been unclear. "Now, if you'll excuse us, we need to keep ahead of needs with our shortened staff. Ms. Li, Mr. Jackson, if you'll accompany me we'll have a brief conference in my office."

Jenkins turned and followed Cassandra Clark, Li and Jackson back inside, leaving the entourage in the garden. Clark spoke to the publishing representatives as they departed.

"It really is a peaceful place," an elfish, petite young lady said dreamily. Though it was not the case, she looked as though she could have been in high school. "The photos I get here are going to be great."

Her infant daughter, in the sling about her shoulders, yawned.

Standing close, Mick Priest gave the child his finger to hold. He matched the young one's smile and mused aloud softly.

"Finally, brethren, whatsoever things are true, whatsoever things are honest, whatsoever things are just, whatsoever things are pure, whatsoever things are lovely, whatsoever things are of good report; if there be any virtue, and if there be any praise, think on these things."

"Spot on for this place," the big man said, joining them. "Was that Scripture, mate?"

"Now, tha' would be tellin', wouldn't it?" laughed another man, bringing his British lilt over to join the other man's. "You're supposed to know for yourself. Right, Padre?"

"I believe we all need to know Scripture," Priest agreed, "if we're-"

"He ain't a priest, ya daft bakery gremlin, his name is Priest," the ebony giant shouted. He laughed at the short but well built Brit with the silver hair and piercing, blue eyes. "Ya don't call him 'Father'. The bloke's a detective."

The shorter man stroked his silver and black goatee, saying, "Sorry, mate."

Everyone seemed to be enjoying the two Brits teasing each other and laughter worked its way through the garden again.

Priest, smile on his face, shrugged and said, "I've been called worse. I'm Mick Priest, by the way."

The men passed around handshakes.

"B'Rone Matwahali," the big man said.

"Paul Blackwood," the other man introduced himself.

"Well read, by the way, at least in the Good Book," B'Rone Matwahali said to Priest, his grin amiable and his cheerful British tone infectious.

"I try," Mick Priest said.

"Ah, nothin' wrong with that," Paul Blackwood said. "World needs some traditional morals."

Priest took a moment to introduce his wife, Sarah, as well.

Another man introduced himself ever so humbly as a 'motorcycle legend' first and a race writer second. Richard 'Rick' Porter brought up something race related with Paul Blackwood then, a man with a keen interest in fast machines, as well.

The blonde woman announced that she was Kess Melkin, writer of horror erotica. She also mentioned she liked to write 'true story erotica', letting everyone know she was qualified to do so with a wicked leer. She then tried to convince Andreya West, the refined young woman, that the garden would be fully complete with a 'bare chested barbarian' in sight.

The lovely West received it with laughter and doubting eyes as she looked beyond her, to Mick Priest.

"I liked your Scripture, Mr. Priest," she said.

"That was Phillipians, Chapter Four, Verse Eight. It was one of my mom's favorite ones. She quoted it a lot in her own rose garden. Great encouragement and a reminder to appreciate the good things."

"Ideal," Paul Blackwood said.

"Cheers," Matwahali added.

"She would've loved this place," Priest said finally.

The young lady with the beautiful baby started firing away with her camera. As lithe and delicate looking as faerie kin, she triggered her picture gun with defined precision. Deft hands snapped photographs and changed lenses in practiced professionalism.

After a number of shots, she even opted out to a smaller camera still hanging about her neck and she started all over again.

"You're so good at that," Sarah Priest commented, "and so young."

She paused to toss back the long, front bangs and tips of her pixie cut. She whipped them backward, out of her face, the purple ends flying about at the end of her light brown strands.

"Yeah, you have to be practiced. If you want to stand out. The mechanical stuff has to be second nature so you can focus on the art, the shot."

Mick Priest wore a genuine smile.

"Your daughter is beautiful."

"Thanks. She's my world. Emma Lee," she introduced with a proud smile. "Oh, I'm Tayla," she added, offering her hand to Sarah Priest first then to Mick Priest. "Tayla Barlowe."

"Sarah Priest," the SBI agent said.

"Mick," her husband responded and took Barlowe's hand, kissing it.

She stared at her own hand as if it was a foreign object when she pulled it back.

"That would be a gentleman's charm," Johanna Crimson, the actress, said from a few yards away. "Embrace it, darling. There isn't much left of it these days."

Tayla Barlowe's entire face was red.

"It isn't a flirt, I promise," Sarah Priest said, leaning in privately. "It's a show of respect for a lady, even a much younger one, like yourself."

She eased as Sarah stepped back, pondering her first ever hand kiss.

"It's different," she said, "that's for sure. I mean, not in a bad way."

"By the way, I like your verse, too," Priest said.

"Verse?" she asked.

He tapped the inside of his own forearm, indicating hers.

Reflexively, she glanced at her arm and a light came on in her deep, brown eyes. She traced her tattoo lightly with one finger.

"Be still," she read, the only two words printed there, alongside a lovely Cross. "How did you even notice it? In the dark?"

"It's what I do. Notice things."

"Does it pay well?" she joked.

Both Priests shared a chuckle with her.

"Be still, and know that I am God," the young lady quoted then.

"Psalm forty-six, verse ten," he elaborated.

She squinted over her soft smile.

"You sure you aren't a priest?"

"Pretty sure," he said with a smile of his own.

"Completely sure," Sarah added. "We are married, after all."

The young Tayla Barlowe returned Sarah's grin and went back to snapping photographs in determined fervor.

"Ya know, quotes are kinda my thing," the young woman noted. "I do a lot of photos with famous quotes in my head, pictures matching literature or Scripture. The art of word and still shots, poised together in a single, solitary frame...my world."

"Sounds lovely," Mick Priest said.

James Wyatt hovered about Johanna Crimson, eyes alert. Both he and Marcus Gibson raked the shadows with hawk stares. Crimson, for her part, sidled over to the Priests, dragging her bodyguards along with invisible tethers.

"Mark Gibson, *Ms*. Johanna Crimson," James said, nodding at Mick and Sarah, "these are two of my best friends, Mick and Sarah Priest."

"I'm just Gibson to most everybody," the older man said as they all began to shake hands. "I'm not one of those 'titles' kinda guys."

"Oh, neither am I," Johanna Crimson gushed, waving away the introduction with one hand and extending the other.

Her slender wrist dangled that gloved hand in a bent, kissable angle.

Priest took the hint and kissed her hand, though he would have done so without the hint. While her eyes played with him, her smirk toying about with her lush, pink lips, she absently accepted Sarah's handshake.

"I believe we'd all agree you're no 'kinda guy' at all, Ms. Crimson," Sarah Priest allowed, pointing out the starlet's jest. "*Person* magazine's Most Alluring Woman of the Year again? How many times is this, now? It has to be some kind of record."

Crimson folded a hand over her chest, finally turning her eyes to Sarah Priest completely.

"I'm touched you've heard," she said. "Of course, I hardly keep up with it. The magazines are so fickle. They love you today-"

"Trash you the next," Gibson muttered.

Crimson cut her burning green eyes at him as Sarah's warm, brown eyes fell upon him, too. Sarah's, however, reflected the man's humor. She offered him a grin to boot.

"Allure being what it is," Mick Priest said, keeping his opinion on that to himself, "it's a pleasure to meet you."

I'm glad to see you're still alive, he mused to himself.

She beamed, folded her arms beneath her ample bosom and cocked a hip and leg to one side.

"Again, I'm touched," she purred, eyes shifting seductively.

"Your acting is top notch. Superior to a lot of the current names in your business. I've yet to find you out of place in a role or unbelievable in one. And your mastery of linguistics, accents, dialects, that sort of thing, that's second to none. I know you probably hear people talk about your beauty all the time-"

"You got no idea," Gibson muttered.

It earned him a dismissive wave from the woman and a giggle from Sarah Priest.

"-but I believe your talent is your shining star," Priest finished.

"Oh, my," she sang, taking a step toward him.

Grip Bridger abruptly broke away from the fringe of the crowd. The security chief touched his earpiece and walked away. The young man had been with them for the entire tour; his departure seemed odd.

Gibson stepped closer to Crimson, stopping her in her tracks.

"Rude, Gibson," she scolded.

The older man glanced at the Priests then looked back into the night.

"He's always like this," Crimson droned, rolling her eyes. "The world is out to get Johanna Crimson. Terrorists, assassins, paparazzi, ex-boyfriends-"

"That boy's strings are pulled tighter than a talkin' doll's," Gibson told Mick, referring to the security agent. "Problem is, he ain't talkin' to us 'bout anything."

"-stalkers, kidnappers, gold diggers, groupies," Crimson was still muttering.

"I know part of his problem," Priest said in a confidential tone.

"Yeah?"

Priest quietly informed him of the find in the parking lot, the mask.

"That useless boy," Gibson growled. "He knows he's supposed to inform me of anything like this! It's in our stay agreement! Kid might not know what that is but-"

"Yeah, we do, though. Calling card of a certain professional."

"If he hasn't told you," Sarah started, "I wonder if he's told the Resort Director. Maybe we should?"

"Yeah, but later," Gibson said and nodded. His eyes narrowed. "You gonna be here a second?"

Sarah Priest shrugged with, "Sure. I can't imagine why not."

"Good. I do my homework. James Wyatt brought your ol' man as his best bodyguard, even if it is unofficially. All well and good. But you're in the SBI, according to my intel."

Sarah arched her brows in surprise.

Gibson continued with, "State Bureau of Investigation. So, with that bein' said, I'm pretty sure I can trust the two of you," he finished. "I won't be long."

With a nod and a gesture of his head to James Wyatt, the two of them left to follow the head of security.

"How do you like that?" Johanna Crimson asked, pouting, closing in on Mick Priest. "My protector tosses me to strangers. I think I may be overpaying him."

Priest stared after the much older man, impressed, pretending not to notice how Sarah aptly slid between him and the approaching starlet.

"I don't know. I think you're getting your money's worth," Mick complemented the man. "He's on top of the game."

"He's the best, if I'm honest. I tease him but...well, there's not another one like him," Crimson agreed, engaging that stunning smile. "But that's a story for some other time. You were saying you're a fan. Are you absolutely loving the third *Velvet Edge* movie?"

Sarah Priest tried to hold back a wicked grin but could not.

Mick Priest said, "No, I'm actually not *VE3* smitten."

Crimson blinked several times back to back, long lashes beating down her disbelief. After a few quiet seconds, her pink lips parted again.

"You don't like *Velvet Edge*?"

Again, he offered no hesitation.

"I did, very much...but just the first one."

Her mouth hung agape as the blinking reoccurred.

Sarah turned away from the woman, smile wide.

"You liked the origin story but not the sequels?" Crimson pushed.

"Exactly. The sequels didn't have any depth, any challenge, for you."

"The sequels earned twice the recognition and grossed four times the first one's take!" she gasped.

"I don't mean it insultingly," Mick said.

"No, no, I love the honesty," she stated. She seemed genuine but sounded like she was trying to convince herself. "I just...well, you said you were a fan..."

"Of you, your craft. Your skill. Not *Velvet Edge's* sequels."

She caught sight of Gibson storming their way in a return trajectory.

"To be continued, Mr. Priest," Crimson said sternly.

"Mick," Priest insisted.

"Mick. Only if you call me Johanna," she said with a slightly disinclined smile.

"Priest," Gibson interrupted pointedly. "Security says he got a call about lights down in the helicopter hangar. James went on with him."

"I'll stay with Johanna and Gibson," Sarah said, being sure to use the starlet's first name, since it had only been offered to her husband. "You go after James."

Mick nodded.

"Who called him, Gibson? I thought everyone was here," he muttered aloud, looking for any missing faces.

"He didn't say," Gibson informed sourly.

"Ladies and gentlemen, please collect your attendees," Jenkins announced loudly upon his return. "The dining room awaits and, by the time you have all gathered, dinner should be ready and served."

Mick Priest was already retreating and never slowed.

"You know, Velvet Edge would've never been able to beat Psionide," a lean man said, smelling the flowers a few yards from Crimson. "As a villain for VE2, he was really watered down."

As the crowd meandered toward the building, Johanna Crimson gave an appeasing smile and a rebuttal of silence to the quiet, dark haired man.

Gibson moved between them, taking Crimson's arm.

"And you are?" Sarah asked, watching him carefully.

"Oh, I'm sorry. How rude of me. I'm Rembrandt Lyles. But you can call me Remy; everybody calls me Remy."

"Among other things," Sarah Priest heard Gibson mutter.

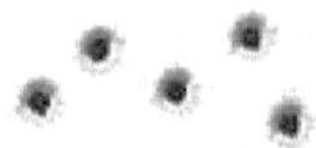

I heard someone calling after me.

Mr. Priest, Mr. Priest.

It was more than likely Jenkins and I could not have cared less.

The stepping stone pathway leaving the garden dotted the ground in pastel yellow octagons. They glowed iridescently in the light of the solar powered walkway lamps. I hopped from one to the next, around the side of the complex, then jogged for the landing zones in the back.

The blacktops looked like lakes in the night. Lights stood in the corners of each of them but they were soft and not terribly bright. The designers had no intention of letting artificial lighting ruin a good night's sleep for the back wing of bedrooms. That suited me well; it made Grip Bridger and my buddy, James Wyatt, all the easier to find when skulking around with a flashlight.

I was surprised there were no lights on the front of the hangar building, however. A flashlight beam, the only light, danced across the pavement at one angle then another and another. It reached out of the open bay, apparently at random.

I slowed the jog to a walk when I reached pavement.

The flashlight beam vanished without a trace.

My spine tingled and I dropped to a crouch. The sweat lining me underneath my clothes suddenly chilled. The mountain air, not cold by any means, raised goose bumps over my form and I shivered. My eyes flitted here and there, looking for any sign of movement, but found none.

Slowly, I moved a hand to my lower back and pulled a Colt Delta Elite 10mm free of its sheath. I crept forward in a crouch.

My usual gear was still up in my room. My own flashlight. My phone. And one of my twin 10mm handguns.

I felt naked.

Nevertheless, I moved. One slow step. Then two. Then three.

Voices, unclear, rode the winds beyond the hangar.

Then something, someplace exploded. Fury bellowed and lanced the quiet calm, silencing cricket songs and whispering breezes.

An explosion rocked the very stone of the mountain and tore the night in two. Its brutal, pervasive eruption echoed from a few miles away. A glow of light plumed brilliantly beyond the trees. The darkness, for a few moments, shuddered and melted in the distance. Fire ignited the hour as if time itself were ablaze.

The light in the distance faded quickly, however, waning in its war with the night. As it did it left behind a new mystery.

Why were the lights dead all over the resort?

Whatever the reason, the distant explosion had erupted in a thunderous crescendo and shook the mountain stone...

...then plunged the resort into a total blackout.

The only light remaining on Shadow Mountain was the distant spot down the road where something burned and it was fading fast.

CHAPTER THREE

Shadow Mountain wore its name with no ambiguity. Its position, even in the daylight, lent itself to a shadowy position among the mountain chain. The night bore the cloak of an even deeper darkness, even in ample starlight. There was just something about Shadow Mountain, something dark, something hidden.

A shining beacon of change in the relative wilderness had been the upstart resort. With the bridge over Nightshade Pass, the Shadow Walker Bridge, it stabbed a bright spot into the heart of the dark mountain side. Power and communications technology for the stable getaway ran through the very bridge foundations. With it, Horse and Heraldry Resort had changed the slope and even the shadows of Shadow Mountain.

That night, however, the mountain took back the nocturnal hour and its namesake as all went black once again.

Mick Priest jumped to his feet as voices rang out a clarion call. In a cacophony of shouted chaos, a dissonance lifted from the main building of the resort. Much closer to Priest, urgent cries rose from the far, darker side of the hangar. A pair of male voices and a female voice vied for dominance.

Then the security specialist, Grip Bridger, stepped clear of the hangar, appearing from its far side. Priest recognized him right away, even in the shadows of the hour. He pointed off toward the fading firelight down the road, shouting with James Wyatt. The night wind carried their voices along with the helicopter pilot's ranting.

Priest jogged over to a stop close by them, still looking about for the source of the flashlight he had seen.

"I'm going to need you to go back to the main building," Bridger said officiously, a palm raised toward the new arrival.

"What was that?" the young woman shouted again.

"You two need to calm down," James Wyatt said again, loudly.

"Butt out!" Gretchen Clayborne railed at him.

"All of you, follow my lead!" Grip Bridger yelled. Then, a lot more calmly, he said, "Mr. Priest, Mr. Wyatt, guests or not, I'm still in charge of your security and your safety. I need you to go back-"

"What's going on down here?" Priest asked, interrupting Bridger.

"And down the road," James added.

The younger man glowered and his voice cracked as he said, "I'm security for this resort. I'll ask the questions."

"Something blew up, way down there, toward Shadow Walker Bridge," Clayborne railed, also ignoring Grip Bridger.

She continued rambling and squawking until both James and Bridger shouted at her to be quiet.

Priest pointed at Bridger.

"Hold it. First, I don't usually play favorites and pull rank but here's the deal: I'm a licensed investigator in this state and Mr. Wyatt is a licensed security specialist. We're working a case at this resort, along with my wife, Sarah Priest. She works with the State Bureau of Investigation and the SBI outranks you all day and night, so let it go. I don't want to hear another word about our safety or your authority."

He let it sink into the young man's comprehension.

"Second, I ask again; what's going on down here? All of it, before the explosion, whatever. Bridger, you took a radio call and came down here. I'm guessing that was Ms. Clayborne on the call. You left your post with Johanna Crimson's personal security detail. I want to know why."

Voices from the direction of the main building rose again.

"Like she's any more important than the rest of us," Clayborne interrupted.

"Gretchen," Bridger warned.

Voices grew closer in the dark.

"Shut up and answer him, Bulldog," James snapped, "so we can move on! We need to find out what exploded!"

"It's all this summer rage," Bridger said dismissively. "So, lightning hit something, popped a transformer! Big deal!"

"I called Grip down here," Clayborne admitted. She continued against Grip's protests with, "I was up here at the chopper hangar 'cause I've been on those little introduction tours a thousand times and I didn't need another one."

"She's not Johanna Crimson's biggest fan, either," James said.

"I was refueling my bird," she snapped.

"She's jealous and for no good reason," Bridger growled.

"I was in my quarters, upstairs, and heard something!" she said.

"Like someone rummaging around outside, out back," Bridger said.

"Then I radioed Grip! Before the earpiece signals went dead!"

"Are you always so skittish?" Priest asked.

"With that skeleton mask we found?" she shouted. "Yes!"

Bridger covered his face with a hand and rolled his eyes.

Priest nodded along slowly.

"Did you relay the mask discovery to your boss? The director?"

Bridger shook his head, saying, "No, I was waiting for more information."

"Which means she couldn't tell Crimson's security. And you forgot you're on tap to do that, as well," Priest finished. "One of you take that mask and leave it with Ms. Clark when we go back up to the resort. I'll get her up to speed."

"What is that mask about?" Clayborne demanded. "Who left it out here? Are they dangerous? Are they responsible for that explosion that-"

"It's a lightning strike! Heat lightning!" Bridger argued over her.

She refused to relent, squabbling on, undaunted.

"Gretchen," Bridger said, "give it a rest!"

"Both of you, give it a rest," James warned.

New voices drew near.

Priest glanced over his shoulder to find Director Cassandra Clark and Tydas Richter striding onto the pavement. Clark was barefooted, having ditched her spiked pumps.

Clark huffed incredulously, looking at her phone screen.

"We've been calling all of you, after the earbuds failed trying to radio you," the director informed, "but none of us can get a signal of any kind! This is impossible! We have our own booster tower!"

"It's all down, the entire cell signal," Richter added. "That's bad, too, since we use our cells to run our radio earpieces. Bluetooth. Progress."

"Update us, everyone," Cassandra said tentatively. "Grip was supposed to be with Ms. Crimson. Let's start there. What brought you down here in the first place, Grip?"

Grip Bridger finally got his chance to do his job and tell the director what he knew. He included Gretchen Clayborne's latest concerns.

Priest told them about the flashlight beam he had seen. Bridger and James owned up to that. They had been looking around the hangar with the main lights out, searching for the source of the night noises.

"I don't understand all of this," Clark admitted, "but I don't have to. Grip, you need to coordinate with Mark Gibson and Mr. Wyatt, there. Get back on the Crimson detail."

"More matters here than Hottie Hollywood," Clayborne snarled.

"We all need to group at the main building, where Grip can help keep an eye on everyone, not just Ms. Crimson. Gretchen, you come to the main house, too. You need to sleep there tonight."

"We have to get in touch with some authorities," Bridger said.

"Let us worry about that," Clark snapped. "You do your job, please. And escort Tye up to the generator building before coming back to the main house. I want that place sealed and secured."

"I'm fine solo," Richter tried. "I'll just run down-"

"No. Take Grip and you two go. Now," Clark growled.

"Someone's gotta lock the hangar down," Richter reminded.

"We'll take care of it," Priest said.

"What now?" Clark asked, Richter and Bridger walking away.

"I'm going to check on Crimson," James Wyatt said. "You ladies can come with me, back to the manor. That is, if you got this, Mick?"

"Not a problem," Priest said with a nod. "I'm going to look around here one more time then someone has to look into that explosion."

James Wyatt left, Clark and Clayborne following closely, Clark looking over her shoulder several times at the detective.

When they were truly out of sight and he was really alone, Mick Priest began to nose around the hangar.

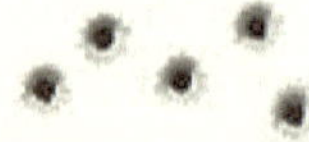

Reginald Bard Jenkins, he thought to himself, *what has Cassandra Clark left to you?*

It was bad enough that the Stable Manor had been reduced to dim, emergency power lighting. Far worse was that the back up lights were only equipped in hallways and corridors.

The lighting, disguised as actual torches, were programmed, battery operated, flickering LED fixtures. Rustic and full of character. Dim and inadequate in an actual power failure.

Other than within hallways and corridors, actual candles and flashlights became necessary.

"Everyone...everyone," Jenkins kept saying, trying to calm them.

That was proving as hard as getting the crowd to come back inside the manor after the explosion.

Hands raised high in the air, he said, "Please, if I could get your attention...everyone, please..."

The crowd rumbled like a storm on the rise. Everyone speaking at once, some loudly, more questions ringing out than answers. With the questions came challenges, accusations and distrust...and, for a formal man of training and service, like Jenkins, the din loomed overhead unacceptably.

"Ladies and gentlemen!" he bellowed finally, his patience ended.

His low, booming voice reverberated within the crystal on the table. Everyone in the large, elegant dining hall fell silent.

That was his second miracle. The first had been wrangling the guests down into the dining hall in candlelight.

"Please," Jenkins followed quickly, his voice a respectful, calm tone again. "Do have a seat. Let's all be patient and I will see to your dinner."

He left with his own candlestick and the others took their seats.

"I bet he kills somebody," Paul Blackwood said with a wry smirk.

"What are you on about?" B'Rone Matwahali asked.

"He's the butler and he just left with a candlestick," Blackwood said, bursting into laughter. As others allowed an uncomfortable chuckle, he added, "If he doesn't, he's missed a fine opportunity, hasn't he?"

More people laughed.

Everyone leaned about, looking around the row of candelabras that stood at attention along the long, cherry wood table. Fine china and crystal glasses lined each place setting, as well, and ornate silver hid within silk napkins.

"I don't care about food," Kess Melkin announced, pushing her plate toward the center of the massive eating space then pushing her bosom about in her low cut top. "I want answers. My phone's got no reach, the power's out and Jenkins-baby says we got no phone lines here that ain't digital, voice-over-internet, Skype, and all like that."

"What difference does that make?" Richard Porter, racing legend, asked irritably.

"No power, no communication," Tayla Barlowe answered. "My husband does I.T. and computer program work; a real tech head. This place would intrigue him...if the place was up and running."

Nonetheless, the talk around the table was about the abrupt exit of the security chief, the detective, the resort director and some others.

Where had they gone? What was happening? What happened to the power?

The topics revolved around leaving, getting answers...and danger.

"Everybody, let's not get ahead of ourselves," Maureen Li, the publishing executive, said. "There's no reason to be uneasy. It's a power drop; they'll work it out. Right now, enjoy the fine meal on its way! How nice is this, anyway? Candlelight, in the mountains, in a super-resort, some of the best literary peers around, lots of book deals to be offered..."

Another voice immediately dropped a no-nonsense statement.

"The event is fully funded already," Victor Jackson reminded. "I wouldn't rush to abandon this luxurious gift."

Uncertain silence loomed heavily for a moment.

The well known starlet on scene rarely left a room silent.

"The rest of you can do as you please," Johanna Crimson then informed the room. "But Gibson and I are staying. To be certain, they'll have the power worked out by tomorrow. I think we all agree that throwing away a weekend's enjoyment over one night's technical difficulties is a bit presumptuous."

"That's the idea, Ms. Crimson," Maureen Li cheered her.

Down the table, an angular face shifted shadowed and obscured eyes. The lean man, Lyles, stole glances at the starlet and her gunhand.

"I'm not sure I'm as good with this," said Gibson flatly then leaned toward Crimson.

Crimson stared through the candlelight at the somewhat gaunt man, Rembrandt Lyles, as Mark Gibson angled his head just for her to see and continued, his voice a hushed whisper.

The whole room suddenly seemed to have an opinion of their own, all sharing at once, but Johanna Crimson just smiled at Gibson and gave no answer to his concern.

Look what I did, her expression seemed to brag at him.

"I don't see a reason to pull out so quickly, either," Tayla Barlowe said and shrugged.

She balanced one of her cameras in one hand and her daughter in the sling, snapped a picture of a candle's flickering flame and nodded.

Richard Porter commented, "If we don't get power back, what are we going to do over this stay?"

"Oh, I dunno, mate," Paul Blackwood chimed. "In a hurry ta drop a vacation and get back ta work, are ya?"

"I know I'm not," the young, elegant West interjected. "I'm not leaving until they drag me out. Work has been murder lately."

Jenkins ushered three serving trays into the dining hall and plates began to appear before hungry, if somewhat disheartened, guests. Jenkins was a pristine master at the table, a serving cloth over his left arm and seemingly endless hands, serving all with speed and precision. With him was a much younger woman, her raven black hair up in a bun, her form outfitted with serving attire.

"I always say, better decisions are made on a full stomach," B'Rone Matwahali announced.

"I knew ol' 'Ricochet' Porter made a lot of decisions. That stomach don't lie!" a woman remarked at Porter's side.

A chorus of laughter rolled around as Rick Porter let loose a few choice words.

"Easy, dobby," she sniped, her voice dripping with Australian flair.

She wore tasteful but provocative clothing made of leathers and lace, high end revealing but not trashy. She had accompanied Richard Porter, the motorcycle race writer, as she had often modeled for the photographs in his magazine articles. He had offered the cover option to her, should he land the lucrative book offer from Gridlock Publishing.

"Keep your blood pressure down. No power, no air conditioning. You get wound up, it's gonna be hot as Great Sandy in 'ere. You stroke out, we get no book offer," the Australian giggled.

"Supermodels," the short, rotund man growled, brushing at his unruly mustache and eyebrows. "More like superbottle, 'cause we both know that blonde ain't factory, it's aftermarket!"

"Whateva, Ricky, whateva," the pretty Aussie answered.

That was why every writer and would be writer had attended the weekend with the publisher's lead agent, Maureen Li. The dangled offer.

Richard Porter and his model associate, Kimber Mobley, writing a 'behind the scenes' of motorcycle racing and the famed names in the sport.

"Hey, ease up, Charlie," Paul Blackwood snapped. "The lady's gorgeous, whatever you say. You're just...loud."

Paul Blackwood, celebrity chef and baker. Star of his own British television series on cooking and author of a whole shelf of books already.

Andreya West tossed her napkin to the tabletop in disgust. She slid from her seat, excusing herself.

"Not eatin' anything?" Kess Melkin quizzed.

"I'm afraid I've had all the high society and cosmopolitan class I can stomach, for now," the eloquent writer said, eyeballing the motorcycle magazine writer, Rick Porter.

Andreya West, linguistic genius. Professor of multiple languages, with understudies in history, chemistry and organic nutrition. Master of Native American histories and the history of language.

Kesley 'Kess' Melkin, horror novelist and writer of erotica.

West then wandered out into the hallway. The historian had been less than talkative, anyway.

"La-di-da," Porter quipped.

"Ay, ya scooter troll," the biggest, most physically impressive man in the room barked. His low voice drew everyone's stare. "Ya need ta lighten up on the ladies."

B'Rone Matwahali. Survivalist. Adventurer. Explorer. Former military. Former freelance operative. Former big game hunter and tracker. British television personality in his own right. Aspiring writer of true to life adventures and how-to novels.

"I agree. Let's all just get along. Make the most of the weekend," Tayla Barlowe said.

Tayla's little girl, Emma, cooed from her sling an affirmative.

"I, for one, wouldn't have it any other way," the diminutive, thin man said, brushing a hand through his thick, black hair.

Rembrandt 'Remy' Lyles. Graphic artist and pop art novelist. Comic book artist, designer and comic book convention mainstay.

He lifted a glass to the room, just as he was lifting hopes of another book deal for his artwork, and many returned the gesture.

Johanna Crimson stared at Lyles with a defiant expression. She did not lift her glass to him. She did not wish him luck. She planned her own book arrangement but had no misgivings about her feelings for Remy Lyles. He was inconsequential in any regard.

"I need to further dinner service," Jenkins said to the room. "Please, converse, entertain yourselves." Then, to the black haired server, the formal man added, "Assist me, please, Ms. Makai."

He rolled away a fine, silver cart with lots of beverage pitchers lining it, the young, olive skinned woman close behind him.

As far as dinner conversation goes, it gradually became lively. The buzz charged the air, opinions and ideas humming with electricity. Mystery and action were the topic of the night.

All the guests remained united in the elegant dining hall with the exceptions of Andreya West. James Wyatt returned with the helicopter pilot and the director and the three of them started explaining what they knew from outside.

The exception, of course, was the mask. It remained on a need to know basis. Like the majority of the aftermarket masks produced for paintball, hockey and extreme sports, it was forged of a high impact plastic or polycarbonate material, complete with dark lenses. Black with a painted skull design on the front and a skull mold, as well, it would have been quite the topic of discourse.

Still, Bridger, Richter, Clayborne and Director Clark had agreed to keep it quiet for the time being. The Priests, James Wyatt, Gibson and his charge, Johanna Crimson, knew about it, too, of course.

They knew...

...and the ghost responsible for dropping it knew...

James Wyatt never really tired of talking. It was a good thing. He told the story of the explosion, the loss of power, the loss of cell signal and the overall mystery multiple times. Guests kept wanting to hear it over again. Mixed into those stories were recollections of 'great' cases he had worked and his honor at being chosen to help protect Johanna Crimson, on scene starlet.

Later, when he had shared all there was to disclose, the murmuring began. Most expressed great concern over the fiery eruption of the night. Some remained carefree.

"It's like a dinner theater," Johanna Crimson said jovially.

"I prefer we come up short on theater and we don't end up short on food," the motorcycle riding legend said.

"Well, you've ended up short but it's through nature. I don't think theater has anything to do with it," B'Rone Matwahali laughed, inciting others to do so.

"Lay off!" Rick Porter challenged. "Not everyone can be a giant."

"You, sir, are living proof," Matwahali laughed further.

"You're both giants in your fields, gentlemen," Maureen Li, the publishing guru, corrected. "Of course, you all are! We need to celebrate such a gathering of talent in one place! We should recall some of your accomplishments!"

She then began to chirp out awards, recognition and accomplishments each had attained.

"And, apparently, we're all cheap dates," Kess Melkin said with a snort. "She foots the bill for a vacation, even one with no electricity, no phones, and no explanations and we all jump at it."

Melkin had a lot more to add, some aloud and some under her breath. She was not alone.

"I am certain we will restore all standards and luxuries," Jenkins addressed them, hands clasped behind himself. Standing at attention by the door to the kitchen hall, he continued, "This has never happened before and I can assure you we are working to return the stars to our 'five star plus', world class stay."

"You sound just like a brochure," said Andreya West, a smile and playful eyes aimed at Jenkins.

She slipped in through the kitchen hall door, bumping him with it.

"Thank you," he replied, meaning none of it.

Then the conversations broke down into smaller, more localized discussions among those seated nearest each other. Shared thoughts became intimated secrets hidden in the dim candlelight.

Mark Gibson leaned close to Johanna Crimson.

"There's too much going on. Too much beyond our control."

"Your control," Crimson said with a sigh and a soft smile.

"Okay," he agreed with a shrug. "There are things I need to control. The more variables, the more chances of somethin' gettin' by me."

Crimson said, "Nothing gets by you at all, Gibson."

At that moment, Mick Priest walked into the dining hall through the door by Jenkins. Again, he was bumped slightly aside. Right behind Priest came Tye Richter and Falgrip Bridger and all took a seat.

"And, at long last, the lost tribe is all reunited again," Jenkins said, snapping his fingers at his server, Ms. Makai.

A cacophony of questions rose to life as Jenkins and Makai moved to serve the last to arrive.

Above the din, Mick Priest raised his voice and one hand.

"I don't mind sharing our information but be patient," Priest informed. "There's no rush; we aren't going anywhere."

And dinner continued.

There was good news. The generator building was fully stocked, up and running. It was self-contained, locked and secure. There was nothing to fear where that was concerned.

There was bad news. Mick Priest had indeed found traces of movement, trespassing, outside the back walls of the helicopter hangar. Hand prints on the windows. Footprints in the mulch beds. An overturned trash can. He had confirmed those things with Bridger. Both had agreed not to tell the gathering at dinner.

Also, Priest had scaled the hangar building's outside stairs to its rooftop observation deck. He used the mounted telescope and binoculars to look into the distant night for the bridge mentioned by the staff members. He could see parts of it, still glowing...in flames.

Though he told Richter and Bridger about the sight before they all returned to dinner, they decided that, too, should be played close to the vest. Priest told the dinner table that the fires in the distance had nearly gone completely out and that, like Grip Bridger suggested, it was more than likely a power transformer struck by heat lightning. Nothing to fear there, he suggested.

But did he believe it?

Yes or no, the guests swallowed it as readily as they had dinner.

The small talk, private chat, group jesting and room wide discussion all served to forge rapport, not only among the writers but with all present. The happiest looking attendee was the attractive Maureen Li. The better the crowd enjoyed things, the more likely she would walk away from the retreat with newly contracted authors.

Candles shrank and little rivers of wax pooled on silver candelabras. The sands of time slipped away. The strange events were discussed and, at least for the night, set aside. The morning would bring clarity, most of them agreed.

The entourage also played a round robin of introductions, yet again.

Aside from flirting with B'Rone Matwahali, however, Kess Melkin had been somewhat reserved, an uncommon state for her. West had been equally subdued. The director stalled the overall room speed and addressed them.

"Why not reintroduce yourselves?" Cassandra Clark asked. "Give us some insights, ladies. You're way too quiet tonight."

"Like what?" Melkin asked, poking about in her purse. Her country accent sharply bent her words, even though she only spoke two.

"Anything. Share what you feel," Clark said.

"Alright. I'm Kess Melkin," she groaned. "Like I told some others already, I write scary stuff, sexy stuff and scary, sexy stuff. Oh, and I won't make it a weekend with no smokes. And I'm out. Just sayin'."

The woman crumpled an empty pack of cigarettes and dropped the film and the paper box on the table.

"I'm sorry," Clark said. "It's just as well; this is a nonsmoking facility."

Melkin adjusted her skimpy top again. She twisted the leg seam of her skin tight, florescent aqua leggings, closed her eyes and swore under her breath. Then she rubbed over her face on the same side that a diamond stud pierced her nose.

"This is gonna be a long weekend," she grumbled.

"One can only imagine," Andreya West said beside her. She smiled for the group, saying, "I'm Andreya West. I write historical fiction and historical nonfiction. I'm an associate professor of Japanese medieval eras and the histories of feudal lords. I hold some other degrees, as well, but that's not what brings me here. Like I said, I write, too."

The director said, "Most impressive, Ms. West. I understand you even mastered Japanese...in all of its dialects."

"That's amazin'. You're so young," Kess Melkin mused. "Imagine all the time you had ta spend in those books. 'Course, it gotcha where ya are. We all write what we know, I s'pose," Melkin leered.

It seemed clear to the others, with Melkin's wide smirk, that she implied her personal experience authorized her to be a master of erotica.

She put on a clear pout as no one followed up on her lead.

"How many Japanese dialects are there?" Tayla Barlowe asked.

West paused thoughtfully, saying, "It's debated. Some dialectic studies are not even counted among the Ph. D ranks. I studied fourteen, only to be told later there were only ten to begin with...it's confusing, on a good day."

"History brought you to bein' a novelist?" B'Rone Matwahali asked.

Even in pondering, her big, sea green eyes distant and thoughtful, Andreya West was beautiful.

"On your way to a master's degree in a field of history, you do a lot of research and writing. That took me to an associate professor's position but left a long road to the doctorate and a fully tenured professor's position. By that time, I was in love with writing and, as Ms. Melkin said, we write what we know," said West. She added with a gesturing, upturned hand, "And, in all fairness, I'm not that young. I'm almost thirty years old."

Melkin rolled her eyes, saying, "Yeah. You're ancient."

"So, how about a weekend rubbing elbows with the one and only Johanna Crimson?" Maureen Li asked the table. She gestured at the actress with a huge smile and began clapping. "A hand for none other than Velvet Edge, herself!"

Others joined the applause. Rembrandt Lyles did not. He folded his arms across his chest, staring ruefully at his plate.

"Thank you, each and every one of you," Crimson said as she feigned a demure, shy shrug. "We're all the same this weekend, you know. We're all just writers, trying to share a part of ourselves with the world." Then, as if popping out of some character trance, she put her hand on Mark Gibson's chest. "And this is my protector, a peerless defense contractor, Mr. Mark Gibson."

Priest met the gaze of Mark Gibson. The man stared at him from directly across the long, wide table. The older man's blue eyes, already piercing, seemed sharper in the candlelight. Sharper...and less than happy at being in the spotlight.

Johanna Crimson nodded when Gibson turned a private word to her but she did not look at him. She stared at Priest, gestured his way and spoke again.

"And how about Mr. Mick Priest?" she said surprisingly. "An associate of my newest guardian, James Wyatt, Mr. Priest agreed to help us for the weekend. The irony is that he's one of us! He's a writer in his own right. Mr. Mikhael Priest," she introduced and applauded him.

Priest waved away the applause, saying, "I'm just a local novelty. North Carolina loves its own. So, my books sell okay, here in state."

Priest met Gibson's eyes when they returned to him.

Victor Jackson spoke on the topic.

"I like your work, Mr. Priest," he noted amiably. "Carolinian or no."

"Oi! What're we, then? A chopped bit o' liver?" Paul Blackwood suddenly teased, gesturing to the other Brit, B'Rone Matwahali. He wiped sweat from his brow, building beneath his silver hairline, adding, "I'm Paul Blackwood, an' I'm on the tele! I got me own cookin' program, the *Blackwood British Baking Show*!"

He reached over and pushed his fellow countryman's shoulder.

Glistening, nervous sweat on his black skin reflected the candlelight.

"For anyone who doesn't know me, I'm B'Rone Matwahali," the large, powerfully built Brit said. "An', fame or no, crowds or no, I still get the butterflies in my gut when I have to do live, public speaking."

It amused the others to see a man as physically imposing as Matwahali appear afraid of something. His reputation added to the irony.

"Matwahali, sweatin' bullets," Blackwood said, grinning.

"Yeah, yeah," the big man acknowledged. "It's a rip, right? Me, nervous?"

"Nah, we all got our *fears*," he answered, blue eyes sparkling.

"You just had to put 'fear' in there, didn't you? I mean, considering the whole '*Wild and Fearless*' thing," Matwahali asked with a knowing smile, making air quotations.

Paul Blackwood chuckled as he ran a hand over his silver and black hair. He was young, obviously having grayed early, even bearing the color change in his mustache and goatee.

"Ya know who this guy is, don't ya?" Blackwood asked no one in particular. "B'Rone Matwahali, the most famous British big game hunter, mercenary and adventurer since Allan Quatermain. He has his own TV show, *Wild and Fearless*."

"Allan Quatermain was fictional," Andreya West replied, pulling her silky hair into a pony tail.

Paul Blackwood answered, "Then I suppose Mr. Matwahali is more like a larger than life Bear Grylls, if Grylls had done mercenary work after his stint with Her Majesty's Special Forces. Besides, who cares if Quatermain was only fictional? He's larger than life, like our friend, here. And nobody can say Sean Connery didn't absolutely bring the role to life in that ensemble movie he did, may he rest in peace."

"Frederick Selous, the British big game hunter and adventurer, was a real person. It's believed that the character, Quatermain, was based on that *real* man," West interjected, her pristine skin glistening. She fanned herself. "Is it getting warm in here?"

"I'm sorry to say, yes," Cassandra Clark admitted. "No power, remember? It's only going to get hotter the longer we're without air conditioning."

Mick Priest watched Gibson signal to him. Subtly, he gestured toward the door to the main hall with the slightest tip of his head.

Priest gave an almost imperceptible nod.

Gibson got up and walked out the door. A few seconds passed and Mick Priest gave chase, telling his wife, SBI Agent, Sarah Priest, he would be right back.

In the dining area, conversations continued somewhat at random.

Out in the hallway, the discourse was pointed.

"Try again," Gibson demanded.

Priest had literally just stepped through the door.

"You first. What's on your mind?" Priest asked irritably.

"Heat lightning? That explosion? I don't buy it. Try again."

"Gibson, I don't know what exploded down the road."

"I think you got your suspicions."

Priest blinked at the other man's single minded insistence.

"I don't know what happened, yet."

The older man shook his head with, "Heat lightning don't hit and make stuff explode so strong that it shakes a mountainside. You know it and I know it."

"What I know is that you're probably right," he conceded. "But that's not something to throw out on that crowd at the table. Whatever exploded took the bridge over Nightshade Pass with it."

"The only ground route up here," Gibson growled.

"And it's only used for supplies and things like that. Guests never come here that way."

Then Sarah Priest interrupted them, stepping into the corridor.

"With the staff suggesting that everyone needs to retire to their rooms, we're about to have plenty of time to look for some real answers," she said. "We need to check out what blew up by searching where it actually happened, not from here."

Priest waved for the two of them to follow him back to dinner.

"...and, by then, hopefully, all will be back to normal," Cassandra Clark was telling the dining hall when the trio entered.

Everyone was present, once again.

"Good, you're back," Cassandra Clark said. "We were just discussing how retiring to our rooms might be the best course of action, at least until tomorrow."

"Badge 'em, Sarah," Mick Priest said to his wife.

"Ladies and gentlemen," Sarah Priest said, flashing her badge, "I'm Special Agent Sarah Priest, with the North Carolina State Bureau of Investigation. In light of tonight's events, I'm asking all of you to stay in your rooms until tomorrow morning. That includes the staff. With the power outage, we feel everyone would be far safer in their rooms."

The usual, expected questions rang out.

Why stay in the rooms? What's there to worry over? What isn't safe about the resort in general? Is there more we should know about?

Before questions could swell to a clamor, Mick Priest added a note.

"We don't want to scare anyone. It just isn't safe to go wandering around the resort with no power and low lighting. For that matter, in some areas, there's no lighting, whatsoever. Hopefully, tomorrow will go back to normal but tonight would be best spent erring on the side of caution. Please."

"If anyone is uncomfortable with the power outage, you can always bunk up in rooms together. All rooms have multiple beds, anyway."

Response to the director was slow to come.

"I can share my room," Paul Blackwood started with a shrug, wearing a wolfish smile. "I wouldn't want any ladies left alone."

"Shocker, that is," Matwahali said and chuckled.

The Aussie model raised an eyebrow at Blackwood and blew a kiss.

"Maureen and I are booked to share," the Chief Financial Officer of Gridlock Publishing said.

Maureen Li rolled her eyes.

"And what if I wanted to start some torrid affair with a writer?" Li teased, giggling.

I would be very grateful I'm not a writer, Victor Jackson mused.

Porter grinned at Kimber Mobley and said, "We can share, blondie."

The model stopped him cold.

"Nice try, Ricochet Ricky, but no," Mobley responded coldly, her accent thick. "I intend to enjoy my weekend."

"Ladies, it looks like the Ricochet Rider is back on the available list," he announced in cringe-worthy fashion.

"Surprise, surprise," Kess Melkin muttered to Andreya West.

The erotica writer, an attractive woman in her own right, then cut a sidelong glare at B'Rone Matwahali. She drank him in, basking in the view of his powerful form and his rich, black complexion, covered in a sheen of perspiration. His rock jaw and chiseled features drew her.

The man caught her look and held it with his own. A grin tugged at the corner of his mouth.

"I'm all alone in my room, too," he announced.

"Now, that's a shame if ever I heard one," Melkin replied. She smiled provocatively and said, "I'd be happy to share mine with you."

Matwahali lifted his glass to her and said, "Cheers."

"Surprise, surprise," Tayla Barlowe whispered to her precious little one, sitting in her lap. Then she added, aloud, "Little Emma and I are in our own room and I doubt anyone else wants to stay up with us when she gets fussy."

James Wyatt said, "I'll be in and out of my room while I check on Ms. Crimson. No need to double up."

"Sarah and I have one," Mick Priest said.

"Gibson is my bodyguard. We're in the same room already," Johanna Crimson said.

Andreya West said, "I'm all grown up and I'm not afraid of the dark. I came here for peace and quiet and a little time away and I intend to have it. I'll be alone."

Cassandra Clark assigned Tye Richter as a temporary roommate for Grip Bridger and asked Pilot Gretchen Clayborne to stay with her. She also asked the lead server, the dark haired Helena Makai, to join her and Clayborne. Jenkins insisted he was fine on his own but Clark would have none of it. She pointed at the Head Chef, a tall, lanky character in an apron and a puffy, white chef's hat.

"Everyone, this is our dietitian and master chef, Avid Swartzovski. Chef Swartzovski, for now, you'll be rooming with Mr. Jenkins."

The thin man nodded without a word. He did fold long, skinny arms over his torso but what that meant, if anything, was left unsaid. The Ichabod Crane double did not even look at Jenkins.

"So, what now?" Andreya West asked.

Marcus Gibson, private defense contractor, jumped to his feet.

"Now, I say we get some truth," he growled in the silence.

Mick and Sarah Priest stared holes right through him.

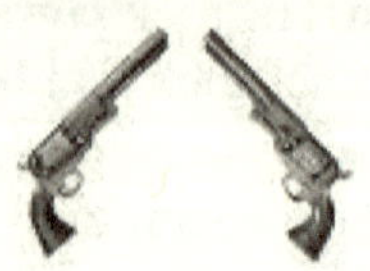

CHAPTER FOUR

"We go to bed," Sarah said sternly, "please."

Gibson looked me right in the eye.

Incidentally, so did Johanna Crimson.

"So, everyone's happy waiting for daybreak?" Gibson asked.

Well... someone said.

I don't really know... another muttered.

Does it make any difference? Who has any better ideas? What's really going on around here?

"I think we can rest easy-" I started.

"I don't. With all due respect to the SBI, I think we can safely say somethin' big is goin' on."

"Gibson," Sarah started again, "we all need to remain calm."

"I'm a private defense contractor," Gibson said. "I work as a full time, live-in protector. *Not* just a bodyguard but a constant protector. I work for a client, goin' with 'er everywhere. Everywhere. All the time."

"Oh, yeah, nothing like a bodyguard at all," James sniped.

"You know what, Ponytail?" Gibson barked, finger pointing.

"Gentlemen," Sarah calmed.

A formerly calm and quiet room was beginning to roil into a dull roar of voices by then.

"Hold it!" I bellowed and the room fell silent.

"Perhaps, Mr. Gibson has a point?" Sarah prodded.

"I've been a Marine Corps Gunnery Sergeant and an Operations Commander for the Marines' Force Recon," Gibson growled, his voice all grit and gravel. "Once a Marine, always a Marine. Warrior for life. I went into Special Investigations for the joint ATF and military task force on stolen military weapons. After that I went into protection with Black Watch. That's the multi-branch, joint military Special Ops unit tasked with protectin' government figures from drug cartels, gun runners, that sorta stuff." After a breath, he said, "I eventually went solo and I got contacts and pull you wouldn't believe."

"The point, Gibson," I said casually. "Quickly."

"Oh, yeah, the point," Gibson nodded with a grin. "Mick Priest, private detective and bodyguard, former employee of the James Wyatt agency of bodyguards and security work. You're a writer, too, but that ain't what got you in hot water with North Carolina 'powers that be' for a while. Overall, a pretty impressive work record. That's what got you out of hot water."

All three of us started to speak but he beat us to it.

"Sarah Melindez-Priest, State Bureau of Investigation Agent, former New Hanover County Deputy, former member of the New Hanover County Sheriff's Chaplain's Office, member of the state Sheriff's Chaplain Offices." He pointed at James and said, "James Wyatt, state licensed investigator, security contractor and bodyguard services contractor. And trust me when I tell ya I know about every person on these grounds this weekend just as good."

Do me! Do me! others urged enthusiastically.

"What's all that got to do with anything?" James demanded, ignoring the voices.

"Johanna Crimson is my responsibility and I take that seriously, like life or death seriously. Especially when it may be. I got a distinct feelin' on all this. It's a feelin' I get when something is in the room with ya but ya can't see it for the shadows. Man like me? I keep starin' until it comes out."

Silence reigned for a moment.

"Somebody say something," Tayla said, hugging little Emma.

"Right. I hate this kinda quiet," Melkin said.

"Is there something ta be said?" Blackwood asked.

"Must be. Nobody's talkin' and that's how you usually know," B'Rone Matwahali said with a nod.

Others agreed. The surge of mumbling began again.

Cassandra Clark locked eyes with me. She wanted to know if we should open the can of worms before sleeping. I could not see much of an option anymore. Gritting my teeth, I could just imagine decking Gibson. Playing the hand too soon. Too soon.

"Take a seat, Gibson," I directed and lifted my hands to everyone. "Everybody, please settle down. Listen. I don't want to repeat this over and over so please pay attention."

It took a moment.

"So, here it is," I said. "There's a possibility that right here, this very weekend, we have a killer among us. It may be-"

"Well played!" Matwahali shouted, a smile on his comely visage.

Then others agreed. Boisterous chatter ran through the room with laughter and relieved tones.

"I told you!" Maureen Li cried. "Isn't this a weekend to remember?"

Someone began applauding and more followed suit.

"No, listen-" I tried.

"Mate, I dunno if you already got a bloke to play along and be your murderer but I'm game!" Blackwood shouted over the others.

"This is just like that movie," someone chimed.

Then someone named another movie, another play, then a television show. Two others named books.

"People!" I called. "Please-"

"We're going to be a part of one of the most classic styles of tale!" the publishing headhunter continued.

"Or just dinner theater," Melkin muttered, her pretty face sour.

The staff all shared quizzical looks as the din increased.

"It could be like the classic, *And Then There Were None*," West said. "The Agatha Christie novel."

Johanna Crimson said, nodding, "And, of course, who could forget the groundbreaking movie? 1945, black and white. Silver screen. Classic. Who could forget Walter Huston in that film?"

"Perish the thought," Melkin muttered to herself, rolling big eyes.

"And what sort of starlet would I be if I didn't appreciate the ones who went before me? June Duprez? Was there a lovelier lady in that era? In any screen era?" Crimson asked.

"I think there was a modern remake, too," Blackwood added.

"The literary works by Christie helped get the whole thing started, what set the standard and the outline for many others to come. It started that format. You know, a gathering, stranded in a remote place where, one by one, the people gathered are murdered. Doyle and Poe wrote mysteries earlier, like *Murders in the Rue Morgue* and all the *Sherlock* tales, but Christie made this format, this set up. The idea became a staple for other books, movies, television shows and plays to borrow and adapt," Andreya West said.

"It's kinda like the board game, *Clue*," said Tye Richter.

"Yes," Jenkins said, drawing out the short word. "Just alike."

His disdain and disagreement were clear.

"They made that into a movie, too," Tayla Barlowe said.

"Now, that's a classic," Kess Melkin said.

Johanna Crimson just clenched her jaw then sighed.

"All of you, drop it!" Gibson roared suddenly, shaking the crystal on the table.

Temper, temper, someone muttered, the only response.

In the abrupt sound of nothingness, he spoke again.

"The boy ain't entertaining us! He's got somethin' to say! Pipe down!"

I cleared my throat, still surprised at the turn the room had taken.

Dinner theater murder mystery, I thought with a shake of my head.

"I'm serious. This is no joke and no program. I am, for lack of a better word...dead...serious."

I raised the black, fully enclosed helmet-mask in the air, glad I had accepted it when the staff offered it. I had told them to hand it over to Clark but she had been less than enthralled with taking it. The candles played off the white, skull pattern emblazoned on the face as they flickered in the dark lenses.

Several gasps and a couple of expletives preceded the oncoming hush. The crowd stared in confusion, disbelief, curiosity, fear and sometimes a mix of them. And the crowd stared in boneyard silence.

"This was discovered on the grounds earlier, out by the landing areas. Unless one of you has an explanation for this little item or you wish to claim it as your lost property, I'll tell you what it may mean."

I waited. No admissions.

"In that case, I'll begin with this. It just so happens that Johanna Crimson has been receiving death threats."

"Lots of us famous types get those," Blackwood said.

"She's getting them from a named killer," Sarah informed them. "The Ghost Revolver. According to my state contacts, one of those masks is left behind at all of this killer's crime scenes. That tells us that it may be a warning or a calling card. The reality is that we know nothing for certain, however. This could be a simple prank...although in very poor taste."

Is she for real? Are you sure this isn't part of a show?

Whispers and suspicions snaked around the table. The crowd was stirring again. Voices slowly came to life from whispers to grumbling.

"And the idea that heat lightnin' managed to drop all communication and power with one lucky strike is either a calming lie or a blind hope," Gibson said, his tone exasperated. "Which is it?"

Then came the uproar.

Before I could shout it down, Sarah stepped up into a chair.

"Stop it!" she howled, bringing them back to earth. "You're gaining nothing! Panic and fear are the wrong responses!"

"Oh, this just ain't happ'nin', no way, no way," Kess Melkin repeated to herself. She rocked back and forth in her chair. "Nope. No way. Can't be. Not here. Not now."

Almost as one the group turned heads and eyes to Melkin.

"It ain't just happening to you, cupcake," Kimber Mobley said.

"We're all here together," Maureen Li added. "For better...or worse."

"I think you'd all agree the most likely target of a nutcase killer would be Johanna," Gibson interjected, putting his hand on Crimson's shoulder. "She's the highest paid American actress. Right now, she's got more exposure, credits and appearances than any of you could imagine. She's got uber-fans, creepy fans, obsessive paparazzi and everything else in between. Death threats, kidnappin' threats...it's crazy. She's recently had mail suggestin' that, because she went through with Velvet Edge Three, she's been marked for death for playing the character."

B'Rone Matwahali nodded to Kess Melkin. She met his eyes, mouthing her previous mantra.

No way, no way. Not here. Not now.

"Maybe everything isn't about Ms. Crimson," Matwahali said.

"Then who's it about, Adventure-Man?" Richard Porter snapped. "I suppose it's all about you and that British silverback, huh?"

"Ay, mate, watch your mouth," Paul Blackwood warned.

"I was thinkin' 'bout Ms. Melkin," Matwahali clarified.

Kess Melkin had lowered her face. She glanced about through the top of her eyes, her look almost one of cowering. Her lower lip trembled.

"You okay?" Tayla Barlowe asked Melkin.

"No," whimpered Melkin. "I...when I was in my teens...I...we..."

I interrupted her, my own stomach in knots out of sheer sympathy.

"For those of you unfamiliar with Ms. Melkin's writing," I began, "her debut novel was about a serial killer in rural Kentucky. It was inspired by her own experiences in her youth."

"I thought she wrote sexy monster stories," my pal James said.

"I do," Melkin growled, trying to recover her voice. "But...the first one was based on my teen friends and me...kinda. I made it into a monster story, a werewolf...but the truth was that there was a serial killer in Knox County they just called the Wolf. Me 'n' my group of friends were stalked by him...by it..."

What're the chances? a woman asked.

How bad can your luck be? a man posed.

Impossible, crept up in the mumbling several times.

"You ain't alone," Matwahali promised Kess flatly. "No worries."

"I want outta here. Now, not tomorrow. Tonight. I don't even have ta pack. Just get me on the road," she whined.

I felt for Melkin. What were the odds of facing a weekend on the watch for a killer more than once in a lifetime, for someone not hired to do so?

"Discretion is the better part of valor," West chimed. "Perhaps an exodus is in order."

Not all were ready to run, however.

"Maybe I'm accustomed to the invisible threat of the unknown. Maybe I'm calloused to dark shadows cast over me that never become tangible," Crimson spoke. "But are we really going to let a trick-or-treat mask and a power outage scare all of us off a mountain? Really?"

"Johanna," Gibson started.

"There's nothing to fear but fear itself," Tayla Barlowe added. "What are we really afraid of? Is there any reason to believe a killer is on the grounds? I mean...other than the mask, that is."

"And how do you even know about this mask thing?" Richard Porter barked. "I haven't heard any big news stories about any-"

"You aren't in the business," Grip Bridger said sourly. The guard pointed to Sarah, Gibson and James then nodded at me. "They do this sorta thing for a living. They ought to know more than any of us. It's their job."

"The Ghost Revolver," Gibson said lowly.

The rest of the room quietened and all eyes fell on him. Sarah stepped down from her chair and locked eyes with me.

"He's a freelancer, another 'contractor', so to speak. His true identity is unknown," Gibson continued. "He's a specialist. Delivers his services to war zones, impenetrable bases, prisons, strongholds, behind enemy lines, inside the most secure locations...and everywhere else. He just 'ghosts' in and out and leaves a trail of bodies, targets and witnesses and anyone who gets in the way. What he doesn't leave are clues, fingerprints or anything that could identify him."

"Including shell casings, bullet casings," I said. "Which is where the name seems to come from. Ghost Revolver. You don't leave shell casings behind if you use a revolver the way you would if you had an auto that was ejecting them as you fired."

"Fascinating," Matwahali mused. "It's hard to believe-"

"I wanna go! Now!" Melkin shouted.

"Stay calm, please," Cassandra Clark said.

"Hold on," Gibson warned them all. "I think Priest has more."

"He ain't alone in that," Rembrandt Lyles interjected.

The thin man ran a finger around the top of his glass, staring into the beverage. Marcus Gibson and Johanna Crimson stared holes into him.

"The Ghost Revolver is a legend," Lyles continued. "Right outta history. Vigilante from the 1800s, bringing justice with two revolvers that are clad in silver and handled in bone. Legend says he's still doing it, his ghost, that is, or his descendants, people he's passed the guns to..."

"Comic book gobbledygook," Gibson growled.

"He's not wrong about the history," Andreya West countered. "It's a real legend, one that's been handed down for-"

"I thought you were a Japanese specialist," Gibson snapped.

She wore a big grin and bright eyes.

"I'm an overachiever," she chimed. "I mastered in Native American histories and southwestern folklore-"

James grinned at her, saying, "I knew it. My people."

"We've got to get a look at whatever exploded tonight," I said, trying to bring the room back to topic. "The glow in the distance...I think the bridge over the pass was destroyed. The whole bridge."

"The lines, electrical and data, and the cellular booster tower are attached to Shadow Walker Bridge," Cassandra Clark muttered. "It would explain why the power and the communications went down. But, for a whole bridge to be destroyed?"

"It was a lot more than a lightning strike," I said.

"So, this is on purpose. A plan," Gibson declared.

"Does anyone come up here by ground?" someone asked.

"Repair crews, builders, suppliers exiting from the highway. The regular mountain roads are not really traveled," Clark said. "Most of our staff and our guests are flown in."

"It doesn't matter. Even if we had transportation. I don't want a crowd of people to get half way to the bridge and find out we can't go any farther," Sarah Priest said.

"We need to know what happened out there," I said. "For sure. Before we talk about leaving and walking and everything else that pops into our heads. We don't even know for certain the Ghost Revolver is here. Everything is just guesswork, right now."

"Does it matter where we face this weekend?" Melkin snapped. "At least we gotta try to leave! Better to face things as they come, in action, not sittin', waitin' on some-"

"*Does it matter?*" James repeated with a scowl. "Yeah, it matters! Defendin' a room is easier than defendin' a car or a clump of bushes!"

Clark and the staffers passed glances and nods.

"We wait."

"No! I ain't dyin' up here! I didn't survive the Kentucky marsh to die on a Carolina mountain!" Melkin cried.

"We wait, Ms. Melkin," Cassandra Clark said.

"Fine," Melkin growled. The woman jumped to her feet, snatched up her chair and put its back against a wall. "But I ain't movin' from right here until we're on the way out. An' I'm watchin' all of ya'll."

West arched her eyebrows high and looked around.

"Fiesty," she noted.

"Sarah, you sit on everybody here. You got the badge and the authority," I said. "James, you're with her. Watch out for each other. I'll take Mr. Richter, Mr. Bridger and Ms. Clayborne to the chopper bay. A short flight down to the bridge ought to tell us more. Scout it out."

"Why not just start taking us all off the mountain with the helicopter?" Melkin demanded.

"Four at the time?" Sarah asked her.

"As long as I'm in the first four, I don't care," Melkin said.

"We keep two SUVs here," Richter told the room. "If the bridge is secure, we can all leave at once. Two SUVs and the chopper can do it."

Melkin did not like it. She was not the only one. No one else had any better ideas, though. So, we slowly broke apart, moving off for our roles.

I wondered what it was all about as much as anyone else. My only clue had been a dream about a dead woman...who was not dead.

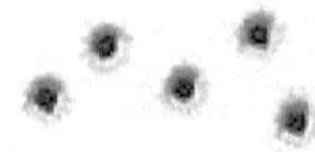

The rooms, from what I understood, all mirrored each other. No need for presidential suites or royal bedchambers. All of them ranked as premiere resort stays. The best North Carolina had to offer. Some of the best in all of the United States. In the top ten worldwide.

I had stayed in nice hotels. I had been to posh resorts and luxury inns. I had to admit, there was something special about Horse and Heraldry. Of course, I owned horses and had been riding half my life, so there was the slightest chance I was biased. Nevertheless, I was impressed from the moment I touched my door.

I admired the iron bound, plank built door in the hallway emergency lighting's glow as I opened it. It stretched seven feet high and barred passage with a barrier of oak four feet wide and three inches or more thick. The balance hinged on perfection; it felt weightless.

Just inside the room, I grabbed up my flashlight and my phone. With the elaborate door closed behind me, it blotted out the hallway's light. I brought the flashlight to life and sprayed it around the room. My bags rested on one of the beds and I rifled through them, retrieving my other Colt 10mm, my lockpick set and several extra magazines for the pistols. I always wore pants with cargo pockets for a reason. Fully equipped, I finally felt dressed.

Then, wielding the light like a sword, I saw the surroundings truly come to life. It washed over wall to wall, horizontal planking, bathing them in its glow. The planks eased the soul with a soft, honey gold color, knots and grains all visible to the eye. They encompassed the high, arched ceilings, too, as much as fifteen feet high.

Shadows played off a tremendous, walk in fireplace dead ahead of the door. It rose to better than ten feet high, a massive wall of rough stone and mortar. It fed into a stainless steel venting chamber that ran horizontally; I figured all the rooms on my side of the building fed into a central chimney someplace through those channels. Two crossed pikes with ax blades and a shield behind them decorated the face of the gray and white stone.

Before the fireplace, in the center of the massive, twenty foot by thirty foot room, a long, leather couch stared into the gaping fireplace maw. The couch had brought its family to stare, as well, since a matching love seat and two matching armchairs kept it company. Four side tables of brass and ebony wood supported thick, glass tops and individual lamps, though the ceiling was perforated with recessed bulb ports.

Against the wall on my right were two beds, a queen and a twin, done up in silk and mock animal skin coverings. Against the wall on my left was a king size bed, dressed alike. All had side tables on both sides, each table with lamps of their own. At the foot of each bed was a rolled arm bench, upholstered in black satin.

To each side of the fireplace, glass french doors opened to the balcony, though it was more of an upstairs walk than an individual perch. The entire fourth floor, my room's floor, had an outside level rounding the building. Of course, so did the third floor, also a guest floor, and the second floor, lined with rooms for the staff. Each level above ground had a line of balconies, uninterrupted and joining every room.

Overall, the word echoing in my mind was simply, *breathtaking*.

Time was an issue, however. There was none available for admiration and study. I moved for the ground floor to meet Richter, Bridger and the chopper pilot, Gretchen Clayborne.

As it happened, they were waiting for me in the main lobby, between the staircases. Grip Bridger stood with his arms folded over his chest. Clayborne was close by his side. Richter, a few feet to their left, held a bag and a flashlight.

"You know, bailing out is probably the best idea," Tye Richter said.

I said, "Leaving is only a good idea if we have a place to go."

Richter shrugged then said, "I'm just sayin'...you know."

"With clear, concise, hopeful statements like that, you could be a weatherman," Bridger growled.

"Hey, if the pay's right," Richter said with a grin.

I swept my light here and there and followed Bridger, our middle man, as Richter led the way. With the dark haired Clayborne on Bridger's arm, we trekked together in the relative comfort of the night air, away from the increasingly stuffy resort building.

"All right, hold up," I said when we got close to the hangar. "Let me take over point. Watch my back."

As if it were scripted, a foundation shaking boom went off in the night, only to be echoed in the distance by smaller ones.

I looked around for danger but Tye Richter shook his head.

"Just thunder on the mountain."

"Are we in for some rain?" I asked.

"Heat lightning," Bridger said. "We call it summer rage."

Carefully, cautiously, we approached the hangar bay entries and Richter pulled out some keys. Bridger held Richter's light.

"Progress is great," Tye said to me. He pointed to a digital keypad, adding, "But power outages are reasons to never give up traditional, mechanical devices. If we had removed the old school lock and key mechanisms instead of merging them with the new pads-"

"Just like the main building's room doors," I said.

"Exactly; we'd be breaking in right now, and I mean breaking, literally. A window, a handle, whatever. I don't mind technology but progress isn't progress without proper fail-safes."

"Made it possible to lock up earlier without keys, too," I agreed. "Set the locks, close the doors, no worries."

"Exactly," Richter said.

Inside the building, Richter took over his light and Bridger drew his weapon. I pulled a Colt to hand, as well. The security specialist and I moved cautiously, checking to see that the four of us were indeed alone, while Richter and Clayborne approached the helicopter. The four of us broke apart in the dark.

While Grip Bridger and I still rousted the shadows for things that go bump in the night, Gretchen Clayborne suddenly cursed and slammed a hand against her bird.

"Well, fellas, that ain't right," Richter called to us.

We rushed back to see his light trained on the pilot's side of the helicopter. Its cockpit door was open, damaged and dangling from one hinge. Gretchen Clayborne was on her haunches, leaning underneath the fuselage of the whirlybird, touching the closest of the fold-down landing wheels.

"The door is torn half off, the wheels are flat, and there's a puddle under here!" the woman howled angrily. "What can-"

"I didn't smell fuel when we came in," Richter spouted, dropping to one knee. "Can't be that..."

He crawled under the helicopter and touched his finger to the liquid.

"I didn't smell anything," Bridger added.

"Hydraulic fluid," Richter growled.

Gretchen cursed.

"We use synthetics. You can barely smell it on your hand, much less in the air," Richter noted.

"Was my bird like this when you locked up?" Clayborne yelled, coming to her feet and into my space. "I mean, you did lock up, right?"

"Ms. Clayborne, calm yourself," I advised.

"He might not have even noticed," Richter said. "You can't smell-"

"You don't *smell* a door hanging half off the hinges!" she screamed.

Richter raised both eyebrows and lifted his hands.

"Easy, Gretchen," he said.

"She's right," Bridger said with a shrug.

"It would've probably caught my attention, the door twisted off the hinges," I said, my own sarcasm rising. "So, no, it wasn't like that. I took my time checking this place. And yes, I did lock it down. Richter just unlocked the smaller entry to get us in. It's simple. We've had a visitor."

"A ghost?" Clayborne snapped. "Fine, let it kill an airhead actress! But why wreck my 'copter? Leave my baby alone!"

She stormed away, cursing, heading for the tool benches, the wrap around cabinetry and shelving.

"How bad is it, Tye?" Bridger asked lowly.

"We can't roll it out of the hangar by hand without tires, and they're slashed. I can still pull it into the open with my tow motor, though. We'd just have to go get it from the generator room."

"Okay, that's not so bad," I said.

He nodded, saying, "Yeah, that ain't the bad part."

"Tye?" Bridger pushed.

"The hydraulic fluid," I said.

"Works the flaps and whatnot," he said. "Won't fly blowin' fluid everywhere."

I sighed.

"Fix it, man," Bridger said.

"He can't," Gretchen interrupted, striding back to us.

She threw a ring of padlock keys at Richter which he batted away.

"Gretchen!" Bridger barked.

"The fluid cabinets are empty, Tye!" she roared. "No oil, no lubes, no small fuels, no aerosols, nothing!"

"Don't blame me!" he shouted at her. "At least we still have the fuel tank...or...do we?"

The young man trotted to a huge, rectangular tank. It stood in the corner closest to the hangar bay door. Up the steps he flew to the top edge where he grabbed at a padlock. It slipped free in his hand. In pieces, one by one.

"No way..." he muttered. "Several hundred gallons of aircraft fuel..."

"Gone," Gretchen Clayborne mewled, teetering on the edge of crying. "Who could've done this? Who?"

Grip Bridger swept his gun all about us again, as if the box had just been pilfered before our very eyes, like the thief would still be standing someplace close by us. Richter, for his part, put his hands on his hips in utter defeat and denial.

"It...just ain't right."

"If I had to guess," I said lowly, "I'd say someone doesn't want us to leave this resort."

"Yeah. I'd bet you're right," Bridger said.

Tydas Richter said, "We still have the Suburbans, the SUVs."

"Unless one of them, loaded with all of this fuel, was used to destroy the bridge," I said with a sigh. "Which would be the another reason someone stole all the flammables. Adding to the ignition and burn on Nightshade Pass."

"Trapping us here...for real," Clayborne groaned.

"We can't even go check on the explosion, to see," Bridger muttered.

"I wouldn't go that far," I said.

They all focused on me at once.

"No one could drive two SUVs at once. It got awfully quiet out here with no air conditioning, no fans, nothing running after that explosion. Whoever took one vehicle and all the fuel-"

"Couldn't have taken both," Richter finished. "They wouldn't have risked getting caught taking another vehicle, in the quiet, with all of us wandering around."

"No, they were too busy trashing my bird," Gretchen said, her lower lip quivering.

"Gotta be a pro," Bridger offered, looking around again. "Takes a truck. Slips in here, takes the fuel. Makes a racket, drawing us down here to check everything and think it's okay...I mean, who thinks to check fuel tanks...and we're busy checking this building while he slips off to wherever he stashed the truck. Drives to the bridge, sets it off, if that's what's been done. We all get wrapped up with talking, talking, talking some more, and he comes in here and lays the beat down on our chopper, knowing we'd all be inside...chatting."

"Who could do all this? Alone? And why?" Richter asked.

"An operative who's the very best at what they do. Efficient. Effective," I said.

"Deadly," Bridger said.

"A ghost," Gretchen finished.

Bridger had railed aloud at the miscreant responsible. The young man promised that vengeance and justice would rain down. Only he did it with less eloquence. Richter had reserved his opinions for himself. His internal thoughts were hardly family friendly. He promised himself he would share them at full volume if they found the perpetrator. Nobody wrecked his hangar. Nobody stole from it. Not without paying the piper. Gretchen had hidden no thought and no sentiment, bewailing the acts, lamenting the damage done to her helicopter and spewing pure hatred for the person responsible.

Priest, on the other hand, took it far too well. Too patiently.

Too patiently, Richter considered. *Man's ire burns that slow...gonna be a furious explosion when he lets go...*

"Okay, Tye," Mick Priest finally breathed.

The detective pointed off in the general direction of the generator building, acres away from them.

"Grip's going back to the manor with Gretchen. You and I are going to get that other Suburban, if it's there."

Bridger huffed and started to protest but all the others shut him down before he got much traction. Moments later, he led Clayborne out.

When Priest and Richter were alone, the detective spoke again.

"Who else has a key to this lockup? And the generator room? And the vehicles?"

Disbelievingly shaking his head, Richter led Priest outside and they started off across the grounds.

"Me, obviously. I have keys to just about everything, within reason," he said.

"Yeah, you're facility operations. You would. I was asking who else."

"Jenkins and Grip, for emergencies, and Cassie...uh, Director Clark. One or two of my regular techs...but none of them are even here. Besides, Mr. Priest, I don't see the motivation for any of our people to do this. You think we're being deliberately cut off, trapped here, right?" the young man exhaled.

"I do," Priest said lowly.

"By who?"

"By whom," Priest corrected.

Richter rolled his eyes.

"Yeah, yeah, writers' weekend. Whom?" Richter asked.

"The question of the hour," Mick Priest said. "So, anyone else you know of with keys to everything?"

"Nope."

"Good to know."

The two men slipped into the generator building by way of its carport door, once Richter had unlocked it. Inside, one stark white Suburban sat where two had once been.

"You called it," Richter said.

"We've still got one." Priest clapped the younger man on the shoulder, adding, "Get your key, bud. You're taking us to the bridge."

"But, even if we find what blew and burned, we're going on for help, right?" Richter asked. "When we get to the bridge, we just cross it."

Priest said, "I have a feeling that's not going to be one of our options. But you never know until we get there."

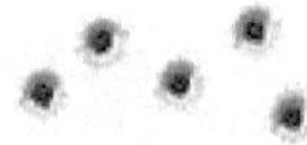

In just the few miles to Shadow Walker Bridge, I developed a new sense of urgency. It welled inside me but was unlike the anxious awareness of the case, what there was of a case. The sudden apprehension settled onto me like a cold, wet blanket, trying to smother my resolve. A weight lodged on my chest. Still, I tried to put it aside as we eased to a stop at the bridge landing...

...what was left of it.

The gaping maw of Nightshade Pass and the fire burning there mocked me, taunted me.

There is no passage here, it said.

The scene was little more than burning devastation. Still, Richter followed my lead when I slipped from the vehicle.

A concussive blast had shattered the bridge landing, stone and pavement thrown far and wide. Fire burned in fuel and oil deposits on the foundations. At one side, the junction service box for electricity and communications lay torn asunder by the blast. The bridge was shattered, too, the very concrete webbed with cracks. While those brittle portions still stood, crossing in vehicles would bring the utter collapse of the bridge. Crossing on foot would be courting death.

The cellular booster tower lay over on its side, a giant slain, bent where it wrapped over the ailing bridge. Its apex pointed downward into the dark shadow of the pass, almost as if gesturing at something.

We apprehensively walked over to the remnants of the landing.

We did not need our lights. Like some great beast slain and cast down from the mountainside, a mangled, burning pile of scrap wreckage covered some rocks near the valley bottom. Flames in multiple shades and colors flickered along the steel remnants, parts twisted and tortured like upturned arms or legs reaching for escape.

"You know what that looks like?" Richter asked.

"Yeah. I do."

A single rear door, blown free of the explosion, offered the answer to what the wreckage had once been, though we knew already. The door, tangled in brush some twenty feet below the ridge, was from a white Suburban.

I ground my jaw against the frustration. I knew what the colored fire meant; explosives, fuels. The burning colors told the sad tale of elements like magnesium, titanium, phosphorus or thermite being present. The prolific and lingering fires testified to the use of fuels to boost them, too.

I jerked about.

"C'mon, Tye," I said and strode for the SUV. "I'm driving."

I looked about again, turning this way and that, frowning in the light of the fires before I closed the driver door. Claws of ice raked down my back and left me with a chill.

No more denying. No more doubt.

A very dangerous soul prowled the mountain. A professional.

"I think I've seen what there is to see here," I said aloud. "Thank you, Lord Jesus. Please help me understand what I'm here to do."

"Amen," Richter said.

Then I put a trail of burning rubber to the road.

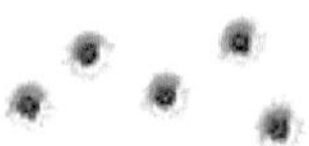

In modern times, the very idea of a haunting, the belief in ghosts, met with mockery. Such stories, once a mainstay of Americana, garnered a dubious reception, at least, and more often rebuttals of logic and *no-such-thing-isms*, whatever their wording. Lingering spirits. The dead at unrest. Those were the topics exiled to campfire stories and tall tales, pulp novels and horror films.

However, a broader definition of ghosts persisted; being haunted meant a lot of different things to different people. Decisions and choices. Paths taken and roads avoided. Things done and things left undone. Memories, yearnings and regrets. All could haunt a person.

The past in general, even distant history, could haunt the living. In perspective, most people lived haunted lives, whether they embraced the idea of restless spirits or not. At Horse and Heraldry Resort, the past had set a collision course for the guests and the staff, no longer a lingering ghost but a coming reckoning.

Candles flickered over fine china saucers and crystal stemware. The silver practically stood at attention in shining perfection. On the table gathered three different types of rolls and buns, one sweet in and of itself, while five spreads made themselves available nearby. Jenkins did not sit even after he and the head server had poured the coffee.

"Would you like to begin, Mr. Priest?" Ms. Clark asked, clearly nervous.

"Sure. It doesn't really matter how or when we start. The facts aren't going to get any better than they are right now."

I spread the cards out, sparing no details. The hand dealt the resort was unkind and there were no draws and no discards. We held a deck of trouble with no power, no communication, little transportation and no way down the mountain even with transportation.

There were numerous death threats on Johanna Crimson and there was a possibility that a famed assassin, a professional serial killer, stalked the grounds. We chewed over the mask found on the grounds and the willful destruction of the helicopter, the bridge and the toppled communications tower.

I had fully expected it to come but the storm of emotions nearly swept the room away. Fear, shock, sorrow, panic. They all made their appearance. Voices lifted in crying and other ones chose rage. In any case, though it was difficult, it all had to be subdued and brought into reason.

The tumult awakened the sleeping Emma Barlowe before being called down and she added her cries to the noise. Tayla Barlowe said she was taking her little girl to a ladies room for changing. Andreya West said she would go along to help.

Cassandra Clark ordered Bridger to escort them. Safety first.

You're safe, right now, in this room, we assured the rest of them. *We have to take it one moment at a time. Be calm.*

A few more moments of chaos until sanity once again took hold.

Kess Melkin adopted her rocking to and fro again and her whispered denials. A fruitless chant, on the one hand, but one that served to quell her yelling and crying.

Back on track, Richter had his head in the game.

"That Suburban would have been perfect for carrying all kinds of fuel, even most of it from the tank, using all of our empty buckets."

"I said the Polo shirts would be the end of me," Jenkins said with a sigh and a dose of sarcasm. "I bet one of them is hiding on the grounds."

"Give it a rest, Lurch," James Wyatt said, wiping his mouth. "Good buns, though, by the way."

"Please, Jenkins," Director Cassandra Clark said. "This is no time for that."

Porter said, "We're all on the choppin' block! You think a killer is gonna leave witnesses? Why do you think he's strandin' us all here?"

"Panic won't fix this," I warned. "It just blinds you, hinders clear thought. Take a deep breath. The only good news is that this particular killer doesn't kill 'innocents' or bystanders, only chosen targets and then only if they're found 'guilty' in the killer's mind. With clear thought and sticking together, we can all walk this through, together, safely."

"I suppose, then," Jenkins spoke melodramatically, gesturing with both hands, "this is the moment someone has to announce that we have a killer among us...and that killer is none other than someone in this very room..."

"Your sarcasm is duly noted...again," Sarah answered. "We've all seen the movies or read the books. Now, cut the clowning."

"Agent Priest," the man droned, "I never...clown. No Jenkins has ever...clowned."

"Has a Jenkins ever shut up?" James Wyatt asked.

"Stop," Sarah chided. "This is serious. Life or death serious."

Several voices attempted to promote personal opinions but Cassandra Clark was having none of it. She held up her hands and waited for the din to lessen.

"You all have a right to know of any legitimate danger. You have a right to heed our warnings and you have the right to ignore them," Clark announced, no hint of hesitation, no visible second thoughts. "And you have the right to choose your own fates. I, for one, will cooperate with law enforcement and defense professionals. The rest of you can let your own consciences be their guides."

"What now, eh?" the model, Mobley, asked. "Sit around and stare at each other, tryin' ta decide which bloke looks the most murderous?"

Other voices rang out with similar dismay.

I said, "Nothing can be done, right now. After daylight, when we can actually *see*, we may find we have more options."

I had no idea what they would be.

"Yeah. And we can see the reaper comin' before he swings the ax! Well, whoever you are, steer clear of ol' Ricochet! Somebody tries to kill me there'll be more 'n' one killer on this mountain!" Porter howled.

Then the shouting. Accusations. Insults. Threats.

"Shut up!" I roared. Before the silence fell, I added, "Stop playing the fools! The easiest way to kill us would be to divide us!"

Crickets.

West, Bridger and Barlowe, carrying little Emma, wandered back into the room just as the tangible quiet settled over everyone.

"Wow," Barlowe said. "Like a tomb in here. Who died?"

"Nobody...yet," Johanna Crimson said with a sneer.

"But we can always hope," Kimber Mobley said and scowled at Richard Porter.

Kess Melkin whimpered, "I don't wanna be on another list. I know it ain't sweet an' all but better ya'll than me...and the rest of ya'll feel the exact same way. Well, all of ya'll but you professional defender types. Why you're different I'll never know..."

"Nice," Bridger said. However, he did not disagree.

"Once again, what now?" Mobley repeated.

"We ain't flyin' outta here...they already told us! One of you nutjobs busted up the chopper and the bridge!" Richard Porter shouted.

"We're stranded here for at least this night," I agreed. "You all want to know what's next? Well, here it is: we spend this night as safely as we can. Tomorrow, in the daylight, we reexamine things. In the meantime, try to be as civil as possible."

"Oh, in other words-"

"In other words, scooter troll, keep your trap closed unless you got somethin' productive to say..." Matwahali trailed in a low rumble.

"There is always the hope that someone will come up to the resort for something; deliveries, travelers looking around, vacationers, who knows? If so, they would find the bridge destroyed and call the local authorities or the closest rescue department."

They stared incredulously at Jenkins.

"And that's likely?" Andreya West asked.

"Well..." Jenkins started, frowning, holding upturned hands out to Director Cassandra Clark.

"No. It's not," she said.

"Okay, alright, but still..." Jenkins tried.

"Thanks for being direct with us, regardless," Paul Blackwood said.

"Sure...that's a real comfort," Melkin whispered, wiping a tear away.

"That might be the only positive note we get tonight," Mobley said.

"This is the part of the story where the guests and the staff turn in for the night. They lock themselves in their rooms, all alone, and hope to last until daybreak," West said with a smile.

She was so calm it was nearly disturbing.

"Wrong," I said.

"We talked about it earlier," Clark reminded. "Doubling up so that no one is completely alone is probably a wise alternative."

"Yeah? Maybe. If the killer is an outsider, prowlin' the grounds, some late arrival or crazed staff member ya sent home, yeah, that might work. But, if it's one of us?" Porter asked, a rueful grin on his face. "Who wants to be roomed up with Ghosty Gunman?"

Again, silence. Like the proverbial graveyard. The exception, of course, was the cooing of lovely Emma Barlowe.

"The only other option," Sarah said after a moment, "would be for all of us to stay the night in groups. There are multiple beds in the rooms. We would be far less likely to be caught alone by the killer."

Andreya West spoke, bringing voice to many of their thoughts.

"I'm confident inside my own room with the doors locked."

"We should go back to our own rooms," Paul Blackwood agreed. "I don't know about the rest of you lot but I know the risks and I'm pretty sure I can handle meself against this barmy lout."

"I'm with the Silver Fox," Kimber Mobley commented. She gave him a wink, adding, "We can still pair up with new friends, if need be."

"Think it over carefully," Sarah Priest said.

"Get over it," Gretchen Clayborne groaned. "We don't need policing. It isn't going to work! Why run around in a rat race, following directions from other people, if we're gonna die anyway?"

"Gretchen, that's enough," Cassandra Clark warned.

"Mr. Blackwood has a point, actually," Johanna Crimson noted. "And so does your pilot. We could all use some rest...and privacy."

"Spoken like a woman with bodyguards," Richard Porter said.

"Bully for her," Paul Blackwood said. "She speaks her own mind. Guards or no, she's right."

"We don't need some kind of martial law," Gretchen said.

"At the end of it all, unless Agent Priest is going to legally sequester us, or whatever, the choice remains individual," Cassandra Clark said begrudgingly. "I can't force anyone to do anything. But, for the record, I support following the lead of the professionals on this."

A few moments of silence ran the show until Clark stood up.

"All of those who want help or observation for the night, please stay and work with Agent Priest. Those who want to go to your own rooms and handle your own well being, follow Jenkins. He and Grip will walk you to your rooms. I only ask that, if you choose to be on your own or with a chosen partner, stay in your rooms until tomorrow morning. Don't wander, don't go off without someone knowing where you are. It's for your own good."

"That it?" Melkin asked then eyeballed Matwahali.

The big man gave her a somber, gentle smile and a nod.

"What else is there?" Clark asked. "Sleep well."

Sure, sleep well, someone muttered.

Why not? someone else asked.

That's right. You ought to enjoy your last night's sleep, another voice mumbled.

Cassandra Clark could not help thinking it was true enough.

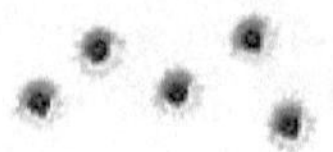

What was that statement they attributed to Agatha Christie? About justice? one of them wondered, walking along with the others. *Oh, I remember. 'Too much mercy...often resulted in further crimes which were fatal to innocent victims who need not have been victims if justice had been put first and mercy second.' My dear Agatha, you spoke the truth. A deep and profound truth for the ages...*

In the crowd, the Ghost Revolver did not even need the traditional mask. The crowd was mask enough, the dark hallway a disguise, a hiding place right in open view.

The Revolver smiled though there was no mirth in it.

CHAPTER FIVE

Cassandra Clark provided the Priests, Falgrip Bridger and James Wyatt with printed layouts of the floors and the room assignments.

Jenkins led the large party to their assigned rooms with Grip Bridger providing security. Mark Gibson stuck close to Johanna Crimson as they made the trek upstairs, unwilling to abandon her though he wanted to be in on the meeting in the Dining Hall.

James Wyatt promised to catch up to him and fill him in later.

Tye Richter, attached to Cassandra Clark, lingered with her. Though she told him she was fine, he pointedly ignored her. He knew she would take on feeding all the horses for the evening, with no riding staff, and he was not about to let her go there alone.

"There are four pages in your layouts that are the four floors here," Clark said, retaking her seat. "They're self explanatory, of course, but the first floor has all of our community rooms and the horses, the tack, all that. The second floor has all of our staff rooms, including my office chambers. The third and fourth floors have all of our guest accommodations, as any of you already know if you've been to your rooms."

"Yeah, speakin' of," James said, "Why did ya scatter everyone around and do it on two floors? I mean, wouldn't it have been easier and simpler to just dirty up one floor of rooms?"

"You'd have to ask Ms. Li," she said. "It was her explicit request for maximum privacy and exclusivity-"

"Isolation," Sarah Priest said.

"Well, okay," Clark allowed. "We did our best to give everyone as much of a feeling of being the only guest here as we could. Per request."

"Somethin' to remember," James growled. "Considerin' she invited everybody here, put the roster together."

"What else have we got here?" Sarah Priest asked.

Richter said, "The other printout is a general grounds layout with building locations. I asked Ms. Clark to give that one to you, too. You might wanna know where things are outside the standard resort building, if you plan to wander, at all."

"Thanks, Tye," Mick Priest said with a nod.

"At any rate," Clark said, "those room assignments won't be accurate. We already heard several people planning to bunk up together, to group together. It's the best I can do."

"We appreciate it," Sarah Priest said.

Then Clark turned to Richter.

"Ready? The babies don't like being fed off schedule."

He nodded, stood and followed her out, waving at the others.

"Nice people," Sarah said.

"I like them," Mick agreed.

"That kid is twisted around her little finger so tight his spine is screamin' for help," James added, eyebrows arched.

"James!" Sarah snapped.

"He hasn't even looked twice at Johanna Crimson! Him and Clark ain't even engaged!"

"So?" Sarah asked with a frown.

"So? Johanna Crimson!" James half shouted.

"James," Mick started.

"Kid ain't in love, he's comatose," James said. " Come on...Johanna Crimson..."

"I'm not distracted by her," Mick Priest stated flatly.

"You're married, Mick," James answered with a wink. "And Sarah's gotta gun."

The shadows enveloped Cassandra Clark where she waited with Tye Richter. In his arms, the moment exuded novel romance. Faux oil lanterns, actually little, flickering, LED lamps, had kicked in upon the power failure. Their intermittent, scarce placement left the stables in a somewhat primitive, shadowy ambiance for two young people to enjoy.

The smell of worked leather and tanning oils wafted on the summer night's wind. Studs and mares snorted contentedly while they ate the sweet smelling grains, bearing witness to the budding love affair but willing to keep it privileged information. Once in a while, they would even look up from their feed buckets, remembering their own trysts in the fields.

On the ground floor of the Stable Manor, both wings of the massive structure were indeed stables. Rustic, roughly hewed beams protruded through old world, plaster walls. Thick, solid wood stall doors and dividers hearkened back to much older, simpler times.

For Tye Richter, a man who loved to work with his hands, those times resonated with him. As for Cassandra Clark, the Tye Richter kind of man resonated with her.

In one of the stalls, a horse neighed and the couple turned its way.

"A little privacy, please?" Richter asked of the gelding.

Another steed bumped a stall door and the vibration tipped over a stack of empty buckets behind them. They clattered to the ground.

Clark peeled herself from Richter's embrace in a snatch as he twisted about to find the source of the sound. Buckets rolled to and fro in the dark.

"Did you have a heart attack, too?" Cassandra asked.

"For *real*," Tye emphasized. "I thought it was some blood-soaked killer."

Cassandra Clark said, "I was pretty sure it would be Grip. Gretchen's always saying he's creepy."

"Why would she say that?"

"He's always sneaking up on her," Clark said. "She calls him ninja creepy, says it gives him pure joy to scare her. Make her jump."

"Cassie, Grip might get a kick outta startling her, goofing with her, but the truth is that she's high strung. She's downright jumpy and she's edgy, too."

"I suppose."

"So, how long can you stay down here?" Tye asked.

"As long as you can," she said, raised her nose in the air and gave a mock glare of arrogance. "I am the boss, you know."

"Um, that's good...how 'bout a raise?" Richter teased.

Cassandra Clark pretended to consider it.

"Do you have any special skills...any talents...the management should take into consideration?"

He grinned and his boyish charm inspired a grin in her, too.

"Would you like a list in alphabetical order or-"

"In triplicate, on my desk by seven in the morning," she giggled. "In the meantime, we should get back."

"Nah, Grip's busy checkin' doorknobs and tuckin' people in. He won't miss me. And Gretchen has Helena in your room. They can keep each other company until you get there."

"Gretchen Clayborne and Helena Makai hate each other and you know it," she said and giggled again. "And we both know Grip Bridger will be calling a red alert if you don't show up where you're supposed to be. I don't want the SBI and her husband sent away on a search and rescue mission for you just because you want to stay down here and kiss."

"Is there a better reason to make people search for you?"

"I'm serious, Tye," she said. "You know Grip."

Tye drew her into another embrace.

"Don't worry, Cassie. It'll all work out."

"Worry is all I can do. I worry even more with no answers than I do with answers. The unknown is worse than all of it...even murder."

"I'm thinkin' tomorrow will bring enough issues of its own, lady," Tye admitted. "Even with no answers, you'll be too busy to stress it."

Cassandra spun out of his arms, started for the stairwell and spat, "Great pep talk, Tye. See you in the morning."

"That's why you pay me the big bucks," Richter countered.

"Be careful," she said, pausing to look back to Tye. "I don't know what I'd do if...if anything-"

"You get back to your room and ya'll keep an eye on each other," Tye ordered.

"I don't take directions from you, Mr. Richter," Clark teased. "I'm the boss, I believe I've reminded you. Resort Director, to be exact."

"Then direct yourself back to your room," he laughed.

She turned and left him there to finish up with the horses.

That blue roan, the gelding, neighed at him again.

"Buddy, your...condition...isn't my fault. You were a eunuch before we met. I had nothing to do with it, so don't blame me."

The horse flipped its head back and forth.

"Don't be jealous, either. Green ain't your color."

Tayla Barlowe, intent on a quiet wandering of the grounds, took photographs to preserve the nocturnal beauty.

The morning usually opened up like a flower and released its colors across the sky and the previous day's beauty had not failed her. In the distance, beyond the rise and fall of mountains and slopes, the sun had spilled its liquid oranges and reds into the sky, filling it with warm allure.

She yearned for shots of the night, however, the clouds and the moon over the mountain. The purple and indigo, even the darkest blacks, thick and wet on the canvas of night. Day and night, light and dark, yin and yang; she would capture it all in her art.

When she hurriedly trotted the outside stairs back to her balcony level, she was still looking over her shoulder, shushing little Emma. Still looking for the perfect shots, all the while quieting her daughter so that she would not be caught out of her room, alone.

Her camera went off again, five or six times in succession.

Barlowe knew she had to return to her room, Room Three, on the west side of Floor Four. She paused on the balcony overlook at its northernmost point, by the outside elevator. That elevator, also powerless, was still and quiet. The overlook protruded there beyond the building itself and she captured an elevated view of the eastern grounds.

Tayla Barlowe abruptly stilled with her camera. A long way off, by the landing pads, a flashlight beam whipped here and there. Tayla froze, for the first time startled. Then, before she could rush for her room door, she saw someone even closer to the building.

Andreya West was strolling on the grass, making her way for the resort stairwells on her side.

Tayla Barlowe adjusted the way Emma was nestled and fired off with her camera again. Barlowe knew, as beautiful as Andreya West was, her picture would add to whatever publication bought the sets. It would be a simple matter of a signed permission form; the class act photographer carried them in ample supply.

"That's gonna be a payday for Momma," she told her daughter in the sling.

Suddenly, something banged on the balcony below and startled Barlowe. She bolted for her room door, the danger on Shadow Mountain more real to her every moment she spent outside with her little girl.

Bridger accompanied everyone to their delegated chambers, with the exceptions of the Dining Hall group, Director Cassandra Clark and his own roommate, Tydas Richter. Some were grateful. Some were polite. Some told him, in no uncertain terms, to go away and stop bothering them.

One person, a famous British baker, even told him the guests would have a 'crackin' good time' without him. He simply smiled and nodded, his eyes betraying his real feeling on the matter.

Afterward, he took up the role assigned to him by Director Clark. Roving patrol, at least a couple of rounds, at least a couple of hours, after seeing everyone to bed. The taste of it stuck in his throat.

Door knob shaker.

He had been a prominent deputy with a promising future of promotions. He had been real law enforcement. Of course, H and H Resort had given him what his friend Tye referred to as a pie job. And they paid him roughly three times what he had made in 'real' law enforcement, so...

...on the rounding patrol he went.

He slowed by Kess Melkin's room but kept moving. With no one in adjacent rooms, the controlled noise of very boisterous laughter and whatnot did not give him pause. After all, the resort's privacy policies emboldened the designers to use such sound dampening materials that the obvious roar inside the room was quite tame outside the room. He heard B'Rone Matwahali's voice in there with her, too, and continued his patrol of the third floor hall again.

Melkin had the last room on the south end of the Stable Manor, on the west side of floor three. The room across the corridor, on the east side, housed no one and neither did the first room north of that one. The room directly north of Melkin was also empty.

She was quite secluded with her new friend.

Though he slowed by every door, opening those he knew were not in use and glancing in the room, his actual concern rested with the assigned rooms. The next designated guest room was the fourth room on the east and had been assigned to the man in Melkin's room, Matwahali. Bridger checked the latch and found the door locked as he had hoped.

The next room watched from across the hall. He checked it and nodded in satisfaction, content with things as he thought they should be. He strode directly to the east run of rooms again, one room north, and paused by the barrier. The British accent in the room gave Blackwood away. Bridger assumed the man was practicing a speech or something, talking all by himself, his voice alone.

Again, satisfied, he wandered north one room. That room was actually Room Four, the next to the last on the eastern side. Bridger listened closely and heard what sounded like a man doing exercises. Satisfied that was Richard Porter, the assigned guest, he cut back across the hall to the door opposing Blackwood's room.

Unassigned, the room should have been closed and empty.

When he touched the handle, the door creaked backward more than a foot and a half.

Not closed. Would that mean not empty?

Bridger kicked it wide and blasted into the room with the light, murdering the dark and its shadows. His Glock at the ready, a very quick review showed him no one and nothing unusual and not a thing seemed out of place. In a word, empty, as prescribed.

The man still did not like it. Housekeeping had prepped all the rooms and he and his security team had closed up all the rooms unscheduled for guests. There it was, however, an empty room, yes, but with an open door and a mocking sense about it.

"Hey, Bulldog," a deep voice called from the hallway.

The voice jolted him about instantly, twisting him back toward the stairwell. His body torqued up, locking him rigid for a moment, causing him to drop his flashlight. He held on to his Glock, however, wagging it about in the dim light of the hall.

"Whoa!" James Wyatt shouted at him.

He snapped his flashlight upward in a way they could both see each other. In a way Bridger could see his Sig Sauer .357 handgun, held down by his leg but very much at the ready.

"I...I didn't see you come up," Falgrip Bridger noted, his body calming. Holstering his 9mm, he sighed, adding, "Sorry about that."

"It's all good," James Wyatt said.

He holstered his gun again as he walked the hall toward the security guard.

Bridger bent over and picked up his light. It would not come on so he shook it. Something inside rattled but it did manage to reignite on the third try.

"I'm headin' up to my floor," James said, "but I figured I'd check where you were on the patrol."

Bridger gestured down the corridor.

"Okay, then. Away we go."

James sliced into the open room with his light.

"You done killin' the boogeyman?"

"Funny," Bridger griped.

Irritably, he snatched the door closed but the uneasy feeling never left him. Was it empty? Still, he moved away with James Wyatt.

The next room north, on the empty side of the hall, was closed and empty. The pair, satisfied, moved on to the rooms considered the first on the floor, Rooms One and Two. They just happened to be the last in the direction Bridger had been going.

At the door on the right, the farthest room north on the east, James Wyatt tapped his light on the frame.

The magazine model from Australia, Kimber Mobley, answered the door in a little, lace nothing.

"Sorry to bother you," Bridger said after cutting his eyes sharply at the defense contractor. "We don't usually knock on the doors while we patrol."

"No worries," she responded. "What can I do for ya?"

"Are you still alone?" Bridger asked.

"Well, yeah. You need a roommate, luv?" she asked flatly.

James Wyatt grinned with a roll of his eyes but Bridger was rigid.

"What? Uh, no, we're...working..." he said.

"We're checking on everyone," James said, trying to give Bridger time to reboot his brain. "Tryin' to make a mental note of where everyone is."

"...for protection..." Bridger said.

"And you want me to protect you?" she answered, feigning confusion and batting her eyes.

"Wh-what? No...no, of course not," Bridger stammered again.

James Wyatt covered his grin with his hand.

Bridger finally got control of his synapses and gave the model a brief speech about opening the door for people, general safety and protecting herself. He then bade the woman a good night.

He was first to turn away and it gave the Aussie a chance to smirk and wink at James Wyatt. For his part, Wyatt smiled, too.

Door closed, the men walking away, Bridger turned to James. He broke the silence when they were half way to the interior stairs, back at the southern end.

"You think she was really coming on to me or just being difficult?"

"Wow," said James Wyatt. "Just...wow."

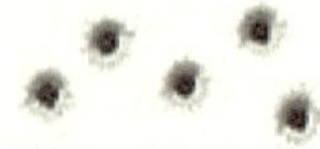

Andreya West climbed the tall flight of exterior stairs back to her balcony level. Reaching the fourth floor, she tossed back the deep brown hair that framed her face, neck and shoulders. Two spaghetti straps held up her silk, peach-toned chemise. It flowed down around her hips and the matching silk sleep pants. Barefooted, she stopped outside her balcony door and sat down, pulled an antimicrobial wipe from the single pocket in her outfit and began wiping the bottom of her naked feet.

West's beauty could make a man's breath catch in his throat. She pondered how she had come alone to the retreat when so many men would have joined her. Sometimes she wondered what she was waiting to find in a paramour. Then she remembered how so many of the men her age behaved. When she chose someone the age gap would probably turn heads.

That made her smile. She knew people always found a reason to gossip. Giving them one right away would keep them busy. Maybe that would get them chatting about something other than her mysophobia.

Ever since an academic reviewer had published part of a private conversation about her fear of germs, it was often all anyone added to her dissertation reviews. Along with the fact that she was vegan. That was such a promoted point of interest. Her eating choices.

With an introspective sigh and a curious giggle, she went into her room and closed the glass, balcony door behind herself. She locked it, out of cautious habit and not in any kind of fear, then strolled for the king size bed.

She had broken the rules already. Her first night there. Her first night ever under lock down, tied up with the precept of a dangerous killer lurking outside the guests' doors. A smile broke over her countenance despite her concentration on the situation.

Breaking the rules. She was hard core.

Some people had things to fear...people to fear...and some people simply feared life itself. Andreya West had never considered herself to be one of those people. If not for the random, roving germ here and there, she could not think of a single thing she feared. And that, alone, made her giggle again.

Outside, footsteps fell gently on the balcony. Someone lurking about the resort was creeping around...someone other than Andreya West.

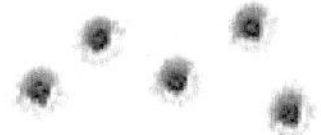

Grip Bridger, on patrol, had already covered Floor Two. He had started on that floor, before moving onto Three.

On Floor Three, after meeting up with James Wyatt and relaying the nothingness he had discovered patrolling Floor Two, they moved on for Floor Four. As boring as it was, James Wyatt had listened politely to the breakdown of Floor Two.

Most of the rooms had been empty, unused and unlocked, just like they were supposed to be. Quite a bit smaller than guest accommodations, they allowed the floor to house a lot more rooms. Occupants also had roommates, using even more of the available space.

Rooms One through Four were for the Housekeeping Department when they were onsite. Room Five gave shelter to the Chef and the Underchef. The Chef was still onsite but the Underchef had been sent home.

Room Six belonged to the Staff Chief, also entitled Staff Director. That was Mr. Reginald Bard Jenkins. The room could accommodate two but Jenkins usually had it to himself. Newly ordered to share by the Director, Cassandra Clark, the Chef was bunking with him for safety.

Rooms Seven and Eight were used by kitchen staff and servers, accommodations for four. Ms. Helena Makai would have been sleeping there if not redirected to share with Clark for safety.

Rooms Nine and Ten similarly served the groundskeeper crew. Eleven through Sixteen made places, again with two to a room, for other general staff like receptionists, guides, escorts and baggage crews. Room Seventeen, a much larger space, offered room for four staff members. The horse and riding crew slept there. Room Eighteen was where technicians for communications, computers and any other high end services would bunk down.

Room Nineteen held four sleeping arrangements. Three security guards and the Security Chief, Bridger, usually occupied that room. With no staff, Grip Bridger would have been alone had Director Clark not ordered Tye Richter to room with him, in the main building, for safety.

Richter, as the Director of Facility Operations, normally slept in a very nice room in the generator building. It also had other chambers outfitted just for his needs and for his maintenance crew's quarters, when they were onsite.

The last room, Room Twenty, located in the far southeastern corner of the corridor, welcomed the Director, Cassandra Clark, at the end of each work day. It dressed itself in much more elegance, much like guest rooms, and offered only space for two to rest. Clark, however, like Jenkins, normally roomed alone. As it was, Clark had welcomed Helena Makai and Gretchen to room with her. Gretchen Clayborne, normally housed in the helicopter hangar's pilot quarters, would not be asked to go the nights alone, just like Richter.

"How many rounds you gotta make tonight, Bulldog?" James asked, as much to quell the man's droning as to actually get a number.

Bridger gestured for the other man to exit the stairwell first. When they both departed onto the Fourth Floor, he spoke.

"Agent Priest and Director Clark suggested at least two rounds."

"About a couple of hours of eyeball time, then," James said.

"It could be worse," the security chief admitted. "People could still end up dead."

"See? That would be worse," James said.

Then they began checking doorknobs to be positive that occupied rooms were locked and empty rooms were unlocked and empty.

Room Twelve, the first room on their right, belonged to Johanna Crimson and her protector, Mark Gibson. Very faint voices, a male and a female, resonated within.

Room Eleven, across the hall, and Ten, one room north of Twelve, were empty.

Room Nine, on the western side of the hall, housed Victor Jackson and Maureen Li. They were present in their room; they could be heard faintly through the door.

Room Seven was reserved for the internet and comic graphic novelist, Rembrandt Lyles. There was no sound from the room but it was locked securely. Room Five, the room north of Seven, was properly empty.

Back on the eastern wall, Room Eight was the room assigned to the Priests, though neither was there. Room Six, the next room north, was an empty room just like Five, directly across the hall from it.

Room Three, back on the western side, was for Tayla and Emma Barlowe and they were safe inside; Emma was making sure everyone knew it, too. The child had healthy lungs.

Rooms One and Two, the last of them, were reserved for James Wyatt in One and Andreya West, across the hall, in Room Two.

The men gathered at the end of the hall, in front of the door to the elevator that did not work, even under emergency power.

"Okay, have a good night," Grip Bridger said.

Bridger gestured at the defense contractor's door.

James Wyatt walked instead toward West's room.

"What're you-" Bridger stalled.

"Lady's flyin' solo, gotta check on her," James said.

"We didn't check all the...You're just trying to get her to the door!" Bridger shouted in a hush. "You wanna see if she's got on somethin' like that model!"

James Wyatt rapped on the door, a rakish smile on his face.

"Don't be silly," James said. "Mobley's pretty and that outfit looked like it was right out of a catalog but West-"

Bridger cleared his throat.

"-could never get all those fine curves-" James Wyatt continued.

"Uh, *Mr. Wyatt*," Bridger pressed loudly.

"-into Mobley's itty bitty...outfit..." James said, slowing down, light dawning in his eyes.

Bridger scratched the back of his head, roughing his blonde buzz cut.

James Wyatt turned around to find Andreya West in her open door.

The woman's dazzling smile was ear to ear. The silk of her peach nightwear, immediately drawing James Wyatt's attention, seemed to glisten in the emergency lighting, particularly against her deep tan.

"Gentlemen," she greeted, a giggle bending the voice.

"See, Bulldog," James Wyatt spat immediately. "She's fine, she's safe. No need to bother her. I tried to tell you."

"What?" Bridger snapped.

"Sorry to bother you," James Wyatt said confidentially to West.

"Oh, no bother," Andreya replied in a near whisper of her own. Her eyes twinkled with mischief and her smile never waned. "Just imagine how much it would've bothered me, though, if I'd been wearing some of Kimber Mobley's tiny clothes, constricting me."

James Wyatt smiled and said, "Yeah. Yeah, gotta hate that."

Andreya West looked past James and met Bridger's wide eyes.

"So, just curious; from one Native American to another, what tribal heritage are you from?" James asked her.

She kept the smile wide but shook her head.

"First, I prefer to say American Indian. To answer your question, though, I'm predominantly Choctaw. Why? What gave me away? Just the primal tan and the high cheekbones?" she asked, giggling.

"You know how it is. Takes one to know one."

"It must," Bridger muttered. "I didn't have a clue."

"Maybe I should get a feather for my hair, like Mr. Wyatt. Goodnight, gentlemen," she said sweetly and closed her door.

"Wow," Bridger said with a deep exhale.

"Hey, have a little respect," James said. "She's a scholar."

"W-What did I say?"

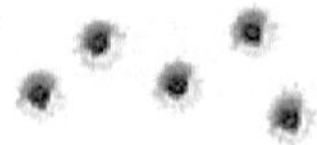

Mick Priest stood very close to his wife, Sarah. He was not just close; he stood with his body against hers. The heat of summer waged war on the little remaining cool of the ground floor. With no power, the resort air conditioning was down. Summer, however, had little to do with the heat radiating from the couple.

Sarah ran a hand over his shaven head, wiping away the sheen of sweat building there. It seemed innocent enough. But she followed it with a rake of her long, red fingernails over his scalp, her eyes suggestive, her lips pursed. Her breath caressed his lips in their nearness to each other.

Mick Priest shivered over the full length of his form.

"You're a cruel woman," he breathed.

"Me?" she asked, her voice heady.

"You know what the nails do to me," he said, his voice low.

"Then we'd better get to work," she said.

"I might ask why but-" he muttered.

Suddenly, she extricated herself from their embrace.

"Because we certainly don't have time for passion until this is over."

"I know. That's why it's cruel," he growled.

"What's cruel?"

The voice jolted Mick Priest back to the moment.

Your arrival is cruel, the detective decided silently.

Cassandra Clark strolled into the Dining Hall, looking around as if to find more guests. When she saw only the Priests remained, she focused on them and made a straight line for where they stood in a secluded corner.

"What?" Sarah asked.

"You said something's cruel," Clark said. "What's cruel?"

"Nothing," Mick Priest said.

"But you just said-"

"Never mind," Sarah Priest said. "Are you wandering around alone?"

"I just finished up the horse work," she said defensively. "Feeding, watering, all that. Someone still has to do these things, you know."

"Wasn't Richter with you?" Sarah asked.

"He's gone up to his room," she informed.

"So, he's out and about on his own, too," Mick said.

Clark sighed, seeing she was getting nowhere quickly.

"Yes, I guess. And I get it," Clark retorted. "But this place has been home and life for a good few years now. It's hard to imagine it as suddenly dark and dangerous."

Mick Priest countered with, "Please, be careful. This isn't a 'what if' scenario. The danger is here."

She nodded.

"Let me walk you to your room," Sarah offered. "I can check on Mr. Bridger, too."

Mick Priest kissed her and the two parted, the ladies heading upstairs and the detective standing alone in the Dining Hall.

At least, as alone as someone like Mikhael Priest could be.

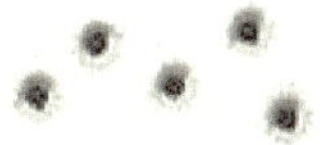

I blinked. That was all it took. A second, two at the most. No longer than two seconds and an admittedly tired blink and the entire night changed. I still stood in the Dining Hall but everything around me shifted into some other world, some other time...all somehow different.

The candles glowed far brighter than before but they threw odd shadows from their ghostly blue flare, shadows that shrank and grew and moved of their own accord. Loud and clear, the ticks of the big grandfather clock echoed in the room. Inaudible though they had been just a little while before, they suddenly clicked away time with an authority, a real presence. The ticktock, ticktock was all I could hear in the solitude, as if it spoke directly into my ears.

"Time," a thick, velvety voice said. "Do you have the time?"

I jolted nearly out of my own skin. My renowned speed and utter instinct brought one of my Colts clear of a holster and my flashlight free of a pocket before I even realized I was moving. Both leveled on the figure sitting at the table. Half of her face remained obscured by shadow, the flashlight failing to scatter it.

I felt that she had been there all along yet had just appeared at the same time, two different realities colliding, merging. Some part of me knew she was coming while the other part of me was startled at her arrival.

Her mane of flame red hair radiated light as if ablaze, shining and sparkling in the the candlelight.

"That is what it really is all about, if you asked me," Johanna Crimson sang, her voice distant, disconnected. "Do you see? The past...the present...the future...time."

"Johanna Crimson?" I asked, seeking some clarification.

If she was Crimson, who walked the halls of Stable Manor with us?

"Time!" howled the apparition but she was not at the table. She cried in an otherworldly dirge, her voice ringing, abruptly right beside me.

I pitched to the right, bowled over in shock. In the seconds it took me to stand again, however, she was gone. I looked this way and that, spinning several times, but the remnant of the young woman was beyond my sight.

"Time," she muttered, the word bitter and distant.

Then, just as it struck midnight, that grandfather clock buckled and twisted. All the glass exploded from it, spraying the room. I barely got my arms up in time to shield myself as the clock tolled the hour.

"Mr. Priest?"

I lowered my arms with a jerk. The room's candlelight was back to normal. I had never moved from my stance where Sarah had left me. The clock had not exploded.

Tayla Barlowe stared at me, four feet away, holding little Emma. The child was wrapped in a blanket and looked like a human burrito. A precious, beautiful burrito.

"You okay?" Tayla asked, frowning in concern.

"Oh, yeah, I'm fine. You guys okay?"

She opened her mouth to speak, paused and said, "Yeah. I mean, we weren't frozen in place with our arms up like Medusa had turned us to stone or something."

"Oh, neither was I," I said, somewhat at a loss for words.

"You sure?" she asked sardonically. "I mean, I just saw you."

"That was...when I'm investigating, when I'm thinking...you know, sometimes I let myself act things out, trying to..." I stammered.

"Acting out what? The eruption at Pompeii?" she jabbed.

I pointed at her, wagging my finger.

"Cute. A better question; what're you doing down here?"

She twisted her lips into a smirk.

"Okay, subject changed," she agreed. She tossed back her purple bangs and said, "I thought somebody needed to know; nobody's followin' the 'stay-in-your-room' rule."

"So I see."

She giggled and mimicked my finger wag.

"And you have funnies, too," she said. "I don't mean me and Emma."

I just waited.

"Okay, we're not in our room, either," she said. "But I'm serious. I went out to get some night shots, some mountain and moon kinda shots, and I heard movement on the balcony under us. I saw Andreya West crossing the grounds in her jammies, too, and I saw a flashlight swinging around, down by the helicopter garage."

I locked my jaw for a moment and slowly exhaled.

"I can't tell you any better than I already have that it's dangerous here, Ms. Barlowe," I said lowly, calmly.

"Tayla."

I just stared at her.

"Wow, have you got a 'dad' look," she complained.

"Tayla, I'm sure people are going to do what they want to do. It's like the people who rush down to the beach to see the hurricanes. The problem is when they get washed away and never come home."

"Morbid, much?"

"Just stay in your room," I said flatly. Then, "I'll talk to Ms. West, too, and I'll check Floor Three. But I suspect the flashlight out by the hangar was Mr. Bridger. He's on patrol."

"You're right," she allowed quietly. "I should be in the room. Me and my chunky monkey. I feel bad, now, reckless...but it just doesn't feel real..."

I touched Emma's cheek and she giggled at me.

"Only they're allowed to be oblivious, Tayla," I said softly. "The rest of us have to be doubly careful. For their sake."

"Just let somebody try to mess with my monkey. They'll get the throat punch of all time."

I could not keep myself from smiling as I said, "In the meantime-"

"Back to my room," she said with a nod. "Yes, Dad."

"I'll walk you," I offered. And I could not resist asking, "Chunky Monkey?"

Tayla Barlowe laughed merrily.

The rooftop of Horse and Heraldry Resort angled at multiple points, bearing a barn-like, gambrel roof line. On both sides, each room and each bathroom had a skylight. The fixtures lined the uppermost apex. A small recess dipped at the foot of each for maintenance and repair.

A few of them cradled nests for various birds...

...while one supported a nest for a hidden predator.

Leaning low in the clouded light of moon and stars, a figure opened an antique, wooden case. Inside it nestled two silver revolvers with bone handles, both a twin to the other and both very old. Quite elaborate scroll work engraved the silver. A cask of black powder joined them in the case with a handful of metal balls, a small tub of primers, a ball mold and paper to wrap very old world bullets. Rich in history, the old hand cannons were 1851 Colt Navy revolvers, forged in .36 caliber.

Gloved hands lifted one revolver, checked the cylinder for a full load and found it ready. The other gun, found lacking, underwent the loading process. Hot after the climb, the black garbed figure pushed back a skeletal mask for fresher air while working with the pistol.

Paper, powder, primer, ball. Then the process continued.

"Justice..." a whisper broke the night. "If revenge is an act of passion, and vengeance an act of justice...if injuries are revenged and crimes are avenged...what can bind all to one?"

But the night had no answer for the barn's rooftop gargoyle.

"It would have to be...time," the whisper answered itself.

CHAPTER SIX

Mick Priest saw the Barlowes to their room and asked Tayla again if she would consider bunking with someone else. He was forced to accept her resistance to having a roommate. That did not keep him from standing and listening at the door to be certain she actuated each and every lock provided.

Then the detective did the only sensible thing. Having seen what seemed to be the restless spirit of Johanna Crimson, he turned for her room and made haste. Long, quick strides carried him to the starlet's room at the far end of the corridor, the last one on the left.

Priest angled his flashlight to knock at Room Twelve but the door swept back before he made the initial strike.

He and Mark Gibson, one on each side of the doorway, jerked back a bit from each other.

"What're you-" Gibson started in a whisper.

"Whoa, Gibson," Priest said at the same time, also reflexively quiet.

"You comin' to get me?" Gibson asked, looking out into the hallway. "Where's your boy, Ponytail? I was gonna check to see if he was out here."

Mick Priest noted the continued whisper so he kept it low, as well.

"I don't know where James is. His room, probably. Maybe getting a shower. And I wasn't coming for you, specifically. Just checking on Ms. Crimson."

"Ain't it grand?" Gibson said with a shake of his head. "Can't run the room lights on the emergency power but they kept the hot water and the water pump on emergency standby? Guess you can be blind but they don't want you stinkin' up the place."

Priest lifted his eyebrows and smiled.

"I suppose. Is Ms. Crimson around?"

"Yeah, course she is. And she's sleepin' away. Somethin' you need?"

Mick Priest hesitated. Was there?

"Some guests have been wandering," he said after a moment. "I wanted to make sure she's okay."

"Well, she is."

"And make sure she's in her room, not wandering like some others."

"And she is that, too. Trust me. I wouldn't let her outta here."

"Gibson," Priest said, his one sided grin rising, "I've gotten spoiled to seeing things for myself."

Gibson paused but allowed himself a smile, too.

"Man after my own work ethic. But, you wake her up, you sing her back to sleep."

The man eased back the door, turned toward the room and pointed at the king size bed. At its head was a cell phone, standing at an angle and glowing as a night light. In the bed was a restless Johanna Crimson, turning over.

"Thanks," Priest said and started to leave.

"Thank *you*," Gibson corrected emphatically. "I feel good knowing you're on the prowl."

Priest gave a nod and left the doorway. Gibson closed it, fastened each lock and wandered back into the room. He tortured himself, imagining sleep.

Mark Gibson would not sleep. He would try, once James Wyatt was in the room to stay, but he doubted his own intent. In situations like the one on Shadow Mountain, he could rarely rest. Sleep eluded him, taunted him on those occasions. It ran about him, teasing him in full view, just out of reach each time he considered it.

Sleep was a dangerous enemy to personal defense work, after all. Besides that, something was off; he felt it. He could not and would not sleep until he knew what the night held.

Johanna Crimson, bestowed the title of the world's most alluring woman several times, turned over in the king size bed. She wore a Bugs Bunny t shirt and a pair of gray and white boxer shorts, all in full view when she kicked the covers away for the tenth time.

Her hair wound about itself in an elastic strap. The beauty aide had cost an inane amount in Beverly Hills when the twin sister to it could have been obtained at any department store. But the one Crimson wore, the bearer of a hefty price tag, promised to keep her movie star hair 'fresh and vibrant, holding to its style' even overnight.

Gibson allowed himself a grin as he manipulated her bed linens and covered her up again. He tucked them in around her shoulders, looking at the tangled, red hair. The beauty item company owed Johanna Crimson a refund.

Gibson chuckled to himself at his unspoken tease.

Remembering the latest interview Crimson had given, the man reminded himself that she was quick with wit and sharp of tongue. Teasing her, much less insulting her, rarely worked all that well. On that last occasion, a thinly veiled insult had been dealt to her by the gaunt faced 'journalist', clearly a day or less away from starvation.

"Ms. Crimson, at your age now, don't you worry far more about weight gain, as your body slows down? The build you've always worn...bravely, I think, considering...well, 'thick' starts to be less of a compliment on exciting curvature and more about needing to shed those unwanted pounds, am I right?"

Gibson remembered Crimson's reaction as clearly as if it were happening again, right before his intense, blue eyes.

"Margie, Margie," Johanna had said with a perfect, precision smile, "the last thing I worry about is weight. I haven't pulled a fabric onto these curves that's had a single complaint and I've worn the best of the best, professionally and in private. And, just between us girls, I've never met a man yet who had a single complaint, either."

She had reached over then and patted the writer's leg and added, "I know it might be confusing to anyone without a defining shape at all. Let me put it another way; if you were a man and you loved excitement, would you rather drive along a straight, monotonous stretch of road with nothing to see or uncover? Or would you want to race a screaming motorcycle into deep, engaging curves, searching and discovering as you went, pushing the limits and laying down in those curves, breathless from the ecstasy, trembling with the struggle to maintain control..."

Gibson laughed softly, looking down at Crimson.

The lady interviewer had immediately called for a break. It was a good thing. Half of her staff needed that break, breathless just listening to Crimson's siren voice. Her less than subtle implications of what men really wanted were not lost on the talk show journalist. The woman had stormed off and left a considerable bit of laughter in her wake.

Of course, the 'honest journalist' would remove that entire exchange from the article. Johanna Crimson had 'turned it on', however. That magical effect she conjured to mesmerize, seduce and charm. Not even counting her physical beauty, her ability to let a raw, sensual energy flow out of her and enchant those around her was literally hypnotic. People never forgot it when they witnessed it...

...and witnesses posted it to every social media outlet there was.

"Gibson," the actress mumbled, face half submerged in her pillow, "what are you laughing at?"

He tugged her covers a bit tighter about her shoulders.

"That last interview. The one for *Shelley of Miami.*"

"I remember. The pop culture rag I shouldn't have even agreed to do in the first place."

"I think I told you that at the time."

"We had the other work in Miami, anyway," she grumbled. "I figured, why not?"

"It turned out for the good," he chuckled again. "All the comments and support for you through everything...we need to send Margie a thank you card."

"Is this what you do?" she asked, raising her head a few inches to free one eye from the pillow. "Stand over me when I sleep, rerunning interviews in your head? If so, I gotta give you more time off."

"You can't afford to have me around any less," he chided, moving away for one of the other beds. "Who else would keep your secrets?"

She sat up a bit in the bed, as far as one elbow, both eyes finally opening.

"I resent that. There is precious little I have to hide."

"True enough, after some of those scenes in VE2," he allowed her with a shrug.

"Hey!" she barked.

"But, still, the world expects starlet material twenty-four hours a day. They got some real misconceptions that folks like you wear the best of the best of the best all the time. Just the pics I took of you in that department store, Looney Tunes t shirt is worth thousands."

She dropped back into her covers with, "Great. An aspiring paparazzi for a bodyguard. Besides, I don't care. I love Bugs."

"You always have, ever since I've known you," he said nostalgically.

Reflexively, he eyeballed the drapes, the curtains and the doors. Always on watch, always on alert. Always protecting her.

"Gibson...you know you're more than a bodyguard, right?" Just the emotion in her voice and the way her tone shifted pulled his eyes back to her. "Way more. You know that, right? I tell people that's what you are and I call you one...but you *know*, right?"

"I know. Go back to sleep, Looney Tune. It's past your bedtime."

She threw a pillow across the room at him without looking. It sailed wide.

"I can't," she admitted. "It's really hot in here. And I can't sleep without covers, you know that. And it's too hot for covers."

Gibson huffed and replied, "Yeah? Take another shower."

Cassandra Clark had felt her stomach draw up inside her when Priest first told his story. Much later, as she found herself lying wide awake in her room, she still felt like she had when listening to the detective. She withered inside, desperately yearning to think of words that would offer Helena Makai and Gretchen Clayborne hope. Instead, she stared at the ceiling in silence, eyes full of tears, while the other two argued in the dark. As a leader, the Resort Director, she felt she had to say something.

Before addressing either of them, however, she slipped back out of bed and into the hallway. Alone, she did her best to breathe.

"Bad news?"

Cassandra literally jumped, coming out of one high heel in the motion. She spun, fell against the wall and gave a startled, stifled shriek.

"Whoa, sorry," the speaker eased, his British accent thick.

He caught her gently and she gauged his considerable strength. While she staggered on the one heel, he never swayed, not even an inch.

She fumbled about, trying to jam her foot back into the lost shoe.

"Thank you, Mr. Blackwood," she said.

Her cheeks flushed with embarrassment as she noticed a touch of anxiety run over her. What was the baker doing out of his room? And on the staff level?

"Well, ya shouldn't be thanking me, now should ya? I nearly scared ten years of life outta ya. Are ya alright?" he asked, charming smile engaged.

She nodded emphatically, saying, "Well, thank you, anyway. And, yes, I'm alright. I'm just...tired."

The very manly Blackwood angled his keen visage downward, looking into Cassandra Clark's downcast face. Stark, crystal blue eyes scoured her face for hints as to just what had her so uptight. The shadows cast from the dim emergency corridor lighting decorated his features with even more character, even more allure. His white, spiked hair and goatee, stranded here and there by black rebels, marked a strong contrast to his tanned complexion.

She moved her eyes up to meet his stare.

Could a man so dreamy possibly be the killer, she thought ironically to herself, *and still smell so good?*

She pulled herself out of his grasp and straightened her dress.

"Are you sure you're alright?" he asked again, a touch of a smile playing at his lips. "You don't seem tired. You seem upset or-"

"I'm good, really," she insisted. Her hands shook with her rising discomfort. "Th-this weekend just isn't going according to the manual. I want everything to be wonderful for you...f-for you all...for all of our guests."

He said, "Ah, don't worry over it. It's a free weekend for all of us. The only bloke who could complain is that Jackson character; his company copped the bill and he has to write the checks. Everybody else is clear."

She nodded for him with a halfhearted smile. He sauntered away, heading back for the stairs. It did not even dawn on her to ask where he had been, wandering around by himself. As long as she survived the encounter it was good enough for her, for the moment. She turned for the room door again.

"Hey, I hate to bother you," Agent Sarah Priest announced, stepping from the darkness of the stairs.

Clark jerked about, startled again. She covered her mouth with her hand and put the other over her heart.

"Sorry," Priest said on her approach. "I didn't mean to scare you."

"It's okay. The shock can't hurt me. I already had a heart attack a minute ago, when Paul Blackwood walked through here."

"Blackwood?" Sarah Priest repeated. "What was he doing down here?"

"I didn't ask. I quietly celebrated not being murdered in the hallway."

Priest looked down the corridor. She eyed the stair landing.

"Agent Priest?" Clark said. "Is everything okay?"

Sarah turned back to Director Cassandra Clark.

"It will be. I just have to look into Mr. Blackwood's wandering now, too."

"Too? What were you looking into when you came back here?"

"Ms. Clark-"

"Cassie, please," she replied with a distressed smile. "We're all in this life and death thing together, right, Agent?"

"Please, call me Sarah," Priest said. "So, I've had a lot of experience with people and human nature. And I know, especially the first night, when you announce a curfew or lock down or anything of the sort, the response will inevitably be-"

"Wanderers."

"Yes. So, at least for a while, Mick, James and I will be periodically making rounds, just like your Mr. Bridger."

Cassandra Clark looked around, glanced back at the room door she still did not want to enter then looked back to Priest.

"Could you stand some company for a while?"

I lit up a list in my hand, provided by the quite cooperative Cassandra Clark. On it, scrawled quickly by the Director, names stained the page in black ink. The names were the people on site known to be armed. I bathed them in the flashlight's bright beam.

Security Chief Falgrip 'Grip' Bridger : 9mm Glock

Detective Mikhael 'Mick' Priest : Two 10mm Colts

SBI Agent Sarah Melindez-Priest : .40 caliber Smith and Wesson

Security Provider James Wyatt : .357 Sig Sauer

Security Provider Marcus 'Mark' Gibson : .45 Caliber Sig Sauer

It is always good to arm yourself; knowledge is a potent weapon.

I took the stairs to Floor Three, praying all the while. God always listens; it is a shame mankind spends so little time talking with Him. God is an ever present help in times of trouble and trouble is always around us.

The moment I stepped from the stairwell landing, the white beam of light from my flashlight pierced the hallway and that was good. The inner corridors were only lit with that dim, emergency lighting and they needed help resisting the darkness. I wielded the light like a weapon and scoured the floor, praying fervently to God. I knew I needed understanding and guidance, like everyone. Earnestly, I sought the merciful Savior's blessing and wisdom. The dreams and visions were gifts bestowed upon me but sometimes my understanding was slow to catch up. I still had no idea why I saw Johanna Crimson dead in a dream. Trusting, I prayed and moved on.

I also prayed for patience. Already I had people meandering about when asked to keep put. Before I ever reached the landing, I heard their voices, so I clicked off the light, traipsing along, careful and blind.

"Are you two okay?" I blurted as I stepped out of the stairwell.

Paul Blackwood and Kimber Mobley visibly jolted. The model even let out a curse in shock.

"Barmy lout! Are ya tryin' to scare us to death?" Blackwood asked.

When he turned about and I stepped farther into the inadequate lighting, however, his tone changed.

"Oh, Mr. Priest. I thought you were the house detective, Bridger. Man's been around enough for one night."

"Tell *me*," the model muttered.

"He's just doing his job," I reminded. "You two okay?"

"Oh, good. Another hall monitor," Mobley complained while cinching the silk robe's sash with a snort.

"Now then, Kimber," Blackwood admonished. "This man cares about us. This ain't even his job. He's only doin' this to help out."

"Sorry, Mr. Priest," Mobley said. "I'm just knackered. Ricky does like to earbash, all them glory stories 'bout racin' days on his bike, an' all that. I had to get loose of 'im so I met with Paul. I guess I'm runnin' low on steam; tired as I am, I s'pose I ain't gonna be tomorrow's mornin' glory, either."

"Not likely any of us will be, that's for sure," Blackwood said.

"Where is the track legend?" I asked.

"Who, Mr. Motorbike?" Blackwood asked. "He told me before we all split up tonight that he couldn't let all the fine eats left over go to waste. Said he'd have to check on 'em at some point."

"You don't get a figure like that without work," Mobley said with raised eyebrows and a suggestive grin.

"Little guy's a bit dodgy, if you ask me," Blackwood added.

"Fair dinkum," responded the model. She swept up her blonde hair in her hands, wiped the back of her neck and let it fall back down. "Good ta know somebody else sees it."

Celestial Seaspray body lotion, a delightful scent, wafted off the model. Mobley and my wife had similar tastes in fragrance. I knew that one well.

"It ain't half hot in here, either, is it?" Blackwood commented and wiped at his neck and chest through his open shirt.

Booze and sandlewood cologne tainted the air, too.

Lifting from Blackwood, I thought.

I smiled, saying, "No offense, but the grounds aren't safe. Heat is the last thing you should worry about. You two should keep that in mind. And, if you see Porter before I do, tell him the same."

"He's right," Blackwood conceded. "Should we hide in your place?"

She giggled and gave him a mischievous look.

"No. Yours. We've seen mine."

And away they went.

I waited by the stairs for them to disappear. Then I walked the hall, looking and listening. I stopped at Room Four, Richard Porter's room, having noted nothing out of the way up to there. Besides, I figured checking on the man's location would not be unreasonable, considering my inside tip.

I knocked on the door to his chambers. No one answered. I glanced up and down the corridor as I thumped on Porter's door again.

"Richard? Mr. Porter? Are you in there?" I called.

Nothing. That is, nothing vocal, nothing physical...

...but the cold chill that ran my spine...

The sensation chased after the sweat under my shirt and I shivered.

"Mr. Porter..." I started.

The air, stone still, slowly turned to ice. Something moved at the end of the hall. It was a blur, a movement, right in the middle of the corridor between Rooms One and Two, in front of the elevator. I spun that way and lanced the shadows with my flashlight.

For a long moment I waited, transfixed in the silence. Nothing...no one...moved. The stillness was thick.

The hair on the back of my neck stood up. My spine tingled. I spun back to the door and pounded it again. Something was wrong.

"Porter, if you don't answer, I'm going to-"

Someone passed through a doorway in my peripheral vision, again at the end of the hall, startling me to silence. In darkness and shadow the person seemed to have walked into the elevator, the elevator that was not working.

I wrenched my torso about and shot the elevator with my light again. Nothing. No one. The doors were closed. I waited for a few moments, all the while feeling as if someone were standing right behind me, watching over my shoulder.

"It's all in the wrist," a voice muttered suddenly.

I snapped about with a violent jerk. The flashlight died in my hands instantly. Its beam evaporated as the darkness washed over me, enveloped me with a cold wave. I looked everywhere for a speaker but saw no one. I spun to my far left, still searching the darkness for a speaker, then turned back to my far right.

"It's all in the wrist," he said, his voice echoing.

I trembled, a sudden, merciless cold piercing my innards, chilling my blood. An unearthly squeal grated through my head. The elevator, inoperable and out of power, rose on a howling cable. An odd fog, glowing in an ambient blue haze, rose from the floor.

I knew what was happening. I knew then, for certain. Porter was dead...to everyone but me...

The smoky light lit the edges of the elevator doors, tendrils of vapor seeping through the closures and reaching. One, two then three taps knocked at the elevator doors from inside.

"Porter?" I called but my voice caught in my throat.

Then the doors slid apart on their own, power or no power, and the waiting was over. A plume of fog belched from the lift car, filling that end of the hall with its blue glow. Short, stocky Rick Porter staggered into view, materializing from the pale haze. His hands reached out before him, as if holding handlebars, his right hand rotating as if twisting a motorcycle throttle.

"Winning, losing..." Porter groaned in his spectral tone, "...living, dying...all in the wrist..."

The heavy man's flesh had faded into a deathly gray and his eyes were dark, hidden. He twisted the imaginary throttle again violently and the bones in his arm popped.

"Porter," I started warily, "can you tell me-"

"Who won?" he asked. His anger grew and he howled, "Tell you who won and who lost?"

Porter, the track legend, the motorcycle guru, staggered from the lift, trailing the clinging, glowing vapor. He dragged one leg behind him in a painfully slow shuffle, Boris Karloff revisited from the Mummy movies. Onward he struggled, pulling that mangled leg, arms outstretched.

"Richard Porter," I said boldly, "think! Remember! Do you know where you are? Who you are?"

A grimace twisted his face to great distortion as his right hand twisted the invisible throttle with a yank. He lumbered forward, shambling with the dragging of a leg. Again, he snatched at the throttle I could not see, though I was sure I heard a distant bike engine revving up that time.

"Porter," I warned, pointing at him. "Try to remember-"

"Oh, you bet! Remember! Remember it all! The winners! The loser..." he trailed.

I was about to speak again when he stopped cold in his stride. A grimace disfigured him to the point that I could no longer recognize his face. His mouth opened wide then widened further into an inhuman gape, a nightmare come to life. He worked the jaw to one side and then another as it continued to elongate itself, the imagery becoming a horror.

Then what had been Richard Porter screamed.

The sound ripped down the corridor so sharply and loudly that it should have stripped away the very wall boards. I dropped the dead flashlight by reflex, throwing both hands up to cover my ears. The sound shook the very hallway, the floor beneath my feet buckling. I fell to one side, colliding with the wall, head first. The blow sent me to my back.

"Mr. Priest?" a woman's voice asked.

The raging apparition had gone.

I refocused, forcing my eyes open, unaware they had even closed.

Director Clark stared down into my eyes, long hair draped about her countenance. She knelt with me in the hallway, concern etched into her lovely features. Reflexively, she tucked part of her hair back behind her ears.

"Mick, are you alright?" Sarah then asked, leaning into view as she crouched beside me, too. "Tell us what happened."

I blinked rapidly, trying to shake the cobwebs. The odd light was gone. Clark held my flashlight aimed upward, toward the ceiling, for all of us to see. It gave illumination to a wide area that way.

"I'm...yeah, I'm good. I think I bumped my head."

"You mean where the wood is cracked there?" Clark asked incredulously, pointing to a split board in the lower wall.

"I have a hard head," I said.

I tried to sit up but Sarah palmed my chest and pushed me down.

"Hold it," she ordered. "Ms. Clark just told me she has emergency medical training. Go slow and let her check you."

"Oh, it's rudimentary but I do what I can." Putting up a single finger before me, Clark said, "Now, Mr. Priest-"

"One finger," I said.

"One finger?" she echoed. Then the light came on in her light eyes and she smiled, adding, "No, not 'how many fingers am I holding up'. I want you to follow this finger with just your eyes."

"Is this a party game just for two or can we all play?" James Wyatt growled from nearby.

I jolted, a bit startled. Of course, all three of us were startled.

"I need to test his responses," Clark answered irritably, tucking more hair behind an ear.

"You good, Mick?" James asked.

"I'm okay," I said.

"Responses are good," James said.

"Hush, James," Sarah said.

Cassandra Clark said, "Follow my finger, Mr. Priest. Prove it."

I did, apparently to her satisfaction, though she still had to offer her best advice, touching the red lump near the top of my forehead.

"The impact you just took to your head could be a concussion," she reminded. "It can be a bad sign-"

"Or just a bad haircut," James muttered. "That guy's head is hard. It's full of rocks, anyway. He'll be fine. Let the man up, already."

"James Wyatt, hush," Sarah said curtly.

I knew James was covering for me, though. He knew of my dreams. My visions. The odd side effects. Sarah would fall into that mode, as well, when she was sure I would be okay.

Cassandra Clark stood, backed away and let me rise with a hand from Sarah and James. She was more at ease when she noted how I seemed stable right away, no ill effects.

"Do you have a lot of black outs? Are you anemic? Diabetic?"

"No, no," I said. "None of that."

Sarah met my eyes and I finally had the chance to give her *the look*.

A flare of recognition, of realization, burned in her dark eyes.

"He probably just tripped up in the dark," she said, quickly covering for me. "He's not one for passing out and all of that sorta thing."

"It's silly but I dropped the flashlight and ducked down too fast, trying to catch it. I rammed my head into the wall. I wasn't unconscious, just stunned."

"Oh," Clark said, seeming to accept it. "If you're sure. You were mumbling something, too. Were you calling for help?"

"Probably that dinner a while ago," James insisted. "He was calling for Pepto Bismol."

Sarah gestured for the stairwell with her eyes.

Yeah, I thought as I matched her stare, *take Clark away*.

"I'm okay, everybody," I said with the faintest nod. "Really."

"Okay," Sarah said. "You know yourself best. We'll be upstairs."

"If you feel off, come and get me. Okay?" Cassandra Clark asked.

"Yes," I said. "And thank you."

"Come on, Ms. Clark," Sarah said. "Let Mick nurse his own bruised head and his bruised pride."

The two of them walked away, giggling, Clark asking questions.

I shook my head, rubbing one side of it.

"James, I'm glad you're here."

"Yeah?"

"I think there's been a murder."

I told him about the vision and asked him to walk with me.

"Where?"

"To the elevator."

We moved to the end of the hall and the elevator doors. A quick examination revealed no perforation in the faux plank doors for a regular key hole, the kind used inconspicuously on elevators for safety. With no lock, we gambled on being able to open the lift car.

The two of us drove our sturdy, sizable pocket knives into the crack of the doors and pried at the seam a bit. When there was an open crack between them, we dug our fingers into the space. Slowly, steadily, we pulled the doors apart. When they were open and stayed that way, we rested.

"Well," James said, his voice aloof, "at least it ain't a body."

Victor Jackson and Maureen Li sat in their room on two separate beds. Li had the biggest, Jackson a smaller one, an exercise in irony. Jackson was a solid, formidable form, while Li was small and delicate.

"Already hot," Maureen said, fanning herself with a file folder.

Li, clearly quite hot blooded, wore a pair of white, stretch yoga shorts and a tank top half shirt. Jackson sat in sharp contrast to Li, his laptop screen lighting his face and the full set of black pajamas he wore.

"I don't know how you can stand to wear all that when it's this hot," she continued and began pulling that long, silky hair up into a bun.

Victor Jackson smiled a relatively uncomfortable smile.

"I'm fine."

"Okay," she said with a sigh. "I suppose we could do a little work since the heat isn't likely to let me sleep. You want me to go over there or do you want to come over-"

Jackson raised a hand in a halting gesture. The woman had already hopped to her petite, bare feet but she paused. The money man offered a polite smile.

"You're fine. Over there. I'm fine. Here. I can hear you. From here."

Her girlish voice became lower, very smooth. Mischief pranced about in her dark eyes.

"Vic, is it possible you're afraid you can't control yourself? Am I just a little too provocative?" she asked, running her hand around behind her neck. "Maybe it's just the heat but-"

"Shhh," he interrupted suddenly. Eyes wide, he shut his computer and the light died.

"Vic, really? I-"

"Be quiet!" he vented in a hush. "Did you hear that?"

"Clearly not," she said, irritated.

"The door to the balcony," he added. "I heard it rattle."

"Not likely," she snapped and strolled to the glass barrier.

"Wait! Don't!"

Li, after stumbling in the dark, unlatched the door without even looking through the privacy drapes. A twist of the knob and she swept the door into the room, her arms outstretched at her sides. Victor Jackson, though expecting the night itself to reach out for her, saw nothing move save a breeze brushing the drapes to one side.

"Nothing there," Li said, turning about to face Victor in the dark. "Nothing but a night breeze...nearly as humid as the air in here."

"Okay, fine," he growled. "But close the door. The last thing we need is outside air if it isn't a lot cooler than the air in here."

She clenched her jaw, wiped the sweat from her neck again and dropped both arms back to her sides.

"True," she agreed. "But, when we go to sleep tonight, if it's not cooler, I'm sleeping out on that balcony."

Jackson reopened the laptop and waited for Maureen to return to her bed. He scanned his screen, trying to intentionally distract himself with the work at hand. Thinking on anything would be better than thinking of a killer on the grounds.

Or Maureen's far less than subtle flirting, the married man thought.

"Let's go over our notes, again, on each of these writers," Maureen Li ordered. "I have to try and remember why the publishing partners picked this group to recruit. I'm running out of generic compliments to throw around and I never even heard of most of them before getting the orders to set this up."

Victor frowned, replying, "Maureen, this was your personal project. You put these together. You had to-"

"Don't be crazy," she snapped. "I knew about Blackwood and Matwahali being on television and Johanna Crimson in the movies. Did I want them? Of course. The others? News to me."

"I don't understand. I thought you chose-"

"No, I got passed the operation from the senior partners. I'm just following orders; digital orders, at that. The leads on this couldn't even be bothered to call me. Everything was done in my company emails."

Victor Jackson scowled at the screen.

"Maureen, even the files have tags on them from our own offices. I didn't relay any emails to you and I sure didn't file anything with corporate, not for expenses or paying the talent or anything else."

"No, it came in already set up, already approved. Don't worry. We were just handed a huge operation free and clear by the seniors. They see our worth, our potential," she said. "And, when it comes to charm to seal a deal, they knew to hand it off to me."

The man scrolled down the list of attendees and probable contacts. Li was listed as the recruiter on each and every name. No one was listed as a fall back agent. No one was listed as signing off on the money.

"This whole thing is set up with you as the sole agent proposing, promoting and handling this contract acquisition. I'm worried about signing off on any-"

"That's why you crunch the numbers and sit and stare at computers. I've got this, Vic."

He did not understand a thing she was trying to tell him. The worst point of it was that he suspected she did not understand a thing about it, either. Something in the business workup was missing.

At the same time, the pair totally missed the sound of the doorknob being tried from the balcony again, as well.

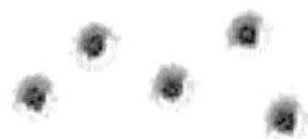

"James...that *is* a body."

We both stood in the doorway to the elevator on Floor Three. Richard 'Ricochet' Porter lay crumpled inside it.

James looked at me flatly, his expression noncommittal. He blinked several times, quickly, the way he always did when he either did not understand something or did not *want* to understand something.

"Naw."

"James, what's wrong with you?" I asked, ire building.

"Think about it," he said. "If that's a body, whoever it is must be dead." He shook his finger at me, continuing with, "If it's a dead body, it can't walk. If it can't walk, we'll have to carry it. And, if it really is Porter, come on, man, he weighs like four hundred-"

"James!" I yelled, shocked at his callousness. "Shut up."

I had thought James could no longer shock me but I was wrong, yet again. I stepped into the elevator.

Porter was propped up in a far corner, bent at the waist, as if sitting. His skin bore a light gray hue, a shade of the dead. Eyes, already discolored, stared in wide open blindness, seeing nothing.

I crouched by his body and checked for wounds and blood. I found nothing. The only oddity was one sagging jowl above his neck. One side of his mouth seemed distended, too, pulled taught. Then I remembered the visions. His twisting countenance. The man dragging the left leg...

"James, check his left boot," I said, still looking around the man's torso and head.

James dropped down and picked up the foot and turned it about.

"He must've dropped the boots at some point, Mick. The man's wearing Cole Haan saddle shoes. And, compared to the other one, this one has scuffs, pretty deep and consistent, all along the inside edge of the sole and toe." James sighed and shook his head, adding then, "Just sad."

"Yeah, I know. He was only in his fifties-"

"These shoes were really nice! Nobody makes a saddle like Cole-"

"James," I warned lowly, "stop messing around! This man died!"

"I happen to know the shoes way better than I knew the man," James said. "You mourn the man, I'll mourn the shoes."

"I need to pray," I blurted out.

"You okay?" James asked, finally genuine.

"No. I'm trapped here with you and I couldn't leave if I wanted."

"That's right, count your many blessings, my friend."

I did a routine check of the dead man's pockets.

"Mick, what're ya doin'?" he asked.

"I figured I'd roll the guy for lunch money," I said.

"Man's got jokes," James muttered.

"You know what I'm doing," I said. "We need every edge we can get. If this guy had anything, at all, that can help us work all this out-"

"Yeah, I know," he allowed. "I just hate it. You ever read *Contents of the Dead Man's Pockets*? It's by-"

"Jack Finney. Yes, I've read it."

"Yeah. Haunts me. I always think about somebody diggin' in my-"

"James," I said with a sigh, "please, concentrate on this dead man."

"Sorry."

A cheap, faux leather wallet with an attached money clip took up the most space. It contained nothing more than a license, two bank cards, two credit cards and a business card with Gridlock Publishing embossed on it.

Three loose dollar bills. Fifty-five cents via several coins.

"Can't write much of a story on that," James said.

I said, "The story I'd write would be on what we didn't find."

"Oh?"

"You notice what isn't here?"

"Well, it's a new age, Priest, ya know? People just don't pack their pockets with papers, forms or notes and all anymore. Everything gets saved in your...oh."

"Yeah. No phone. No PDA, no tablet...and no room key."

He whistled.

"Ya gotta wonder where it went."

"I think we know. The killer. I just don't know the last of it."

He nodded in grim awareness with, "The who and why."

"And maybe even the how. He seems like he could've died from something like a stroke," I told my partner.

"That ain't murder. You don't kill somebody with a stroke. Unless you count the people who've been feedin' this guy for decades."

"Still, no stroke took his room key and his phone from his pockets. Someone rummaged the outfit."

"Who'd rummage that outfit?" he grimaced.

I snapped a look back at James.

"Priest, I didn't know 'im. You're not gonna make me feel guilty for bein' detached, even with those schoolmaster eyeballs."

"Just...move him."

"Do you really wanna move 'im?" James asked.

"Preservation of evidence. Preservation of the body."

"I paid a pretty penny for these ostrich leather boots. If I get any dead guy goo on my boots-"

"Shut up, James," I said again.

"You're so irritable. Vacation don't agree with you. How you wanna do this, anyway?" he asked as we maneuvered into the space. "Wheelbarrow, dining cart, luggage dolly..."

"How about with respect?" I said. "We carry him."

"Mick, it's a long way...wait, where we goin' with 'im?"

"The only place with cold storage. The kitchen. That whole system is set up to run on the emergency power."

"Aw, naw, no way. I can't put a body in with food-"

"James, we'll have to do some rearranging. I'll handle it. You just help me carry him. You get the feet. Can you manage that?"

"Yeah, yeah. I can. It's just..."

"What?"

He sighed and said, "It's already humid. We'll be all sweaty by the time we get there and-"

"James..."

"Okay, okay..."

James finally quietened a bit once we hefted the rider and started downstairs. Not that James Wyatt ever goes completely silent.

En route, we met with absolutely nobody. I was glad but curious; I had not wanted to offer a spectacle but I wondered about the Security Chief's location and the progress of his rounds. When I mentioned it, James told me about walking with him on Floor Three and Floor Four. It was good to know he was on the job.

"Mick, about the boots," James stated along the way, "for the record, I don't really like throwing around money figures. It's rude."

"Okay..." I muttered, rolling my eyes.

"I mean...you know. But we're friends."

"We are," I agreed.

We left Floor Three's landing.

"So, you wanna know how much I dropped on the boots? I feel like I can tell you, as long as we've-"

"Not really."

"No, it's okay, I don't mind. Just between me 'n' you."

We passed Floor Two's landing.

"Come on, you like 'em, you probably want some, I don't mind-"

I looked over my shoulder, taking a deep breath, and said, "James, really. It's all good. I really don't."

"Mick, ol' buddy, jealousy is an ugly thing," James Wyatt said.

"I'll have to make a note of that."

We emptied onto the ground floor and trudged the last of the journey for the kitchen with James huffing. He wiped his brow and smoothed his ponytail as soon as we put him down.

"You gonna be okay?" he asked me, as if I were the one panting.

"I think I'll make it," I said. "You sit and rest. I'll make us a spot."

"You sure we need to do this with him, though?" James asked.

"We need to store him, stabilize his condition-"

"He's dead. It ain't likely to change, much."

I waved the conversation away and turned to the coolers and the freezers. With multiple, walk-in coolers in the kitchen, not to mention freezers, consolidating all the food stuffs provided a challenge but it was doable. Once that was done, I pointed to the empty cooler.

"Okay, James. Get the feet."

Then we packed Porter into the empty cooler. With that done, the two of us stood outside the makeshift coroner's storage. He stared at the closed door. I stared at a particularly big dry goods cabinet. We were looking but neither of us were seeing, our focus on a man's mysterious demise.

"You call it, Priest," he said finally. "What're you thinkin' on?"

"Kimber Mobley."

He waited.

"She told me Porter wouldn't leave her alone, kept talking her ears off. I got the impression it hadn't been very long since he'd been talking with her. Porter, our dead man, a man who looks to have been dead long enough for his color and eyes to shift."

James checked his phone.

"Time's blowin' by, Priest. It's after one in the mornin'. She could've been around him hours ago. And he was alive not that long ago."

"How do you get that?" I asked.

"Bulldog told me when I met up with him earlier. He said some of the guests were less than grateful for his rounds."

"Porter?"

"Nah," he admitted, "but our resident knob shaker said he heard the round racer grunting in his room. Exercising, he thought."

I squinted and cocked my head.

"Porter. He's where the mystery begins, James."

"What now?"

"You're going back to check on Johanna Crimson. Ask her and Gibson what they know about Richard Porter. Don't tell them he's dead; you may want to ask about other people to keep Porter out of focus."

He nodded with, "What're you doin' then?"

"I'm going to his room."

Mick Priest split directions when he and James Wyatt reached Floor Three. His friend was on his way to Floor Four. Priest stayed on Three's corridor and went back to Richard Porter's room. Finding the door locked, he employed his lockpicks, making short, clean, undamaged work of the break-in.

Once inside, his spine tingling, he waited in the darkness to see if Porter would speak again. When he did not, the detective kicked his flashlight to life and eased deeper into the chamber. Slowly, methodically, he dug around in Porter's things and the things native to the quarters before the race legend had arrived. From bed to bed, seat to seat, desk to wardrobe the man scoured the room using a proverbial, fine toothed comb.

When he had nearly finished, Porter's things had told no singular tale. One small sportsbag, completely full of snacks, drinks and diet pills, summed it all up nicely. Porter was overweight. He often thought about and talked about food. Any former athlete his height and weight would likely be pondering a diet, too. Grip Bridger had heard him doing something. Exercising seemed more a possibility in light of the bag than it had at first mention.

The one thing that caught Priest's attention as noteworthy was the office-sized trash can, completely full. No longer than they had been there, Porter had filled a whole trash can. Curious, Priest lifted it to a nearby tabletop.

Candy wrappers in lots of brands and sizes papered the interior of the can. Four empty energy shot bottles rolled about in the bottom. Seven diet soda bottles, different flavors and empty, also, chased the smaller shot bottles around in the bin. A lot of soda for one person.

Priest moved some of them around. Two of the soda bottles had lipstick on the mouth. The cosmetic was present in two different shades. Porter had not been wearing lipstick, so he had entertained in his room. Mobley had said she had been talking with him. But two shades? Two women, or one woman, two different visits?

It was something to remember.

An empty, slender medicine bottle, prescribed to Porter, peeked from beneath candy wrappers alongside its larger partner.

Lisinopril. Metformin.

Priest made a mental note to ask around, to find out if anyone knew what those medicines were used to treat.

Then, lastly, he retrieved three magazines from the trash bin. All of them were *Dirty Rider, Dirty Writer* issues. Two had articles about Richard 'Ricochet' Porter, track legend. One had an article written by Porter, as well, proclaiming it to be his premier column. All three had a very familiar cover model on a speed bike, Kimber Mobley.

Interestingly, his debut article focused on none other than Johanna Crimson. The periodical wanted to show the behind the scenes action of *Velvet Edge's* motorcycle stunts.

Priest slipped those into his back pocket, wondering if he had found the link between a hired killer, a stalked celebrity and a dead man. Whatever the case, it was a start. And there was another name provided for the detective right out of those pages. The model, Kimber Mobley.

Mick Priest thought of the irony in it all. He had never written a traditional 'whodunit', had never had the urge to do so and had never imagined that changing. The formula was too set, too overdone. The backdrop, a secluded location, beyond outside help. Enter a group of stranded strangers with a killer, stalking them from within. How could it be done with a freshness?

Of course, he enjoyed reading them, even collecting old radio versions to which he listened intently. But they were just simply not his creative forte. He had always wanted to leave that classic to masters of the mystery craft and their ink dipped feathers.

From what inkwell had the event at hand been drawn? Onto what paper were their intertwined fates scrawled? What were the odds that a writers' retreat would become such a formatted classic and who was the scribe putting quill to parchment?

Whatever the story, someone had to rightly divine the truth within the mystery and split fact from fiction.

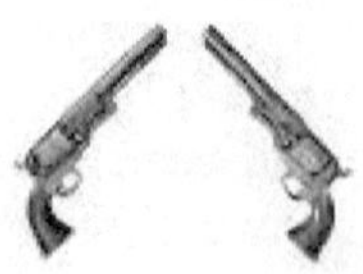

CHAPTER SEVEN

On Floor Two, the staff floor, a tall, manly presence stopped before the door to Cassandra Clark's room. Assigned there were Gretchen Clayborne, the pilot, Helena Makai, the head server, and Clark herself. Clark, however, was still out roaming with Sarah Priest of the SBI.

The man knocked gently on the door.

"Ms. Clayborne, are you awake? Ms. Makai?"

Clayborne and Makai were under direct orders not to open the door. The pilot knew the caller by voice, however.

"Ms. Clayborne? Ms. Makai?" he called.

The pilot yanked the door open with a head cocked to one side.

Jenkins jumped at the sudden movement, hand lifted for the next tap.

"Oh...did I wake you? My apologies."

His formal tone was as distinguished as it would have been if it were the middle of the day.

"No, Jenkins, I was up," she countered, stepping back. She gestured for him to come inside and said, "Why do you ask? I didn't get to the door fast enough?"

"Oh, well, no...not that," he answered hesitantly, careful not to stare at her. "You're already in your...informal attire."

She looked down at herself quickly with a light huff. She had been lounging, girls' sleepover style, with Makai.

"It's okay, Jenkins, you and I are both adults. I'm not trying to show off my undies and I know you'll behave like a proper gentleman."

"Indeed, and never anything else," he said curtly, as if the idea were somehow impossible. "Where is Ms. Makai?"

"Helena's in the shower. She's takin' her fair share of time, too. Seems like she's been in there since we got to the room," she said.

Gretchen went to the balcony doors and pulled them open, fanning herself with the thin, pink fabric of her sleeveless night shirt. She also constantly pulled the tale of it low enough to cover her purple 'undies'.

"Ms. Clayborne! What are you doing?" he pressed and surged forward, taking the door in his own hand. "This is hardly appropriate!"

"Sorry, Jenkins," she said. "I didn't mean for the shirt to come up but I can't do pants, right now. It's just too hot and I'm not a summer girl."

Sweat ran from her temples, over her jaw and down her neck. She kept a hand on the tale of the shirt, holding it down, while she wiped perspiration away with the other.

"I didn't mean your clothes," he snapped. "*Or* the lack thereof. You cannot open this door! Anyone could-"

"Jenkins, I'm a helicopter pilot," Gretchen said. She strode defiantly onto the landing with, "I don't do well locked up in a cage. I'm glad the water is on emergency power but how many cold showers can I take?"

"Ms. Clayborne, I must insist!"

He was chasing her onto the overlook when she rebuked him.

"Won't do you any good, Jenkins. Now, look at that sky."

The moon watched the resort from high above, seeing all but telling no tales. Its soft light, in the moments the clouds allowed it, embraced Clayborne's swaying body. A night wing cried out someplace nearby and an owl, demanding identification, gave answer in the form of its question.

Who? Who? it asked. Who, indeed.

"Gretchen Clayborne," the pilot answered. "The grounded wing."

"Ms. Clayborne, you need to come inside," Jenkins said.

She leaned over the landing rail, looking out into the night sky.

"Nope. If somebody's gonna kill me they can do it while I enjoy the night, not when they come for me in some little hiding place. No thanks."

"Ms. Clayborne...Gretchen," Jenkins said, well out of his comfort zone, "I sympathize. But we have to stay inside. I know danger when I see and hear it. Something dark is-"

"If you say 'afoot' I'll throw you off this balcony."

The prim and proper man straightened, folding his hands behind himself and lifting his chin.

"Indeed?" he asked. "Then let me say something dark is-"

"How 'bout just don't say it at all? My boyfriend is the Security Chief, remember? I've heard it all tonight."

"Speaking of Mr. Bridger," Jenkins said, changing the subject, "he told me you might be the most likely to wander."

"Really? That's Grip, for sure. But, in all fairness, why aren't you watching over Cassie, wherever she went?"

"Mr. Richter, Chef Swartzovski and I are all taking shifts sleeping and watching this floor. I am the Staff Chief. I do not watch over just one person. I care for all of the staff here, as if-"

She laughed with, "Yeah, that's exactly right, *as if.*"

When she brushed her damp, shadowblack hair back from her face and pulled the hair into a ponytail, Jenkins stretched his neck and pulled at his tie. He nervously averted his eyes from Clayborne's arching form. His salt and pepper hair was damp with sweat, too.

"Whatever does that mean?" he asked regally.

"Jenkins, you're sweet on Cassie."

"What?" he half shouted at the suggestion, looking all around. "What...how could you say...that's absurd!"

His exasperation made her giggle even more.

"C'mon, let it go," she admonished. "This whole 'too professional' thing you do-"

He reeled as if struck, biting back with, "My dear girl, I am a professional!"

"-and this 'doting dad' routine-"

"Ms. Clark is much like a daughter to me!"

"-nobody's buying, Jenkins!" she insisted. "She's like a daughter *in age* to you but that's as close as that gets! Admit it! I don't know why you try to hide it-"

"You have no idea-"

"Agreed! I got no clue, Jenkins! Why you can't embrace your feelings, instead of swallowing them down like some bitter medicine, I will never know!"

"There are no feelings to swallow...my feelings...there are feelings but they are not...I am a man, Ms. Clayborne, but I..."

He lifted his face to the overcast, night sky and sighed. He stared wide eyed into the darkness.

"It is a complicated emotional balance. I can't expect you to understand."

She left the railing and moved close to him. Closer than he found comfortable, truth be told. She put a hand on his broad chest.

"Matters of the heart are complicated, Jenkins. That much I do understand...without an explanation."

He met her eyes with his own.

"And I think you don't want to muddy your professional admiration and your friendly affection for Cassandra with messier, unstable things like romance and attraction."

His lips parted ever so slightly.

"Personally, I think you'd like to be more to her but you're hung up on age," she finished, patting one side of his face.

He rolled his eyes as she turned away from him and went back to the balcony railing.

"Preposterous," he challenged in utter chagrin.

She looked over her shoulder, eyes bright in a beam of moonlight.

"Okay, Jenkins. But let me say this. Cassie and I are the same age."

"And?" he asked, shaking his head.

"Women our age are tired of boys, Jenkins. We're tired of trying to drag them to their full potential. We're tired of trying to get them to be adults. A real man – a mature man – is incredibly attractive."

He swallowed hard at his disbelief.

"I hardly understand what it is-"

"You're not old, Jenkins. You're...well, let's throw it out there. You're hot. Not boy-band hot, not jerking around at the club hot; you're grown up hot. Where proper, professional, sophisticated and manly come together, you're it. And we won't even talk about the glinting silver in that black hair."

He could not help adjusting his collar and stretching his neck again. His discomfort amused her, too, even if she was being honest. Her grin was ear to ear.

"I don't know about Cassie and Tye," she said. "But I know about me and Grip. If he doesn't change, and I mean grow up a lot...well, you're the kinda *man* we want our *boy*friends to grow into."

"You flatter me too much," he said after a moment. "But it's been quite some time since someone did. I appreciate it."

"Jenkins, it ain't lip service. You're a strong, charming *man*. I'm sure you get your share of feminine attention. You probably just don't notice when you're being flattered by somebody."

The idea gave him pause.

"I'll tell you a secret, just between you and me. Okay?"

"Of course, my word as a gentleman."

"Cassie was pretty drawn to you when she first started here."

"Oh, please-"

"The truth, honest," she said. "But she felt like you didn't really see her as a woman, more like a girl...or..."

"A daughter," he exhaled.

"So, she wrote it off. When Tye expressed an interest they kinda clicked. I don't say it to make you regret anything but, maybe next time, pay attention, Jenkins. Don't write yourself off as 'out of the running' until you're told you are."

He joined her at the railing and, without warning, something within her stirred. She took a quick breath.

He gently put a hand on each side of her face and she made no effort to pull back. He lifted her face upward and her pulse quickened.

"You are a very sweet young woman. Thank you."

She took another quick, needy breath as her heart raced. Where had the sudden feelings originated? Had she always had them or had she talked herself into it on that balcony?

He kissed her forehead while she was lost in thought and released her. She shivered, a chill running her frame.

He smells like cedar and starlight... her thoughts rambled. *...starlight? What am I thinking? Who can smell starlight?*

She adjusted her t shirt again, pulling it down. Inside, different sensations and inclinations battled for dominance. Curiosity and concern over her willing response to him. Worry over her dedication to her relationship with Grip Bridger. Surprise at her new admiration for Jenkins.

Disappointment...and simultaneous relief...at the kiss being only on the forehead.

He really is a sexy thing, she thought.

"Now, Ms. Clayborne, I must insist you go back inside," he said, returning to business.

"Did you come over here just to stomp out my escape from all this?"

"Of course," he said with raised brows.

She smirked.

"Okay, Jenkins. You win. For tonight."

"A man takes victory where it can be found, my dear," he said.

Both went back inside and one of them locked the landing doors with clicking tumblers.

Pressed against a doorway, four doors down the outside walk, a watcher stepped gently from the shadows. Garbed in all black, the shape bore a mask with a white skull.

Then the figure strode away boldly. Making purchase on the outside stairway, the living night trotted down it as quickly as possible in silence. Soft soled, leather boots absorbed impact and sound and the shadow only stopped at ground level. A black overcoat whipped about the figure like a vicious storm cloud, threatening and concealing at the same time.

The arrogance! the ghost thought in surprised ire. *Locked doors and roving butlers! Do they really think those things can stop the Revolver? They'll find out soon enough!*

Gloved hands flipped out the cylinder of a silver revolver, ages old. It held a full load of paper cartridges from the late 1800s, one through six, ready to bellow. Then, with the cylinder rolled back into place, the ghost stuffed the pistol into a vertical holster beneath the long, black coat. A bone handled twin to the hand cannon rested in a copy of the holster under the other side of the coat.

Cold eyes stared up at the balcony doors from behind the skull mask.

Let them sleep. Let them relax. Then justice can fall...finally.

Then the figure was on the move again. In moments, the shape was one with the night and disseminated into shadow and mist.

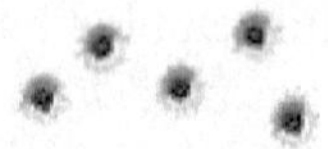

A storm brewed someplace over the mountain. The 'summer rage', as they called it, had begun to give way to a real storm building, a rumbling giant with thunder and lightning in its grasp. The pressure was different, the atmosphere new, the utter feel of the night foreign.

Of course, I had just left a dead man in a cooler and ransacked his room. The night had definitely changed.

Floor Three held Richard Porter's room, a place waiting for an inhabitant never to return. It was also the floor holding a room for the model, Kimber Mobley. Her name and Johanna Crimson's name were connected to Porter in print, in the magazines I had found. I wanted to speak to both of them and chose Mobley first. I was closer to her room and Mobley had claimed to have seen Porter most recently.

As luck would have it, too, the model seemed quite taken with the famous Paul Blackwood and his room was on that same floor. If she was not in her own room I was only two doors down from another chance to find her.

I stormed down the hall of Floor Three.

Suddenly, the night thickened,. I felt as if I struggled to march underwater. It was as if time slowed down to a crawl. The emergency lighting flickered but not in quick flashes. It burned for a second or two, died for a couple then came back on again. Over and over. Like seeing lights blink in slow motion.

I held my flashlight fixed on the corridor. Dust particles drifted in the beam in a dreamy state, scarcely moving, simply suspended in space before me. I blinked against the illusion, pressing ahead.

Porter, a woman's voice whispered from everywhere in the darkness. *Ricochet Ricky. Racing genius. Buncha codswallop. Pervert, ta be sure. Better lock up the kiddies.*

"Where are you?" I demanded, spinning around. I found no one there, though I recognized the voice. "Mobley? Where are you?"

The door at the far end of the hall, the one on the right, creaked and swept open. An unearthly fog rolled out of the room, an indigo haze lighting it.

A chill bit into my spine, paralyzing me for a moment. Then tremors shook me. I locked my muscles against the shaking, steadied myself and moved for the end of the hallway. Once at the door, I swept the light into the glow and the fog dissipated.

I entered the room slowly, cautiously, wielding the light.

Finding no one, I yelled, "Kimber Mobley! Show yourself!"

"She's dead," a disjointed, feminine voice said.

The warbling tone, not to mention the abrupt speech, caused me to jerk with a start.

"...very dead..." the voice trailed strangely.

I whipped around, gun in hand just that fast. The flashlight beam simultaneously blinked out, replaced by a dim, gray hue.

Kimber Mobley lay on her left side. She propped up on an elbow, stretched out on the bed closest to the door. The corridor itself seemed to glow behind me, a weak, grayish light emanating from it, too, like my flashlight. The weak light scarcely helped her appearance, raising her own gray skin tone to a lighter shade of pale. A gory wound marred her upper chest, flesh torn open, all the blood dried to black.

She wiped at her lips, smearing a bit of inky black there.

"I'm a mess, huh?" she asked, her voice thick with a dark intent.

"Kimber," I started.

"I know, I know..." she said, gravel rasping in her throat.

She wiped her hand on the bed. A strange, twisted smile wrenched her mouth to one side. She then began to pull herself toward the edge of the bed frame, one hand over the other.

Her detached voice said, "...I make one beautiful corpse..."

The terror, most palpable, drenched me. Unable to move, unable to flee, my heart hammered the inside of my chest.

"...so, how 'bout a kiss, slick?"

Her otherworldly voice taunted me, her disjointed jaw not moving.

I tried to look away but could not. Her eyes held my attention, the empty holes in her face burning with fiery yellow light.

"Give me a kiss, yank!" she spat, her voice low and rumbling.

Her body twitched erratically. She flew from the bed to the floor with a thud. Hand over hand she grabbed for traction and, as if in fast motion film, she raced ahead in an impossibly quick crawl.

I was frozen, held in the grip of some unseen force, when God reminded me not to fear. In a recollection of Scripture, I knew the weapons of a Christian's warfare are not carnal but are all the mightier, mighty through Him in breaking down strongholds and supernatural power. Faith came alive in me and surged like a raging flood.

"You have no hold on me, in the name of Jesus Christ! Be still or be gone!" I roared.

The dim light flared brightly then disappeared altogether.

I blinked several times in the dark, the glow gone, the apparition banished. I thanked Jesus Christ and Father God for His protection from whatever had been in Mobley's form. Not all spirits were ghosts, not all visitors were from above. Some dreams bore a darkness unspeakable...

I touched my Cross.

When my eyes popped open, I stood just inside Mobley's room, the model dead in the floor. She had a large wound, like a gunshot wound, in her upper chest. I bathed her in my flashlight, the weird glow and the fog gone, my light back to normal.

I locked my jaw against the emotion and retreated for Paul Blackwood's room. I no longer hoped to find Mobley there. All that remained was to find the man with whom she had been most engaged since our arrival.

Mick Priest departed Mobley's room in a hot streak. Jaw set, eyes intent, the detective stormed his way for Paul Blackwood's room.

Time was slipping away. It was a scarce couple of hours before dawn. With every passing moment it felt to the detective like the answers themselves were slipping from his reach.

How much should he reveal, he wondered. Whom should he tell about Porter and Mobley? Would telling Blackwood cause problems if the man was actually the killer? If he was not the killer? Every case, every situation was different.

Nevertheless, Priest police knocked on the man's room door without hesitation. He would play it by ear but play it, he would.

No one answered the investigator's summons, however.

Priest rapped on the barrier again with the butt of his flashlight.

"Mr. Blackwood," Priest called loudly, knocking again.

"He ain't there, sexy," a voice twanged from the end of the corridor.

Mick Priest, true to his reputation, had shockingly fast reflexes. Blindingly fast with his hands, the detective drew one of his weapons and his flashlight. He leveled both on the speaker in the blink of an eye.

In front of her room door, near the stairwell, Kess Melkin froze. She blinked, awed at his speed, never having noticed him flinch. The gun was simply there, all of a sudden, no explanation and no warning.

"Whoa," she gasped. "Easy, tiger. It's just me."

Priest lowered his weapon.

"I see. Why are you out and about, Ms. Melkin?"

"I ain't, not really. I just know the baker ain't in his room."

"Ms. Melkin-"

"I heard ya bangin' and figured I'd save ya the trouble," she said, shading her face.

He lowered the light out of her eyes.

"Where is he?" Priest asked.

"Him and B'Rone went down to the kitchen for a snack," she said with a shrug.

Her relatively short hair was wet to her scalp. It ran water over her face, down her neck and shoulders and soaked the top of her strapped, summer shirt.

"Both of them?"

"Well, yeah," she acknowledged, a curious expression stamping her features. "Why not? Safer in numbers, right?"

Priest said nothing for a moment.

Then, "Yes. Numbers."

She frowned and said, "Me 'n' B'Rone were gonna go but the baker man came down from the model's room. He said she was gonna getta shower and wanted to know if we wanted to go with him to the kitchen. I didn't know the showers were workin' so I ducked out of it. No way I'm passin' up a shower when I can just have B'Rone bring me somethin', ya know?"

"Yeah," Priest allowed. He looked up and down the corridor again with the flashlight then started down the hall for Melkin. "Any idea how long they've been gone?"

"Been a long time," she said. "I'm a girl who likes her long, hot showers and they left before I ever started."

"When they come back up-"

"I'll tell Blackwood you want him," she said when he reached her.

"No," he corrected immediately. "Tell him to stay in his room. I'll be back. And-"

"Okay, okay, Mr. Fun Police," she mumbled. "Me 'n' B'Rone stay inside, too, right?"

"It's for your own safety," the detective warned.

Then he disappeared onto the stairwell, thinking fervently of how he needed to get his allies in the game.

In the northwest corner of Floor Four was Room One. That was James Wyatt's room. In the opposite corner, in the southeast point, waited Room Twelve, where Marcus Gibson watched over Johanna Crimson.

Mick Priest was destined for James Wyatt, to get him up to speed and set him back onto Crimson's watch. However, stepping onto Floor Four, he spotted his beautiful wife and her tag along, Cassandra Clark.

"Hey, baby," Sarah Priest called.

She had just closed the door to the room she and Mick shared.

"I'm glad I ran into you two," he responded as he closed the distance between them. "There's something you need to know, right now."

"Mr. Priest? What is it?" Clark gasped.

"Who?" Sarah asked, ahead of the curve.

"The model. Kimber Mobley."

"What about her?" Clark asked flatly.

"Ms. Clark, be patient. I'll tell you. Probably more than you want to know. Kimber Mobley is dead." He waited a moment then added, "And Richard Porter was already dead. Earlier. I just wasn't sure there was foul play involved with him. With Mobley there's no doubt."

Clark covered her mouth.

Sarah braced a hand against her forehead.

"This is impossible," Clark declared finally.

"Where?" Sarah asked.

"Killed in her room. We moved Porter's body to a makeshift morgue, a cooler in the kitchen. I'm going to get James before I move Mobley. Sarah, I need second eyes on Porter, another opinion about his death. Then you'll have to examine Mobley."

Clark gagged as if she might vomit.

"I'll go now," Sarah said calmly. "If you'll walk Cassandra back-"

"Isn't she a medic?" Mick Priest countered.

"I'm the closest thing to a medic here at the resort," Clark nodded. "I was a certified EMT before I took this job and, in college, I helped with sports medicine as a trainer."

"Emergency Medical Technician and a trainer. That makes you our resident specialist," the detective decided.

"Mick, she's not exactly accustomed to-"

"I'm fine. Gretchen and Helena have each other in the room, they're fine," Clark said defiantly. "I started this round with you. I can finish it."

"Cassandra," Sarah started.

"I'm fine," she said again.

Sarah nodded, glanced at Mick and started off for the lower floors. Cassandra Clark gave close pursuit, though she muttered something about her job requirements.

Mick Priest then hit Room One first, looking for James Wyatt, banging on the door. If he was not in his own room Priest would move on to Crimson's.

Nevertheless, James answered from inside his own room.

"What in the world..." James asked in a fog.

James Wyatt managed to get the room door open but leaned on the knob for support. Sleep weighed his eyes to half mast. Bare feet peeked from the pants legs of the defender's jeans, pants that drooped from his slender frame sans the belt. Tattoo ink ran his bare torso.

"Sorry, James," Priest said. "We got a serious situation."

"I hate you, Priest," he mumbled. Then, "Oh, uh, I mean, sure thing. Let me grab a shirt...some socks, boots...my brain..."

In a short few moments, the professional defense contractor joined the private investigator and the two marched the hall. Priest brought James Wyatt up to date on his discoveries. He told the lanky man they had another body to move, one Kimber Mobley.

"Did you mention Porter to Crimson?" Priest asked him.

"Yeah, and she danced around it. Maybe she remembered him, from somewhere, some time...but, in her defense, she does run with a lotta people. If I had an option, I'd forget about Richard Porter, too."

"Look, I want you to check on her and Gibson. Secure the room. Ask about Porter again, directly. If you get nothing, toss it to them that he's dead, see how it hits them."

James Wyatt nodded his head.

"You're the investigator and the interrogator. What then?"

"Meet me in Mobley's room. Gotta go through it and move her."

He gave a little resistance to the plan, particularly carrying another body. None of that mattered, however. What mattered was wrestling with whatever waited in Kimber Mobley's room.

Clues, evidence...entities...all have to be brought under control, Mick Priest thought. *The Revolver has to be stopped.*

Then the two split again.

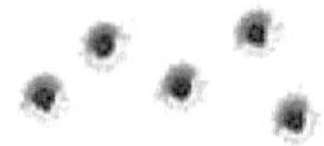

"I appreciate your help," Sarah Priest said, stopping at the cooler door. "And, again, I apologize."

Clark took a deep breath and sighed.

"I don't really want to see a dead man," she said, not for the first time. "I have no urge whatsoever. I'm no doctor, no nurse..."

"Cassandra," Priest calmed, handing her a pair of nitrile gloves. "We wouldn't ask if I didn't really need a second pair of eyes. Trained eyes, knowledgeable eyes."

"I'm not a coroner. I was an EMT."

"Cassie," Sarah soothed. "It's okay if you can't do it. You're only here because you insisted."

"Okay, yeah, I know," Clark nodded. "I've dressed wounds, stopped bleeding, given IV fluids and dressed sprains, breaks and tears...but I don't know dead. I'll do my best but I don't know dead stuff."

"You're all we have," Sarah said. "Just take a look."

Looking up at the ceiling, she smiled ruefully.

"When you put it like that," Clark said.

Glad she had changed out of her dress, she was nonetheless regretting the thick top she had chosen. She pulled the loose, v neck blouse away from her damp skin.

The women shared a soft, nervous laugh.

"You look like you're going to puke," Priest teased.

"Yep. Facts," Clark continued.

"But you're ready," the agent said confidently.

Clark nodded and said, "As ready as I'll get."

Sarah Priest threw open the metal door.

Clark recoiled almost instantly. Sarah was no stranger to death and its accompanying factors but Clark could never have been prepared.

"What...is that?" she gagged, both hands clamped over her nose and mouth.

The cold of the cooler had slowed, if not halted, decomposition. The death had been only hours prior, not even a day; the smell was not that of a corpse breaking down. The smell originated in the body where the muscles that held fecal matter and urine in place had utterly failed; the floodgates, so to speak, had let go entirely. Also, upon death, the general human smell amplified, ramping up things like body odor and the emanations of bad breath. All of that had infused the cooler space before chilling down and it lingered, abated but still virile.

The stains on the corpse's clothing testified to the origins.

"Is he rotting already?" Clark half shouted.

"No," Sarah said. "The body released the bowels-"

"Oh, no no no no no-" Clark chanted, her hands going to her ears.

"Easy, Cassie," Priest calmed. "I said he wasn't rotting-"

"Bowels, guts, the stuff inside," Director Cassandra Clark stammered as she backed away from the room.

Sarah Priest closed the door again and followed her.

"But it's okay. We aren't going to dance with him. We just need to check for cause of death."

"That smell could've done it!" Cassandra barked.

Sarah tried not to laugh. Stifling it caused her to merrily chirp.

Cassie Clark, even in a state of such disgust, giggled in response.

"So? You good?" Sarah Priest asked.

Clark looked at her as if she had lost her mind.

"Good? No," Clark said. "Not at all. What I mean is, on a scale of one to ten, of how desperate I am to just run out of here, I'm at a twelve, easy. Sarah, there's a reason I gave up the EMT thing. A really good one."

"You can do this," the agent said.

Clark twisted the gloves in her grasp, clutching at them like a drowning woman holding on to a life preserver. She held them up.

"You're even prepared on vacation," she said. "Thank goodness."

She stretched the purplish gloves onto her hands as Sarah Priest donned her set. Then Priest held a jar of petroleum jelly out between them after dabbing some of it on her upper lip, underneath her nose.

"This I borrowed from Tayla Barlowe," Priest commented. "Never knew a new mother without some."

"What is it for?" Clark managed.

"Put some under your nose. It won't take a lot but don't skimp. Be thorough. It'll help keep the smells at bay. Masks the scent."

Cassandra slathered on a thick worm of the gel across her upper lip. Some of it actually squished into the edge of her nostrils.

"I'm...good. I won't say ready. But...I suppose I'm good."

Sarah Priest nodded and swept the door open again.

"You are such a liar," Cassandra Clark said once they were inside again.

The cooler door slammed shut and, as if on cue, Clark leaned over, braced her hands on her knees and gagged. It was not the first time.

"It'll pass," Sarah lied, trying to suppress her grin.

"Liar!" Clark screeched, giggling despite her nausea. "The jelly didn't work, the smell isn't dissipating, I'm not getting used to it...you are full of false hope!"

"Well, you know, nothing's one hundred per cent."

"Yeah, now that I believe."

Sarah took a photograph with her phone as Clark struggled to contain herself. She took several more, yet additional angles of nothing telling and nothing discovered, but she had to start somehow.

"They make stuff specifically for blocking the scent of things like decomp. You know, decomposition. Crime Scene Units, coroners, a lotta times they need stuff. Some of it comes in tubes, like lip balm, and there's lightly scented nose plugs-"

"And you have none of it," Cassandra Clark said and sighed. "You had gloves but not that?"

"I'm on vacation."

Then, giggling, the women stripped Richard Porter bare and began to check him over, recording it in photos.

Strange as it was, examining the naked corpse proved to be a bonding experience. Their banter flowed naturally; one would have thought them to have known each other for years. They endured the dark activity with a newly forged friendship, born in the fire of the distasteful.

When they were certain they had finished, Clark turned back to Porter and shook her head a final time. She had checked all she knew to check with her emergency background. There was no hint and no clue as to the cause of death of one Richard Porter, aside from the facial distortion. The former EMT only managed to offer one thing after all was said and done.

"His face," Cassie Clark started, leaning over on her knees and trying to swallow down another gag. "That twisted expression, only on one side. My uncle died of a cardiac event...I don't remember which kind...but he looked like that."

"Stroke?"

"Maybe."

"Or heart attack?"

"Could...could be," she managed between gags.

"Do you think it could have been a-"

"Sarah!" Clark urged, covering her mouth. "One of them. I don't know. Now, I need to go."

Sarah Priest snapped a last photo, one of Cassandra Clark propped over on her knees.

"Just waiting on you," Priest said and walked out of the room.

"You're a liar and I hate you," Clark said, stifling a chuckle.

My flashlight lit the space like stark, white napalm igniting a grassy field. It flowed like a liquid, burning away the darkness. Regardless, the aftermath of Kimber Mobley's violent end was hard to miss.

More than a scuffle had transpired. A fight had clearly erupted. A struggle for survival had exploded in that room and left in its wake all the telltale signs. Nightstands lay broken, a coffee table crushed, legs from them all pointing in skewed directions. Two of the beds had been pushed out of place and one was overturned, covers apparently lost in the combative tornado. Lamps, broken on the floor, told the violent story, a story to which Mobley's lifeless form penned the epilogue.

The young woman's blood pooled in the floor beneath her. It painted the gruesome scene red and smeared its vulgar crimson on almost everything nearby. Her upper chest, blown open by heavy caliber bullets, released her lifeflow all over everything and I knew the room was the initial scene. Her body had not been moved.

I stared in silence. My silence, not hers. She screamed out for justice through her spilled blood. In death, she begged for vindication.

"Give me time," I said.

She had been someone's daughter. Someone's granddaughter. Sister. Lover. Friend, and on. Aside that, no matter whoever, whatever else she may have been, she had been made by God and He loved her. Whoever had killed her and stolen her life had worked an unforgettable evil reaching all the way back to the days of Cain and Abel. Like with Abel, Kimber Mobley's blood cried out.

I examined her body and her wounds. Finding nothing of import on the outside, I set about scouring the room for anything that could be a clue. I started with her bags, throwing them onto a bed and zipping them open.

In short order, I emptied all of Mobley's luggage onto one of the small night tables. Each piece of clothing, each article of personal hygiene, every bit of makeup and perfume got the same intense, focused examination. I sought anything and everything that could be considered noteworthy.

Unfortunately, the only notable clues in the cases suggested she had come expecting an intimate liaison. She had far more lingerie packed than daytime clothing and it was not typical sleepwear. It was all of the playful, entertainment variety. No one wore things so uncomfortable as some of those costumes to spend the night alone.

Also, there were far too many party drugs packed in false makeup packaging for any one person, even an addict, to use in one weekend. She had planned for a few intimate friends.

I pulled the luggage apart completely, finding little else. Eventually, I turned my attention to the room and its wreckage from the fight. I carefully checked under and on and inside every bit of furniture and movable décor.

At a loss, I was finally about to evacuate the room, having already opened the door, when I lost the light. My flashlight never flickered. It simply died. Everything fell black. The very atmosphere darkened to pitch in the blink of an eye. It seemed no light at all existed.

"Doesn't make sense," a raspy voice said from behind me.

He struck a lighter as I whipped about and the otherworldly, gray flame burst into life. It colored his already lifeless face with a morbid reflection as he lit a cigarette. The tip flared a bright white then faded back to gray when he pulled it away from his lips.

"Porter, do you know where you are? Do you know-"

"Oh, I know. Just doesn't make any sense," he repeated, his voice strangely echoed. "They always said these things would kill me..."

He doubled over with boisterous laughter and ragged coughing.

"Think, Porter."

He lowered the cigarette and I could no longer see his face, just his glowing hand by his side, as he continued.

"After all this time...why?"

Though he was not drawing from it, the glow of the cigarette burned with a piercing white light.

"Why what?" I demanded. "Why kill you, Porter?"

"For my sins!" he screamed.

The entire chamber trembled with the tremor in his voice.

The light dropped to a faint glow at the end of the cigarette. Then it turned red. An ambient glow surrounded it with a faded, graying orange.

"What sins, Porter?" I pressed, unable to see his face.

The cigarette lifted to be smoked again, red lips making purchase upon the filter. The full, plump lips were not Porter's, though, and the orange reflection lit another face. Blood red eyes, mimicking the lips, stared at me from Kimber Mobley's stricken countenance.

"Wouldn't you like to know?" she growled, her voice an animal in chains.

I grabbed my Cross where it hung about my neck and stepped back from her grisly visage. My flashlight swept upward, coming back to life, just as the rest of the lighting did. Porter and Mobley were gone...

...if they had even been Porter and Mobley...

Sins of the dead. More secrets. More mystery. I needed answers. Something to build on.

I opened Mobley's door and bailed into the hallway.

Immediately, I jolted. James Wyatt stood close to the door.

"Hey, Mick," he said. "I was comin' to find you."

"Yeah?" I asked.

"Yeah. Let's move Mobley, get it over with. Won't be too long 'til mornin', ya know."

"I was going to sit down with you and Gibson and Crimson first," I said.

"No good," he said. "She's asleep and he's already secured the place, put his back against a wall. Be a little while yet before I relieve him, if he sleeps, at all. Old man's like a robot, Mick. I never seen anything like it."

"Did either of them say any more about Porter?"

He chuckled.

"I'll tell you on the move."

Mick Priest and James Wyatt again set about moving a body. There was less banter between them. Priest wondered what had quietened his friend. Was it because it was a second body? Was it because the victim was a woman? Was it because of the obviously bullet related wounds, bringing home the certainty of a killer? Either way, James Wyatt was just a little more business than before.

They still talked en route to the cooler, however. The talk centered on Johanna Crimson and Mark Gibson. It seemed they did have more to reveal than previously unveiled. The two despised Richard Porter, the short story told. He had tried to cross Crimson via the article interview and his own vulgar flirting. He had tried to cross Gibson when the man called him on his behavior...and that had not gone well for him.

Priest nodded, not surprised. He would follow up on it in person.

He and James met Sarah Priest and Cassandra Clark in the kitchen. They were having a cup of coffee. The men handed off possession of the model's body and turned that inspection over to them.

Before leaving, Priest had questions.

"Have either of you seen Blackwood or Matwahali?"

The women had not.

"What about Bridger?"

Not lately, was the generalized response.

"You call it," James Wyatt said.

"Let's make some rounds," Priest said. "Knock on these quiet doors. These men have to be someplace."

Again, the men set themselves in motion.

Sarah Priest and Cassandra Clark offered well wishes as the men left then donned the nitrile gloves again. Again, the petroleum jelly in the edge of the nostrils. Again, time taken for Clark to mentally brace herself. Then the two invaded the big, makeshift morgue...the larger of the resort's walk-in coolers.

Clark immediately shivered and, oddly enough, giggled.

"What?" Priest pressed.

Goose bumps raced over the director but she smiled even wider. Her outfit glistened quickly as a sheen of sweat froze in the soft materials.

"It feels glorious in here! I almost forgot there are dead people!"

Sarah laughed openly. In moments the cold would be ridiculously uncomfortable, the real feeling of the low digits setting in on them. At that second, however, Clark was absolutely right. Sarah Priest was a hot blooded woman and she had been suffering in the humid resort night.

Her tank top was not just damp, it was completely wet. It stiffened as her perspiration crystallized in it.

"It's like a reverse spa," Sarah said.

"I know!" Clark said excitedly. Then she sobered and her face lengthened. "With dead people."

"Speaking of..." Sarah Priest answered with a nod.

She led Clark to the bodies lined against the far wall.

Richard Porter wore nothing. Sarah Priest and the director had stripped him down the first time they had checked him over. The cold had done nothing for his color.

Kimber Mobley had to be disrobed. By the time the two women had her bare, the cold in the cooler had both of them shivering. Clark stepped out first to don the meat locker jacket and whatnot hanging by the door and, before she was done, Priest was already doing the same.

"Gets cold fast."

Priest nodded, saying, "It does."

When both were back inside, Clark's smile over the icy temperature lost, they resumed the exam. They started with a review of Porter, a 'just in case'. It took mere moments to reassure them there was nothing new to discover, at all. Muscular tensions and slight contortions of the face and limbs supported the death by stroke theory that was only a theory.

They then turned sadly to Kimber Mobley, clearly killed with a firearm equipped with large, round bullets.

"I can't believe it," Clark muttered. "She clearly took a beating and then, to be shot like this, multiple times..."

"The evil that mankind can do. Desires. Urges. Dark drives and motivations. Believe it."

"How could all this happen to her without someone hearing it?" Clark demanded.

"Isolation. Dispersion. No witnesses to offer input, no one to come to another's aid. The only answers are often ones offered by the victim. The dead victim. That's why we dig."

The women examined and measured the bullet wounds, following Sarah Priest's lead for her experience. She took note of entry angles, depth and shape of bullet wounds and probed inside the wounds for solid, misshapen lead rounds.

In no time Sarah pulled a considerable wad of lead from one wound, rounded and not jagged. It was far bigger than the bullet lead Clark had seen in her life.

"You said we'd find whole bullets and not shrapnel. Not broken up bullet fragments. How did you know?" Clark asked Priest as she dug around in the corpse's flesh again with her fingers.

"Elementary, my dear Watson," Sarah said in a British accent.

Clark groaned, asking, "You just couldn't help yourself, could you?"

"Apparently not," Priest admitted.

The Director took the big, somewhat flattened, lead ball in an upturned, gloved palm.

"Seriously. How did you know the bullet wouldn't be in pieces?"

Sarah Priest rested her hands.

"I know a bit about forensic police work," she said, not arrogantly but more like a warning. "How much do you want me to tell you? I hate rattling on and having people around that are too nice to say they really don't care to hear it."

"Share. I'm interested. Honestly."

Sarah started checking another wound, saying, "Okay. Don't say I didn't warn you."

Sarah completed the removal of the bullets from Mobley and started photographing every wound on her. Scrapes, bruises, cuts, whatever.

"Bullets? Ballistics?" Clark prompted.

"Yeah, okay," Sarah Priest said, snapping photographs. "In the old days, like the 1800s, the Civil War period, that sorta time, guns fired big, round metal balls for bullets. A lot of documentation references them as 'cap and ball' guns, because of the way gun powder was applied and ignited and for the fact that the projectiles were simple, round balls of lead."

"Okay."

"Those balls were already big, blunt, round and soft. On impact, they flattened out a lot, spreading. So, when they hit a person, they did a lot of tissue damage, bringing a lot of trauma. They had a tendency to spread out, doing a lot more bruising before pushing into the flesh."

"Like being punched with a big fist instead of poked with a knife. Knife slips inside, fist impacts," Clark said, content with her analogy.

Priest lifted her eyebrows and nodded emphatically.

"Hey, good, yeah. Exactly. Well, modern bullets are more loped, like little cones-"

"Longer nose, steeper point."

"Dead on. You like firearms?"

"Not really," Cassandra Clark said with a chuckle. "I like police dramas on television."

"Okay," Priest laughed. "Well, the modern bullets are forged harder on the outside for quicker, better penetration, so you get less bruising and impact trauma."

"Okay, so...this is an old ball bullet?"

Sarah nodded her head, saying, "Yep."

"Okay, I follow you, so far," Clark said.

"As you can see, with a cap and ball round, the wounds have large, colored rings around the entry point. All bullet wounds have bruising around the entry points. An abrasion ring is a narrow band of stretched and torn skin where a bullet pierces through. A contusion ring is a much bigger band of bruising that encircles the point where a bullet, like a lead ball round, passes through, the band reflecting the impact trauma. Mobley has clear contusion rings, a whole lot of bruising."

"So, not pointy bullets. Not modern bullets. Cap and ball bullets...old fashioned bullets."

"Yes," Priest said.

"But modern bullets are forged harder, made of harder metals, whatever. Why would they have been broken up if you'd found those?" Clark asked. "You said they'd be fragmented if they were modern."

"Ah. Good question."

Sarah put her camera down and whipped out her Smith and Wesson. She jacked the slide and kicked a round free to the frozen floor. Then she put away the weapon and handed the free round to Clark. It had an advanced nose and was smaller in diameter but the end had been hollowed out, leaving a cavity.

"These are modern rounds and are made to do that very thing intentionally. They're called hollow points. They became popular for two reasons. First, they spread out really fast and do quite a bit of internal damage, more than even the old cap and ball would when it spreads. Only, it does it once it's inside the body. This gives more knock down, impact power than a hard, pointed bullet would, because it won't just pass straight through."

"Okay, right."

"That's the second reason, too. When shooting a target, the last thing you want is for a bullet to pass clean through and hit something or someone else. The hollow point normally doesn't kill secondary, accidental targets even if a piece of it should pass far enough to hit one."

"So, no exit wound but the huge bruise spot-"

"Contusion ring."

"Yes, that. You knew it wasn't a hollow point 'cause of a lack of shrapnel and it wasn't a regular, modern bullet because it wouldn't have had the contusion ring and it would've had an exit wound...you then knew it was an antique bullet."

"I surmised."

"What a guess," Clark remarked.

"I had a clue already," Priest admitted.

"Do tell."

"This rumored killer? The Ghost Revolver? The name says it all, really. The killer is believed to use a revolver. An antique, black powder revolver. The scenario here matched 'cap and ball' rounds and cap and ball rounds were not used with handguns that came after antique, black powder revolvers."

"Have you ever been wrong?" Clark asked, impressed.

"I thought I'd spend this weekend in romantic bliss," Sarah said.

Clark chirped with laughter, saying, "That's an emphatic *yes*."

"Yep."

One pervasive, driving urge, a relentless desire, pushed Kess Melkin out of her bedroom once again to wander the corridor, completely against the rules. It was a mental need, an emotional attachment and a physical addiction all conjured up in the same smoke. Her need for a cigarette. Unwilling to wait any longer for her amorous room guest, the big man, B'Rone Matwahali, she slid into a tight, red skirt, almost knee length, and yanked on a lacy, black tank top. By reflex, she finger fluffed her short hair before grabbing up knee high boots. In bare feet, she strode out into the hallway and made for the stairs, shapely hips swaying emphatically. Her intent was having a cigarette no matter what, whether she had to lie, cheat, steal or seduce her way to it.

Melkin stopped short at the stairwell, looked both ways, up and down, and listened. She found it empty and took the moment to sit down on the landing and slip into her boots.

"Ms. Melkin," Falgrip Bridger greeted lowly.

She jumped from her bottom in a shocked jolt, hit unevenly on the heeled boots, slid to one side and toppled backward. She went right back down onto her bottom. To her credit, she made no sound, jaw locked against the sudden fright.

"What's wrong with you?" she snapped angrily, a heavy hush spewed between clenched teeth once she had settled to stillness.

The young man could not resist his smirk.

"I only said your name," he responded quietly. "I wanted you to know I was in the hall with you. I didn't want to startle you."

She cursed then gave a snide smile, saying, "You dropped the ball."

"I did. I'm sorry," he said, yet there was mirth in his eyes.

"I think you enjoyed it," she said.

She accepted his extended hand and let him pull her to her feet.

"My girlfriend says I love to scare people."

"Is that a confession, Hall Monitor?" she asked.

He paused but eventually nodded.

"Probably. Let me make it up to you."

"And how would you do that?" she asked.

"I can choose to not bring this up to the Priests."

She twisted up a scowl.

"Tattletale. Okay, deal, on one condition."

"What's that, Ms. Melkin?"

"Walk me outside for a couple of minutes. You escort me so I can go and you can be sure I'm not killin' anybody."

"I don't think-"

"C'mon," she urged. "One smoke. I know it's against the rules but what's the biggie? You gotta admit, you got bigger worries than me an' a cigarette."

He shook his head uncertainly.

Her big eyes held his, however...and she did have a point...

"Okay. One. Then you go back to your room."

She threw a big smile behind her wine red lips.

"I'll owe ya one," she said and tickled his chin with a single finger.

He wondered if he might have gotten himself into trouble.

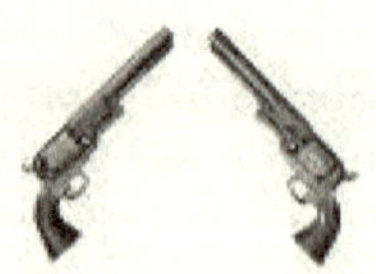

CHAPTER EIGHT

Thunder rumbled and growled in the distance, someplace just beyond the faintest of colors being born over the mountains. Someplace, a real storm stirred, not just summer rage. Someplace, morning was on the way, too, the arriving sun seeking dominance once again. Soon enough sunrise would begin burning away the mists on the mountain, evaporating them like the ghosts of a previous night.

Grip Bridger looked around the rose garden again, stealing peeks at the horizon. He did his best to pretend he was just watching over Kess Melkin. He pretended he was simply protecting her but there were two additional truths hovering within his mind, try as he might to deny them.

He was covering for Melkin to smoke on resort property, first of all. The cigarette butt she had already tossed into the bright red mulch was proof enough of that, never mind that she had lit another right behind it. He was breaking rules for her and doing so almost without a thought.

The second point of his own distraction was the raw, sensual allure of the woman. Gretchen Clayborne, his girlfriend, was pretty. Kess Melkin was different. She was older, more viscerally and blatantly sexual. Clayborne was a peer. Melkin was a huntress, her demeanor itself seductive...and Bridger, willing to admit it or not, was fascinated.

I'm in High School again, in love with the teacher, he thought. Of course, it was anything but love and he knew it.

"Ms. Melkin, we need to finish up," he said finally.

His sigh bore a regret at the idea of potentially disappointing her.

"Relax, Boy Scout," she teased.

"It'll be dawn soon," he reminded. "I don't want to end up playing chaperon to every guest here."

"Ohhhhh," she said. "I'm...special?"

She blew smoke in his direction from the pucker of her full lips. Her eyes seemed to draw him in.

"Yes. No. I mean..."

She cackled then giggled for a long moment, drawing on the cigarette. She blew out again, cocked her head to one side and winked at him. She then thumped away the second butt.

"All done, cutie."

"I see that," he noted.

Gesturing with his left hand, he escorted Melkin back into the ground floor of the resort. Just inside the open, double doors, she drew up short, spinning about. Bridger bumped into her, chest to chest.

"Thanks for this," she said airily, eyeing him through the top of her eyes. "I do appreciate it."

His heart surged and he feared she would hear its thuds within his chest. His wide eyes fixed on hers.

"No problem. At all. Glad. You know. Glad to help with-"

She put a flat hand on his chest, right over his heart. Had she actually heard it pounding? Suddenly, she bounced her short, curvy self up onto her toes and kissed him.

That is when B'Rone Matwahali turned into the corridor near them. They split apart like magnets repelling similar charges.

"Okay, 'ere," the big man said, striding up to them. He handed a platter of food to Melkin. "Take this, will ya?"

An abruptly nervous Bridger swallowed hard. He nodded at the famous explorer and adventurer and looked away for the stairwell.

"I'm glad you're here," he lied. "I was walking Ms. Melkin back to her room but I need to finish my rounds. If you could escort her..."

"Oh, glad to," Matwahali said jovially. "Thanks for seein' her about, mate. I told her to stay put but she's a headstrong one."

Melkin whipped her head back to Bridger with a sly grin.

He would not meet her gaze.

"You should really stay inside and safe, too," Bridger told the man.

"Yeah, no worries. On the way, now. The bakery gremlin will be along, too, once he packs away a little more food."

"Bakery...gremlin?" Bridger started with a confused grimace.

"Paul Blackwood," Melkin said.

"My pal's still scavengin'," Matwahali said, pointing at the Kitchen. "We came down, gonna take goodies upstairs, but we started pilferin' on the scene. Well, ya can't eat inna kitchen, that's what Paulie says, so we took a load of it outside and sat for a bit. Then, when we came back in, I had ta get Kess somethin' and he stayed on to eat more."

"I'll see him up," Bridger said. "You two go on ahead."

"Thanks, mate."

They offered a final farewell and started the stairs.

Bridger had just turned about and began his walk for the Kitchen when he heard it. A fluttering wing, the whipping of a sail. Both, neither. Nothing, maybe. Or something.

Whatever it was or was not was just outside. In the garden.

He whirled about and rushed a few steps, back outside, back into the garden. Sounds, too faint to make out for certain, seemed to move farther away. He pursued the unknown into the garden and the shadows playing there.

His right hand eased back to his gun, reflex and training overriding conscious intent, as he pushed his coat back behind the holster and out of the way. The hot, night air threatened to drown him as his breathing quickened.

The talk was over, the suspicion blown away like vapor in the wind. At that moment, the danger on Shadow Mountain was all too real and a stiff dose of fear came, uninvited and mocking.

Grip Bridger pulled his gun free slowly. With it leveled out before him, he followed it like a compass needle, the bore always leading the way. The sound he had heard was not a night sound. A nature sound. A common sound for the resort. It sounded a lot like some fabric material whipping in the wind, like some pirate's flag blowing beneath the moon.

Then the long, black coat, a physical shadow that cloaked an individual in the garden, merged again with the night itself. It hid a watcher among the flowers and the bushes.

A pair of silver revolvers slipped free of the black folds and the hammers rolled back.

Thunder went off in the night again, summer rage bellowing.

Thunder went off in the night again, summer rage bellowing. Other ominous, rolling voices joined in, however. Volatile, percussive cries, closer to the earth and the resort and the inhabitants. Thunder, yes, but singing a dirge of baritone fury with booming, audible violence. The gun handlers on the mountain knew the explosive voices too well.

Gunfire broke the last tendrils of the night.

Mick Priest raced through the resort with James Wyatt close on his heels and Sarah Priest right behind them. Experience had taught many lessons and one of them was knowing how sound echoes and flows. All three of them knew immediately that the shots rang from outside the building, close to the ground, near the gardens.

The rain had just begun softly drizzling when they reached the roses.

"James, that way!" Mick Priest pointed and yelled.

James Wyatt turned to the right ninety degrees and pressed through the bushes, gun in hand.

"What about Crimson?" Sarah asked, coming up beside her husband.

"James said Gibson had her secure for the night," Mick Priest replied. He readied both of his Colts and asked, "Where's Clark?"

"She's just inside. I told her to stop any others from coming out."

"Go back with her. You got the badge and the authority, Sarah. Make sure we don't get a crowd out here in the way."

She did not like the plan. She nearly said so, it was evident in her dark eyes. Sarah Priest did not want to leave her husband's side. However, she knew he was right.

As she eased back, Mick moved again, further into the flowers and the shrubs. He crept in a crouch, guns ready, eyes sharp. A newly assertive wind raked through the garden, however, and brought a load of slightly intensifying rain. Priest had to wipe his shaven head with a forearm to keep the downfall out of his eyes.

A flicker of lightning blinded him for a moment, too, and he stilled. The flare gone, he blinked it and the rain away and looked about himself. He found nothing out of place until he glanced behind himself.

Falgrip Bridger stood perfectly still, as rigid as stone, less than fifteen feet away from the detective.

Priest jerked about, reflex bringing up his weapons. He lowered them instantly when he noticed it was Grip.

Bridger did not react, at all. He did not blink and did not wipe his face as the rain came harder. The young man simply posed motionlessly.

"Grip, didn't you hear the shots?" Priest asked. "Crouch down! We don't know...we..."

Priest slowed as he noticed Bridger's lack of response and lack of recognition. The young specialist stared blankly into the night, looking beyond the garden and beyond Priest.

"Grip?" Mick asked.

The young man jerked suddenly, his left arm snatching out to the side, bent at the elbow. He pointed behind a particularly large spate of underbrush, his body shifting in a twitching motion, like a marionette on strings.

"Oh, Grip..." Priest muttered quietly.

"Hey," a voice said in Priest's ear.

Priest jerked to the side so violently that he nearly fell over. His heart, feeling as if it would pop, pounded in his torso with the shock.

"Take it easy," James Wyatt said quietly. "It's just me. I didn't find anything, though; how about you?"

Mick Priest looked back for Grip Bridger and the man was gone. More to the point, he had never been there. Priest then waved James Wyatt forward and led him behind the shrubbery.

There, half stuffed into the bush, Grip Bridger's body sat in a limp curl of himself. Gunshot wounds marred his back, three of them, and blood soaked his jacket.

"Naw, not Bulldog," James said quietly.

"Check for his piece," Priest said.

James Wyatt rolled the young guardian out of the brush and onto his back. He rifled inside the man's jacket and probed his pockets.

Thunder boomed. The rain intensified to a steady, albeit moderate, cascade, finally cooling in its touch. The temperature began a fall.

"Holster's empty, Priest," James said darkly. "And that ain't all. His pockets are empty, too. No phone, no keys, no nothin', man."

Mick Priest locked his jaw, muscles tensed on his face. Fierce eyes burned hot in the cooler air, staring intently at the young, dead man. For a long moment, his silence howled a mournful refrain as the rain steamed upon his head.

"Mick?" James said after a few moments.

Nothing but jaw muscles working and a burning fire flickering in the detective's eyes even hinted that the man was alive. Otherwise, he was stone.

"Priest? We goin' sideways?"

"Already there," Mick growled.

James Wyatt popped his neck to one side then the other.

"For just such a time as this..."

James Wyatt and Mick Priest stormed back into Stable Manor from the garden entrance. The two men split the falling veil of rain outside the entry and appeared inside, apparitions come to life from the very weather.

Just inside the open room, a crowd had gathered. They had been quickly corralled by Agent Sarah Priest and Director Cassandra Clark, with help from Staff Director Jenkins and Facility Operations Director Richter. For a moment, the audience fell quiet at their appearance. When the shock passed, they greeted the men with gasps and murmuring.

Then, of course, the questions.

What was that? Was that gunfire? Was anyone hurt? Who was shooting? Are we in danger? What did you see? Has anyone seen -

"Quiet!" Priest bellowed, his voice resonating deeply.

Again, shock. Again, silence, with the exception of little Emma Barlowe. Priest had nearly awakened her. She tuned up for crying, lying in the sling over her mother's chest.

"Clark, get everyone to the Dining Room," Priest ordered. "Now."

He and James Wyatt had been taking a mental roll call in their minds. Both of them had already ascertained how many of the guests and staff were not present and who they were.

"James and I can collect everyone who didn't come running down here for the show." Then, to James Wyatt, Priest said, "Start knocking on doors."

"And if they don't respond?"

"Start knocking on heads."

On the stairs, James Wyatt started, "Any particular way-"

"Start however you want," Priest said, his voice a guttural warning. "I'm bringing Blackwood."

No one had balked while the men were still present. Their look and their demeanor screamed no nonsense, deathly serious intent. Once they went up the stairs, however, the murmuring started.

Who does this guy think he is? They can't make us do anything. What are they hiding? Why won't they answer our questions? What makes him think -

"Due to circumstances soon to be discussed, I am turning any and all authority I have here, as Resort Director, to Special Agent Sarah Priest of the SBI," Clark announced loudly. "Please follow her instructions."

Sarah Priest nodded when their eyes met.

"All of you, please gather in the Dining Room. There is much to discuss."

"Or what?" Maureen Li interrupted Priest. "Some of us aren't morning people. I need to go back to bed if we're not all in danger or anything."

She's right. The agent is just trying to help. We have rights, though.

Sarah spoke without moving. She did not even blink.

"You can gather willingly for a little while or I can sequester you by state authority and I can lock you down for the rest of your time here. The choice is yours."

Ouch. She ain't playin', is she? Let's not push her. I told you.

As one, they moved for the Dining Hall.

That left James Wyatt and Mick Priest to rally the last of the inhabitants, those missing from the curiosity convention.

The young scholar, Andreya West, had not come downstairs. Marcus Gibson and his employer, Johanna Crimson, had failed to appear, as well. No doubt they were safely holed up in their room. James figured to get all three.

Paul Blackwood, also absent, had landed in Mick Priest's sights and James Wyatt did not envy the man. Mick would collect him...one way or another...and bring him along.

"I just wonder what the Brit did," James muttered to himself after he and Priest had split directions.

It was simple mathematics. Fractions.

The common denominator.

Paul Blackwood would not stay in his room, choosing instead to wander. He claimed to have seen Richard Porter, alive and well, more recently than anyone with the exception of the model, Kimber Mobley. Blackwood confirmed Mobley's tale of being the last to see and speak with Porter while he was alive, though it remained to be seen if that was even possible. Porter wore death as if it had been on him longer than that.

With Mobley dead, Paul Blackwood became the last to see her alive, too. Added to the aloof attitude he wore like a cologne...

...Mick Priest wanted answers from the British baker.

The detective banged on the man's room door. It was not a *knock knock, are you available* kind of rapping, either. Priest pounded it with the butt of his fist and the tip of the flashlight shaft, held in that hand.

He was quick to strike again, too, when the baker did not respond immediately, and his pummeling rattled the iron knocker on its hinge.

"Whaddaya want? I'm tempted to knock on your head the way you're...knockin' on my...door," Blackwood trailed.

He quietened and calmed once he had the door open and saw Mick Priest. There was something about the detective's glare.

"You asleep, Blackwood?" Priest spat quickly.

The baker wiped his eyes and pushed his hand back over his head, ruffling the spiked, silver hair. Then he gestured at his body. He wore nothing but boxers and a white gold chain around his neck. Silver chest hair sprinkled a very fit, solid torso, something viewers of his television show never saw beneath his button down shirts.

"I wasn't dressed this way for company, mate," he sniped. Then he chuckled and winked, adding, "Unless my Aussie friend was inclined to come back over."

Kimber Mobley.

"Yeah...she's busy," Priest growled.

"Okay," Blackwood offered with a scrunched face full of confusion. "What can I do for *you* in the meantime? I guessing you didn't just-"

"Did you hear anything unusual? Just a few minutes ago?" the detective pushed sternly. "How hard were you sleeping?"

"Hey, what is this? What're ya playin' at? This is me vacation time. I don't know how you lads in the States do it but we don't get up at the crack o' dawn when we're on vacation."

"Today, you do," Priest said. "Get some clothes on; we're all going down to the Dining Hall."

"All? Who's all?" he said.

"Everybody who just heard those gunshots, Blackwood. Everybody who ran downstairs to see what they could see. Everybody, almost...but you."

Don't go sideways, Priest told himself.

"I ain't heard no gunshots, Priest," Blackwood snapped, "and besides, maybe I got more important stuff to do than run up and down stairs. I ain't shot, so I figure I'll mind my own business. You know, like you an' everyone else should do."

Priest's eyes narrowed and he took a deep breath.

"Blackwood, I'm gonna tell you right now, since you don't wanna hear it with the group. Richard Porter is dead and you might be the last person to have seen him alive."

"Codswallop," he barked. "Sweet lil Kimber had that privilege, I believe. So, you can-"

Here we go.

"She's dead, too, lover boy," Priest rumbled.

The Brit staggered with the news. He turned ice blue eyes this way and that, as if looking for the woman. For a moment, Priest thought it would shatter the other man's confident veneer. He expected the blow to bring Blackwood's compassion to the surface and torpedo his indifference. It did not. The man recovered almost instantly.

"Well, not that she wasn't a lotta fun," he said, shrugging as if shaking off any required concern, "but we weren't gettin' married! I mean-"

Sideways.

"Blackwood, get some clothes on!" Priest roared. "There's a resort full of folks downstairs and not a single one is getting a pass on this little gathering! We're gonna get some answers tonight and I, for one, wanna hear yours, first hand!"

Paul Blackwood was solidly built. He was quick, too, when he decided to press his luck. Perhaps he thought no one could talk to him that way, that his celebrity status afforded him exclusion. Perhaps it was the early hour or the inconvenience of being bothered with the deaths of people insignificant to him. Maybe, just maybe, he believed his own press and the rumors in the media. Entertainment outlets touted him as far more than a famous baker, that he was a tough guy with a new action movie coming down the line. Whatever it was, it was foolhardy.

The kitchen king lunged at the detective with an open hand, trying to shove him out of the doorway. To his credit, he twisted his body with the motion and leaned into it. It would have been a powerful push if Priest had not simply rolled the man's arm to the side, letting Blackwood stumble forward.

In the same motion, Priest whipped his own arm up and brutally caught the Brit across the upper chest. The strike bowled the man over backward, nearly turning him for a flip. Blackwood crashed and tumbled backward, rolling back into the room, and Mick Priest followed him inside, slamming the door behind them.

"You...you can't...what're ya...do you know..." Blackwood gasped and wheezed.

"Get dressed or I'll drag you, in your underwear, down every flight of stairs between us and the others," Priest growled menacingly.

The Brit, flat on his back, let his head drop to the floor with a thunk.

The tatters of that first night on Shadow Mountain, stretched threadbare and their seams split, disintegrated into a new day. By the time I ushered a dressed and rueful Paul Blackwood into the Dining Hall, morning had touched down upon us with a returning heat. The fog and mist turned to vapors lifting from the grass and the trees. The mountain itself looked as if it were being seared under the brilliant light of the sun, the rising moisture like ghosts being driven from the land.

If only it were that easy, I thought.

The sky remained angry. Clouds gathered like an army amassing forces for war. Thunder rumbled instead of battle drums even as the sun found places to burn through on occasion.

Summer rage, someone was saying in the Hall.

If I never heard that local colloquialism again it would be too soon.

In any sense, it was not very long before nearly everyone had settled down again. Jenkins, an exception to the status quo, worked busily with the server, Helena Makai, to hand out food and whatnot.

The chef, alone in the Kitchen, stirred up our consumables with a passion and efficiency.

I glanced around the Dining Hall and took a head count. Johanna Crimson, close on the arm of Gibson, was the last person to join us. Ms. Makai seated them near James and Andreya West and put their plates down on the table.

It was settled. Grip Bridger was the only person absent, with the obvious exception of Kimber Mobley and Richard Porter. And I knew where they all were, even though we were destined to move Grip soon.

Sarah raked the Hall with hawk's eyes. I had noted her deft intellect and intuition when we first met, working in Wilmington's blood rains. She never ceased to impress me. I would not like to be an outlaw with an agent like Sarah Melindez-Priest chasing me. No sleep, still sharp.

Unlike Sarah, James Wyatt was exhibiting his lack of sleep with red eyes and a resentful countenance. He was alert and aware but he hardly looked it. The man reminded me of a bear prodded out of hibernation.

"Bon appetit," Jenkins said from the Kitchen door. "Ms. Makai and I will be in and out to check on you all."

"Good," Cassandra Clark said. "We'll send our praises to our chef through the two of you as we go."

Clark looked worn and haggard. She had spent the night wrestling the dead for answers with my wife. It had clearly taken a toll.

I stood up, saying, "We need to get down to business."

"You can eat as we go along," Sarah told them.

Anxiety stilled most guest and staff voices. It had done a number on their appetites, too. Most poked at their food with a fork, eating nothing.

Blackwood found his voice with, "Agent Priest, I wanna file a complaint on your husband."

No one commented, no one even muttered.

"Right now there are more important-" Sarah started.

"More important to you 'n' him, sure, but not to this bloke," Blackwood interrupted again.

"Hey, Slick, close your mouth. This is listen time, not talkie time," James Wyatt warned, the bear provoked.

Blackwood opened his mouth to jab back but Gibson cleared his throat, scouring the man with his blue eyes. B'Rone Matwahali cut his eyes that way, as well.

"Please," Sarah said, "let's focus. We have some horrible things to tell you. Then we have to make some command decisions."

"You should know," I said, "there are two guests dead."

That drew a sharp breath and whispered names from everyone.

What about us? several voices asked. *What's going to happen?*

A wave of uncertain mumbling and the first whimpers of crying washed around the room. I paused for a moment.

Blackwood ground his jaw intently. A woman had been killed just a little while after the two had spent private time together. The pale Brit turned a light shade of green beneath the sheen of sweat on his face. He covered his mouth with a hand as ice blue eyes stared blankly at the ceiling, his head tipped back. He seemed capable of vomiting. Was he putting on a show, quite the actor, after all?

Matwahali, not the sort to be spooked, shook it off.

"No one panic. You need to use jungle logic, here. Survival logic. Seems we have a hunter in our midst. A wolf. A leopard. That makes us a herd. We just have to adopt herd behavior. Hunters drop members of the herd that get separated from the band. Nobody let yourself be caught alone. Simple."

Disbelief and confusion reared their ugly heads. Both fed the commotion and the newly clamoring voices as they fought to be the loudest and, by proxy, be judged correct. The room ran thick with livid debate, fraught with an absence of information, much like political pundits in the throes of campaigns.

"Hey, loud people!" Tayla Barlowe shouted, her young voice breaking piercingly. "Shut it!"

Everyone fell silent, more from surprise than having been persuaded. Everyone except her own child, however, who began to cry in her arms.

Mumbling to herself, Barlowe got up and left the Dining Hall. She was pursued by Jenkins, at a wordless order from Cassandra Clark's eyes.

"This'll go faster if we could finish telling you what we know. Then you can ask whatever you like. Fair?" Sarah asked them.

The greater majority nodded along.

"Good. Mick will break it all down for you."

She shared a look with me and got up, headed for Gretchen Clayborne and led her out of the Dining Hall. The room heard her covering with some talk about the helicopter but I knew what she was doing. It would be far more in the vein of mercy to tell her about Bridger's murder one on one, not have her learn it with the crowd.

"This is unreal," Andreya West blurted out in the quiet of the pause.

"I understand," I told her. "But it's still as real as any of you. As real as I am. There's a killer on these grounds, make no mistake."

"What do we do? What's gonna happen?" Melkin demanded quietly.

"We look out for each other. Watch over each other," I told her. "And we arm ourselves with all the available information."

"You're gonna suggest bunkin' up again at bed time, too, ain't ya?" Melkin asked.

"Sounds like the smartest idea," Matwahali said with a shrug.

"Until you find out your chamber mate is the killer," Li huffed.

A lot of sharp looks cut across the room at her.

"Hey, I don't care. I ain't worried. Victor and I are in a room together and we came with each other. We know we're safe," she said.

"I would recommend, before grouping in pairs with a stranger, staying alone. That's just my thought," Director Clark said. "Agent Priest, earlier, suggested all of us stay in one large location so we-"

She was drowned in a noisy sea of opinions. One of the prevailing ideas was that staff security, Grip Bridger, should be tasked with watching over everyone, however they believed that to be possible.

There was no good time to announce his death. I chose to reveal it then, before going any further.

"There's more. You should also know-"

"Oh, more good news?" the relatively quiet Rembrandt Lyles interrupted me. "Do we get to vote who takes the chop next? Like that survival show, voting people outta the camp? But survival here means literal survival."

Sarcasm dripped from his Carolina accent like thick syrup, just not as sweet. Until then, I had not heard enough from him to know he had an accent. Or a dark sense of humor.

"Any intelligent questions before I go on?" I asked.

James Wyatt gave Lyles the finger drag across the throat gesture.

"Okay, here it is," I said flatly.

Then I dropped the low down in full, as for the where and who. Richard Porter. Kimber Mobley. I reminded them of our situation with the isolation and the bridge condition. All I knew of it, anyway.

Someone asked anew about the gunshots in the garden just as I was about to share it all. Down the hallway, out of sight, Gretchen Clayborne called out the young Grip's name in a baleful, desperate banshee's wail. It was a signal echoing through the resort right on time.

Before the room could rise up, I told them about Grip Bridger.

The shock of the macabre events left the room still and quiet. Even the staff, ones I expected to cry out, seemed unable. The revelation had knocked the wind from their lungs, stealing the words from their mouths. Only stricken faces and watering eyes responded...in utter silence.

An ominous, smothering silence.

B'Rone Matwahali eventually spoke first. Even so, he took a long time beforehand.

"And now?" is all he finally said.

"Somebody needs to go down to the bridge and check it out, now that it's light outside," Tye Richter said. "Normal protocol would mean Grip was going but..."

"He ain't up to it," Mark Gibson remarked dryly.

"The rest of us need to stay together and stay safe," Cassandra Clark said.

Her voice cracked under the weight of her emotion, prompting her to cover her mouth with one hand. Richter put an arm around her.

"Sarah and I are going to ask some questions," I said. "And we're going to get answers. Serious, helpful answers. If anyone has a problem with that, they'll have a much bigger problem than they realized, and we'll still get our answers. It's time to meet this thing head on."

"If you won't need me for that," James said, "I'm down for leading our expedition back to the bridge. If anyone feels like they might be some help..."

"I'm all over that," Matwahali said. "I've rappelled with the best."

James Wyatt locked eyes with me. I nodded.

"I don't suppose you brought any adventure gear," James muttered.

"You lot brought pistols, mate. It's what you do. Blackwood Bar-b-que probably squirreled away a spatula or two," Matwahali said. "Well, I carry survival gear everywhere. It's what I do."

"Fine. You're with me," James said.

He and Gibson shared a glance.

"Go to it, Ponytail," Gibson said. "We're good while you're gone."

"Please, before launching any major operations, eat your meals," Jenkins urged. He had just returned with Barlowe and her daughter. "Whatever waits in Nightshade Pass is not likely to go anywhere."

So we did, advice taken. Even Chef Avid Swartzovski joined us for the breakfast fare. Not everyone had an appetite, of course. After Sarah returned with Gretchen Clayborne, Jenkins joined the broken lady pilot in a far corner. He chose to be a comfort over eating his food.

It was odd the way the crowd ate in pure silence. If looks could kill it would have been a mass grave. The events had stolen what blind confidence they may have had. Distrust and suspicion marred every face, danced in every eye, made every accusation in utter, boneyard quiet.

After a time, one of her own staff missing from the table, Cassandra Clark addressed the room. With a tall glass of something stronger than juice, she made a toast.

"To Falgrip. May he be at peace. May justice be served."

Sniffling and a few whimpers played a background for the soft, mournful crying of Clayborne.

"I'd like to suggest that all of us stay together," Sarah said. "In one or maybe two groups, at the most. We need to take care of each other, watch over each other. Everyone watching everyone. Keeping in mind, it would allow all of us, the armed individuals trying to protect you, the ability to relieve each other for sleep here and there."

"Why would anyone need to go it alone, anyway?" Cassandra Clark asked with a sigh. "Sarah is right-"

"Then you stay with her, cooped up for easy chicken huntin', Clark," Kess Melkin growled. "But I didn't survive bein' hunted by the Wolf of Knox County for some paycheck killer to take me out in the Carolina mountains! The cops didn't save any of us back then and I ain't waitin' on 'em now, either! I take care of myself!"

"She has a point. I've survived far worse in guerrilla-overrun, wild terrain, all on my own," B'Rone Matwahali added.

"So, it's all about ourselves? No group concern?" Andreya West asked. "Even if some of us are independent and capable, what about the others? Maybe we should group up to help them if we don't need to do so to help ourselves."

Then, guest emotions high, the tension blew through their dams of self control and threatened to drown them. Everyone shouted to be heard at once as they accused and argued and denied. They each railed at the others, voices indignant, angry and enraged. Many were fueled by real fury. Many statements were spawned out of strangling fear.

We need the protection! I'm fine on my own! How many are armed?

Even more passionate were other outbursts, the ones about noises in the night.

I heard someone on the balcony! I know it was you! Were you outside my door last night? Someone tried my door handle!

I made a mental note of those.

"Shut up!" the young mother yelled suddenly. "Stupid!"

She shouted again at all of them as her baby cried.

"Her little girl was sleeping!" Andrea West yelled at the mob.

The chaotic rumble did not falter that time. The din growing louder, Barlowe snatched herself from her seat and stormed for the Kitchen, baby Emma in her arms.

Emma cried enthusiastically, quite the healthy lungs in full use. She was, after all, a very young child. The crowd in the Dining Hall did not have that excuse for their blaring, prattling rancor.

"Quiet, all of you!" I bellowed furiously.

My deep voice raked over the room with its grit and gravel. It echoed against the fine, polished woods in the room. If any missed the first roar, the reverberations brought the meaning back around. Big eyes and concerned faces looked all around until they found me, the source.

"People," I started again, my voice still low and rumbling, "I suggest you finish your food...quietly. A lot is going on. We're still cut off from the rest of the world, we still have dead, we still have a killer on this mountain."

First, no one said anything, instead looking around at each other with gaping mouths. Then they all tried to speak at once, yapping over each other, growing irritated, and a few shouts broke out again.

Johanna Crimson said something into Gibson's ear.

Andreya West left the table for the Kitchen.

"It's like the first grade with you people!" I railed loudly. "Show each other some respect! There's a killer among us! Think about it! The person you mouth off to might be a maniac! They might come back around and get you in your sleep!"

"Mick!" Sarah said through clenched teeth.

James cackled.

A hush fell on the room like a blanket but Director Clark spoke through it, brow furrowed, lips quivering.

"Mr. Priest! That kind of speech is not only unkind and frightening, it is reckless and-"

"We got way bigger problems than words, Director!" I yelled. "Sticks and stones can break your bones but the Ghost Revolver might kill you!"

"Mr. Priest, I must say-" Jenkins tried.

"Yo, listen up," James Wyatt barked, eyeballing Jenkins. "Everybody, use your mouths to finish your food, not *say* stuff."

"When you're done, we're gonna break into groups," Sarah declared. "We're gonna stay in groups for the time being, at least. James Wyatt is opting to go down to the bridge. Mr. Matwahali has chosen to go with him. I would like to send a person on the staff...Mr. Richter? Would you go along?"

Tye Richter nodded.

"Good. The rest of the men can group with my husband, Mick, and you ladies can meet with me."

"With the exception of me 'n' Johanna," Gibson said. "I'd rather she didn't leave my sight."

Sarah directly cast an unapologetic gaze onto Gibson.

James and I eyeballed him, too.

"Your rathers will have to take a back seat this time, Gibson," Sarah said. "Mick and I are going to compile notes and a timeline; it'll be best for everyone to be on their own, answering for themselves. There will be far too many of us in each group to be in danger."

"Not everybody wants to-"

"It ain't a suggestion, Kentucky," James snapped on Melkin.

For once, she fell silent. Everyone else followed her example. James and Gibson passed a look back and forth and James shrugged.

"Well, it ain't."

I waited, watching faces and body language, giving everyone time to process things. Tayla Barlowe then returned to the table, Andreya West with her. West carried little Emma.

"She's sleepin' again. Can ya'll hold it down this time?" Tayla asked.

I huffed to myself. One could only hope.

The Head Server, Helena Makai, got up and began clearing place settings. More food remained than had actually been eaten. Jenkins, seeing that no one was still feeding, gestured at the chef to help Makai. Then he pulled his formal jacket back into place, adjusting his cuffs and pretending the heat was not an issue.

"Jenkins, forget the jacket," Cassandra Clark suggested.

"Indeed," he said. "I think not."

James Wyatt stood and pointed at B'Rone Matwahali.

"Ready, big man?"

The other man nodded, rose, and Richter stood in response, too.

"Let's *all* go outside," Director Clark said. "At least we can feel the wind out there. We can see the gentlemen off that way, too."

Jenkins bowed slightly, saying, "I will stay to help clean up but we will not take long. I wish all of you a safe day."

James and I brought up the rear of the caravan, stopping to look back at the remaining staff members. James winked at Jenkins.

"C'mon. You can say it."

"I'm sorry, what is it I can say?" Jenkins asked him.

"C'mon. *All of you*, really? You can cut loose. Just say it, Jenkins."

"I'm sorry, Mr. Wyatt, I don't understand."

"Really? C'mon. Ya'll. Not *all of you*, it's you all. Ya'll," James coached with a sly grin.

Jenkins looked as though he had swallowed something bitter.

"I think not."

James chuckled and raised a fist to the man.

"Okay, Jenkins, it's all good," he said amiably, regarding his own fist with a quick nod. "C'mon, pound it, man."

"Again...no."

Jenkins raised an eyebrow in disdain and dropped back from us. He joined Helena Makai and Avid Swartzovski in the Kitchen.

Then James and I made one last detour once we were alone. With heavy hearts and gentle respect, we moved Falgrip Bridger's body.

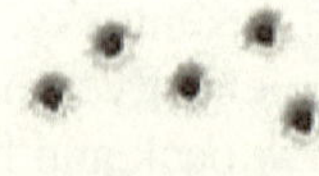

To the southeast of the main building, at least an acre away, a stone outcropping reached upward from the greens of the area. Designers included the stone formation in construction rather than attempting to flatten the area when they razed much of the surroundings. White and sandy colored rock protruded from the ground in large and small shapes, allowing much of the definition and identification up to the imaginations of the observer. However, several things had been decided by the builders.

Cut into the rock here and there were flat planes for lying down in the sun. Other sitting style, man-made shaping had been achieved, turning spots into bench appearances and individual seats. The crowning outlay was a pond, carved into the very stone of the outcropping. Water from the pumps came up to keep it full, with level switches to turn them on when needed. The carved stone had also been sealed, to prevent losing the water, and circulation pumps kept it fresh. The water was crystal clear and showcased the stone beautifully.

"Anyone for skinny dipping?" Kess Melkin asked with a lewd grin, unable to restrain her more primal tendencies. "That should change the boys' minds and bring 'em up to join us."

None of the other women switched gears as fast as Melkin. They still bore the haunted look of the hunted...and the mournful.

"Everyone, get comfortable," Cassandra Clark instructed, "just not *that* comfortable. Let's do our best to help Agent Priest."

Sarah Melindez-Priest, special agent with the North Carolina State Bureau of Investigation, stood atop the apex of the formation. On the wide, flattened spot, a tall flag pole reached for the clouds and hefted the American, North Carolina and resort logo flags high above the sitting spaces. Priest leaned against one side of the pole.

She watched the group of men walk Richter, Matwahali and her husband's long time friend, James Wyatt, down to the generator building to see them off before she turned to the women and spoke.

"Ladies," she addressed, "we need to establish timelines-"

"You want alibis. Where we were. When. With who," Melkin interrupted.

"With whom," Andreya West said.

Melkin rolled her eyes.

Priest, to her credit, did not flinch.

"Exactly," she said.

The ladies looked around at each other, some surprised, some irritated, all suspicious.

"You brought us up to a movie set for the Flintstones to ask questions?" Johanna Crimson quipped suddenly, chirping with laughter.

"Why not start with the on-scene actress?" Tayla asked.

"I have nothing to hide, Agent Priest," Johanna Crimson challenged.

Priest met her eyes and nodded.

"Okay. We start with you."

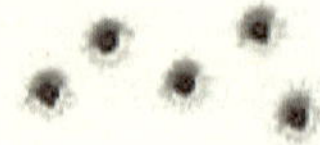

"So, all you did was rough Blackwood up," James said to Mick.

Priest squinted in the daylight as they walked toward the horizon.

"So far."

"You think it's him? Really?" James asked.

"I think he was one of the last present with two people who are now dead. I think he was out wandering alone when Grip was killed."

"Coincidence?"

"I don't believe in coincidence," Priest said.

"That's what Gibson says, all the time," James said. "Thing is, coincidence does occur, Mick."

"A lot less often than intent" Mick said, "especially in murder."

The band reached the area with the SUV and Richter shook the keys in his hand.

"Mr. Matwahali, Mr. Wyatt, would either of you like to drive?"

"Nah, Tye," James Wyatt said. "You're staff. You got the keys." Then, to Matwahali, "It seems you're ready."

The big man wore his gear and his climbing lines over one shoulder.

"I, for one, like to think I'm always ready for anything. I feel good about today. We aren't exactly on the endangered species list, yet."

Richter got in and started the vehicle. Matwahali took the passenger seat and James, after shaking Mick's hand, got into the back.

"Be careful," Priest reminded them.

"My middle name," James Wyatt said.

Then the SUV pulled away. The remaining men began a stroll to their destination, a placement of black iron tables and seats half way between that building and the helicopter hangar. From where they were, they could see the arrangement quite clearly. It rose up atop stark white stepping stones that mapped out the shape of a horse's head and mane.

There was mumbling on their way but Priest ignored it. He was still trying to process what James had told him about Gibson and Crimson, in exchange for the 'skinny' on Blackwood, as his friend had posed it. James had relished the idea of the somewhat arrogant Blackwood on his back.

As for his part, James had rousted his two from the room when they had not come downstairs. Gibson, considering it was James, had opened the door quickly and easily enough. After that, unfortunately, James had felt stonewalled. The answer to why they had not been curious about the gunshots, why they had not come downstairs and why Gibson still did not want them to venture out of the room were all the same answer.

"I can protect her better from the room. Make 'im come to me," the champion had hailed. He had offered no compromise.

"Other people are dyin' outside the room, Gibson. I know that ain't a reason to wanna come out, but there's more to it than all that. Don't you think there might be safety in numbers? That being said, don't you think you might be able to help other people, too, while you help Johanna?"

"Are any of them my personal responsibility?" Gibson had asked.

His cool blue eyes were colder than usual, James told Priest later.

Gibson had added that Johanna Crimson was targeted specifically, he believed, and any others had been distractions or casualties of some convenience; knowing too much, seeing too much, hearing too much. As far as he was concerned, Crimson was the real target and she was the one they should concentrate on defending.

James had ended the confrontation with a warning about Sarah Priest, her badge and her direct order to come downstairs.

"Andreya," James had shared, "was infinitely more cooperative. Even though I interrupted her shower."

Soon enough, Mick Priest was certain he and Gibson would likely clash. On the white stones of the Horse's Mantle, as the resort called the sitting area, Gibson was certain to be resentful of interference. It did not matter. It was time he learned that there were more lives at stake than Johanna Crimson's. Mick would be happy to show him the bodies to prove it.

The summer heat tired of restraint and ramped up considerably. The air was post-rain steamy, muggy. A majority of those present at H and H Resort congregated outside in it, talking and tossing ideas back and forth. The congregation, split into two, found the perfect auditorium seating in their halls of nature. The men met in iron and the women in stone. With the air conditioning down at the locale, outside was still more amenable than inside, despite the rising sun.

It was hot in the vehicle traveling the roadway, too.

"Great time for the AC to drop," James Wyatt noted.

Tye Richter pounded the dash and shook his head.

"Tell me about it."

"Windows it is," Richter decided.

"You two," Matwahali said and laughed heartily. "You think a North Carolina mountain is hot! Try the terrain I've survived, carrying packs as big as one of you on my back!"

"No, thanks," James said.

Windows down, the trio continued for the pass. They arrived in short order, unceremoniously greeted by destruction.

Mangled wreckage smoldered at the bottom of Nightshade Pass. Not much could be said for the remnants. Twisted steel and shattered glass littered the rocky landing of Shadow Walker Bridge, too. The original, nearby structure was unrecognizable, the rubble left behind hardly any bigger than a handful of shrapnel in any given spot.

At least the fire had starved and died since Priest's visit.

The little building that had served as a security checkpoint at the foot of Shadow Walker Bridge had utterly exploded. As the base foundation for the power and communications tower, it had erupted into shards and scrap and dropped the tower down across the bridge. Its cataclysmic end brought a stark ending to the reliability of the bridge, as well, not an accidental event but a calculated one. The foundations housing power, communications and the cellular booster tower were soundly destroyed.

They had, in fact, been the true targets of the fury executed upon the little checkpoint building. It was clear to anyone with tactical thinking.

Down in Nightshade Pass, the aftermath of ruthless destruction sent up a cry for help in the form of rising smoke. The lifeline to the outside world had been shattered. Shadow Mountain, despite the resort residing upon it, once again stood dark and alone.

"I can see a vehicle frame down there," James told them.

"The other SUV," Richter said. "Like we figured."

B'Rone Matwahali, silent giant, led the jump. He and Richter made short work of it. James Wyatt stayed up on the landing, covering them and watching over the drop lines. Matwahali was a master on the ropes and Richter was a quick study.

The pillar foundations of the bridge had been damaged in the explosion and the collapse. Fissures and splits many would have missed never fooled Matwahali. He pointed them out easily and confidently. It was just as they had feared.

The bridge was unreliable in the very least.

It was more likely a death trap if used.

On a torn bumper, not far from the skeletal husk of the resort vehicle, a blackened, company plate displayed the burned remnants of a number. It had HH and M in its makeup with random numbers.

"Horse and Heraldry, a Maintenance designation," Richter said.

Matwahali nodded with, "No doubt, now."

"Was there ever?" Richter said.

Matwahali bent down to the grass.

Glittering in the sun, like stars having fallen to the earth aflame, bent and battered, perfect little circles littered the grass of the valley. Among the mess of shrapnel and auto parts, he picked out a few.

"Coins?" Richter asked.

Matwahali shook his head. He fished about in the scrub, gathering small pieces of dense looking plastics and wires.

"Not coins," he corrected Richter, showing him what he had gathered. He wiped a hand across his brow, pushing the sweat back. "Mr. Richter, after a blast like this, for us to put hands to this much intact triggering and penetration debris, I can only come to one conclusion. There was a lot of plastique discharged here. A lot, Mr. Richter."

"Plastique?" the young man asked.

"Oh, yeah," he said. "Plastic explosives. All this bit? These are the ruined pieces of high grade, military blasting triggers. I've seen enough in my day to know. This was professional. Professional and hooked up."

"Why? Why this much firepower to target some writers? A movie star? Television stars? It doesn't add up."

B'Rone Matwahali held out the bent, scorched, thin metal circles.

"Wait 'til I tell ya what this lot is," he said.

"Yeah? Let it wait. I have a feeling we've done all we can from here. Let's head back up and you can tell me and Mr. Wyatt."

James Wyatt waited on the upper ridge of the pass and watched from there. Had James Wyatt been the killer they would have been prime targets, climbing back up from the pass on vulnerable time. On the contrary, however, James helped them by watching over, clearing and maintaining their lines.

When they were all atop the ridge, James nodded at Matwahali.

"What've you got?"

"Bad news," the big man started.

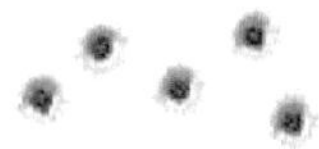

Helena Makai said something softly in her native Romani.

"We only want to kill the ones we love," she repeated in English.

Chef Swartzovski said, "Then I have had *so* many women love me."

Makai giggled at the scarecrow of a chef.

Jenkins carried another candelabra to the table and refreshed the candles. He tugged at his clingy clothing, wet with perspiration.

Jenkins said, "Good job, Mr. Swartzovski, Ms. Makai."

"I'm afraid," Makai admitted. "A real killer is here. It is a reality."

Swartzovski regarded them both with large, baggy eyes.

"But who is this killer?" the chef asked. "Not one of us, to be obvious. We're here all the time. So, which of them is it?"

"I don't think-" Jenkins began.

"It has to be a woman," Swartzovski declared.

"Oh?" Makai replied, eyes wide and eyebrows arched. "Why?"

"Please," Jenkins moaned, rolling his eyes. "I don't think it is good practice to speculate. It can only lead to confusion and resentful-"

"I think it is a man," Makai said.

"And what man?" Swartzovski demanded of the dark eyed woman.

"I believe it is the small man, skinny man," she said.

"Ha! The artist! Drawing his monsters and men and then killing people?" Avid Swartzovski guffawed.

"Who then?" Makai shouted. "If not him, who?"

"Please," Jenkins calmed.

"It is plain to see! The publishing woman, Li! She brought everyone here and now they die one by one! Who else would have a reason to kill more than one person here this weekend?"

"Stop it, now!" Jenkins bellowed suddenly.

The other two jumped nearly out of their skins, voices gone.

Jenkins took a deep breath, straightened his jacket and sighed.

"We simply cannot engage in this kind of reckless thinking. You will have each other afraid of particular guests with no real reason. Please."

A long silence ensued.

Then Makai said, "You didn't see the picture the man was sketching at the dining table."

Swartzovski lifted his hands and let them fall.

Jenkins rolled his eyes, yet again. Something, however, gnawed at him. Something Avid Swartzovski had said. It had been Ms. Maureen Li who brought everyone to the resort for the weekend...was there more to it than anyone realized?

CHAPTER NINE

Sarah Priest lifted her hand to shade her eyes even though she already wore sunglasses. She fanned her face with her other hand then lifted her ponytail from her neck. Sweat trickled down her back, tickling her spine.

Most of the time, modern amenities and technology allowed background work to be done remotely. The internet, social media, digital records and information databases made a lot of old fashioned, investigative leg work nothing more than a little typing. Sarah pondered the irony of the mountain situation. Every amenity had been built into the rustic palace but it had just as simply been stolen from them. Cut off from the world the way they were, the need to fall back to old school methods stood out as singularly clear.

Remember me? the old methods asked. *Return to the basics.*

"Agent Priest?" Tayla Barlowe said after a time.

"Sorry. What was I saying?"

"All I heard so far was blah, blah, blah," Kess Melkin muttered.

The closest person to her was Andreya West and the scholar gave her a sour look, to which Melkin returned a sarcastic smile and wink.

"You were telling us about the way information will help keep us all safer," Tayla said. "And you had said we should share anything that might be important, about ourselves or others...and you had agreed Ms. Crimson could start."

Pulling up a handful of water from the stone pool, the young mother let it run down over her little one's hair and head. The child sat happily splashing in the water where her mother had placed her, close to the edge.

"The photographer with the photographic memory," Maureen Li quipped to the nearby actress, Johanna Crimson.

Sarah pulled a stretchy cord from a pocket. Quick, deft practice guided her hands as she whipped her caramel mane up into a bun. All loose strands gone from her face and neck, she wiped the sweat from her skin where the hair had been, even running her hand down over her chest and wiping the moisture from the opening of her low cut shirt, too. The pond was looking like a great idea.

Game face engaged, she spoke again.

"Thank you, Tayla. Obviously, no one wants to die on this mountain," she said. "I think you'll each be able to agree that the more we all know, the less secrets there are. And, the less secrets there are, the less ways there are to conceal the identity of our killer."

"Well, she ain't wrong," Gretchen Clayborne said.

Director Clark gave her pilot a warning look that spoke volumes.

Pay attention and participate but keep the sarcasm at a minimum.

"I can start by saying that I'm not this Ghost Revolver," Crimson said almost jovially. "As it has been rumored that the Revolver has accepted a contract put out for my death, it should be clear I would not bring all of you up here and kill some of you to cover a plan to kill myself. Besides, if I did kill myself, how would I collect the contract fee? It hardly seems worth it on my end."

She swirled her bare feet in the stone pool, on the opposite side from the Barlowes. Her nonchalance garnered her a few stares. She continued, undaunted, unabashed.

"Second, I can promise you that Mark Gibson is not the Ghost Revolver. I have known him most of my life. And he never leaves my side! He couldn't kill anyone without my knowledge."

Several whispers and remarks came under the breath of speakers.

Sarah Priest called them down and asked for courtesy.

"When I shower, if the ladies' room has windows, he requests that I leave the door ajar so he can hear if anyone crashes through to get to me," Crimson said. "If it has no windows, he has me shut and lock the door and puts his chair's back against the door, and waits for me to finish. The man has been more than family to me and is never more than one closed door away. Then, for the obvious, if he wanted to kill me, he wouldn't have to come up here with me to do it."

"But it would make a nice cover," Melkin said.

Crimson turned an emerald earring in her right ear.

"Brilliant," she mewled. "You've broken the case."

"Do you have anything else to add? Things you've seen? Noticed? Heard? Any suspicions?" Priest asked.

"I'm not the suspicious type. I pay Gibson to be suspicious enough for both of us."

Several of the women laughed softly.

"Okay. Where were you when-"

"Agent Priest, when Kimber Mobley was killed, I was with Gibson. He was with me. The same applies to Richard Porter. And, unfortunately for the young protector, the same applies to Mr. Bridger. And we didn't come down for the gunfire because Gibson frowns on me running out to investigate shootings. It's his job to keep me clear of them."

"How well did you know Mobley? Porter?"

Crimson rolled her eyes with, "I hate speaking ill of the dead but you're pushing me into a corner."

"Force yourself," Li said snidely.

The actress pulled a handful of water up and poured it down her shapely legs.

"I didn't know anyone here well and definitely no one any better than I knew Kimber Mobley." She wiped over her brow and touched an earring again, attesting, "Mobley and I have been around each other at galas, premiers, parties and stuff like that. But I don't...didn't...*know* her. I knew of her reputation as a hedonistic pleasure seeker and a gold digger but she was nothing but professional around me. I don't know what more to add."

She smoothed her hand down her legs.

"What about any more guests?" Priest pursued.

"I may have crossed paths with the television twins, Blackwood and Matwahali, in studios and whatnot. I seem to remember them in that respect but I can't be sure. I meet a lot of people, famous and otherwise."

"Richard Porter?" Sarah asked again.

Crimson met her eyes.

"He was a mean, fat little man with no talent and no class."

"Ouch," Andreya West said. "What did you really think of him?"

"I didn't think of him, at all. He was assigned to do an interview with me for a motorcycle rag about the stunt riding in the first *Velvet Edge* movie. I love motorcycles and I did my own riding and my own stunts. He refused to believe me and I walked out of the interview five minutes into it. The mongrel 'journalist' still published his 'interview' with the magazine by writing up three pages of a conversation that never happened. In this article, he also implied that I flirted with him."

"Would've been motive enough for me," Kess Melkin remarked. "Guy was totally creepy. I wouldn't hang with that guy for cash money."

"I sued him and he was released from his contract, the magazine printed a retraction and an apology and my motorcycle skills became famous. I would've had no reason to kill him. I haven't given him a second thought in years."

"I appreciate your candor," Priest said. "How about Rembrandt Lyles? Your face said a lot more than any words could about him."

Johanna Crimson took the sucker punch on the chin, no time to deflect it, no time to roll with it. It gave her pause and a case of stuttering.

"W-what? Who? Oh, the artist," she floundered. "When was this?"

"You know, in the garden, on our arrival tour."

The thespian waved about royally and snorted.

"I can only think I was unimpressed having a comic book doodler here with literary intentions. I've never met the man."

"Doodler?" Tayla Barlowe commented. "His graphic art is top notch. He can do with pencils and charcoal what I can only do with a camera."

"Well, there you are," Crimson said with a laugh. "See how little I know of him? You should ask Tayla if you have questions about him."

Agent Priest smiled knowingly.

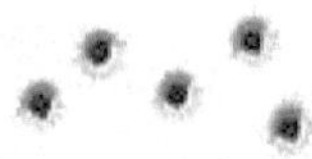

At that time, in the men's camp, Mick Priest and Mark Gibson were sparring verbally, as well.

"I still don't buy the use of splittin' us all up," Gibson said. Again.

"We know, mate, you've said it enough. But here we are. Answer the bloke's questions and let's get done."

"Maybe I don't blindly follow anybody who tells me to," Gibson snapped at Blackwood. "Maybe I like to-"

"Hear the sound of your own voice?" Remy Lyles interrupted.

"You think so, chicken scratch?" Gibson barked.

"Hey!" Mick Priest yelled. "Drop it. We're already separated, we're already working this investigation this way. Be a help, not a hindrance."

"You're Ms. Crimson's protector, right?" Victor Jackson asked.

Gibson and everyone else turned to face him where they sat.

"Of course. That's what I been sayin' to everybody."

"Okay, but I don't get is why she's content with the question and answer time as it is, if she's the one who needs protection, and you're the one who seems scared to be on your own."

"Exactly," Paul Blackwood chimed. "Cooperate, already."

"Oh, just play the game. Fine. Until I get tired of it. Then you can look for me to set the rules," Gibson warned.

"Why don't you just answer the questions?" Priest asked.

"What? Which question was it you-"

"Do you have any personal suspicions? How well did you know the victims and how well do you know the rest of the guest list?" Priest asked again. "Have you noticed anything suspicious here?"

"I know of and about the entire guest list this weekend, as well as all the staff, full time and temporary hires," Gibson said. "I told ya, I'm the best at what I do. I know everything there is to know before I let Johanna Crimson set foot in a situation. I got contacts and resources-"

"Here we go, again," Remy Lyles groaned. *"The best there is, was or ever will be at what I do..."*

"You know what-" Gibson started with clenched teeth.

"Enough!" Priest reminded. "Mr. Lyles has a point, Gibson. You've told us your credentials several times and you still haven't told us anything useful."

"Useful," Gibson said lowly. "Okay. Let's start with the vics. 'Ricochet' Porter was a bloated, smelly, washed up racer with one foot already in the grave and more enemies than friends!"

Others tried to call him down for his slander but he got louder.

"It's a fact! The man burned every bridge he ever crossed in racing. Sponsors, teammates, track handlers, you name it. He only got a line on writing about it, instead, when his health sidelined his career. Diabetes, high blood pressure, rheumatoid arthritis, liver cirrhosis and congestive heart failure had him limpin' on borrowed time! Didn't straighten him up, though. Porter started doin' the same ol' thing with other writers, contacts, magazines and whatnot, too, dirty dealing with everybody. It's just who he was."

"I take it you and Ms. Crimson had negative dealings with him."

"What? Not really, Priest. I try to steer her clear of that type. We had one issue with him but the court cleared all that up just fine."

"What was that about?" Priest asked.

"Old news," Gibson said. "Man lied about some things in an article. It's done; the lawsuit saw to that. It ain't like we killed 'im for it. That was years ago."

"Slander, libel, copyright lawyers. Crimson's got some of the best."

Remy Lyles locked his sleepy, brown eyes with Gibson's blue fury.

Priest was about to comment when Gibson continued.

"The Australian supermodel, Mobley. Woman was a-"

"Careful, old man," Paul Blackwood stalled.

Mick Priest found himself surprised. Either Blackwood was a consummate actor in his own right or he genuinely did not want Kimber Mobley disparaged. The baker's bright blue eyes twitched with emotion.

"Mind your business," Gibson warned. "The woman was a total professional every time me 'n' Johanna ever crossed her path. She wasn't drunk or high at events when just about everyone else was. Now, we never had much interaction with her, other than business, and she had a reputation as a real wild one. But we never saw that side of her."

"Good," Lyles commented. "At least, your legal team didn't sue her for anything."

"There's some bad blood, some history there," Victor said.

"Do you two know each other?" Priest asked. "I noticed a moment ago that Mr. Lyles has heard your humble speeches before. About your talents and your professed credentials."

"He ain't worth knowin'!" Gibson yelled.

"Oh, who is, compared to Queen Crimson?" Lyles prodded.

"That's it-" Gibson started, coming to his feet.

"Hold it!" Priest shouted.

"Or what?" Gibson yelled back, his hand on the pommel of his gun.

Priest looked down at the table at which he sat then looked back up at Gibson pointedly. Gibson glanced at the table level, following Priest's eyeline. Mick Priest held both of his 10mm Colts in his lap, just below the ironwork table.

"Take your hand off that heater, Gibson," he growled. "And sit back down. Please."

Gibson ground his teeth for a moment, immobile. He drew a long breath, angled his head to one side and raised his eyebrows. Suddenly, he dropped his hands to his sides and sat back down with a raspy laugh.

"Since you said 'please'..."

Paul Blackwood blew a long held breath out in a silent whistle.

Gotta be crazy, pokin' Priest like that, he mused.

And he knew. Personally.

"So, we talked about Porter and Mobley," Priest said. "We were moving onto any other guests. How about you tell us about Mr. Lyles?"

"I thought you wanted to know about things I'd seen and heard. Things that caused me suspicion. I couldn't be suspicious of good ol' Remy Lyles *doing* anything. He's never *done* anything to speak of in his whole life."

"That's rich, coming from you," Rembrandt Lyles barked quickly.

Priest was about to dig deeper when Gibson veered off topic.

"Mobley and Porter were pretty tight, right?" Gibson said offhandedly. "That Kentucky writer, Kess Melkin, seemed to take to both of 'em pretty good. I saw 'em all cozy up a couple times. Seemed a little odd. Melkin and Mobley started their little doin's with the Brits, Matwahali and Blackwood, at the same time, too. "

"What's suspicious in that?" Blackwood asked. "Men and women fancying each other?"

"Just the quick connection between Melkin and Mobley, that's all. One of 'em is dead; we gotta ask questions. Fact is, you got pretty tight with Mobley pretty quick, too."

Blackwood jumped to his feet, shouting wildly.

Mick Priest put one of the Colts on his table without a word.

Paul Blackwood heard the clack of gunmetal on the iron table and calmed down immediately. He sat back down but kept eyeing Gibson.

"What's between you and Gibson, Mr. Lyles?" Priest asked. "Or is it between you and Ms. Crimson?"

"Two different issues, I'm afraid. One with each of them," he said.

"Wouldn't have been if you hadn't been all stalkerish about it."

The man huffed at Gibson and waved the topic away.

"Same old story," he grumbled. "Same old Marcus Gibson."

"Why not tell me the story?" Priest asked.

His tone suggested it was not a request.

"The kid made a stupid gamble with business," Gibson said, suddenly interested in sharing. "When he lost, he kept followin' us around to signin' locations, film locations, you name it, tryin' to stir bad publicity and bad news. I had to explain to him just how that was going to grind worse for him than Johanna and he tried to sue me and her for assault and who knows what else. Her lawyers handed him a good whoopin' and sent him on his way, no free ride over the business deal, no free ride over the false assault charge, have a nice day. That simple."

The men expected an outburst decrying it all. Instead, Lyles was quiet and calm, his eyes fixed on Priest. He wiped over his slightly gaunt face with one hand, rubbing his scruff.

"Mr. Lyles?" Priest said.

"I created the character *Velvet Edge*," the thin man said.

"No, you drew it, you didn't create it!" Gibson shouted.

"Gibson, you had your say," Priest warned.

"Well, he just drew it, Priest! For a writer he knew!"

"I did draw her, that much is true. I was the first artist to ever pencil what *Velvet* would look like. I brought her to life on the page for the world to see-"

"Mr. Lyles, I write. I understand the artistic expression. Let's not wax on too much, though. Tell me about the conflict, your issue with Ms. Crimson and Mr. Gibson, not your artistic vision."

"Okay," he told Priest. "I drew her for the first time, gave her form and design. Identity. What I first-"

"Spit it out," Gibson said. "You and your deadbeat cousin, Greg Rhyme, were poppin' out indy comics from the basement of your aunt's print business. To call it small time would be a compliment!"

"A lotta great mags started that way!" Lyles shouted back. "We were getting a following, too, thanks to social media and-"

Gibson looked right at Priest and cut off the man's tales again.

"They got a lucky break when a rep for Regal Crown Comics picked up a character they were doin'. Bought the title and the character outright. Cousin Rhyme had the copyright control since the digital media was bein' hosted on auntie's computers, the print was bein' done in auntie's workspace and Rhyme was the duo's mouthpiece. Since there was no formal copyright up to that point, sellin' was fair game."

"I've never contested the sale or the copyrights! I got my fair share of things and I've never debated that!"

"On the title and the title character," Gibson said. "Where you lost your mind was on *Velvet Edge*! She was a background character you two ran for three issues in a dead end story line! Your partner gave verbal ownership of that character, too, in a casual meeting with RC Comics! The character was never meant for more than background!"

"So, you say! So, my old partner said! But my heart says otherwise! She was the only character he ever let me set up visually and envision the backstory! She was my creation! He had no right to sell her to RC Comics-"

"Oh, good grief," Gibson complained, rolling his eyes.

"-and RC Comics had no right to change her story and the essence of who she was-"

"You see this?" Gibson asked the men.

"-and they had no right to sell her to the movie studios to be stripped bare and treated like a sexpot-"

"Whoa, mate, calm down!" Blackwood ordered.

"-and kept away from me-"

"Mr. Lyles!" Priest shouted.

All of them paused, silence falling again.

"It's like when Archbishop was crippled," Lyles muttered lowly, wiping a tear from his eye.

"What?" Paul Blackwood asked.

"A famous, bigtime RC Comics character they wrote into a wheelchair," Gibson said.

"They wronged him! They wronged the fans!" Lyles shouted.

"Take it easy, Mr. Lyles," Victor Jackson said, eyes concerned. "You're putting fan back in fanatic."

"Puttin' the loon into lunatic," Blackwood said.

"In the end, he couldn't get any of the pie once 'his' character hit it big," Gibson said flatly. "The man started harassing Johanna, as if she had anything to do with it. Things went bad for him from there."

"She has executive production control!" Lyles barked. "I didn't want money! I just wanted to be involved, creatively! To have anything to do with *Velvet's* world would have been enough! I created the character!"

There was a wild abandon in the little man's eyes. A fever gripped him, a passion that had long given way to obsession. His lip twitched as his face teetered between sadness and anger...and perhaps a touch of madness. Artistic madness, at the least.

"Mr. Lyles," Priest started lowly, "just how angry with Ms. Crimson has all of this made you? How much responsibility do you really feel she holds over this character's acquisition?"

The man bit at his lower lip and wiped the running sweat from his face again. He shook off the grip of his intense focus, forcing a chuckle and a smile. He shook a finger at Gibson.

"Well played, Gibson," he said. "Just like at court. Drawing out my creative passions so all the stiffs would think I was nuts."

Victor Jackson tapped his temple with a forefinger, eyebrows arched.

Lyles missed the motion, too distracted with chuckling and shaking his own finger at the aging bodyguard.

"Lyles would have to have enough ambition to get outta his momma's basement to be a famous assassin, Priest," Gibson said, surprising everybody with the defense.

Lyles cursed at him, causing Priest to call him down, again. Everyone ignored the man, anyway. Gibson just continued in a much louder voice.

"The Ghost Revolver is supposed to be world wide! An avenger, taking payment for hits but only on the guilty! Those who've escaped the law, somehow! Does this kid look like a mighty vigilante to you?"

"Life's funny that way," Priest muttered.

"What way?" Lyles asked, suddenly more curious than anything.

"Things are rarely just what they look like."

"Looks like we got more party members coming," Victor Jackson said, pointing across the property.

From the main house, Jenkins and Swartzovski strolled in the grass. Driving straight for them in the SUV were Matwahali, Richter and James Wyatt.

"The gang's all here," Gibson said.

"This is to die for," the Head Server, Helena Makai, said.

Her raven black hair pulled up in a bun, she rubbed over bare, tanned shoulders, cooling them with the water from the pool.

"I sure hope not," Johanna Crimson muttered. "This is quaint and everything but I've never been in a pool worth dying for."

Makai grimaced at her own choice of phrases.

"True," she said meekly.

She had taken off parts of her server's uniform, the jacket and apron, and wore just the black skirt and white, off-the-shoulder shirt. From the time she had reached the stone pond, she had seated herself at its edge and inserted her feet and legs.

Jenkins and the chef had escorted her, of course, so she would not be alone, then they had taken their leave, heading for the Horse's Mantle and the men waiting there.

"She may be the latest to arrive but I'm still next," Maureen Li said flatly. "And I only knew the writers here and their personal guests by reputation. I didn't have a relationship with any of them. Some of them I had barely heard of. I'm not a killer and all I wanna do is get off this mountain alive. Can you imagine the shame? A seventh generation, Chinese descendant of a world famous martial arts clan master, not to mention a publishing executive with three degrees, getting murdered on a hillbilly mountain in a redneck state? I gotta get outta here."

"That's it? That's all that's struck you about this whole thing?" Gretchen Clayborne asked. "And what was all that on the helicopter ride in to the resort? If you didn't know all these writers, what was all that about 'handpicking greatness' yourself?"

"Sales and marketing," Li spat immediately. "Schmoozing, pitching. Business. Plain and simple."

"You're the publishing contact who arranged all this-" Clark started.

"You sound like Vic," Maureen Li said with a boisterous laugh. "He swears I put it all together, too, but most of the name suggestions were sent to me in my inboxes, with contact information and recommended offers. All the info about this place and the recommended times, the whole enchilada. I figured it was just another preset arranged by our higher ups so I launched it. I get a lot of my arrangements that way. I just sign off on them and put them in motion. I mean, I knew Ms. Crimson, Mr. Blackwood and Mr. Matwahali but I didn't know the rest of them from any of the staff. I didn't even know Ms. Crimson was planning to write a book. No offense to any of you; just business."

"None taken," Crimson said with a shrug. "I really hadn't told anyone about...my intention..."

Her look became one of a haunted reflection.

"Seems that presses us to ask, how were you asked here, then?"

The women looked around at each other as Agent Priest's words faded in the hot summer breeze.

"Maybe we should all ask that of ourselves," Andreya West said.

"We might just find we won't like the answers," Melkin said.

"I won't lie. I didn't like her answers. I'm very uncomfortable with it all," Victor Jackson told the men.

"So, let me get this straight," Paul Blackwood gruffed. "You're the accountant assigned to Li's operations in Gridlock Publishing. Li is one of their top headhunters, a...what did you call her?"

"An acquisitions agent and editor."

"Yeah, that's it, mate. She sets up these little soirees to woo and lure talent and you try to keep her on budget, within contract limitations."

"Exactly."

"And you tried to get her to go over the figures and she balked?"

"Yes. She told me that the plans and propositions and the talent list came down to her from higher up, via *Workforce*, an email, instant messaging and business database source we use. I told her it didn't make sense. The information and figures relayed to me all match but they cite Maureen as the originator of the documentation. Maureen insists she did *not* organize or devise any of it but it was sent to her in form. That's her reasoning for not feeling the need to justify any of the costs involved; she swears it came down already approved."

"Odd," Mick Priest said. "But thanks, Mr. Jackson."

"Victor, please," he corrected.

Priest nodded with, "Mick."

"Hand 'em the run down," James Wyatt said to Richter.

"About things makin' me suspicious or what?" he asked.

"Start with the bridge findings," Matwahali suggested.

"You're the expert there, big man," James said. "You take that."

B'Rone Matwahali, having tossed his shirt and his adventure gear before exiting the SUV, swept the sweat from his ebony form with large hands. The bulging, roping muscle ran rivulets of perspiration over hills and valleys cut into his torso.

"The killer here is a professional," he spat matter-of-factly.

"You sound sure," Gibson noted.

Matwahali tossed a handful of debris and wiring onto his table. He pointed at Tye Richter and the staffer tossed a handful of the small, circular metals they had found onto his table.

"The grubber's out here usin' plastique," Matwahali announced.

"Plastic explosives," Gibson exhaled.

"Ain't all. He worked his into the shurikens."

"The what?" Blackwood asked.

"A shuriken is a bladed, metal star thrown in martial arts."

"You're right," Matwahali answered Remy Lyles. "But certain plastic explosives, set up a certain way, are nicknamed shurikens. And they're specialty do ups, too. They're wrapped and encased with all these little, round, metal circles, thin like coins. The same way other bombs get wrapped or built with pellets or nails for shrapnel. Only, there's way more force with plastics, so there's way more little 'coins'. It's sophisticated shrapnel. They fly off and get better velocity and distance, almost like hundreds of little shurikens thrown with the force of a bomb."

"A professional and a specialist," Mick Priest thought aloud.

"That ain't all, Mick," James Wyatt said.

Then he relayed all there was to say about Nightshade Pass.

"Creepy down there, too," James noted. "I stayed up on the top of the ledge while Tye and B'Rone dropped into the Pass. I had the worst feelin' while they were down there. If I hadn't been there and the killer had been waiting for us to check out the bridge, sittin' up top would've been a great vantage point for killin' us off. Made me wonder, if this guy's such a pro, was that part of his plan at some point. Sittin' on the ledge, shootin' down into the Pass from a little nest."

Mick Priest paused then looked over his shoulder, back toward the main building. He scoured the balconies and the roof with fierce eyes.

"A nest..." he muttered.

"What?" Matwahali asked.

"Nothing," Priest said. He turned back to the crowd. "Jenkins, Richter, Chef, any thoughts, suspicions or observations of interest?"

Each responded in the negative, at least, for the time being.

Priest stole a look back over his shoulder, back at the resort building. His eyes focused on the tip top of a tower shape, where the outside elevator went all the way up to a rooftop landing of sorts.

Nest.

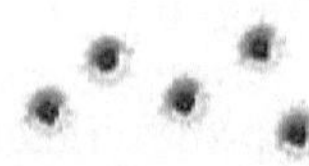

Helena Makai was the latest arrival. Agent Sarah Priest handed her the metaphoric baton, as it were, inviting her to share anything out of sorts, anything that put her ill at ease. The woman felt she had nothing to share. While they were on staff members, the group decided Clark and Clayborne should have their time, as well. Unfortunately for the investigation, those women held no clues close to the vest, either. They did discuss noises and bumps in the night.

"Oddities, not much more," Helena Makai admitted.

Suddenly, Agent Priest shifted gears.

"Ms Melkin, would you like to share anything?"

The woman jumped in her seat when Priest spoke her name.

"About what? What can I tell you? That I don't wanna die up here? I ain't got no insights to anybody's secrets, if that's what you mean. I didn't know none of ya before I got here. I shared a smoke or two with the model, sneakin' one when we could, but we wouldn't exactly be bosom buddies if smokin' wasn't involved. Of everybody I'm gettin' to know here, the only one I care to keep knowin' is B'Rone. I hate that people are kickin' out but better them than me."

Several remarked about her callous, hateful attitude but she did not hear it. She was too busy condemning herself.

You know why Grip Bridger was downstairs before he died, she told herself. *Walking with you. Your fault. All for a cigarette. All for you.*

She wiped a tear away and looked back toward the main house.

"Pleasant," Sarah Priest said. "Where were you hiding with Ms. Mobley to sneak cigarette time?"

"With one of the horses," she admitted.

"You were smoking in the stables? Around the hay? It isn't bad enough you were smoking but you risked burning everything to the ground for it?" shouted Cassandra Clark.

The women expected some tirade from the Kentucky native but she disappointed them. Instead, Kess Melkin laughed hysterically, unwilling to fight back with the Director.

"Yeah, I guess so," she muttered while laughing.

Tears filled her eyes. She remembered the kiss she stole from Bridger before he died, the feeling of his young lips on hers.

What a sin, risking fire...I'm so sorry, Boy Scout...

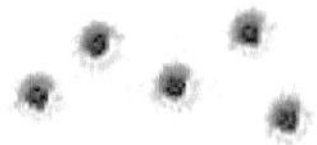

The hour thickened even more with its humidity. It was not just hot, echoing the sentiments of the heat lightning's thunder so loud in the distance. The air was hot and moist, almost damp. It offered the sensation of nigh drowning on dry land.

Only B'Rone Matwahali seemed immune to the heat. When Priest asked him if he could share thoughts and feelings, he replied with a fresh, unencumbered energy.

"I don't suspect any of us," he informed the group.

"Well, somebody's up to somethin', mate," Blackwood reminded.

"I don't see any of us as killers or fiends. I'll say that first, so anything else I say won't be taken as an accusation. As for bein' up to somethin', we're all up to somethin' most every day of our lives."

"You know what he means," Victor countered. "Someone is killing. We have dead people to prove it."

"I can't imagine any of us in that role," the big man said again. "But there are things I've noticed. People have been wanderin' about and that includes me. I've heard and seen 'em. Me, Kess Melkin, Paul, here, Andreya West and the late Kim Mobley and Grip Bridger. Only one thing could've struck me as suspicious in all that and, forgive me, Paul, it was when you disappeared and Kess and I were waitin' on you to come back from the Kitchen-"

"Oh, nice, that is!" Blackwood yelled.

"But I said I didn't think anythin' bad of ya, you daft-"

"No, I'm suspicious! Of course, you didn't tell us all about Melkin wanderin' off by herself and you findin' her alone with Grip Bridger down by the garden entrance, did ya? That ain't a little odd, B'Rone? Your little lady's with 'im right before he buys it?"

"Well, she wasn't with Mobley right before she died but I remember who was!" Matwahali roared back.

"Gentlemen!" Mick Priest yelled. "Enough! One at the time, please."

The Brits stared venomously at each other.

"B'Rone?" Priest asked.

"It's true, Kess was with the security guy by the garden doors. She smelled like smoke; I figured he let her go downstairs for a cigarette, probably took her himself to keep her safe. And it's also true that the Blackwood baker admitted he left Mobley 'dead tired' in his room before he and I went for a Kitchen raid!"

Blackwood and Matwahali passed curses back and forth.

"Enough!" Priest reminded and the two quietened.

"Looks like it's your turn," James Wyatt said to Paul Blackwood. "Wait for the bell and come out swingin', ol' boy."

"It's not nice to tattle," Tayla Barlowe told the women. "That's how I'm going to raise little Emma. But I know there are times that giving information is necessary and good, not snitching. I hope ya'll see the things I say as trying to be helpful, not trying to blab."

"We will," Sarah Priest said.

"We understand," Andreya West said.

"Good...since the first thing I gotta say is about you, Andreya."

Andreya chirped with laughter and nodded.

"Go on, feel free."

"I saw you wandering the grounds, all the way down in the grass, after we were supposed to settle in. You had on your pajamas and you were barefoot, gliding in the dark without a care in the world."

"I was," West said with a nod.

"What were you doing?" Cassandra Clark asked.

"She just told you," West fired back with a giggle. "I was bored and hot. I wanted out of the room. Frankly, I wasn't taking the danger thing too seriously...I regret that, now. But I needed to stretch and move. I didn't see anyone else or hear anyone else and I certainly didn't kill anyone else."

Tayla Barlowe then shared a sound she had heard on a lower balcony, a story repeated in the men's camp and in the women's camp several times over. The wandering killer was not an accomplished sneak and was certainly no ghost, if the stories rang true.

"Ms. West, do you have anything to share?" Sarah Priest asked.

"I don't, to be honest," she said. "Noises, like so many others. Nothing deep or meaningful, no strange encounters, no dark figures in my doorway, no skeletons under my bed. Sorry."

"Don't be sorry. Good news is always...good. I do have a question of my own, a point of curiosity, however."

"Of course," West allowed.

"Where were you when the shooting started last night? The shooting that claimed Bridger's life?"

West visibly saddened.

"I was indulging in another shower. I heard it over the water but I didn't really know what it was. I had just dressed when Mr. Wyatt came to my door to find me. Poor man; Bridger was a kind soul, too."

Gretchen Clayborne held her jaw locked against the emotion.

"Yes. Yes, he was. If that's all, for now," Clark said, "I say we go to the real pool. We may already have missed lunch but the pond is only whetting my appetite for a deeper swim."

She patted Gretchen's leg in a comforting gesture.

"Real pool?" Priest asked.

"Yes, south of the Generator Building. Inside the gymnasium."

The heat lightning flirted constantly, suggesting more rain could come, but it did not. Just the oppressive pressure and the hot feeling of breathing under a blanket visited Shadow Mountain.

"Mr. Blackwood, would you like to share anything-"

"Not really," the Brit interrupted Mick Priest. "I can't really think of anything you need to know, anything important. At least, nothin' that's any business of this lot."

James looked to Priest.

Priest sighed.

A gust of particularly hot wind seared their eyes and all squinted.

"Where were you when those gunshots echoed from the garden?" Priest asked him.

"What?" he asked, blue eyes big with surprise.

"You didn't hear him or you didn't understand the words?" James asked. "I mean, you been pickin' up what we're puttin' down pretty well, so far."

"I was in me room, where ya found me, I would think," Blackwood said, ignoring James Wyatt. "I done told ya, I ain't heard no gunshots, Priest! If I did I must've just wrote it off as thunder on the mountain. And I was honest with ya. If I had known 'em to be gunshots, I wouldn't have run up and down the stairs lookin' for a shooter! It don't sound heroic but I ain't gettin' shot for a stranger."

"When and where did you last see Richard Porter?"

"In the corridor, down from Kimber's room, a little while before you saw us in the corridor," Blackwood insisted. "He was annoyin' Kimber pretty good so I told him to scoot."

"Told him?" James Wyatt asked. "Or made him?"

"I gave him a little shove, ya know? Get the point across? He simply wouldn't let up on Mobley! Pushin' his luck! But I didn't hurt him. I just turned him around for his room."

"You know what he wanted from Mobley?"

Blackwood raised his eyebrows.

"What do you think he wanted?" he asked incredulously. "What every man wanted with Kimber Mobley!"

"When and where did you last see Ms. Mobley?" Priest asked.

Blackwood cleared his throat and said, "What B'Rone said was true. I was braggin' 'cause, right before he 'n' I made our Kitchen run, me 'n' Kimber had been...in my room. She was tired and said she was set for sleep. That's...the last time I saw her. She was gone when I got back. I was surprised but I thought she'd just gone for a shower."

He braced a hand on his forehead.

"She'd go back to her own room for a shower?" James asked.

"Why not use yours?" Priest clarified.

"Come on!" Blackwood shouted. "It's just us, just the men, here! I don't believe you don't see what I'm sayin'! We had a snog but neither of us were down for a snuggle! We were happy with our own rooms, our own space! We weren't gettin' married, fellas!"

"Where were you so long afterward, mate?" Matwahali asked him.

"I was wandering about. I don't sleep so good, to be honest. I take a lotta walks. I slipped away from you guys and went for a walkabout, as Kimber would say. That is the truth, I mean it."

"I believe ya," Matwahali said.

James looked at Mick Priest but Priest said nothing. The man stared off across the grounds. In the distance, the women were marching their way and he had caught it in his peripheral vision.

"Time to regroup," Priest told his old friend.

The Horse and Heraldry Gymnasium stood as a stalwart sentry, the structure farthest south of all the property, and a keen lookout, stationed alone. Ship lap planks armored the behemoth, beige undertones sending it off to battle in an earthy color and a muted shine. Though not tall, reaching upward only one story in height, it was quite long and wide.

Inside it, spread out in a single floor, many rooms and spaces forged the floor plan in a maze of interconnected chambers and hallways. It was a busy and full blueprint from beginning to end.

A lovely skylight peered down on the Olympic swimming pool and its junior partner, a children's pool, in a chamber placed in the dead center of the layout. Grecian columns stretched upward from the aqua tile flooring, yearning to grasp the frame of the skylight in many outstretched, white fingers.

A full gymnasium bordered the pool chamber on one side. Mirrors lined its every wall and the ceilings, too. An attached hallway led to two doors on the left and one on the right, entryways to showers, a steam room and a racquetball court.

On the other side of the pool chamber rested a large room full of hot tubs, the waters kept roiling on a regular basis. With no power, however, like the heating elements for the pools, the Jacuzzi tubs' turbulence and temperatures were dead in the water. A hallway led from there to two locker rooms, one for gentlemen and one for ladies.

The locker rooms were expansive; departments in each were like massive stores. Racks and racks of robes, bathing suits and towels held all sorts of sizes and colors and styles for the discriminating visitor and guest. And for the absent minded, since it seemed they were for those who came to the resort without packing those items.

As a whole, the inhabitants of the resort, staff and guests, had come down to the structure for a respite from the heat...and the situation. No one wanted to consider it anymore. No one wanted to think anymore.

That is, no one who was not tasked with protecting everyone.

Mick and Sarah Priest spoke with James Wyatt while everyone else picked out pool wear and other amenities in the emergency lighting. They compared notes, too. It was necessary that they compared and compiled; all the tales did not tie together.

Johanna Crimson did not tell the same versions of things as Mark Gibson, however slight the variations may have been. Mostly that centered around Remy Lyles. Crimson had come out directly and said she knew nothing of Lyles while Lyles and Gibson held different stories.

Maureen Li and Victor Jackson definitely saw things differently, even if the facts were similar behind the way they told their stories.

Kess Melkin omitted any mention of being with Grip Bridger just before his demise, while B'Rone Matwahali and Paul Blackwood, via Matwahali, knew she had been.

Matwahali had also placed Paul Blackwood as having been by himself for a time, which the pale Brit admitted was true.

Tayla Barlowe had told the tidbit of information about Andreya West with West quick to confirm, too.

There were mentions of noises in the night with disagreements on times, locations and sounds. The group could agree that there had been noises of some kind, at some time, in some volume, that resembled something but that was all. It was not case-breaking proof of anything.

With their collective minds geared up, the trio divided again.

James Wyatt stayed with the gathering as they lounged in the pool area, reminding them that everyone had to stay together. He told the Priest couple that he would use Gibson as armed backup if need be.

In no time, Sarah Priest would be tasked with taking the staff back to the main building. Lunch had already passed them and there was work to be done. She planned to visit Bridger's body with Cassandra Clark, anyway, once Clark and the rest of her staff were settled again.

Mick Priest told the others that he would be around...

CHAPTER TEN

Not a living soul at H and H Resort understood why the emergency power did not run at least a few air conditioning units in the guest and staff rooms. Of course, one would have to admit lights in the rooms, not just in corridors, would have been warranted before air conditioning. H and H did not have those, either.

Sarah Priest, Special Agent with the SBI, reached up behind her head and lifted her thick hair off her bare neck and shoulders. Her body was wet with perspiration. Her tanned skin glistened in the sun, a shimmering sheen of sweat covering her. There was little wind and none of it cool when it did blow. Still, it was cooler outside and that is where she chose to wait for Cassandra Clark.

I won't waste the time, either, she thought.

Sarah Priest slipped sunglasses into place after dropping her hair. She ducked then between the flowers and the greenery. Amid bloom and bush and betwixt scrub and vine, she prowled like a cat, hungry and fierce. Priest followed the gardens in a spiral, making circles that radiated farther and farther out from the resort building as a launch center. She looked for tracks and trace, letting her patterns overlap and double check each other.

In a red bed of mulch that clumped at the base of a yellow rose slept a single, pristine 9mm round. The shiny, unfired brass cartridge glinted in the daylight almost as if winking at Sarah Priest.

Here I am. Take me, hear my secret.

She checked all around the small area first, careful not to step down in any other footprints, then leaned in and took the bullet. The single 9mm round would have been lost forever in the scarlet mulch, nearly invisible beneath the shelter of the yellow rose, had it not been for the gifted observational skill of Agent Priest. People had always told her she had the eye for detail and detective work long before she had acquired an investigator's badge. Things always seemed to just jump out at her.

"Thank you, Jesus," Sarah prayed.

She knew God had preserved the find for her and any gift for the work she might hold were gifts from God.

God had saved something else for her to find, also. A couple of cigarette butts lay in the mulch, hidden from the naked eye until an observer leaned down to grab the bullet.

The bullet had scraping on the shiny casing, as if it had been loaded and unloaded, though not fired from a gun. A very small smear of something brown was on the butt of the casing where '9 M M' was stamped. On the cigarette butts, in lieu of any browns, a glossy, blood red smear held lip prints.

Sarah extracted her phone from her pocket and snapped a couple of pictures, from the bullet to the find location, from the small stain on the shell to the cigarette parts. Though she hated it, she had no way of legally preserving the evidence on hand. She tucked it all into a pocket in her tight pants.

The 9mm was the caliber of round Grip Bridger used. There, near where his body had lain in the garden, the cigarettes suggested a feminine companion. With the stories in mind she and her husband had shared with each other, she felt the identity was simple enough.

Kess Melkin.

Sarah Priest spun and headed back inside to find Cassandra Clark.

Is it time to eat? Did we miss lunch? What are they serving?

The questions were asked, at one time or another, by everyone, with the exception of Paul Blackwood. The baker maligned the very notion of looking forward to resort foods. He understood the need to eat, however, so he still followed the rest back to the main building. Not that he had a choice.

Stay together. No drifting, no falling behind. Safety in numbers, remember that. On the reminders went.

Along the way, Blackwood listened as they cursed hunger and the heat, quietly agreeing but unwilling to lend his voice to the group.

Cassandra Clark and her staff already had the Dining Hall prepped when the guests arrived again. They had artistically provided and displayed the meal before Cassandra left them to walk with Sarah Priest. All were hot and miserable. Sweat covered them, wet their clothing and left each of them sticky and uncomfortable...just as it did the guests.

It was particularly hot for the jacketed Jenkins.

At least the meal impressed the incoming arrivals, with or without Paul Blackwood's admission. Despite his prejudices, he recognized how the presentation offered a meal for the eye as well as the body. It was such a lovely display that most completely ignored Jenkins as he slipped in and out of the Dining Hall, getting water for his face and neck.

The young helicopter pilot paid more attention to Jenkins than anyone. Helping Jenkins seemed to help her deal with things. Each time he slipped out she worried for him.

Eventually, he slipped away and remained gone for some time.

Nevertheless, on proceeded the meal. On came the heat, an unwelcome guest. The muggy, sticky temperature settled in at the dining table and refused to leave. Hospitality aside, that was one guest no one felt obligated to entertain.

Mick Priest was the only person who did not come to the meal. Agent Sarah Priest knew her husband. She knew he wanted to sneak about without an audience and would be more than likely going through the guest rooms, though it concerned her. Like James Wyatt and herself, Mick had already been without sleep all night, though James had managed a nap. It was a good thing for James, too, since he hopped up each time someone had to be escorted to the restroom. Once in a while, people excused themselves before James could get back with the last traveler.

Sarah Priest sighed, thinking of her husband. No sleep, little food, and murder. It sounded like her love was in his element, yet again.

A man swore under his breath about the air...again. He swept a handful of papers off the nearby desk in the ample light of the windows and the glass doorway. The papers he sought eluded him still. The drawers taunted him, too, all locked. The computer, dead with no power, was not an option.

Frustration took hold of the man and he slammed his fist onto Cassandra Clark's lovely desk. Gone were the days of filing cabinets.

Where were the contracts? Was there anyplace else to look?

A deep breath later, struggling to retain his refined composure, he wiped the sweat from his forehead just below the peppered white hair.

"Hot under the starched collar, huh?" a sultry voice asked.

Jenkins, the office invader, turned just his head and gave a mocking smile to the open doorway.

"Is that sophisticated southern humor?" he asked.

"Hey, Kentucky's actually in the middle of the map," Kess Melkin remarked, blew the man a kiss and winked at him. "Not that far South."

"I stand educated," he replied, shaking his head.

"What're you diggin' around for?" she asked.

"Contracts, Ms. Melkin. Legal agreements."

"You really are bored, huh?" she asked.

"Ms. Melkin, Director Clark is too kind, too trusting," he said. "She sees the best in people. I see what there is. And I don't like what I see in your benefactor, Maureen Li. She is the most abrasive, the most arrogant, the most-"

"You don't like her," she said.

"It is more than that. I don't necessarily like any of you, where simple liking is concerned. I don't really *know* any of you," he said.

"Relax, Geeves," she said and cocked her head. "I, for one, ain't in love with you, either."

"Heartbreaking, to be sure," he mumbled. Then, "At any rate, there is something about her. I feel it in my very core. I thought, if I could find the original contracts, perhaps it might cast a light upon her. Maybe unveil some agenda or ulterior motives. Constantly wanting meetings with Ms. Clark, ridiculing the stay, insulting our resort, our prices..."

"It is kinda cursed, Jinkies."

"It is not cursed!" he snapped. "It is being sabotaged."

"Like you said," she chimed wryly. "Heartbreakin', ta be sure. Don't matter to the dead."

"No. No, I suppose not."

Lighting the corridor, a flashlight beam flared down the hallway. It came from the direction of the stairs and was visible to Melkin and Jenkins through the open corridor door.

A startled Kess Melkin chirped a curse and spun about to run. She jostled Jenkins, causing him to drop a sheaf of papers. In her urgency to flee, she tangled herself with the Staff Director.

The light bobbed and swept close outside the open doorway.

Irritated and afraid, Kess Melkin surged with adrenaline and tore free of Jenkins, shoving him backward. Jenkins dropped the papers he had in his hands and slipped on the loose pages.

As he toppled he swore at her.

The woman broke into the hall as if breaking from prison and crashed right into the arms of Mick Priest. He had just reached their doorway, flashlight in hand. She inadvertently knocked it to the floor.

"Oh, Mr. Priest!" she shouted. "It's you! Thank goodness!"

"Are you alright?"

"Sure, sure thing," she insisted. "I'm fine, really."

The color in her face had drained away in her fright. Her cheeks, however, were red and flushed with the heat and from having wrestled Jenkins. Sweat dampened her hair around her face. She breathed heavily.

As her proximity to Priest settled in on her, she could not help but be impressed; she had driven full steam into him and his strong body had stopped her in her tracks. Her impact had not even swayed the big oak.

Then Jenkins appeared in the doorway.

"Jenkins?" Priest said, wondering what was happening.

"Crazed minx!" Jenkins shouted angrily.

"Whoa," Priest calmed. "Mr. Jenkins, Ms. Melkin, explain."

The two rattled on, loudly overrunning each other and arguing for the majority of the exchange.

Priest, getting the gist of it, tried to mediate without losing patience.

"Both of you, calm down."

Jenkins turned about angrily and went back into the office.

Melkin, for her part, had not been willing to step back from Priest, leaning against him. He moved back to make room.

"So, what brings you up here?" she asked, stepping directly to him, pressing into him again.

"Looking for clues to our situation," he informed, again backing away from her.

"Hmmmm, ours? You mean, yours and my situation? Together? I feel...special," she said airily.

She nibbled at her lower lip, looking provocatively upward through the top of her eyes, head leaned down.

"No, not just concerning you and me, Ms. Melkin," he clarified. "This situation involving all of us."

"Ouch," she said lowly and patted his chest with an open hand. "Ms. Melkin? Drop that stuff, Priest. You can call me Kess."

She batted thick, black lashes and offered a truly cute pout face.

He picked up his flashlight.

"Ms. Melkin, what exactly are you-" he started.

"Kess," she insisted.

Priest regarded her with a raised eyebrow when she neared him, again standing far too close. Before she could speak further, her lips still in a full pout, he blinded her, point blank, with his flashlight. She fluttered her eyes and stepped back, lifting a hand between them, and he took the opportunity to talk.

"There's a killer on these grounds," he said. His voice was very low but placid, unsettling her in its calm. "Why don't you shift into neutral? I know you're smart enough to get it; now, idle down."

"Okay, okay," she said, hands raised in surrender.

He lowered the flashlight.

"Point taken," she continued. "No flirtin', I get it. But, since you're all business, I'll tell ya, Geeves was up here riflin' through Clark's paperwork. I was just passin' by this floor on the way up to mine when I heard the stuffed penguin rustlin' around."

She seems genuine enough, thought Mick Priest. *But, like Joseph in Potiphar's house, I'd better keep my running shoes on around that woman. Her behavior is all over the map.*

Priest said, "Why aren't you with the others?"

Melkin said, "I left 'em to sneak a smoke-"

"By yourself?"

"Yeah. Then I was goin' up to my room and change, get the sweat and smoke off, so I don't get busted."

"Where are the cigarettes?" Priest asked.

"In the horse stables, down at one end," Melkin said. "Porter smelled smoke on me our first few hours here and pulled me aside. Told me he stashed a pack down there, hid 'em in one of the feed buckets. Me an' him and Mobley have all...had all...slipped down there for a smoke at one time or another."

"Oh, there's a shock!" Jenkins shouted from the office. "What else has she done?"

"And what are you doing, Jenkins?" Priest snapped, leading Melkin back into the room with Jenkins. "Does Ms. Clark know you're up here? I'm willing to guess she doesn't."

Jenkins rattled off a lot of excuses about why Clark needed protecting from herself, her own kindness and her willingness to believe the best in the worst people. Priest got the general idea that Jenkins thought Li was up to something and Clark was too innocent to see it. The man also clearly believed there might be some secrets about Gridlock Publishing and their arrangement with Horse and Heraldry Resort.

"Did anyone know you were sneaking off?"

The man straightened up rigidly and cleared his throat. He started to speak, lifted his eyebrows and exhaled without any words. Then he gathered himself, straightened his formal jacket and donned a faint but polite smile.

"I do not *sneak,* thank you very much. I also do not *creep, slink, stalk* or *lurk-*"

"Let me go at this another way," Priest said. "You can tell Clark you were doing this yourself when we get back downstairs or I will. And neither of you, for any reason, wander off again. I mean it."

"Cassandra...Director Clark just doesn't-" the man of etiquette began.

"Are we clear, Mr. Jenkins?" Priest asked.

"We clear, Jinkies?" Kess Melkin mocked.

Jenkins scowled at the Kentucky native.

"Crystal."

"Good," Priest growled. "Now, I'll escort you back to where you belong. And you *will* stay there, both of you."

Both Melkin and Jenkins nodded, Jenkins with a rueful expression and Melkin with a sarcastic sneer just for the Staff Director.

Nevertheless, in no time, Priest had them back with the group.

He gave his old friend, James Wyatt, a hard time for losing two of those in his charge. He owned it, to his credit, but was quick to share the blame with Mark Gibson. It seemed they had debated several times the better handling of Johanna Crimson. It had been in one of their engagements that the two had slipped away.

Gibson, for his part, offered no apologies and no remorse. He had no qualms in reminding everyone that he was there to keep Johanna Crimson safe. As long as she was secure, he considered himself to be batting a thousand.

Mick told James to watch over everyone as well as he could...and to watch Gibson with fresh eyes. Not as an ally. Not as a helper. As a very mercenary sort with singular concerns.

He said that right in front of Gibson and Crimson. Crimson seemed disappointed in her man. Gibson flushed an angry red and squinted at the detective as if taking aim from a great distance, a proverbial sniper in the trees.

Cassandra Clark took part in a brief whispering session with Reginald Jenkins. He looked the part of a sorrowful child but she simply smiled, cupped a hand on one side of his handsome face and comforted him. Then they parted.

When the older man charged off to work Agent Sarah Priest appeared at her side.

"Shall we?" Sarah asked and gestured for them to move.

She had already plotted a bit of work for the Resort Director and prepped her with a speech. Sarah wondered if the speech would work when they walked out of the Dining Hall and Clark looked at her own, shaking hands.

"I can't really say I'm ready," Clark said, walking along with the agent. "We've done this already but, not to sound unkind, those people weren't my friends. We weren't close. What if I can't handle this?"

Sarah Priest closed the Kitchen away from everyone else.

"Cassandra-"

"Cassie, please," Clark reminded. "It's what my friends call me. And we may not have known each other very long but you're the only person I've ever examined dead bodies with. That's gotta qualify us as...close."

Sarah chuckled, saying, "Okay. Cassie it is."

"Just don't call me Regan," the other woman said, rolling her eyes.

"Regan?"

"Cassandra Regan Clark. I have no idea what my mother was thinking with that one."

Sarah pulled open the cooler...freezer...morgue.

"We have to check Grip for any clues, any trace. Just like the others. I also want to check the bullet wounds-"

Clark said, nodding, "I understand. But I have to ask a favor."

"Okay."

"We had to undress Porter and Mobley. If we have to undress Grip, can you handle that part? I knew him a little too well to be stripping him on top of examining his body. It's awkward."

"I understand. Think of it this way, though. It's only awkward for you. He won't know the difference."

Turning, she led Clark into the freezer.

Naked and in truly unappealing color, Porter and Mobley offered a blunt 'welcome back' to the women, delivering a rush of memories from both silent examinations. They lay on their backs, right where they had been left, and neither posed a problem for the living women.

However, Cassandra Clark drew up short at the sight of her friend, Falgrip Bridger. He was prone on his back, as well, a newcomer to the party, still dressed.

Sarah had already shared a bit of gel for Clark to put under her nose so she then handed away a pair of gloves. She donned her own, too, staring at Bridger's form.

Clark pitched her head to one side and had to look away but Sarah Priest drove forward another few feet. She knelt with the body of the young man and paused still, her hand on his chest. Softly, she prayed that the man had not been in terrible pain as he passed and that there would be justice.

"Amen to that," the resort woman whimpered, choking back tears.

186

I ground my teeth together, considering the loss of life and my turning stomach. Senselessness. Murder. Violence and hate. Things God taught against, all wrapped up in a neat package weekend. It disgusted me and I quietly mourned the dead as I stalked the resort anew.

I wanted to search the rooms. I knew I needed to do just that. Some clue or proof of the killer's identity had to be found, somehow.

Before I could, another point kept pressing in on me, a hunch, a feeling. It would not relent, like a bit of sand in the eye. I could see beyond it but I could not deny its urgency.

Something James had said about Nightshade Pass. How the killer could have easily eliminated them. From a distance, from the upper ledge, when Matwahali and Richter went down into the pass, shooting them would have been a simple act. The bridge landing would have made great high ground positioning for a sniper and the Shadow Walker bridge would have been good bait. What he said made perfect, logical sense. As an assassin, it's what most would do. Find high ground. Make a base...a nest.

I quietly prayed as I turned my attention to higher ground.

The overlook outside Floor Two carried me to the next set of stairs to Floor Three's balcony outcropping. That outer ledge led me to the stairs rising to Floor Four's overlook, too. With each new ascension, I drank in the grounds from an elevated vantage point, trying to see anything that would be a clue...or a clue to any place our killer might perch.

I saw nothing from that highest outer balcony on the eastern side, however. The roof itself would offer even higher ground and a way to move onto the highest western balcony, too, so it called to me.

Here I am. Take what I know.

Since I knew elevator systems had to have rooftop, penthouse workrooms, I knew each elevator system would have some access to the actual roof. Each outer ledge had an elevator location so the outer elevator cars could access each floor, too. The eastern balconies of each floor had their elevator landings on the southern face. I trotted down the balcony to the southern tip and found the nonworking elevator car.

Beside the immobile, glass walled, see through lift, an access ladder rose up to the resort's slanted top. It was iron and bolted well to the wall facing. It had a circular cage welded around it so a climber could not fall off backward.

It also happened that the ladder scaled the outer wall of what was Johanna Crimson's room. In moments, I scaled that wall, also.

The sun brilliantly lit the metal roofing with light and heat and dancing reflections. Despite sporadic cloud coverage, I had to shield my eyes with one hand to see in the radiance of the sun itself and the roof's shining glare. Every top floor room had two skylights, a large one above the main room and a lesser one above every bathroom. Both glasses crowning each of the rooms glinted with a searing white light, too.

That is, almost every one. The small one right before me, just off the roof landing and topping the bathroom of Johanna Crimson, was dulled.

I crept over to it and found out why immediately. In the one foot recess created by the skylight, a box over half its size blocked it out. It was an antique wooden trunk that looked to be a hundred years old or more. The iron hinges and the clasp told that tale easily enough. I checked it and found it unlocked so I threw back the lid.

Nest, I mused morbidly. *A hunter's nest.*

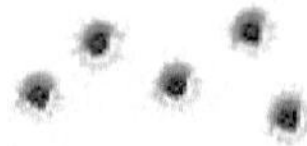

Back in the Dining Hall, Melkin would not look up from her plate.

The very late lunch conversation revolved around Falgrip Bridger, the Security Chief, like heavenly bodies orbiting a black hole; the situation was a macabre mystery and drew everyone down into it.

People had just seen him. It had not been long. They had just spoken with him, shared something with him, interacted with him. Gretchen Clayborne said she had just kissed him...

There had been no time for a man so young to die.

No one, however, had seen him after a certain point. No time after Bridger had taken Kess Melkin downstairs and then agreed to wait there for Paul Blackwood as B'Rone Matwahali took her back upstairs.

Of course, that was a secret...so she believed.

She kept her eyes down on her plate. The silent unknown surrounding the man's end rattled her cage far more than anyone's questions could have. Still, she did not want to address questions. Not again. Not like she had back in her teenage years. She tried to keep from breaking down, blinking away tears of fear while gnawing the inside of her lips. She was scarcely hanging onto her demeanor.

Looking for an escape, Kess Melkin cleared her throat emphatically. If she could not avoid attention she would control it. Normally, sex and sensuality kept her masks in place pretty well. The room was not open for that, however. She swore quietly and bitterly and abandoned her fork, spearing a piece of the roasted duck she had not been able to finish. Leaving it on the plate, she eased her chair back a bit and stood up, drink in her hand.

"Here's to us. The Second Survivors," Melkin announced.

Andreya West crossed her legs in a very ladylike fashion.

"Second Survivors? Who are the first?"

"And what did we survive?" Tayla Barlowe asked.

Melkin put down her glass after draining it dry. She had not even spoken before Jenkins was there, filling it again.

"I'm from a little place in Kentucky called Flat Lick. When I was a teenager, me 'n' a group of friends ended up gettin' stalked by a serial killer. Those of us still alive call ourselves the Survivors. I'm wishin' ya'll the best up here this weekend. I hope we'll all be the Second Survivors by the time it's all said and done."

She dropped back to her seat.

"Hear, hear," Matwahali said loudly, lifting his glass.

"Ah, a fellow parliamentarian," Paul Blackwood chuckled. "Hear, hear, as well!"

Before any lighthearted returns were launched, Tayla Barlowe spoke.

"Tell us about it," she said to Melkin.

And the room went tomb silent.

"I don't think we need to impose on-" Jenkins attempted quickly.

"I'd like to hear it," B'Rone Matwahali interrupted. "We got us a haunted weekend. What's one more ghost story?"

"Everyone," Jenkins started again, "I would be surprised if-"

"It wasn't a ghost," Melkin said flatly, soberly. "But, if you wanna hear about it, I'll tell you...about the Wolf."

Flickering candlelight both lit and shadowed her face in a shifting mirage. Onlookers stared intently, even Jenkins, though he had apparently opposed the retelling of her claim to fame.

Her book, *Wolfen Shadows*, shared her story with far more people than she ever could have in person. Still, telling it again, herself, Melkin trembled. It was like revealing it for the very first time...again.

"Flat Lick's a little bitty place," she started. She mumbled something about a cigarette then took a long draw from her drink. She then said, "But the Wolf of Knox County put us on the map."

Kess Melkin wove a web of intrigue. A thread of horror and injustice followed the narrative and everyone in the Dining Hall followed along with her story. Almost every person present decided to buy her book as soon as they could, most of them making that decision before she was half finished. By the time she reached the climax, her audience had experienced more than a tale, true or not. They had experienced a part of Kess Melkin, for better or for ill.

She seated herself to a round of applause, oddly enough. Applause for having survived? Applause for not being one of the Wolf victims? Applause for entertaining everyone with a terrifying life lesson? Perhaps it was a little of all of those.

The best part, she told herself, *is now they ain't got proof what the tears are for, if they ain't for the scary story and my sad past. I can wipe 'em at will, nobody the wiser.*

She still knew, however. She knew all too well.

Inside the chest hid several black cloaks and hats. Black overcoats nestled down in the blue lining, too, with black boots and gloves of many varying sizes. Black tactical masks, made of high impact polyarmor and dark lenses, lined one side, their painted white skull faces staring upward. Underneath it all was a wooden case just as old as the chest or even older, measuring about one foot by one and a half feet wide and only a few inches deep. Priest recognized its design. It was a pistol case from the 1800s, designed to hold a matching duo of pistols and the necessary tools and so on to make bullets for them.

He opened the cherry hued, wooden case and found identical blue lining, matching the trunk. A bit of gunpowder and lead balls were inside, squeezed into little compartments, along with a little powder horn and a bullet mold. For all that waited inside to be discovered, however, neither of the guns from the gun compartments were present.

"Arms loaded, killer armed," Priest muttered. "Not the best news but at least we know."

Then he considered anew the specific location. Had the killer simply climbed that very ladder and picked the first skylight for nesting? High ground from which to hide and plot and watch? A little recess to keep things from sliding or slipping? Or was it more? It was a view into Johanna Crimson's room. The main target, so they had all thought. Was it proof? Did it confirm the suspicions? Or, if not coincidence and not an indicator of the endgame, was there another purpose in the position?

The answers were not spelled out in the trunk. Priest took the gun case and tucked it under one arm. Then he unceremoniously pushed the chest to the edge of the roof and slid it over the edge. It crashed heavily to the Floor Four overlook, just outside Johanna Crimson's room, and skittered all the way to the balcony rails. It held form, old world strong.

The detective climbed down to the balcony again. Priest then dragged the trunk all the way to his own room's glass, balcony door. He put it inside the room then hid the double gun case inside there, as well. He tucked the small box up behind the mantle space, just inside the fireplace's gray mouth.

"Now," he said, "back to the rooms."

He passed through his room for the inner corridor. Floor Four greeted the detective with more of the resort's general hospitality. The heat was thick enough to cut. The darkness lingered in palpable clouds, undaunted by the emergency lighting. And the abandoned state meant every little creak and squeak could be a killer creeping nearby. Once in the corridor, he nevertheless walked briskly to the northern end and began the process of searching rooms.

He did not search the room assigned to James, however. He started across the hall with Andreya West's room.

The lockpick kit sliced into the keyhole surgically. How many times can someone pick locks before it becomes another mindless, autopilot action? However many times it took to master, the man had long completed them. Priest breached the door so quickly that having a key would scarcely have made it any faster.

He closed the door to the hall.

Mick Priest was not sure what to think. He looked around one last time, checking for anyone else present, regretting his snooping before he even started it. He hated to go through everyone's things but there was little choice.

He grabbed one of her three sizable, high end suitcases.

Priest rifled through the first and second suitcases quickly. If he did his job well, and Priest was very good at what he did, no one would ever know he had come and gone. For that, Mick Priest was truly grateful. The two suitcases were the more personal cases, with intimates and undergarments and a lot of other clothing onto which he would have never wanted to put his hands.

"No more secrets," the detective bemoaned. "Not even for Victoria."

Priest then opened the third and last suitcase. He shuffled things about in the case with both hands, taking a mental inventory of the contents. Mostly there were certificates and copies of diplomas and declarations to the woman's sheer genius. She was more than a linguistics and history scholar; she held degrees in all sorts of things. From chemistry to literature, all the way around the classroom and back, she had 'been there, learned that'.

In every field she had contacts and numbers, too.

"This woman's never spent a day outside a class, either learning or teaching," he muttered. "And she carries the proof around with her."

About to repack the suitcase, duly impressed, he stopped. A fold of red silk caught his eye against the black, satin interior of the suitcase.

He unfurled a bit of the red silk, exposing two fire hardened, wooden escrima staves.

Priest brushed his fingertips along the staves.

Each had a metal cap on one end. One had a threaded protrusion and the other had a threaded bore, allowing the two to be screwed together as a single staff. The etching in the wood and their rich, golden finish were impressive.

Authentic.

Short, wooden weapons of the Filipino Martial Arts, they looked to be quite genuine relics. Whatever name to the FMA arts one wanted to apply, eskrima, arnis or kali, all bore stick fighting in their heritage. Many masters felt the art called silat was also close in style and tradition. Mick Priest, however, had never studied any of those. He had an awareness, a knowledge, of their styles and existence but that was as far as his understanding took him. He certainly did not know why the scholar, a professor, had brought them on vacation.

"And I'm not likely to find out standing here," he mumbled, alone.

He abandoned the room for the corridor again. Next on the agenda was Room Three, once he again skipped James Wyatt's space, Room One. That was Tayla and Emma Barlowe's quarters. He almost skipped that one, as well, disbelieving a killer would bring an infant along, but he immediately refocused.

Thorough, he reminded himself.

He still found nothing of import, however. Having perused his way through Tayla Barlowe's room and her things and having reached completion none the wiser, he slipped into the hallway, yet again, and moved southerly. He skipped the empty rooms and his own, Room Eight, and that put him on task for Room Nine.

Maureen Li and Victor Jackson had that room.

Inside it, Priest scoured everything, grateful for the blazing sun outside and the glorious light shining through the windows and the glass doorway. He was not so thrilled with the rampant heat and the sweat he kept wiping from his eyes, though. The burden of the shaven head. He did his best not to drip on their things as he probed their bags.

Where the case was concerned, the luggage disclosed no secrets, exposed no hidden agendas. The search revealed no dark backgrounds, no surreptitious dual identities.

The detective only managed to uncover the fact that Victor Jackson, always presenting himself as a gentleman, was quite modest with his sleepwear and his underclothes. Forced to room with a female coworker for the weekend, it was clear he was a professional...

...while that lady boss wore animal print spandex, red leather bustiers and black thongs, none of which Mick Priest wanted or needed to know.

Still, having acquired little from the expedition, Priest did gain one potentially useful insight from the work. He found that Victor Jackson had a series of backup batteries for his laptop and multiple notebooks, clearly intent on working over the weekend and having access to his information and his databases.

Maureen Li had not even unpacked her laptop and she had not even brought a cord for it. It was painfully clear who had the dedication in the pair.

He left for the last the empty rooms on that floor then went to Room Twelve, Gibson and Crimson's room. Priest made short work of the lock and pushed inside.

As he started his search, he could see the actress breaking into outrage in his mind. How she would have protested his search. How Gibson would have agreed with her, just a bit more understanding because he had been on the job. How they would have come around once they thought about things. Perhaps...

It did not matter how they would have felt, however. Priest never slowed. He tossed their bags and their whole room. The truth was pretty ambivalent, anyway, unable to be defined in their belongings. There were oddities but not heart stopping revelations.

Gibson carried a book with him, though he hardly seemed the reading type. *The Path of Forgiveness*, it read. More than the title, for Priest, the description jumped off the cover. It was a very long piece about the samurai in Japan, their code of honor, *Bushido*, and the part forgiveness played in it.

For her part, Crimson struck out into the strange and unusual with her bags, too. In one of them, lining the entire base, her high school annuals and her college yearbooks stood ready for reminiscing. In another bag some compact photo albums and a couple of scrapbooks held onto the past dearly.

Priest frowned when he thumbed through them; earmarked pages actually focused on pictures of Crimson, herself, not others she may have wanted to remember. The detective found it hard to believe even a starlet could be so self-obsessed. Keeping all that history so close at hand just to look at herself? Not even Johanna Crimson would do that.

Yet, there they were. Odd. Not shocking, frightening or telling. Odd.

Then the man put everything back as it was.

I was never here, he thought. *At least, that's the story.*

Priest then left, having done what he could do. He did not just leave the room, however. He took to the stairs again, heading for Floor Three.

Cassandra Clark shivered violently but it was more than just the cold of the cooler getting to her. She covered her mouth with one hand.

"I wish you didn't have to do that," she said, eyes closed.

"Me, too," Sarah said. She pulled away more of Grip Bridger's cold, stiff clothing with, "But you never know what's beneath the surface. Investigation is far more than chemical spray tests and microscope analysis, like on television shows. It starts right here, in your hands, under your nose. Everything looked at so that nothing is looked over."

Bridger had been very wet in the rain. When he was placed into the cooler, the deep cold had stiffened all of his garments and made them difficult to move. Sarah Priest, to Clark's chagrin, had simply begun cutting them away from his cold, dead body and tossing the parts to a far corner.

Clark looked up at the ceiling where the air ducts blew frosty wind downward and several little fans circulated it. She cleared her throat.

"I can check the pockets you're tossing away, if you like," Clark offered her teammate.

"Thanks, Cassie, but James gave him a thorough search."

Clark's hands trembled. She tried to steady them but found no way to still the tremors.

"I...I just can't..." she muttered, turned and fled from the cooler.

"Sorry, Cassie," Sarah Priest whispered to herself. She sighed. "Some people aren't cut out to...what's...this?"

The SBI specialist leaned down close to Bridger. She had him undressed and had been looking at his face, thinking of the young man he had been when he was alive. That is when she noticed it. She leaned closer, putting her face uncomfortably close to his. She sniffed, too.

"I'm sorry, Sarah," Cassandra Clark blurted, plunging into the cold room again. Then, "I was just...w-what're you doing?"

Sarah Priest turned around to Clark, her eyes wide and her expression excited. She grabbed Bridger by the jaw and tipped his head to one side, to face Clark.

"Cassie, what does this look like to you?" she demanded.

Clark covered her mouth with her hand again, sickened.

"What does what look like?" she asked, eyes squinted almost closed.

Sarah pointed with her free hand.

"Look at his lips," she ordered. "What does that look like? Blood? Marinara sauce? Broken blood vessels near the surface?"

Clark crouched and leaned close to her former friend. The sickness waned as her interest piqued. She gently touched Bridger's face and stretched the skin around his mouth. Along both lips ran a smear in the red family of colors, thin and only on the very surface.

"Nothing medical or biological, I don't think," Clark said. "If I had to guess, I'd say lipstick. But you should be able-"

"No tests, right now. No microscopes and no chemical analysis. In other words, yes, you do have to guess. What do you think it is?" Sarah pushed.

Clark locked her jaw and grimaced as she ran her fingers along the man's lips. The velvety, almost oily, blood red substance came off on her digits. She pulled it close to her own face, gazing into its imperfections, when she sniffed the air.

"This is lipstick."

Sarah nodded, asking, "Do you recognize it? Is it a color Gretchen Clayborne uses?"

"Never. Gretchen hates reds, especially fire engine and blood tones. Bright is not her thing."

"And the scent," Sarah said. "Does Gretchen-"

"No," Clark said. "Gretchen doesn't and has never smoked, that I know of. But someone here does and she wears fire engine red lipstick."

"Kess Melkin."

"Time to ask her some pointed questions," Clark growled.

"Yes," Sarah agreed. "But, first, the bullet wounds."

Clark winced when Sarah popped out her knife.

Floor Three, I considered, stepping from the stairway landing.

The first room off the stairwell, on the left, was Melkin's. A quick pick and I was inside it, violating privacy and trust.

Melkin's clothes draped over everything in the room. All kinds of items clung to all sorts of furniture. She had to be changing clothes every ten minutes or modeling them for someone...

...and my eyes rested on one of the nightstands.

B'Rone Matwahali's leather bracer, the etched one he wore over his right wrist, lay by the bed, laces unfurled.

They certainly are hitting it off, I thought.

Her things revealed no secrets during the search, however. Too many copies of her own books littered the place. The ghosts of far too much smoking haunted the paper in the books and the clothes all around the room. The liar in the room, an overpowering lilac perfume, tried to deny the cigarette smoke but I was not fooled. Both spirits rose from the past, returning from their graves, to fight for dominance. Those scents wafted here and there in ample amounts.

It made the Kentucky writer an unlikely operative in tackling Porter, considering he always reeked of quite strong pain liniment when he was present. Forensic transfer being what it was, had she rolled about with him, his smell should have been lingering. And Mobley, for that matter, had worn a sea-inspired scent that was nothing if not potent. In Melkin's chambers I could not detect even the faintest whiff of it.

And I found nothing else to record. At an end of the search, I retreated from the room.

Being thorough required at least a passing, breeze through search of the empty rooms on the floor. I checked out the four empties next in the hallway before ducking into B'Rone Matwahali's chambers.

Getting in was much like penetrating Melkin's. Lockpicks. Patience.

Searching the room was similar, too. Personal items. A mess. Putting everything back just as I found it. Nothing odd...unless a whole suitcase full of adventure gear and equipment was odd. Still, it was nothing out of the ordinary for the big man's world. And, had it been a big secret, he would not have offered its use. He had voluntarily revealed it, using it at Nightshade Pass. The only thing that gave me pause was a large binder tucked beneath a coil of climbing rope, a machete and a voltage meter.

Explosives : *The Right And Wrong Way*, the cover read.

It would have been a red flag moment if the man had not been ex-military, ex-paramilitary and an admitted contract soldier. In light of those things, the finds meant little. Just one more sticky note to paste onto the refrigerator door of my mind.

Then I started the hall again.

I slid inside Paul Blackwood's room and closed the door.

Reflex grappled me to a sudden stop. The hair I did not have stood up on my neck and the back of my head as I froze just inside the doorway. The room languished for a lost moment, adrift in Mobley's perfume. The scent was as thick as the fog rolling onto shore beneath a pirate's moon. It mingled with Paul Blackwood's own cologne but I caught it right away. Mobley had been there. The smell was intense. She had been there for some time. Often.

It was hardly news, though. Just confirmation.

I reviewed all of Blackwood's things but I found nothing that spoke to me of any dark tidings. The most oddest discovery in his room was the sheer amount of clothing. He was not as messy as Melkin but he had fully intended to change clothes as much.

I could not help but feel empty handed as I pulled back to the corridor. Door closed on Blackwood's things, room sealed again, I checked the other empty rooms on the floor. It did not take long.

Then the last room, Room One, wiggled its metaphoric finger at me.

It lured me. Beckoned me. Challenged me.

Last one on the floor, Detective, it taunted. *Better make me count.*

I stormed the door, ignoring any and all of the hesitance. I had barely pushed the picks into the lock when the door creaked back out of my reach. Half expecting to see the registered guest, Rembrandt 'Remy' Lyles, holding the handle, I was surprised when I looked and found myself still alone.

Caution ruled the day, however. I carefully pushed the door completely back and clear, looking around inside the room. Sure I was indeed alone, my nerves easing, I went inside and closed myself off from the hall.

"Now, Mr. Lyles," I said, "what do you have to say for yourself?"

Remy Lyles rose to his feet.

James Wyatt stared at him conspicuously, wondering what the introverted cartoonist was doing.

"I have a story, a true one, like hers," he said.

Others stared at him then, too. Some of them wondered if it had suddenly become 'open mic night' for scary stories. Others wondered what morbid story haunted the thin man with the Voltron t shirt.

"Share," Tayla Barlowe urged.

"Really?" Maureen Li asked with a curled lip. "You want one of our 'not a writer' guests, an artist, to tell us a story?"

Remy eased back down with a 'no hard feelings' shrug.

James was about to berate the publishing headhunter but one of the Brits beat him to the assault.

"More than we want to hear your input...but there it is," B'Rone Matwahali said.

"Great adventurer, huh?" Li asked. "You certainly haven't been around enough to know you don't attack those who write your checks-"

"Let me stop you there," Matwahali warned lowly. His eyes, fierce, offered no chance of jest as he said, "I've been around enough to know I wouldn't do business with you, Li, if there were no other publishers left. Your whole bit's been dodgy from the jump and, with your attitude, you've bein' a proper charlie."

"You should talk! *Yúchǔn de!*" the print executive retorted, breaking into her first language.

"What did you call me?" Matwahali demanded.

"I don't think it was 'mate', big man," Paul Blackwood said.

"Yo, shut up!" James Wyatt shouted. "Let's hear from Remy."

"Hear, hear," Paul Blackwood said, leading several others to encourage the artist.

Mark Gibson and Johanna Crimson were not in that crowd.

Remy Lyles stood again and cleared his throat.

"Oh, honey, you don't have to stand the whole time," Kess Melkin said. "Relax."

He chuckled, tilting his head in deference. Taking his seat again, he began.

"It's about the killer they've been sayin' could be on these very grounds. It goes a little something like this."

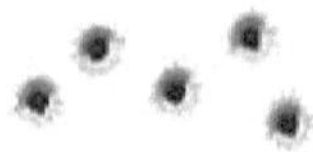

They decorated the room in a morbid sort of celebratory recognition. Pinned to walls. Strewn across tables and sofas, chairs and the beds. Stuffing several portfolios that lay open on the floor by the balcony doors. The artwork by a young man with a clearly questionable taste.

In black and white sketch work with thick lines and splashes of a single color, crimson, depictions of the larger than life killer, Ghost Revolver, were everywhere. He stood above bloody victims in picture after picture, revolvers smoking, shadowy cloak billowing in the wind.

And the white skull face peered from each stylized portrait.

"Remy Lyles," Mick Priest muttered, "who's your hero? As if I didn't know. The legend is real, if no place else than in your mind."

The detective shook his own shirt by the collar, trying to get some air down into it. He wiped the sweat from his slick head.

The ghost watched him from every wall, it seemed, as he started a deeper search. Bags. Drawers. Desks. Tables. Pencils and charcoals filled an attache case, a supply of bright red inks tossed into the bag for good measure. Lastly, the portfolios fell open in the hands of the detective to reveal more of the same. But they shared something new, too.

In each one, there were mock covers of a Ghost Revolver comic book under the brand of RC Comics. There was a mock graphic novel cover with the Revolver battling Velvet Edge, too. The brand logo was Gridlock Publishing.

CHAPTER ELEVEN

"It started way back in the late 1800s. We're talkin' cowboys and Indi...ans...and horse 'n' buggy days." The young, scruffy pencileer choked down his apprehension at taking a perceived misstep. "Sorry, Mr. Wyatt," he countered himself. "I meant Native Americans."

"Remy, do I look politically correct to you?" James scoffed, shaking his long pony tail and the feathers at the end of it. "Most people accuse me of bein' a stereotype on purpose. Do I seem like the sensitive kinda guy who'd have a meltdown every time I hear a word or an expressed thought I don't appreciate?"

"W-What?" Lyles stuttered. "Well, no..."

"Have I said I'm offended by the term Indians? Redskins, even?"

"No, I just-"

"Good, 'cause I ain't. I'm a grown man, not a crybaby."

"Okay..." Lyles allowed, unsure of where to take the discussion.

Andreya West, unafraid to give audible voice to her own thoughts, spoke directly into the mix, grinning, sparing no sarcasm.

"Thank goodness you straightened him out, Mr. Wyatt. We wouldn't want him running about trying to respect you without permission."

Chuckles and giggles ran the room.

"Yeah, okay, laugh now. That's just how Washington football lost its title and logos," he said with a pointed finger, shaking it.

"Shut up," Johanna Crimson said with a grin of her own. "There's enough murderous intent at the resort without political debates."

Again, laughter. It was a needed medicine.

"Hey, I'll make you a deal. When somebody says somethin' about your heritage or ancestry, you decide if it's offensive. When they say somethin' about mine, let me worry about it. I don't need surrogate sensitives taking offense *for* me."

"He's right, you know," Andreya West interjected suddenly. "The Washington Redskin logos and artwork were originally done by a Native

American, Walter Wetzel. He often said how proud he and others were to see a positive representation of his people on such a big stage."

James nodded, impressed by her knowledge.

"The Blackfoot heritage," he said.

"Social activists hoped to better that heritage," Paul Blackwood said. "Didn't I read that the ol' boy's own family didn't love the logos?"

"In Wetzel's own words, 'radicals'," James quipped. "And the vast majority of his family and friends were very proud. His family's been robbed of that now. Like a lot of us. I was a proud Redskin fan, Blackwood, and I'm a Native American. It's *my* heritage, not the inheritance of a buncha emotional children tryin' to think for the whole world."

Andreya West grinned with, "My heritage, as well. And, for the record, I agree with Mr. Wyatt."

"Hear, hear," Wyatt said with a grin of his own, mimicking Blackwood.

"Hey," Tayla Barlowe interrupted. "Can we hear the story, now?"

The room, uncomfortable in the face of open and cordial discussion, unanimously agreed with the young Barlowe. After all, much of America had lost the ability to discuss controversial topics. Somewhere along the way, the people had bought into the lie that to disagree was to despise. Too many also could not face a differing view without breaking down. Instead of standing up for a viewpoint in the face of opposition, the new approach was to hide behind labels and imagined 'safe spaces'. Many called for others to be silenced rather than hear their point and one could only assume it was for fear of being wrong.

"Okay," Lyles said again, just as slowly as the last time. "It was the late 1800s. America was still wild out West and men lived hard and fast. A lot of 'em believed in 'natural law, tooth and claw' more than any courthouse, legal law and order. Cattle drives and shootouts and gangs of rowdies kept growing legends about cowboys and their adventures. A lotta people don't know it but newspaper reporters and pulp writers from all over the world took up stories about gunfighters and Native American conflicts. They even came all the way to America to compete with American writers to get interviews and firsthand experiences."

"They found out how bad those men on those drives smelled, too, all the days on end, working without baths, and how most picked up lice and other parasites from the trails-"

"Oh, wow, that's not disgusting at all," Andreya West cut into Tye Richter's impromptu input. "Thank you, Mr. Richter."

"You should've been along for some of the expeditions I've been on," Matwahali said.

"I honestly don't think so," West countered with a grimace, scratching her shoulder out of psychological impulse.

"Anyway, out in the wild, western frontier, lawmen were few and far between. Men tended to handle justice a little quicker whenever possible. Always tryin' to pass judgment on their own when they could get away with it, bypassing sheriffs and marshals and their deputies."

"We've all seen Gunsmoke reruns," James Wyatt said.

"And your movie, Ms. Crimson, *Georgia's Gunmaiden*," said Paul Blackwood enthusiastically.

"At least in that one the women did more than teach school or dance in the saloon," Kess Melkin lamented. "What is it with so many westerns and the whole male dominated-"

"And white dominated," Gretchen Clayborne noted.

"That's not the same," the pale Kentuckian countered.

"And I wonder why you'd feel that way," the dark beauty, Clayborne, replied.

"It was a different time," Andreya West said.

"You're defending them?" Melkin asked. "How can you? A woman with so many degrees-"

"Degrees in history," she answered quickly. "Times have changed and continue to change but we can't change history. And we shouldn't, either. You cannot make movies or anything with any integrity, at all, if you change the past to suit current preferences."

Melkin rolled her eyes and said, "Please."

"When something needs changing, we need to first remember it as it was, so we know how far we've come and so we won't find ourselves going back there. Rewriting history, which started in entertainment but has bled over into political activism, is frightfully dangerous. If we forget what came before we may repeat it," West elaborated. "Also, if anyone is allowed to rewrite the past now, someone will be allowed to rewrite the now when it is passed. We will start a cycle of useless endeavor. We will find ourselves constantly having our achievements erased because of our shortcomings for the sake of someone's future feelings."

"Thank you, Moral Majority," Kess Melkin said with a huff.

"No, she's right," Matwahali said flatly. "Just visit Egypt. Proof is all over the tombs, the pyramids. A lotta times, when a new Pharaoh rose up, he'd send his crew in to carve the history of those before him off the hieroglyphic walls. I've seen 'em with my own eyes."

The whole room turned to him, surprised he had countered Melkin.

B'Rone Matwahali nodded emphatically.

"I mean it," he doubled down. "I traveled with a Nigerian priest and relief worker for a while. He told me a saying honored by his people.

'The child of an elephant will not be a dwarf.' He also used to say, 'When the music changes, so does the dance.' He was spot on."

"What's that got to do with cowboys?" James Wyatt asked.

"It's about history," Victor Jackson answered thoughtfully.

"All I heard was somethin' about the Elephant Man dancin' to music."

"No, Mr. Wyatt," Andreya West said. "*The child of an elephant will not be a dwarf.* That means what comes from one thing will not be so far different than what started it. Hate breeds hate, anger breeds anger and so on. So, if there is war in the past and we continue doing the exact same things we will get more war. That sort of thing. It's about learning from our history."

"What about the dancing music?" James pressed.

"*When the music changes, so does the dance.* Once times change and the status quo changes and so on, the people in it change. It's about history changing, hopefully for the better, and people learning from it, gaining new ideas," West said.

"Whatever. Back to you, Gunsmoke," James said to Remy.

Chuckling, Remy Lyles said, "So, we're all on the same page. There was a lotta vigilante justice. Some of it wasn't justice, at all. Some of it was wrong and was dished out so quick that the wrong people dropped to the end of a noose or fell at the end of a barrel, innocent the whole time. Worst of all, even court appointed lawmen were guilty of rustlin' up a posse and exacting their own brand of justice a little too quick. A lot of 'em got away with doin' it. Some didn't. That's what gives birth to this story."

"I can't wait," Kess Melkin groaned.

"Hush," the young Tayla Barlowe chided. "We were quiet for you."

Several chuckles snaked around the room.

"Picture it. Bandera, Texas. Originally named for the red banderas, or flags, that signified the boundaries between hunting grounds. The place saw a lotta bloody battles between Apaches and Comanches and the Spanish Conquistadors, way early on. Later, though, it became a serious, iconic old west town, famous for the staging of massive cattle drives."

James Wyatt pretended to suddenly wake up from a loud snore.

Remy Lyles smiled, nodded and continued with, "Okay, moving on. I won't bore anyone with a history lesson of the other locations in this story. Amarillo, Texas. Deadwood, South Dakota. Silverton and Durango, Colorado. Cody, Wyoming. The story chases a handful of gunmen, bent on revenge, through these towns and a lotta others."

Kess Melkin moaned, "I hate stories that read like a road map."

James Wyatt snapped his fingers and pointed her way.

"What she said."

"In Texas, a little south of Bandera, was a tiny outpost of a town called Wet Rock," said the thin, elfish man. "The corrupt local township, run roughshod by its local sheriff, framed an innocent man for a huge cattle theft. A whole herd was rustled. Thing was, this man wasn't even a cowboy, a ramrod or part of a drive. He was a farmer, a 'sodbuster'. The man couldn't have rustled all that cattle. He didn't have enough friends to help him pull off something like that. All he had was a lotta land. Of course, that land is what the township had decided it wanted. So, they arranged the rustling of a herd, got the bankroll from the crime and laid the blame on this farmer, Rod Miller."

"Dirty sneaks," Paul Blackwood frowned.

"Crooked brigands," Matwahali growled. "Land grabs. Reminds me of the cocoa farmers' plight I fought for in my military days."

Lyles said, "The sheriff, a man named Bond Warner, badged up a few 'upstanding' townsfolk and rode out. They didn't bring him in; they hung 'im in his own barn."

For a minute or two, everyone was quiet.

Mark Gibson conferred with James Wyatt in a whisper, making sure he was staying on the scene. Then he thumbed over his shoulder toward the outer hallway.

"Gonna step out," he told James. "Too much coffee today."

James nodded with raised eyebrows.

Be careful, the look said. *Pay attention.*

"I need to tag along," Andreya West said, nodding at Tayla Barlowe. "Let me know what I miss."

Gibson gestured to the door and led her out.

"Well, nobody cared about Rod Miller, other than his wife, Eleanor, and his kids, so the town thought. For the most part, they were right. They let the woman and the kids go, thinking it would be the end of it. They didn't know Ellie would go straight to the only family she had, a distant relative she had always shunned for his chosen profession. The man was a hired gunslinger, as fast and as deadly as they came," the artist said, pretending to draw an invisible gun from his hip.

"I feel trouble saddlin' up," Tye Richter commented.

"Ouch," Gretchen Clayborne said to Richter. "Saddlin' up? Really?"

Richter chuckled and several others joined in the fun.

Lyles said, "Unlike Rod Miller, that man had allies. They all worked in the same profession. They operated as a band of quick draws, the Ghost Revolvers, mainly 'cause no one knew their real names. Ellie's black sheep relative, for one, had left his legal name behind. He had picked up a Native American name from the Choctaw during the time he spent in their territory. They called him Hanta Illi; the white folks called him Hantilli, from lack of understanding the language."

"What's that?" Tayla Barlowe asked.

"They were calling him the White Death," Lyles told them.

"Well, close enough," Andreya West said with a knowing smile.

"Now you're talkin', man," James said. "We went from Gunsmoke to movie-of-the-week."

"It's a loose translation," Remy noted with a shrug and a nod for West. "He was well loved in the Choctaw nations, though, 'cause he fought for 'em in tribal skirmishes and against white threats. His white name was lost before his legend even took off."

"One man's mercenary is another man's freedom fighter," B'Rone Matwahali said.

"I believe the term is terrorist, not mercenary," Blackwood said.

"Watch your mouth," Matwahali warned.

Remy Lyles kept going with, "Funny enough, the wife's maiden name has been lost to time, too, so people can't research and uncover the gunman's given name, even now. Check it out, though; we know what he did. He gathered the Revolvers and rode hard on Wet Rock. They took a terrible revenge on that little town, puttin' down every man involved in Miller's hangin' and then every man with power or prestige. They gathered up the women and children and put them in buggies and pointed them for Banderas with an order. Tell the story. Tell how the Ghost Revolvers brought 'justice'. And tell them that justice would ride hard on the sheriff next."

"They didn't get the sheriff?" Paul Blackwood asked.

"Naw, you know the mastermind always runs," Tye Richter said.

"He did," Lyles admitted regretfully. "He had gone to Banderas. The tale says one of the Revolver group must've sent word ahead, betrayed the band, warned the sheriff. It didn't stop them, though. They chased him right on to Banderas where he had put together another posse, including a couple of tin star deputies from there. The Revolvers burned 'em all down but Bond Warner, the sheriff, got away again. That's when they started chasing the man through all those towns I mentioned earlier."

Tayla leaned forward on the table upon her elbows, face exuding a rapt fascination.

"Along the way, Sheriff Warner kept gaining the trust and loyalty of other lawmen; gullible ones, anyway. By the time the chase circled back around and came close to Amarillo, Texas, Warner had more allies than the Revolvers. Hantilli's riders had lost a few despite their expertise. On the way toward that last, fateful town, the Revolvers split up, hoping one group or another would catch Warner. They say the team that separated from Hantilli got cut down in an ambush outside Wellington Way."

"Buggers," Paul Blackwood said.

"Hantilli rode on with his last two allies, one of 'em only an informant from back in Banderas and not even a gunfighter. Then, in the light of a campfire just five miles from Amarillo, the last of the Revolvers stood down a charge of ten deputized gunmen. They were the last of the sheriff's compatriots. Hantilli's 'informant', it's said, slipped away into the darkness just before the fight...and disappeared."

"Benedict Arnold Cowpoke," James Wyatt said.

"Good enough for story time, since we don't know his name, either," Lyles said. "The keynote point is that the last man standing was Hantilli. He killed Bond Warner that night, in that gunfight. But his urge for revenge and his own 'justice' had been driving him and he wasn't ready to stop. He turned his attention to the informant he suspected was a traitor. That night, he cursed the man in the dark, by the firelight. He covered his face in ashes, masking it to resemble a skull, and laid down an oath."

"Of course he did," Jenkins said with mock severity. "What would a firelight cursing be without a solid oath and macabre face painting?"

Gretchen giggled, reached back and popped his arm playfully.

"Hush," she said, motioning for him to be quiet.

"Indeed," Jenkins allowed. "I will take my leave. I need to gather a few things, put a few things away. If it is acceptable, Mr. Wyatt, I will take Ms. Makai and Chef Swartzovski with me on my quest."

"Sure, sure," James said. "But nobody wanders alone and you don't wander far...again."

The narrative paused for a time while Jenkins and his team cleared the table of the finished dishes, tended to refills and the like. Once they disappeared, some small talk ran about the room before being reigned in so that Rembrandt Lyles could continue.

"C'mon, Remy," James Wyatt said finally. "Get back on your horse and finish this."

"Back on your horse," Tye Richter said, chuckling. "I like that."

Lyles nodded, cleared his throat and actually got to his feet for the rest of the tale. He hunched over a bit and pointed across the room to no one, playing the part of the Ghost Revolver as he imagined him.

"I know what you did! Run, little man! Run as far and as fast as you can! Even when I'm a ghost I'll be hunting you and one day you'll see these revolvers and you'll know it's your time!" Lyles shouted, trying to deepen his voice.

He shook his imaginary judges, or revolvers, in the air.

"And my work won't never stop! As long as I breathe and, after that, as long as I can pass my 'judges' on to other men, my work will never stop!"

No one had time to offer a review of his performance. B'Rone Matwahali asked a question before anyone could blink, clearly enthused.

"So what happened to this guy, the Death Man?"

"No one knows, for sure. Legend says he kept on dealin' out his own brand of 'justice' for years, takin' up this cause or that one," Remy said and shrugged. "Legend also claims those guns kept appearing long after the man called Hantilli was dead, handing out vengeance in a cloud of smoke and a thunderclap, each time in the hands of a skull faced apparition. There's great debate between enthusiasts as to whether the successor Ghost Revolvers are people chosen to take up the guns or if they're ghosts of the original band."

Many in the room noted how well the tale had captured the mood.

"All that scores your fish 'n' chips," Paul Blackwood mused, "until you remember this yank is the inspiration for a very real killer for hire...and some of us are already dead."

"The Revolver, whoever it is-"

"Whomever," Andreya West corrected, striding back into the room.

Melkin rolled her eyes and grumbled.

"Whomever," Lyles stood corrected, "carries those shining 'judges', only goes after the guilty. Trying to bring justice to unjust situations. I've done a lot of research and it proves that the latest run of Revolver retribution is one of the most righteous, at least, where vigilantism is concerned..."

"And the murders up here this weekend?" Victor Jackson asked.

"Not to mention the target on my back," Johanna Crimson said.

"That's easy," Lyles chimed almost pleasantly. "Nobody's *all* good or *all* bad. Seems like some of us are finding our sins catching up to us this weekend, whatever they are; we're paying the piper for the dance."

"Oh, nice, that is," Blackwood murmured.

"Poppycock," Maureen Li growled.

"By the way, it's our fault we're gettin' killed," Melkin mocked, a venomous look tossed at the man in the Voltron shirt. "Whatever."

Then, finally, the room silenced.

He reached out with both hands, pretending to hold the ghostly revolvers. He imagined shooting one with his right hand and let the invisible pistol recoil, lifting his arm upward.

That is exactly when a thunderclap boomed someplace outside the dining hall. Not outside the building, however. Upstairs. Inside.

Everyone jumped, startled, and several let out a shocked cry.

James Wyatt shouted for everyone to get down, his gun in his hand, as he rushed a corridor doorway. He put himself in that opening, watching the hall and the room at the same time.

"What happened?" Remy Lyles gasped.

"Gunfire! Upstairs!" James Wyatt roared. "Stay down! Everybody!"

Lyles fell to a crouch, hand over his heart.

"Thank goodness...I thought my finger had killed somebody..."

The North Carolina State Bureau of Investigation's Agent Sarah Priest pulled off a nitrile glove. After digging wads of lead from Grip Bridger's corpse, wiping down the wounds and covering him, she had scarcely cleaned the blade of her knife when her accomplice spoke,

"Is he..." the resort's director, Cassandra Clark, asked, still facing the other way.

Sarah said, "Yes, Cassie. He's covered."

Clark turned and put her hands on her shapely hips.

"Is it the same with him?"

"Yes," Priest answered. "Old style bullets. Three."

"Poor Grip," Clark said.

"Yeah," Sarah Priest said with a deep sadness, turning to leave with the other woman.

That is the very moment thunder boomed someplace inside the resort. Both women jolted violently. Sarah Priest's .40 Caliber leaped to her grasp so quickly that Clark almost did not catch the movement. Sarah grabbed Clark by the shoulder, spun her about, and pushed her back into the cooler.

"What was-"

"Gunshots!" Priest railed. "Stay here! Turn out the light and hide!"

The agent tried to make her exit but Clark grabbed onto her thin, tight top. It nearly tore off, several stitches popping loudly.

"Wait! I can't stay here! These are dead people!"

"They're already dead, Cass! Worry about the living!"

And Priest disappeared into the heat.

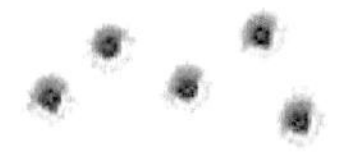

If he had not already been finished in the artist's room, the gunshots would have wrapped up the search for him. At the very first boom, Mick Priest snatched a Colt from its sheath. He crossed his wrists and leveled the 10mm and the flashlight together then rushed down the hallway, searching, following the sound.

The second boom resonated from someplace below, someplace on the Second Floor, and it spurred Priest into a breakneck run. He soared onto the stairway almost in flight.

Footfalls already thumped from the Second Floor hallway. Priest heard them from the stairwell. Sharp voices carried dire warnings between two people. He already recognized the vocal combatants by voice.

"Okay, Agent!" Mark Gibson shouted. "Listen!"

"*Que pasa contigo?*" she shouted at him. "What're you doing? *Es estas demente?*"

"I don't speak Spanish!"

When he spilled onto the landing, Mick Priest's flashlight scattered the darkness in a brilliant sweep. Both Gibson and Sarah Priest whipped about to see Mick Priest bound onto their floor then turned on each other again.

"What were you doing?" she demanded.

"I'm tryin' to tell ya," Gibson said.

"What's going on?" Mick asked when he reached them.

"I shot the Ghost Revolver," Gibson said.

On the Ground Floor, in the dining area, James Wyatt flipped on his 'responsible adult' switch. He ordered everyone to crouch in a single corner of the room, the southeast corner, where he could watch over them and observe each line of sight to all of the room's doors. James held his Sig Sauer at the ready and his flashlight, too.

"I got twelve and three," Remy Lyles informed James Wyatt.

He meant he would watch two doors, one on the north side of the room and one on the east. It may have seemed he had seen military or police service. The truth was that he had learned it from video games.

"Nine and six," Wyatt confirmed his own responsibility. He would watch the south and west...with real life experience.

Johanna Crimson said, "What about Gibson? He was probably-"

"He's a pro," James Wyatt calmed. "Don't worry about him."

"Him? What about us?" Kess Melkin barked.

James shouted, "Gibson, Mick 'n' Sarah are out doin' their best! That leaves me with ya'll to do mine! Now, stay calm!"

"That's okay! You got this!" Remy Lyles shouted.

"Now the man's cheerleading," James muttered. Then, "Everybody, be quiet and stay still. You're fine as long as you maintain your positions. Let me watch the doors and don't make me second guess any movements. If you're still and quiet I won't be distracted."

"Yeah, and he won't accidentally shoot you."

"Remy," James growled, "that's not helping."

Cassandra Clark broke from the Kitchen door to the Dining Hall only to freeze in her steps. She stared, eyes wide and mouth agape, at the open bore of James Wyatt's Sig Sauer.

"Lady," James warned in a low rumble, "that ain't wise."

Then he lowered the gun.

"What were those shots?" she asked. "Where did they come from? Was it the killer? Where's my staff?"

"Ms. Clark, hush," James said. "One at a time, okay?"

"To answer her question, the members of staff are here," Jenkins answered.

The man appeared abruptly, leading his group in a mass crouch, back through the Kitchen door. Each seemed very skittish, looking about in every direction.

James slowly lowered his cannon, yet again. He locked his jaw against the strain of overriding his reflexes.

The returning crew had nearly caught a few warning rounds.

"Where were you?" Cassandra Clark snapped.

"Daft berries," Paul Blackwood barked. "Wanderin' around, tryin' to get shot...you do know our protectors are American, right? Guns? Bullets? Friendly fire? Any o' that ring some bells?"

Jenkins rocked forward on his toes dramatically then fell back to his heels, his hands clasped behind his back.

"Hiding," he said. "We've been hiding. Gunshots inspire that in the unarmed. And yes, Mr. Blackwood, we're aware of all the nationalities here this weekend. As for Americans, I am one."

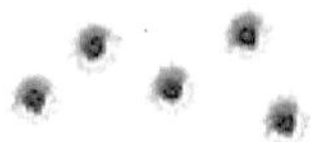

Sarah and I stood at equal distances away from Gibson.

"You wanna repeat that?" I asked as Sarah angrily holstered her weapon. I was not so quick to tuck my Colt away from sight.

Gibson sighed and reluctantly holstered his Sig.

"Our friend, the Revolver," he said. "I was shootin' him...sorta."

He kicked a pile of black garb with a booted foot and a hooded, polyarmor mask rolled free of it. The mask, a hole opened right between the lensed eye holes, matched the torso of the black sweatshirt lying under it. The shirt had several holes, however.

A wooden hangar dipped to one side where it had been splintered in Gibson's spattering of rounds. The rounds had clearly murdered a hangar of clothing and a mask suspended to resemble the killer. It had been draped from Resort Director Cassandra Clark's room door. It had been shot down into a lump on the floor.

"*Eres estúpido o algo?*" Sarah shouted, her Spanish banner unfurled.

"Hey, hey," Gibson calmed, his eyebrows sewn close together.

"I could've shot you! *Tonto!*"

"Hey, I'm sorry, but I was doin' my best to-"

"What, kill a bystander?" Sarah shouted. "Look at the strafing!"

He and I both glanced by reflex at the door and wall behind the clump of clothing. There were at least ten craters in the structures where his bullets had either passed through the decoy or had missed it.

"I ain't used to shootin' it out with empty shirts," he growled. "Besides, ain't everybody in the Dining Hall where they were supposed to stay while-"

"Like you?" Sarah snapped.

"I had to use the boys' room, lady. I heard somethin' on the stairwell. I came out, saw a cloud of black and it was gone. I trotted up the stairs and saw it down here, in the hallway, and I recognized the costume. I popped him. Well...them. The clothes."

"You see well enough to hit it from the stairwell in this dim light but you couldn't see it was a flat hangar wearing clothes?"

Sarah was on target about the low lights. The emergency lighting was all there was in the corridors with the room doors closed. The rooms may have been getting sun but the hallways did not.

"Instinct," he said and huffed. "Been doin' this a long time."

"Hold it," I suggested lowly, staving off any more back and forth. "What's done is done. I'll walk the hall, Sarah, if you want to go back to everybody. They may need to see that badge in order to calm down."

She ground her teeth then, through a locked jaw, said, "Okay."

"I'll go back with you, Agent Priest," Gibson said. "I wanna go check on Johanna with my own blue eyes."

"I figured you'd want a chance at dropping this perp," I countered.

"Ain't nobody, not even a ghost, hanging around after I dumped a whole magazine down the hallway. Man's gone, Priest."

I gestured Sarah over and whispered in her ear.

Gibson watched us suspiciously but I did not care. Sarah had to know about the wooden chest and the hunter's nest and I did not want Gibson to have that same bit of information. Not until I knew more. I also told Sarah to tell James.

She took the moment to inform me of the lipstick on Bridger's lips, as she and Cassandra Clark had discovered in our morgue. Lipstick not unlike the shade worn by Kess Melkin, not unlike one of the shades I had found in Richard Porter's room. It was, according to Clark, not a shade worn by Bridger's girlfriend, Gretchen Clayborne.

"You can come with me," Sarah then informed Gibson. "But, if you pull that gun between here and there, I'll shoot you myself."

Sarah strode away with the exchange of information and the intent of bringing our friend James into the loop. Gibson pursued her down the hall, mumbling irritably.

He was dead wrong on ghosts not hanging around, however. I had realized something or someone was present while Gibson was still talking; for me, the temperature had plummeted. The hair on the back of my neck rose in alert. For lack of a better phrase, the silence was louder than before.

Then I saw Grip Bridger.

Standing in the Security Chief's room door to the hallway, a specter stared back at me with empty, filmy eyes. The dead face of Falgrip Bridger watched me. He was a blur, his appearance faint, somewhat diaphanous. There but not there. Present but someplace else.

In the fleeting moment I looked away, making sure I was indeed alone with him, the apparition faded. Another glance both ways down the hall told me Grip was already gone. I hoped he might still be lingering, however.

I touched my Cross and prayed to the Lord Jesus.

Priest crept down the corridor, searching, looking anew for Grip Bridger. The silence hovered about him, followed along like a partner, an understudy. It watched him, as if learning, studying him. It remained invisible, curious and persistent. Other than that, Priest was alone.

As alone as the man, Mick Priest, could be.

Bridger, of course, had faded momentarily.

It drew Priest down the corridor. He stalked the dark hall, stealth shielding him like a trusty cloak. Senses on high alert, he broke the supernatural silence; all the normal, ambient sounds seemed to have been stolen away from the corridor but Priest would not abide the resonance of nothingness, the ballad of a tomb.

"Bridger," he quietly called. "Grip Bridger, talk to me."

His voice sounded flat, contained. No echo pursued the initial sound. His nerves danced on the end of a string. Though he got no answer to his calls, he did not believe he was alone.

And he was a man who would know.

The thought had taken strong root in his mind when a creaky hinge announced itself. Chills ran Priest's body. The dead man's room door opened gradually, slowly, the hinge grinding. It was not sunlight that spilled from the chamber but an oddly dim, blue glow.

Priest opened his mouth to speak but found his breath short, his voice tight, strained.

A figure materialized suddenly, a hazy silhouette carved out of the light. The form was leaving that hallway, however, entering the room and escaping Priest once more. Then, just as startlingly, the door slammed shut, extinguishing the light from inside. Like a candle, it went out, blown into oblivion by a nonexistent wind.

"Priest..." Grip Bridger called distantly, his disembodied voice born on the shadows.

Mick Priest locked his jaw. He pressed onward, undaunted. He reached the door in the corridor and, with a hasty breath, stepped through it. He broke into the bedchamber, expecting the glaring sunlight that should have been more than prevalent in the room. However, he was forced to blink rapidly, trying to regain his sight. The room draped him with nightshade instantly; he had stepped not only into a different place but a different time, too, it seemed.

He lit and spun the flashlight about, its silvery white searing the darkness and evaporating it. That's when the beam fell upon the gray face of the dead Security Chief, Falgrip 'Grip' Bridger.

Priest shivered despite his attempt to hold himself rigid.

"Grip?"

"Ironic," Bridger said, his voice echoing distantly, carrying the weight of a thousand regrets. "I was supposed to protect everyone..."

"It's not your fault, Grip."

The flat, vacant eyes focused on nothing in particular.

"I couldn't even protect myself..."

The specter looked at his hands abruptly as if unable to believe they were his own. A bit of the light from the flashlight permeated them, dissipated them, and breached the rest of his form, too, filtering through him in places.

"I'm dead," he said sadly, his voice an unearthly, solemn lament.

"Yes, and I'm sorry."

What else is there to say to that? Mick Priest wondered.

"I was there but I barely remember it. The moment."

He pointed toward the closed door.

Mick Priest turned about and the night changed.

Grip Bridger had just told Kess Melkin to go back to her room. Mick could see it in a misty, foggy hour lost to their past.

Then Bridger heard it. A fluttering wing, the whipping of a sail...something. He stopped and whirled about, staring into the garden and the shadows playing there. His right hand eased back to his gun, pushing the coat out of the way. He was alone in the moment.

B'Rone Matwahali had just taken Melkin up the stairs. Bridger promised to see Paul Blackwood back upstairs as soon as he found him; the baker was wandering around alone. But the sound...

Bridger pulled his gun as he stepped out into the night and into the flower garden. With it leveled out before him, he followed it like a compass needle, the bore always leading the way. It pulled him in and out of the flora of the garden as he searched.

The sound he had heard was not a night sound. A nature sound. A common sound for the resort. It sounded a lot like some kind of material whipping in the wind. A flag, blowing in the wind?

It sounded that way still as he heard it again, right behind him.

A long, black coat cloaked the individual who slipped close behind the young specialist, the fabric swishing against itself. A big, silver revolver slipped free of the black folds and the shadows.

Grip turned around with a jerk, gun hand extended. Of course, he never expected to find someone so close, someone in striking distance. He had already begun to squeeze the trigger on the Glock when the skull faced mystery lunged forward. Nimbly, gracefully, the assassin grabbed onto the Glock's slide and jammed it backward, kicking a round out of the chamber. In the same motion, the strong hand rolled the weapon upward and back and twisted it from Grip's hold.

The slide slammed back to readiness, catching the meat of the killer's gloved hand between the thumb and forefinger. The Glock fell end over end to the ground, landing near the bullet that had been ejected.

Bridger, in his own reflex, countered by grabbing the ghost's gun, the shining revolver. The hammer fell as the Ghost Revolver pulled the trigger but Grip Bridger's little finger lodged under the hammer. It failed to fire and Bridger snatched the pistol away from the shadow.

The shadow pressed the attack without the gun, however.

A vicious kick caught Grip Bridger in the gut and he had not even doubled over before a wicked punch caught him alongside his head. He tried to bring his hands up to shield himself only to be grabbed by the wrist and rolled over, through the air, to his back. The wind gushed from his lungs and he gasped for air as the ghost wrenched the revolver from his hand.

Something inside him told him his swollen pride would get him killed. He could not relent, nevertheless. Though he knew he should call out, bring others into the fray, he opted for determined stealth. His inner, disgruntled police officer, still striving to prove himself, would have no help. He would bring down the international killer on his own, reclaim his status and his honor, or he would die trying.

Of course, no one ever *really* believed they would die trying something.

The Ghost Revolver rolled back the hammer again and snapped the trigger. The gun misfired. It offered a weak puff of smoke, the only admission of its impotent aggression.

Bridger desperately raged to his feet and lashed out in retaliation, kicking at the killer's gun hand. His foot landed a solid blow and the glinting revolver flew free, lost to the rose bushes. He followed up with a right cross that the killer ducked. He threw a left jab that grazed the killer's mask. The shooter spun around, however, rolling with the momentum. Bridger surged on the inside with renewed confidence and immediately lunged for another strike.

The ghost ducked his arm so easily that his thrust looked apish and slow. The shooter responded with four strikes to the man's torso, none of which Bridger could block or parry. He staggered in a drunken charge and tried a floundering, off balance kick.

The Ghost Revolver caught his leg at the ankle, however, and dropped to the ground in a spin, wringing the leg around at the knee. Even as Bridger shouted a pained curse, the killer kicked outward, driving a boot into his supporting ankle. It did not break but it gave way and dropped Bridger to his back, both legs tormented.

Raindrops started to pelt them as the mist gave way to real precipitation. Lightning arced again between the ominous clouds. Looking up at that scary sky, half blind, Bridger suffered his first flush of real fear. He knew he could die in the fight. He did not suspect. He did not consider. He did not wonder. He knew he could die right there.

The killer drew the second silver revolver from the shadows worn like a death shroud and thumbed back the hammer. Grip was on his way to his feet in a panicked shamble when the lightning arced across the black sky and thunder shook the earth with a mighty eruption.

With the thunder came the pain. Bridger fell again to his back, the breath knocked from him, his strength stolen, his body failing him.

Blinking in the rain, he saw plumes of smoke clouding the killer's pistol hand in ghostly, clinging tendrils. The gun had fired anonymously, its voice masked in the thunder.

Then the Ghost Revolver holstered the pistol and walked away in the direction of the lost weapons.

Bridger grimaced, his voice caught in his throat. He was not finished, however. He swallowed down the fear, the shock and the pain, struggled to his feet and held what he thought might be his last breath. He clenched both hands over the bullet wound and staggered after the shooter.

Mick Priest shivered violently, watching the events unfold from the sidelines, unable to help, unable to move. He felt the cold rain, the palpable fear and the raw, brutal pain inside Grip Bridger.

Still, all he could do was watch...and mourn.

Falgrip Bridger made an incredible, brave attempt, though he never caught sight of the shooter again. He followed the elusive, phantom shadow but could not catch up to it. After a few moments, thunder bellowed again. It was the thunder held by the killer's hand. Bridger staggered, shot more than once from behind.

It was more than he could survive. Bridger collapsed in the rain, dropping face down in the mulch. Then the shadow grabbed him and rolled him into a bush.

Mick Priest jolted back to awareness. It was hot and bright, daytime again, in the staff room. He tensed his jaw against the emotional surge within himself.

"Go rest, Grip. Well done."

The dead man had revealed an incredibly important clue to the identity of the killer, the Ghost Revolver. All Priest had to do was find the guest present with a slide bite on one hand, the place where the Glock's mechanism had pinched the meat of the dominant hand.

Then Mick Priest thanked the Lord Jesus Christ and Almighty God for the gift of the vision and divine direction. He initiated the rest of the search he had planned for that floor with a new zeal, finding some progress in the gift of knowledge from God. He knew it was more than time for due diligence in searching Floor Two, the staff floor.

It was dark in the open corridor. Floor Two allowed no real light in the hallway with the rooms closed. Only the dim emergency lighting burned. The figure rushing its shadows checked room after room, entering each and lingering, then evacuating soundlessly again.

The darkness watched the shadow, a part of itself.

The figure wore all black, like a dead thing wrapped in a nightmare. The Revolver crept patiently, teeth clenched behind a skull mask, the shadow far from reckless. Quiet, controlled. Ghostly...the word of choice.

Detective Mick Priest, the Ghost Revolver thought bitterly. *Hot on my heels. That's bad enough. But he took the gear. The gear! The powder, the balls, the reloads, the box! I should've stayed when I saw him drop the box...and dropped him.*

Then the phantom stopped at the doorway through which Priest had last passed.

No. That's not the way. Only for the guilty.

The ghost stared at the closed door in an uncanny silence. Silence and an unusual feeling. Admiration.

Only the guilty. Not the Priest.

CHAPTER TWELVE

Kesley Melkin **was** among the most vocal of the congregants. None of them were sitting; all were standing on their feet, most offering unnecessary opinions and suspicions, many with great fervor. Melkin lead a verbal rebellion, thick with demands and ultimatums.

Agent Sarah Priest had just arrived on the ground floor, whispering her updates to James Wyatt, when the usual conflict took over the raucous debate.

We need to get off the mountain. There's no way out! There's a killer here; we would be better off running around outside! We should lock ourselves in our rooms! At least, if we're alone, we can trust ourselves!

All the voices bled together, the fluid sounds muddied by all the soils of argument and perspective.

A frustrated Tayla Barlowe, holding a crying child newly awakened and frightened by the din, shouted at the crowd. They heard none of it. She turned and stalked from the room, carrying her little one.

"Please, people!" Sarah Priest shouted. "Hold it down! One at a time!"

She nodded to James Wyatt and pointed at Barlowe. James immediately gave chase.

He was not alone. Andreya West and Johanna Crimson, of all people, followed the young mother, as well. That carried Mark Gibson out into the hallway, too. Cassandra Clark gave Jenkins the eye and sent him to aid the restroom expedition even as Rembrandt Lyles joined the excursion, for reasons unannounced and unrevealed.

Sarah Priest stood within the group and raised her hands. In front of her rallied Cassandra Clark, Gretchen Clayborne, Paul Blackwood, Maureen Li and Victor Jackson. Behind her stood Kess Melkin, B'Rone Matwahali, Tye Richter, Helena Makai, and Avid Swartzovski.

"Listen," she calmed. "All of us-"

"No! You listen!" Kess Melkin yelled, grabbing her arm.

Sarah rolled her arm out of the woman's hand instantly, reflex arcing voltage through her musculature. Before anyone could even speak, Priest swept about and nailed the woman with an inverted fist, driving the knuckles upward into her solar plexus. The writer from Kentucky toppled backward onto her bottom, gasping, the breath knocked cleanly from her.

"Stay down," Sarah warned flatly, finger pointed, her other hand on her gun. "My one and only warning."

B'Rone Matwahali crouched with Melkin, checking the woman and her labored breathing.

"Are you crazy?" he demanded.

"We're at odds with a murderer," Sarah Priest growled. "You don't get physical with me unless you're ready to face the consequences."

"Oh, no, I wasn't talkin' to you," he countered, shaking his head and pointing at Sarah. Then, looking at Melkin, he said, "I meant Kess; are you crazy? Manhandling a state cop? What's wrong with you?"

Fighting some air back into her lungs was difficult but she managed.

"I'm...worried!" she choked. "I want...answers!"

Sarah said, "Keep your hands to yourself."

"You knocked the...breath...outta me!" Melkin said.

"Must run in the family," Blackwood said. "Her ol' man did the same to me already."

"Back to the point," Sarah Priest growled, eyeballing Blackwood, "we all want answers. We won't get them tonight. Be patient. It's hard, I know, but there's no other option. Now, calm down...everyone."

She looked around at their faces, pondering the next move. It was clear that the mob mentality was becoming unstable, divisive. For the first time, she wondered if they would all be better off locking themselves away from each other. Abandoning the large crowd. Isolating. Someone had said it already in the ocean of voices.

We should lock ourselves in our rooms! At least, if we're alone, we can trust ourselves!

Maybe that voice was right.

"Here's our new plan," she announced. "We spend the rest of this afternoon together, whether here or not. We have our dinner time together. Then we split up tonight. Lock ourselves in our individual chambers. The best of both ideas; together, keeping an eye on each other, until time for sleep. Then we can separate, securing ourselves away from each other."

"Just what do you-"

"She's not finished," Clark interrupted Maureen Li.

Priest nodded at Clark.

"Thank you. My husband and I, with James Wyatt and Marcus Gibson, will make patrols, keeping watch."

"Fat lotta good it is, too," Blackwood balked, visibly discontent.

"You ain't stopped anything, yet," Melkin agreed.

"Kess," Matwahali warned lowly.

"Grip was armed, too," Gretchen said. "He...died on patrol."

"He died doin' what he believed in," Tye said softly.

"Sure, that makes it all better," the chef, Swartzovski, mumbled.

"The man gave his life trying to keep others safe," Victor Jackson said. "He died a protector. That matters. It means something."

"Means he died."

"Avid, hush," Cassandra Clark said, calling down the chef. "Mr. Jackson is right. And Agent Priest is right, too. We don't have many options. The question is," she trailed, lifting her arms in a shrug, "where would you like to spend the rest of the afternoon? Since lunch was late, we'll push back dinner a bit later than usual."

Gretchen Clayborne slammed her hand down on the table in front of her. Her face drew up into a grimace. Then the tears broke free, dammed no longer behind eyelashes and trembling eyelids.

"Lunch! Dinner! Afternoon plans!" she railed. "How dare you? Any of you, especially you, Cassie? People are dead! Grip is dead!"

The young woman bolted from the room just as James Wyatt and a few others returned.

"Gretchen!" Clark shouted.

"Where is Ms. Clayborne going?" Jenkins asked, entering the room.

"Never mind," Sarah Priest told him. Then, to James, she said, "Take roll. Keep everyone here. I'll get Clayborne back."

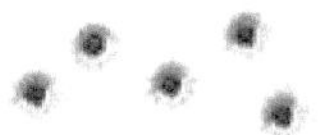

The young pilot leaned her damp forehead against a wall. Sweat trickled from her hairline at her temples, glistening against her very dark, brown skin. She watched the open door to the outside world with her peripheral vision, poised in the corridor nearest the gardens. The place where Grip Bridger had always stolen single flowers for her.

The place where he had died.

She locked her jaw against a torrential storm of emotion. A storm of more than one emotion; love was not all she wrestled for control. There was love, of course, between the two. But, for the lovely pilot, there was anger.

What were you doing? she demanded silently of a dead man. *Why were you so careless? You were a professional!*

There was sadness. Misery. Mourning.

Now, we'll never see each other again...oh, Grip...

There was confusion and uncertainty.

Why did you leave me like this?

Most distressing of all, however, there was guilt. Guilt over the strength she still clutched inside her, the will to continue without him. The ability to already see beyond the pain and the dark horizons of loss. Guilt over her own concrete constitution.

Why am I so settled? she interrogated herself. *Why am I not completely broken? What's wrong with me?*

She slid herself down the wall and sat down at its base. All the questions swirled about in her mind, time and again, yearning for answers she did not have.

To add to the tumult within her, thoughts of the powerful frame of the formidable Jenkins rushed her mind, too. How it would be to let him hold her, comfort her. To lean into his broad chest, to rest in his strong arms...and more guilt came along with the musing.

I did love you, Grip, she swore with unspoken assurance. *But...*

"It's a terrible thing, losing someone to violence," Agent Sarah Priest said. Her stroll brought her close to the garden doors and she added, "I know it hurts, Gretchen, and I'm sorry."

Gretchen Clayborne got to her feet, wiping her eyes. She adjusted her garb a little, composed herself and met Priest where she stood.

"I'm sorry I ran. The way I blew up. The things I said."

"Don't punish yourself over it. You're dealing with something no one should have to deal with. It can't be easy in any sense of the word."

"No, it's not. Not at all."

Several mockingbirds screeched outside, sharing the gossip overhead and out of sight. Sarah did not even offer a glance. An owl, roosting someplace out there and watching on with yellow, saucer eyes, asked for whom the women lamented. She issued no reply to that nosy fowl, either.

"I'll be praying for you," Sarah said. "For your peace. Comfort. For your part, you should go easy on yourself. These events trigger a lot of emotions and they don't always make sense. Be patient with yourself. Remember, you're human. Give yourself time to grieve, your own way."

Clayborne was quiet, her face downcast.

"Sometimes I wish I had faith in something, some way of knowing there's more to life than this, that there's hope..."

"You don't have that? A belief?"

"I do...I mean...it's hard to describe," the pilot said. "It's not a faith, exactly. Not like you seem to have. I have this...idea, this suspicion."

"Oh?"

The pilot took a deep breath before speaking, gesturing about nervously as she began.

"I think it's kinda obvious there's a Creator. It stands to reason, since there's a creation. I can't grasp a 'something spawned out of nothing' mentality. All the scientists who spout that are ignoring...well, science. It violates the very laws of science, you know? The first law of science is that for scientific theory to be scientific fact, we have to be able to prove it and we have to be able to repeat it. No one has ever, ever, witnessed something coming from nothing. I mean-"

"Gretchen, breathe," Sarah encouraged, pausing her. She could tell the young woman was distraught, hiding from the feelings, masking them with distraction. "You don't have to-"

"No, no, it helps," Clayborne said, gesturing for Sarah to continue the discussion with a rolling hand.

"Okay, so, at the very least, you believe in Intelligent Design. There is a Creator behind the laws of science, physics, biology and all that."

"Yeah," Clayborne said. "I don't see any other viable belief options. Science itself, with all we understand, defies the theories of random creation from nothing."

Sarah Priest nodded.

Clayborne said, "My ex...my ex before Grip was in debate in college and was pre-med. He used to get me to help him research Intelligent Design so he could debate other groups about it. It worked against him since, the more we looked into it and the other options, the more I.D. made sense to me."

"Searching for the truth is how we make discoveries. You've already discovered that man doesn't have a fraction of the answers. I mean, it's crazy arrogant for men to say 'there is no God' when, if we're honest, there's more out there that we don't know than there is that we do know. Acknowledging that, how can man say God does not exist, particularly in the realm of what we don't know?"

"I think that's the position that got me kicked out of my ex's life."

"Sad. For him. That he couldn't allow you to think."

"Yep. Makes it look a lot like he was afraid his supposed truth was wrong. He sure didn't like it when I pointed that out, either."

"I'm sure. Deep inside, you suspect there's a Creator, a God. Greater Faith will come as you continue to search and learn. Just don't stop looking. He's there, Gretchen. Waiting for you. Waiting for all of us."

The young lady remained silent for a moment.

"Gretchen?"

"Grip's really dead," she said lowly.

Then she fell into Sarah Priest's arms and began to weep.

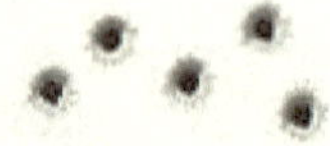

It was not long before the staff and the guests were all back in the Dining Hall, all present with the exception of Mick Priest. Almost unanimously it was decided that the gym and the pool called to them. They would spend the remainder of the day and a portion of the evening in that pool and in that gym then return for a late dinner. After that, all would turn in for the night, locked in their rooms, alone and safe...or as safe as they could be.

Sarah Priest sent James Wyatt to find her husband, Mick, and share the plans. She would oversee the expedition. When James made it out to the gym, she would accompany the staff back to the main house for dinner preparations.

The plans were set.

But the best laid plans of mice and men...

Mick Priest knocked on the door slowly, solidly. Grip Bridger was not likely to reappear but the detective still tried rapping on his room door one more time. The searches of rooms on Floor Two had been over for some time but he stood in the young man's doorway, door open and in his hand. Priest waited, quiet and still, wishing there would be more. With nagging chagrin, though, he finally eased the door closed.

He had discovered nothing. On the entire floor. Nothing more than on any other floor. Less than he had on others, to be realistic.

Funny, he thought to himself. *Grip isn't still here but I could've sworn I wasn't alone on this floor. If I had hair it would be standing up.*

Priest wrote it off as the presence of his friend, James Wyatt, having left a lingering sensation. James had just come upstairs to tell him about their planned exodus back to the gym and the pool then left him, again.

Priest gave a mental shrug. Whatever the case, he panned his light down the corridor and reluctantly started for the stairway.

Cutting through the inky shadow with his light, Mick Priest made haste for the Ground Floor. The man did not start where the stairwell landed, however. He wandered the main hall first, shining his light this way and that, until he reached the other end of the corridor. He then started at the northern end of the building with the informal foyer.

The foyer, a greeting lobby of sorts, held post just inside the resort's front doors. Elaborate décor welcomed all who entered with black and white marble construction, red velvet window treatments and cherry wood doors. The elevator grounded itself there, when working, and lifted to the other floors.

A quite expansive tack and feed room, connected by two separate doors with wrought iron hardware, reached across the building just as the first lobby did. Both stretched across the structure's floor plan from one stall aisle to the other.

The kitchen, running lengthwise with the structure, bordered another room on the east. That room, the same size as the kitchen, was the staff Dining Room. Priest would have greeted the staff members he passed in his trek, had there been any. Floor One was abandoned, however.

South of those rooms stood the main Dining Hall, centralized in the structure. In all its elegance, it opened to the corridors on both sides of it and the horse stalls beyond them.

The two rooms following the hall were the high tech conference room and convention center room, filled with communications equipment and computer interfaces and big screen monitors. Some of the most comfortable, yet formal, seating available filled those two rooms. Comfort while sitting was all the tech locations had left to offer with no power available.

The very last room worked as another gathering place, a focal point and a huge lobby. Marble, torches, tapestries and paintings sang of its grandeur and two spiraling staircases, in a choral echo of the selfsame song, lifted from its floor in arcs on each side. They intersected into a landing that opened onto Floor Two and continued to the other floors.

Sadly, none of the ground level rooms brought any revelation.

With a deep breath and a shake of his shaven head, the detective decided to walk the aisles on the eastern and western sides of the central room formation. Before going too far, he prayed as he always did; for guidance, for insight, and for a revelation. Then, taking a bit of a respite in the peaceful animal housing, he wandered the two corridors. He took his time, speaking to the horses and offering scratches to the equines interested in receiving them.

He stopped at the elevator end of the floor, talking to an Appaloosa mare about the case. A clap of thunder boomed outside. The mare jolted, dancing sideways, and knocked over one of the feed buckets propped atop her gate. The bucket toppled onto the stepping stone aisle, bounced once and rolled away from Priest.

Left in its wake, a pack of cigarettes lay on the stones.

Mick Priest thanked Jesus Christ for answering prayers.

The detective rushed to the pack and reached down in one swift motion, grabbing for them...

...and everything went black. The emergency lighting, extinguished in a split second, left Priest on his own. He groped about for the invisible pack but found nothing.

"What're you gripin' about, Kentucky?" a man's voice asked irritably. He sounded as though he were far away, under ground or within a box. "They're free."

Priest snapped to his left. Rick Porter held those cigarettes out toward Kess Melkin. An odd, dim glow lit him and the Kentucky writer where they stood.

Melkin answered, her voice distorted, as if underwater.

"They smell funny. I need a smoke but not that bad."

"I can't smell anything," his voice responded. "You'll wish you'd had one once tomorrow morning rolls around. That director's got eyes in the back of her head and she's got that stormtrooper security guard. You ain't likely to find any others here without getting caught."

"We'll see. Security-stiff Bridger is still a man. I bet I could get him to get me some hisself," she said. "Besides, Andreya might watch my back. I'll get her to start lookin' and we know nobody could tell her no."

She faded into the ether as she walked away from him, swishing this way and that. He stared lewdly after her, shook a cigarette from the end of the pack and lipped it. Fishing for a lighter, he spoke again, careful to hang onto the cigarette with his mouth.

"Hey," he said loudly, "when you get desperate enough for one, I'll have a couple saved for ya! Providin' ya don't tell the bookworm about these! Our little secret, Kentucky, you, me 'n' Mobley!"

He struck a light as the glow began to fade...

...and Mick Priest opened his eyes. In his hands were the cigarettes.

He smelled something odd, too.

"Pain liniment," he whispered. "Not exactly the cologne of champions, Porter. But I know you had interactions with Melkin, now, along with your history with Mobley. Considering I already had questions about her and she's the one of the three of you still alive..."

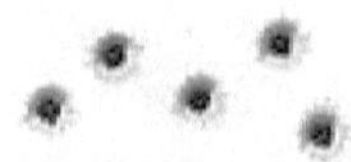

Suspicion walks her own path. Shaped by influence and lead by experience, she is oft the companion of detectives and researchers and scholars, alike. A necessary accomplice, a boon to their work. Prodding them, pushing them, urging them to ask the next question. The right question. And, while she might accompany those who are simply paranoid, insecure or distrusting by nature, she causes them a great deal of unnecessary anxiety and misery. She is an unsettling voice, a needling worry. Nevertheless, for trained seekers, for searchers, she is a keen comfort in mysterious times.

Mick Priest had known suspicion most of his life. It was a part of his nature; a man prizing truth will be counseled by suspicion. Being a detective simply enhanced his already curious, attentive demeanor. His ability to see just below the surface, to mentally carve beneath the skin of the apparent, was simply augmented by suspicion.

Case in point: Mick Priest was chasing a hired killer, an assassin. This mystery gun traveled the world, hitting slippery, elusive targets. The kind of targets with too much wealth or prestige to be convicted. All around the globe the operative traveled, dispensing brutal, final justice. Most detectives would not have been quite as thorough as Priest. They would have investigated every guest at the resort, certainly. They would have even suspected nearly every guest, at one time or another. They would never have suspected any of the staff, however. And they would have never, ever investigated all of the staff and their chambers. Why would they? Could a full time employee of a resort actually get away enough to tour the earth, meting out vengeance for hire? The consideration would have been futile legwork in the eyes of most detectives.

Mick Priest, suspicion along for the ride, was not most detectives and he was nothing less than meticulously thorough.

He had checked all the quarters in the resort proper, guest and staff, alike. He had peeked under every napkin and rummaged through every flower pot throughout the rest of the rooms, too. Then, as the day was drawing closer to its sister, the night, he walked out to search the outbuildings and the staff quarters within them.

He checked Tye Richter's place first.

It was neatly kept and unusually impersonal. The chamber could have suited anyone working in Facility Operations. The books, the magazines, all the accouterments spoke to a technical mind.

Not a particular technical mind but a keen one. Not a murderous mind but an intense one. Dedicated. Invested. Intent on being present. Not one bent on traveling here and there to kill.

Priest locked the Plant Operations building again, having picked the locks to get inside it. Then he made his way toward the hangar and the upstairs apartment belonging to the pilot, Gretchen Clayborne.

Loath as he was to go through her things, especially as it was nearly impossible for her to even be a suspect, he opened up her place just as he had Richter's. He chose being painstakingly thorough over any chance of recklessness. Using his light, he stabbed about the apartment for anything of import, following the ignited blade here and there, peeking inside this and that.

Thick, black drapes dangled from silver rods and covered every window, including the glass panes in the outside door to the overlook. It reminded priest of the rooms belonging to people who worked nights. Was Clayborne a night owl? Would it mean anything, either way?

Old, white paint splotched the horizontal planking of the rustic walls. The brown showed itself through in places, in varying degrees. If the worn look was intentional, it had been done well. The walls looked to be genuinely old, their paint dying away, even though the chestnut color of the trim and doors seemed quite fresh.

The sitting area had leather furniture that matched the rooms of the main resort. The tables matched, too. Black and white photographs plastered the walls with all sorts of moments and personalities. They had an aged look that complimented the planking very well, from the eight by tens in rough cut frames to the multiple pictures in collage frames sealed away in polished silver.

Mick Priest rounded the room, glancing at each point captured in time. The flashlight glimmered from the silver frames while reflecting from the glass faces and soaking into the raw wood of others. The light spilled over them one by one, illuminating the portals through time and space. Many focused on Clayborne and what looked to be family and friends, with casual and formal, intimate shots from her life.

Many showcased couples shots with the young lady and Falgrip Bridger, some of them alone and some with other couples. Priest sighed with a sad pang in his heart.

Autographed photos of noted personalities also filled some frames, like the ones of Dr. Ben Carson, Gal Godot and Denzel Washington. Autographed photos of people taken with Clayborne, herself, often with her pilot's gear or her helicopter in the backdrop, filled others. Rosario Dawson, Johnny Depp, Jason Statham and Halle Berry were in the mix. It seemed the young lady was accustomed to rubbing elbows with fame.

Priest slowed at two in particular, however.

One showed the dark and lovely Clayborne arm in arm with a man also in flight gear. He was none other than B'Rone Matwahali.

Close by it, Rembrandt Lyles hammed it up with the young pilot. In the background, behind a milling crowd, a sign for Gridlock Publishing glittered in the night lights.

Suddenly, a face jumped out at Priest. Near Lyles, off to one side and engaged in a conversation with someone else, a familiar woman's image sprang to life in Priest's memories. She was there in the photograph's cool black and white and in his memories in living color.

Brenda Lynn Wright; a politician, activist, speaker and writer. Author of *Uphill Is Harder In The Dark*. Mother of one victim in the 'Blood Rains' serial murders in Wilmington some years back. Card carrying member of the criminal organization, Belladonnai Violettes.

Priest tapped his finger on the glass absently.

Now, who let you out of prison? he wondered. *I guess maybe they didn't have quite enough on you, personally. But here you are, staring me in the face, hanging out with a man all tied up in this vigilante case. That's what you and your flower power gal pals were all about; working your own ideas of 'justice'...small world, huh, Ms. Wright?*

It was a possible coincidence, of course. Something in which Mick Priest put little to no stock. He moved his finger to the grinning countenance of Remy Lyles. He tapped it twice.

"And you, Mr. Lyles, will hear about this," he muttered aloud.

A thought dawned on Priest like a light shining from above. He turned quickly to the bookshelves on the opposite wall. On a high shelf, poised between the works of several other North Carolina writers, *Uphill Is Harder In The Dark* stood cover to cover with Kess Melkin's *Wolfen Shadows*. He was not sure what it meant, if it meant anything. But it was interesting and knowledge was power, leverage.

Then Priest paused and chuckled lowly. Down the row a bit was a bent, dogeared copy of *Nine Mile Road*, one of his early mystery novels.

"At least, she read it more than once," he said, noting its condition.

Moving on, Priest found nothing else of interest to the case in the chamber.

When he left the hangar, having searched her rooms, he carried no more insight than he already held. All he had managed to take from the search was the knowledge of the photos and an element of her privacy he never wanted to invade anyway.

No people. No bodies. No costumes. No distinct clues.

Finally, he turned back for the main building.

It was just as well. The day grew too tired to continue. Its light dissipated, relinquishing its dominance. Shadow Mountain prepped a drawing of the curtains once more, readying itself to embrace the night and its vanguard of shadows. Though not quite nightfall, the day's slumber had begun.

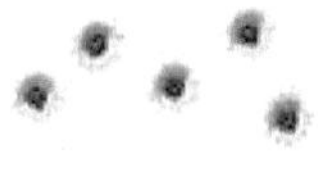

The Dining Hall held its silence in the face of everything. The brutal imagery, conjured up in the minds of those present, was enough to quell the most talkative natures. The pool outing at the gym had taken most of the energy they had left and the situation had taken its toll on their minds. Gone was any giddy sense of mystery. The thrill of the unknown, the excitement of potential but unlikely danger, paled and faded in a death of its own. No one wanted the mystery. No longer did anyone yearn for a brush with death, for the sense of survival adventure. Death had manifested itself as all too real and wore the white face of a skull...and it had a name.

Fears of personal mortality draped over the room like clinging, heavy shrouds fit for corpses. Most pondered the fleeting time of life, wondering when they, too, would be wearing a literal shroud, knowing it would come. The events at H and H Resort had concreted that in their minds. All were together there for the meal and shared the thick, palpable dread, with the exception of Mick Priest. He was still on the prowl.

Of course, he would be along soon enough.

The last of the day finally spent, sunset a memory and dusk passing into darkness, the night had started to settle low on Shadow Mountain. The nocturnal hour spread its wings out over the land but brought no cool, no respite. Thick, steamy heat threatened to smother the resort in the suffocating embrace it offered.

The heat and the darkness amplified the quiet stillness. Every time someone moved and made a noise someone else jumped, reacting with a start. Uneasiness stalked the dining room more aptly than any hired killer. The congregation dealt with it all in their own manners.

Tye Richter busied himself stirring his coffee. He sat closely with Director Clark, listening to her narrative about cleaning up the mess in her office. Jenkins had made it when he had been rifling through her things.

"You should make Jenkins clean it up," he said to Clark. "He needs to explain what he thought he was doing, too."

She huffed with a mild amusement, shaking her head.

"What?" asked the young man.

She said, "You're protective of me and I appreciate that. He cares, too, just in a different way. Like a dad, or something, a big brother. Whatever it is, you two need to understand that you're on the same side. You're a lot alike."

"I don't know," he said.

"You two should talk things out, get on the same page. You're both great at your work and you're both very important to me." She winked at him, adding, "Again, not the same way, but both important."

"Yeah. We need to talk, I guess," he said and sighed deeply.

Stuffed penguin thinks he runs this place, Richter pondered. *But, if Cassie thinks so much of him, maybe I'm not givin' him his due.*

Then Mick Priest entered the room abruptly, tossing the Hall door wide. Multiple gasps of surprise echoed one another as more than one person twitched with shock.

"Proper Charlie, tryin' ta give somebody a heart attack," Paul Blackwood muttered. "Carryin' that torch, pokin' about in the dark..."

Priest went straight to James Wyatt. Many eyes followed the detective but he ignored them. He and his old friend discussed a few things, covertly, then James nodded as Priest walked away from him.

On his way around the table, the detective tossed an open pack of cigarettes onto the table in front of Kess Melkin. She stared at them, unwilling to look up, while most of the others stared at the detective.

"Mr. Priest, smoking is-" Clark started.

Priest shot her a sharp look and lifted an open hand, as if blocking her very words. Then he simply moved to the empty seat by his wife and sat down. He whispered a few things to her.

That garnered him more than a handful of curious onlookers.

"Have you any news for us?" Matwahali asked, willing to break the somber quiet. "I'm afraid the reality of loomin' death is-"

"Not enough," Priest spat boldly. "Not enough to get all of you to open up, to play it straight. You people need to wise up, cooperate. This ain't a dime store novel. The folks dying? They're real people, whether you knew-"

"If you got all the answers-" Kess Melkin challenged.

"Answers?" Priest growled lowly, fixing his gaze on her. "No, I'm short on answers. What I have are questions. I don't know if you people care about answers but I figure Kim Mobley would like some! You guys wanna come into our makeshift morgue and talk to her?"

Boneyard silence.

"No? How about Richard Porter or Grip Bridger? You wanna talk to them? You sure weren't there when it was time to help me carry their bodies! Hey, maybe you're available to go sit and talk with them, now!"

He drove his hand down onto the table with his last word. Silverware and glassware jumped and jingled around the table. Little Emma Barlowe whined a bit, stirring, but did not completely awaken in her mother's arms.

Sarah Priest shifted, perhaps about to try to calm her husband, but James Wyatt caught her attention, inconspicuously clearing his throat.

He's fine, James mouthed just for her. *He's just gettin' goin' good.*

"No? No on that front, too?" Mick Priest demanded.

"Mr. Priest," Director Cassandra Clark finally answered, the only one willing to be vocal. "None of us are happy about any of this."

Priest pointed to Kess Melkin.

"How about let's not talk about 'being happy with this' and we start with some hard, fast facts. Melkin, you're linked to Porter and Mobley, two of our dead people. Linked by your sneaking around and smoking."

"What're you tryin' to say?" Melkin asked, finally lifting her head.

"I said it, plain enough for everybody," Priest snapped. "Why don't you tell everybody the rest of the smoking connection?"

Matwahali leaned forward over the table, close to Melkin.

Priest said, "You know, too, don't ya, big man? You wanna tell it?"

The big man looked at Melkin, looked back to Priest and back to Melkin, who then bit her lower lip as tears ran free.

"Kess?" Matwahali said. "What does he want me to tell? Is it just about the wandering around-"

"Grip took me downstairs last night!" she howled suddenly, tears streaming down over her face.

Tayla Barlowe stood as little Emma began to cry. She went out of the room and Andreya West was hot on her heels. Jenkins met Cassandra Clark's eyes and then gave chase, too.

"I just needed a smoke! He looked out for me so I could smoke down in the rose garden! I didn't wanna leave him down there by himself but he told me to go back upstairs with B'Rone!"

"Yeah, he told us he'd wait for Paul!" Matwahali shouted. "Blackwood was dillydallyin', slow comin' back from the kitchen!"

Why didn't you tell us? You knew this the whole time? He's dead because of you! came hisses and murmurs. Curses fouled the air, too. *Maybe she's the killer*, someone even added bitterly.

"Easy! Easy!" Matwahali roared at that point. "Kess ain't no killer!"

Sarah Priest placed two cigarette butts and a brass, 9mm shell casing on the table. The shell had a small droplet of blood on it.

"Maybe not, but she sure could've helped us make sense of these," the agent from the SBI said flatly. "This is your shade, isn't it?" she asked, holding up a lipstick stained butt.

"Yes! It's mine, okay?" Melkin cried.

"Good to know. It's one of the shades on the bottles I found in Porter's room," Mick Priest said.

"Yeah, yeah, me 'n' Mobley had a cola with him. We were all gripin' about the no smokin' rule and he was tellin' us he'd stashed a pack. And, yeah, before you ask, it's these!" she snapped, slapping the pack off the table. "Things smelled horrible! I couldn't smoke 'em."

"Why was your lipstick on Grip Bridger's lips?"

Sarah Priest asked it with a perfect, deadpan blindside.

Melkin coughed and began to stutter unintelligibly.

"When did a kiss occur, Ms. Melkin? Before the smoking? After? Was it a bribe or a thank you?" Sarah Priest pressed.

Gretchen Clayborne came out of her seat, hands balled into fists.

"You better have a good answer, you dirty-"

"Hold it!" Clark yelled at Clayborne. "Calm down and sit down!"

"Answer 'em, Kess," Matwahali said. "I'd like to hear this myself."

"It was just a friendly 'thank you' peck for lookin' out for me!" Melkin yelled, finally finding real words.

Of course, it had only been a thank you kiss and stopped there because Grip Bridger had not carried it further and because Matwahali had come along just afterward.

"B'Rone was there! He can tell ya!" she added.

"Careful who you tie yourself up with, mate," Blackwood commented, directing it at B'Rone Matwahali. "All o' this 'cause she couldn't stay put?"

"Oh, do talk, ya silverback gorilla!" Matwahali snapped. "You 'n' me both were out and about when she was, raidin' the kitchen! And you've said yourself you won't be told where to be and when!"

Blackwood opened his mouth to speak but Mick Priest interrupted.

"Time and again you were out, alone," he said. "And you were with Kimber Mobley shortly before she was killed."

"That's right," Gibson chimed into the conversation.

"And either you or Mobley were the last to see Porter alive," Priest continued, "that we know of."

"What? What're you tryin' to pull?" Blackwood shouted.

"I think that's what they're askin' you," James Wyatt said.

"I have no reason to hurt anyone!" Blackwood howled. "I have probably the least involvement with anyone here, too!"

"Mr. Blackwood, you were in the same town as Mr. Matwahali for work or conventions over twenty times. Your television productions have shared studio locations seven times in the last four years."

The voice of Victor Jackson silenced the room like a gavel strike.

"W-what? Oh, really? S-so what?" Blackwood shouted.

"You were in a celebrity motorcycle race with Richard Porter twice and you've been featured in the same parent company of magazines that employed Ms. Mobley more than ten times, including an article and a shoot on your personal motor vehicle collection. In that layout she modeled with your sports cars. Richard Porter wrote up the interview."

"Now, hold on a minute!" the baker said. "Where'd you get all that?"

Jackson looked at Agent Sarah Priest and her husband, Mick.

"I crunch data, numbers," he said flatly. "I've been prying into the files given to me and Maureen by Gridlock brass."

"Well, well," Mick Priest said. "Welcome to the team, Vic."

He then turned his focus back to the crowd.

The awed crowd stared back in silence. Maureen Li, the exception, stared with fiery eyes at her assistant, Victor Jackson. She glowered his way, fuming over something she was unwilling to speak.

"You all have ties to each other and to the dead in all sorts of crossed paths and mutual histories, with the exception of the staff. I'd start offering a little honesty, if I were you. The truth just might get some of us out of here alive," Jackson said.

A previously vocal group with defiant eyes was awestruck, mute.

"Even so, some of the staff may have more connections than any of us knew," Mick Priest noted.

Gretchen Clayborne shifted just her eyes toward the detective.

"You've been in my loft," Clayborne said to Priest.

"I have."

"Why?" Tye Richter asked.

"Who do you think you are?" Chef Swartzovski snapped.

"He had my authorization," Clark said. "If you have nothing to hide, what difference does it make? I told Mr. Priest and Agent Priest to do whatever was necessary. They've been through all our rooms."

"All our rooms?" Maureen Li chimed. "Guests, too?"

"Yes," Mick Priest said flatly.

"How dare you?" Li railed in self righteous indignation. "I should-"

"You should be quiet, for now," Mick Priest said. Then, nodding at Gretchen Clayborne, he said, "We were talking."

"About?" Clayborne answered wryly.

"Connections."

She huffed then said, "I've met some of the people here. I've even worked for some of them before this weekend. I'm a pilot for hire and a really good one. I'm also very trustworthy and I can do work for celebrities without talking about it, talking about what they were doing."

"You don't have that naggin' need for fifteen minutes of fame," James Wyatt said with a nod. "Same here. Makes good workin' rapport."

"And that's why I haven't brought up working for anyone here," she added. "I got nothing to hide but I got nothing to admit, either. No matter who I've worked for or haven't, I ain't involved in any crimes."

"You do have interesting interactions, though," Priest said. "You and Remy both."

Lyles spat, "Me? What's this about me?"

"Why not you?" Clayborne bit. "It's okay for him to come at me?"

"You both associated with a writer involved in a rogue justice group, a vigilante group, if you will. Brenda Lynn Wright-"

"I met her once!" barked Clayborne. "I wanted her to sign a copy of my book! It just so happens-"

"She has a limited amount of time off, anyway," Clark said in Gretchen's defense. "I think you can look beyond our staff, Mr. Priest."

"It ain't a secret that I knew Wright," Lyles interjected. "I sought her out for interviews. Her and a buncha her fellow conspirators. I wanted all the real life research I could get on actual vigilantism before I started work on Ghost Revolver stories."

"That much is clear," Priest said. "I've been in that shrine to murder you set up in your room. Remy, that's pretty twisted."

"I'm an artist, not a killer," the thin man snapped. "I think you can keep on searching if you're looking to put a name behind that skull mask. Just sayin', ya know?"

"And with whom should he start?" Johanna Crimson asked with a smirk. "I move around the most, travel most. I probably, statistically, land in towns frequented by the others quite often. I was probably around cities where this illustrious assassin made hits. Does that make me this Ghost Revolver? This vigilante you keep describing, the vengeful righter of wrongs?"

She and Gibson shared a mocking laugh at the idea.

"So far, the files would agree with you," Jackson allowed.

"Oh, the files are what they are. Let's talk a little more personally where Johanna Crimson is concerned," said Priest.

Gibson started to bow up but Crimson put a hand on his arm.

"I am one of my favorite topics," she said with her defiant smile.

"Let's keep things calm-" James Wyatt started hesitantly.

"No, no, Mick's just getting going," Sarah Priest reminded flatly.

"There's something off about you, Ms. Crimson," Priest charged. "I just don't know what. But it's there. Like when we were kids and we'd color."

"Color, Mr. Priest?" she asked.

"Yeah. With crayons. You can color over some things but, if you color something too dark, then try to color over it, lighten it, it just won't take. It's like using a blue over black; you can do it all you like but it won't change a thing. Something's colored you. I just can't see it."

"What can I say about such brilliant insight?" she asked, arms lifted.

"Maybe we should shift gears. Absolutely nothing has happened to you or involved you but your bodyguard believes you're the central target of the Ghost Revolver. Three dead and you're the target? I mean, I found the revolver case and a trunk of 'bad guy stuff' on the skylight above your room but you're the number one target? Why is the best assassin in the world not even able to make an attempt on you?" Priest pushed.

"Maybe I'm just lucky," she challenged. "It stands to reason-"

"What's this about a trunk on our skylight?" Gibson yelled, rising to his feet. "And when were ya gonna share that tidbit with me?"

"It was your room," Priest replied. "I thought maybe you knew."

"You know what, Skippy?" Gibson barked.

"No, tell me!" Priest yelled at Gibson. "Why don't you tell me something I don't know? Tell me a secret, Gibson!"

Gibson faltered and fell silent at the turn.

"Either one of you," Priest calmed, looking at Crimson. "Why don't you tell me, tell all of us, which story is the true story involving Mr. Rembrandt Lyles? Between the two of you and Lyles we've got three or four stories about your mutual pasts rolling around."

"I told ya, already," Gibson barked. "The brat's got no-"

"Gibson!" Crimson snapped, green eyes afire.

"The lawyers were clear, old man," Lyles shouted at Gibson. "You start talkin', I can start talkin', and ya'll don't want that."

"Suffice it to say, we have had legal conflicts in the past and we are unable to elaborate on it in the public forum. Either way, I hardly think Mr. Lyles is the Revolver, nor would he wish harm upon us...just as I would wish none upon him."

"That makes one of us," Gibson said. "I do agree that the boy ain't no killer for hire. He'd have ta get a job and get out of his mom's basement, first."

Lyles jumped to his feet, one fist shaking, his wrinkled, Legend of Zelda t shirt flapping.

James Wyatt rolled his eyes.

"Really, Beavis? Sit down!"

The man took his seat.

"But you have been talking, haven't you, Mr. Lyles?" Priest asked.

The fluffy haired man trying to comb a hand through his hair.

"I...well, I don't know...what do you mean?"

"Our dear staffer, Ms. Clayborne, was very sour about Johanna Crimson gracing all of us with her presence," Priest said. "Is that because you told her all about the behind the scenes battle for Velvet Edge?"

"What?" he asked, looking at Gretchen Clayborne.

Clayborne simply shook her head, saying nothing.

"No, Remy, Gretchen didn't tell me," Priest said with a smile. "The picture clued me in. You, her, by her 'copter at one of the Gridlock gatherings. Was that when you went in for talks about your new graphic series? The Revolver, I think it's called."

"Kid, how crazy are you, anyway?" James Wyatt asked. "You plannin' to make a comic on a real world vigilante? You want a target on your back you can't wash off?"

"He's lost his mind," Gibson said.

"He got the idea from someone else recently cutting a deal with Gridlock. Am I right, Remy?"

Rembrandt Lyles stared at Priest, unable to answer.

Gretchen stared at Lyles. Gibson stared at Priest. Crimson stared at Gibson. The rest looked from one to another.

"I know Brenda Lynn Wright and I know what she was, who she was," Priest growled.

"We both do," Sarah Priest added. "The things in which the woman was involved and willing to be involved..."

Mick Priest added, "I have no doubt that she put the whole hired operative in your ear, Remy. Like Gibson, I don't see you as the hitman type. Unlike Johanna Crimson, however, I wouldn't put it past you to hire one, not just write about one."

"I don't have to sit here and listen to this," Lyles barked and stood.

"Sit back down or we'll sit you down," B'Rone Matwahali said. "All of us want an answer, little man."

"It ain't true!" he shouted. "Okay, Wright couldn't shut up about secret societies and their use of professionals! It gave me an idea for a comic, not a killing! I'm not crazy!"

"This Wright woman, she openly talked about assassins?" Gibson balked.

"Yeah," Clayborne admitted. "She was loony. But Remy's not. He's an opportunistic liar but he's not crazy."

"Oh, wow. Thanks?" Lyles said.

Crimson crossed her arms, starting, "Did it ever occur to you two-"

"What happened to your beauty mark?" Priest asked suddenly.

Caught between calling down the others and watching Gibson, Crimson's reflexes got the better of her. Her right hand went up to her chin without her consent. Those bright eyes betrayed her; she had not expected the question and she paused to ponder the appropriate answer. As she fought the hand and arm back to her side, she tossed back her thick, flaming hair, digging around for her confident smile.

"What of it?" Gibson demanded angrily, rising to his feet.

Sarah Priest of the SBI placed her Smith and Wesson .40 Caliber onto the tabletop. She motioned for Gibson to sit back down.

Crimson pulled at her man's arm until he sat down again.

"Gibson, hush. Mr. Priest has a right to ask questions if it helps the situation here," she said softly. Then, "I don't know how it matters here but I had that and several other beauty marks removed, Mr. Priest. We do live in an age of cancer scares. We have to be careful.”

Priest held up three fingers for the crowd.

“There you have it. Three truths from Ms. Johanna Crimson. One,” he declared, index finger wiggling, “We don't know that removing beauty marks matters here. Two. We do live in an age of cancers. Physical. Emotional. Mental. Spiritual cancers. It's all over the place, literal and metaphorical. And three. We have to be careful. That's not me saying it,” he said, nodding to Crimson. “That's Johanna Crimson. We need to be careful.”

“What's your point, Slick?” Gibson asked, brow furrowed.

“Piece it together, sheesh,” Tayla Barlowe said.

The group looked her way as she came back with little Emma.

She added, “What? It's like people get old and forget to think.”

“Hey!” Gibson warned.

“He's sayin' Ms. Crimson is cautious about spots on her skin without knowing if they're even dangerous; being careful. He's reminding us, when we got multiple corpses, we *know* there's danger here and *some* of us don't wanna be careful. He's pointing out that we need to be safe, as safe as we can be. And part of that is being honest, working together.”

Murmuring, mumbling and general grumbling followed.

“Indeed,” Mick Priest said with a succinct nod. “Indeed. And while we're telling the truth...” Priest growled, pulling a magazine from his back pocket.

Crimson visibly blanched as he slid it across the table to her. She placed a hand over it, stopping it.

“There are a lot of rumors that surround someone famous,” Priest said. “Magazines, television, internet. Some of it is downright strange.”

“Gossip,” Johanna Crimson allowed. “How wild it can get.”

“Only thing that ever competes with the supermarket rags of the old days,” Gibson said, “is the internet. The internet is the new tabloid, only every nut with a WiFi connection can have a platform.”

“Have you seen the write ups that say you're actually dead?” Priest asked bluntly.

James turned his eyes toward his partner.

Crimson cocked her head to one side, eyebrows lifted high, lips parted in dumbfounded shock.

“Well, at least you can prove that one wrong just by bein' here, there, or anywhere,” Gibson said and drank some coffee. “Pretty clear you ain't dead.”

He never looked at Priest. He never looked at James Wyatt. He did not even look up at Johanna Crimson. He just stared straight ahead, just over his coffee cup, peering through the steam. The ice blue eyes focused like lasers on something no one else could see.

"Mr. Priest knows that," Johanna Crimson finally said. "If he sees me he knows I'm alive. After all, it isn't like he can see the dead."

James Wyatt drew a deep, thoughtful breath and Mick Priest shot a warning look his way.

Keep your mouth in neutral, the sharp look ordered. *Not even a joke.*

"Rumors," James mumbled, shaking his head.

"Why don't you tell us how you felt when Richard Porter confronted you with those crazy rumors. You know, when he was sent to interview you for this motorcycle magazine," Priest said and tapped the periodical.

She rolled the publication in her grasp.

"Mobley's a feature model in that one, too," Priest added.

Crimson and Gibson looked at each other for a moment.

"It says inside she played a background part in your first Velvet Edge movie. It quotes you as saying how she was a natural for acting."

Crimson found her voice, lifting fiery eyes.

She growled, "I've forgotten more magazine interviews than most people have ever read. Where Richard Porter was concerned, I couldn't forget well enough or fast enough. I knew him and I disdained him."

"Creepy letch," Gibson said, eyes colder than ice. "We had a run in and I told him if I ever saw him around Johanna again I'd put lead in him and dump him in a river. Don't mean I'm some Ghost Revolver and it don't mean I killed him. Johanna, either, even if the little troll did try to take a crazy conspiracy theory and make it journalistic reading."

Priest chuckled, pointing at Gibson.

"That's the kind of honesty we need. Cutting to the heart of it."

Priest and Gibson stared at each other.

"Tayla, where are Jenkins and Andreya?" Sarah Priest asked.

"They're comin' in a minute. Jenkins agreed to walk Andreya up to her room really quick."

Clark and Sarah Priest shared a look and an eye roll.

A woman who looks like that can get away with murder, their mutual looks seemed to say.

"Is there more to reveal," Maureen Li asked, "or are we done?"

"Oh, there's more to consider. How about you, Li?" Priest asked abruptly, moving his eyes across the room to her.

"W-what about me?" she asked.

"Share the truth. Who really put this party together? We've heard you take credit in front of all of us but, when you're alone with Vic, you've admitted some disturbing things. Like it was just sent to you, already put together. You just put it in motion."

It was a random sucker punch but verbally boxing with the woman with gloves on would get nowhere fast.

She stuttered, stammered. She tried to deny it, mock the very idea and pretend to not understand how anyone could think it, all at once. All the words collided and formed a traffic jam in her mouth. The struggle silenced her with the inability to speak one thing above another. She stalled, mouth open.

A moment passed then she cleared her throat, eyeballing Jackson.

"Fair enough," she spat. "The truth is...I don't even know. Not for certain. I just got the suggested contact information and started the ball rolling. I thought it was a legitimate assignment and I made it happen."

Victor Jackson cleared his throat.

"Okay, I put Vic on the job and he made it happen."

Thunder gave slow chase to more heat lightning outside. The group could not see the lightning but the thunder bore it witness. Like the killer in their midst; they could not see one but the bodies gave the proof.

When Priest did not speak on it immediately, Li continued herself.

"What else do you want me to say?"

Priest wiped the sweat from his face and his slick head. He dripped with perspiration, like many in the room.

"What else do you feel like saying?" he asked.

"I'm not some crazed killer, if that's what you mean," she said.

"Oh, since you say that, of course, you're all clear," Remy Lyles said sarcastically.

"Your intense, unfettered devotion to helping Victor dig into those files, those contacts and those instructions would go a long way toward helping us," Priest stated. "I want to know every bit of information you can resurrect from your correspondence, your directives and-"

"Fine, done," she said, hands tossed into the air. "Never mind that we have confidentiality obligations..."

She drifted out when the eyes of the room fell on her like toppling monuments.

"We'll do all we can," Victor Jackson promised.

Clark, after a deep breath, said, "I think, after all we've heard and all that's happened, we'd be smart to listen to the Priests. It's time for total truth, no secrets. Something you hide may very well kill you. Does anyone else have anything they'd like to share?"

Everyone looked around, examining fellow faces and mumbling.

"Calm down, everybody," James Wyatt ordered. "This ain't a posse saddlin' up to run one of you outta town. We're examinin' facts."

"Well, here's a fact for ya, mate," Paul Blackwood growled. "I'm done with this. I move we adjourn this little sewing circle and lock up."

Quite a lot of support for the idea was vocalized.

Mikhael Priest slowed the motion, however.

"Before we turn in, tell us why you think you were the last to see two people here prior to their deaths."

"Priest, I told ya, it's just my bad luck! I didn't know Porter would be kickin' the bucket soon after me 'n' Kimber saw him last, and she was with me when I saw 'im, for the record! As for Kimber, I wouldn't hurt her. We were getting' on famous-like! I swear!"

"It might not've been just Mobley and Porter! It might've been all three!" Kess Melkin snapped. "We don't know he didn't get the drop on Bridger!"

"How do we know it wasn't your boyfriend?" shouted Blackwood. "After all, B'Rone is the only one here who could get away in that helicopter without the help of the staff pilot! He's a pilot, too!"

The room turned its stares to Matwahali.

Is it true? Does it matter? Why didn't he tell anybody? Who knew?

"It's true enough," Matwahali acknowledged, "but it was never a secret. I can fly. I ain't hidin' it. It hasn't come up."

Where was he when the helicopter was sabotaged? Maybe he knows how to fix it. Maybe he should be watched. Who shouldn't be?

"We understand your fears," Sarah Priest said. "But be as calm as possible. Be alert. Be safe. And, since we're being bluntly honest, remember this: if I find you wandering around by yourself and your behavior is in question at all, I will respond accordingly. With extreme prejudice."

Tayla Barlowe arched her brows and said, "I think Agent Priest is right. Caution. Ya'll behave yourselves."

"A wise young woman," Director Clark noted. "Because I don't believe Agent Priest is bluffing."

Mick Priest then positioned himself by the door to the hallway.

"We found blood on the bullet we believe came out of Grip's gun, by the way. Sarah showed it to you all a little while ago. We believe the blood stain came from the attacker's hand when they wrestled over the weapon. There was blood on the slide of his gun, telling us it was more than likely a slide bite."

He had lied. They had not recovered the gun.

Mick Priest said to them, "Stop here with me on your way out. We'd like to see your hands."

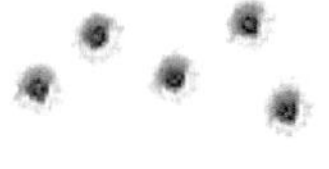

No one had a provable slide bite, truth be told. Many had scrapes and cuts and marks. None had a specific wound that looked the part.

The only standout exception was none other than Paul Blackwood, a man with immaculate, manicured hands...and one pinch mark marring the image. Still, it was not proof of anything.

I let them all go by.

Sarah had stopped Cassandra Clark and spoken to her in the hall. Tayla Barlowe paused behind them, holding sweet Emma, trying not to crowd them. She was waiting for Sarah to take them up to their room.

Cassandra Clark, alongside Tye Richter, started upstairs but Sarah stayed. She said something to Barlowe and started back to me. Barlowe approached the horse stalls.

"I'll be along in a minute," Sarah called. "Right behind you."

I watched with a smile as Tayla held Emma out to see a 'horsie'.

"I'm on my way upstairs, baby," Sarah said to me.

She stepped right into me, against me. Flattening a hand on my chest, right over my heart, my wife whispered in my ear.

Yes, I nodded. *I'll walk Tayla and Emma up*.

It seemed Sarah and Cassandra were going to look for Jenkins and Andreya West. Sarah knew I would, too, while on Tayla's floor, anyway. She and Clark would cover the others.

"I have to go. But I'll miss you tonight, love," Sarah said softly.

"You two need to get a room," Tayla Barlowe said from down the hall. "Sheesh."

"Girl's got good ears," Sarah said of the young mother.

"She should," I said, feigning irritation. "She looks enough like an elf; ought to have those pointy, elf ears, too."

Barlowe turned our way, smirked and tilted her head to the side. Then Tayla brought Emma down the hall to us.

Sarah kissed me then walked away.

"Alright." Tayla Barlowe turned her face to little Emma and said, "Alright with you, little monkey?"

The baby said something no one could understand.

"She says 'great'," Tayla said, giggling at my raised eyebrow. "She thinks five more minutes with the 'horsies' would be nice."

"Yeah. That's pretty much what all girls say."

CHAPTER THIRTEEN

For many of the guests of Horse and Heraldry, as well as part of the staff, that was that and enough was enough. They just did not want to play anymore, electing to take up their proverbial ball and leave the court. Mentally, at least. Going back to their rooms, feeling like prisoners in a zoo for endangered animals, most decided they were finished with it all. They were tired of being ordered around, tired of being scared, tired of being hunted, haunted or both.

Of course, the idea of being killed was just enough to put them in the rooms and into cooperation.

A hesitant *rap, rap, rap* on the door drew Kess Melkin's eyes, though they were far from closed from the start. She went from staring at the ceiling to peeling the varnish from the door with her gaze. Lying on the bed, unwilling to undress and relax, she gave a hushed answer.

"Who is it?"

"Kess, we needa talk," a muffled voice called from beyond the door.

"B'Rone?" she confirmed.

"Kess, open the door," B'Rone Matwahali said. "C'mon, woman. You know it isn't me what's killing and I know it isn't you. Let me in. If we stick together, an' we get on pretty well, we got two sets of eyes to watch over us. The odds are pretty good."

She thought to herself, *He gave up his own room to come to mine.*

Melkin got up, unlatched the door and pulled it open.

"C'mon in," she said. "But no funny business."

The big man said, "I understand. We need ta be-"

She cackled. Embracing him, she shook her head.

"What're you, crazy?"

Then she began kissing him.

Down the hall a few doors, Paul Blackwood opened the balcony doors to the night and left them that way, escaping onto the overlook. He cared little if the lady agent, her husband or the Resort Director liked it.

Let them squawk, he thought to himself. *Rangy bunch of Americans. Pure palaver, hiding in the room. I know a bedroom door wouldn't stop me if I wanted someone else dead...*

Shirtless, the baker wore his thick form well. The muscle flexed beneath the surface when he moved, impressive and powerful. It was rare that anyone got a long look at him in the buff, despite his Hollywood ranking; the man was fond of very expensive dress shirts and was rarely seen without one. He knew, on the balcony, he was alone. No one could see him.

The overcast sky actually looked cooler, even if it was not. The humidity remained, the air thick and sticky. It prompted the baker to wipe sweat from his bare flesh fairly often. The wind gave no help against the heat, either. All was still. Deathly still. And hot.

A floor away, James Wyatt took a turn guarding the illustrious actress and that gave Gibson a chance to rest. He kicked back in their room but still did not sleep; his eyes stared blankly at the ceiling, instead.

The rest of the conglomeration of staff, invited guests and guests of invited guests were supposed to stay in their rooms, for safety. Not all did. It was human nature, always pushing boundaries.

Boundaries like thou shalt not kill.

"Ms. Barlowe-" I started, throwing open her room door.

A foundation shaking boom went off like a bomb, rattling the window glass. It naturally drew our attention to the windows where we saw the subtle flash in the clouds.

"It's Tayla," she corrected.

"Tayla," I said, feeling a little deja vu.

How many times had we covered the name thing?

She closed the door behind us.

"Thunder's comin' on again. Gonna keep little Emma up all night."

"They call it summer rage up here," I said, panning my flashlight around the chamber while she readied a light of her own.

"I guess if you give it a special name it isn't as scary," Tayla said.

"I guess. I'm going to have a look around while you try to settle Emma," I said.

She answered with an appreciative quip of some kind. I was listening but I was not; my focus bore down on the safety of the room. I took my time checking it and the bathroom, the locks on the doors and the storage and everything else. The room was as secure as it could be.

That really did not say much to me. The balcony doors and windows were glass and that was a weak point in any defense.

"Ms. Barlowe-"

"Good grief, Dad," she barked at me. "It's Tayla."

"Okay, okay. I was just going to say you're more than welcome to sleep in the room with Sarah and me. There are plenty of beds in every room and you wouldn't be alone."

She giggled again, a musical sound if ever I heard one.

Adjusting her glasses, she said, "You take this dad thing for real, don't you, Mr. Priest?"

"It's Dad. Or Mick," I said with my own trademarked, sideways grin. "And I want you and the monkey to be safe."

"We're good, I promise. She'll be up most of the night-"

"Sarah and I will, too, making rounds, checking on things."

"Dude, it's all good. I know where ya'll are. If something goes hinky, I'll be on your door like a bad paint job. But I'll feel really bad if we keep ya'll awake for nothing. Now, go check on Andreya. If it makes you feel better, stop back in on your way back to work."

I shrugged with, "I offered."

"We appreciate you, too," she assured me as I started for the door. "But who knows? We might have all kinds of girl mischief planned, just me and Chunky Monkey."

Sarah Priest and Cassandra Clark combed through the lower floors together. Clark took the lead, saying she knew likely places to find her head man, Mr. Jenkins. While they did not find him any place Clark expected, they did discover more about each other. It was a bonding time. Sometimes life and death events worked that way, forging friendships and lasting associations that long outlive the event itself. The two women felt that growing friendship, at least one small goodness born in the middle of all the grief and horror.

They shared a bit of their pasts, their current lives and their hopes for the future. Clark was adamant that Tydas Richter was a part of that future for her. She admitted, too, that she often found older men attractive, as they had always been more her type. She considered herself an old soul. Tye was an exception, she insisted, down to earth and stable.

Clark also confided that Reginald Jenkins was a very attractive man to her. If he had not been more of a father figure to her, it may have gone another way, but that was neither 'here nor there', she said.

"But there's just something about salt and pepper hair, especially if there's more salt than pepper left," she said quietly with a soft laugh.

"Oh, not for me, girl," Sarah Priest said. She took a deep breath and held it, clawing the air with her nails, and added, "Bald or shaven, for me. The feel of it in your hand, under your fingers, raking your nails-"

"Whoa, keep it G rated," Clark halted with a girlish giggle.

"Hey, I'm married. It's all allowed," Priest chimed merrily.

They left the stairwell landing, stepping out on Floor Three, when Jenkins appeared at the far end of the hallway. He strode purposefully toward them, head up and proper.

"Where have you been?" Clark admonished when they were only half way to him. "We've been worried!"

Sarah simply watched him like a hawk.

Jenkins bowed his head when he reached them and folded his hands in front of his waist.

"Yes, yes, I know, and I do apologize," he answered humbly. "It was quite reckless of me, I see in hindsight. Let me explain."

Andreya West's room was across the hall from Tayla Barlowe's, just one room north. Andreya West, however, was not answering her door. Priest had no idea if the woman was there but he was only about five seconds from breaking into the chamber.

He knocked again stiffly. He gave the 'cop knock' with his light. Again, Priest got no answer. It did not sit well with him so he took out the lockpicks. A few pings, scrapes and clicks later he had the door open slightly and was peeking inside.

"Mr. Priest?" West greeted from behind him.

He jerked about rigidly and did a double-take, from the woman to the door gap and back to the woman. Priest then wiped a hand over his own forehead, sweeping back the sheen of sweat.

"I'm sorry. Did I startle you?" West asked with a giggle.

"Yeah, I'd say so. You know, there are very few people who can walk up on me like that. Usually I-"

"I'm hard core," she said with a big smile. "Total ninja."

Priest could not help returning the smile. Hers beamed infectiously.

"Okay, we can go with that, then."

"Yay," she said and cocked her head to one side. "We agree."

"Ms. West, I was concerned-"

"Is everything okay?" she asked immediately.

"-so I opened your door...and was going to check on you..." Priest finished, fading.

"Oh. All is well," she said with a shrug. "Come inside, won't you?"

She eased by him, pushing the door fully open. She waved for him to follow her into the room, which he did, and West closed the door.

"Have a seat," she offered.

"Thank you," he said, sitting in one of the chairs opposite the leather sofa, where she perched.

He found it difficult to be angry with her. He was not even annoyed at her, despite her aloof actions, endangering herself and perhaps Jenkins, as well. There was something genuinely likable, admirable, about Andreya West, the intelligent, articulate, cheerful scholar.

"Was there something I can do for you, Mr. Priest?" she asked, big eyes wide and engaging in the glow of the flashlights they both carried.

"Ms. West, you gave everyone a scare, you and Jenkins, both. Where is he, by the way?"

"He's on his way back downstairs to give everyone my apologies."

"For?"

"All this," she said and gestured at Priest. "I knew we were going to lock ourselves in tonight, that much was already decided. I simply did not wish to go back to that crowded nonsense when Tayla, Emma, Jenkins and I had already emerged with an escape. I offered to walk Tayla and Emma up to their room but she was willing to go back and suffer the rest of that rhetorical mishmash before being sent to our rooms."

She shrugged again, pulled her hair into a pony tail and tied it back.

"And Jenkins?"

"Jenkins insisted on bringing me up here if I was coming alone but then he insisted on waiting for someone else to come up before he left me. We heard the noise when others got up to this floor; I think we heard, at least, James Wyatt opening up his room and you and Tayla when you came up. So, he's gone back down."

"That was irresponsible on his part."

She frowned, head cocked to one side.

"I thought it quite gallant, even noble," she commented.

"I don't mean accompanying you," Priest corrected. "I mean walking around on his own. It was dangerous, for his sake. There's an armed assailant here; as far as I know, Mr. Jenkins is not armed."

"I'm sorry, Mr. Priest. It's my fault, really. I'm not good at just sitting. Staring. Lounging. I'm very active."

"Martial arts?" he asked innocently.

She tilted her head a bit and gave a slight squint with her smile.

"And you know that how?"

"Lucky guess."

"I think we'll come back to that."

"But you were saying?"

"I hate sitting around unless I have access to things I can research and I abhor pointless debate and arguments that lead to no effective end."

"You know there's a killer here, Ms. West. You have to be careful."

"Andreya."

Priest gave a courteous nod with, "Indeed. Andreya. Call me Mick."

"Yay," she said joyfully with a big smile. "We're friends."

"Agreed. But there's a killer on the grounds, Andreya."

"So everyone keeps saying."

"You don't think so?" Priest asked.

She said, "I don't have any doubt, since you found dead people."

"But wandering around was still worth the risk?"

"Mr. Priest," she said with a subdued smile, crossing her legs and folding her hands around her knees, "I'm sorry. Mick, I didn't go far. I tried to escort the Barlowes to help them, too. And I only came up to my room, the very place we were all going to be sent, anyway." She laughed lightly, saying, "Good grief. I'm fine. Mr. Jenkins is fine. Tayla and her little one are fine. I think it's all going to be fine."

Priest looked around the room as he nodded.

"I see."

"But let's return to the other item," she said flatly. Her eyes were sharp and piercing, even though humor curled her full lips as she added, "Why not tell me how you really knew I trained in the martial-"

"I rifled through all of your personal things, tossed your room and tried to find something to implicate the killer. I've been through every room. I noticed the escrima staves," he spat matter-of-factly, right off the cuff.

She tipped her head toward him, the smile intact.

He never flinched but took on a direct stare.

She huffed and said, "You *do know* that's illegal, of course."

"Nope. I had to have permission to search from the owner of this property, or a qualified representative of said owners." He smiled, adding, "I did."

"As long as you asked nicely..." she trailed, rolling her eyes.

The man wiped over his shaven head again then rubbed his hands together. West never lost the smile as she watched him, eye to eye.

"Had you asked, I'd have told you to rummage away. Pillage the goods, Mr. Priest."

"Mick," he countered with a grin.

Andreya West rose and pulled a couple of her suitcases onto a bed. The scholar took out a very chic, pale blue top, a sleeveless, linen blouse. It belted at the waist and had tails in the front and back that would drop down over her hips. With it she acquired shadowy gray, stretch leggings with a herringbone stitch pattern.

Then she pointed at the other suitcase.

"Now..." West mumbled thoughtfully. She did so as if to herself, though she was smiling at Mick Priest. "...accessories, they say, make the girl's outfit..."

She pulled the escrima sticks free.

Priest gave a shrug of his own.

"Fashion is often a transition born of necessity."

West giggled, grabbed up her last case and moved for the bathroom, only stopping once she reached the door.

She turned back to him and said, "Thank you for putting everything back the way you found it, Mick. At least, it was all as I left it. I do hate a mess. For now, though, I need a shower."

He sat forward in his chair with, "All joking aside, all pleasantries shared, please be careful, Andreya. There's a very dangerous person on the loose."

"Then lock the door on your way out. And thank you for caring. We're lucky to have you and Sarah here with us this weekend," she finished, sliding into the bathroom and closing the door.

Victor Jackson stared incredulously at his laptop screen. He blinked rapidly, as if that would somehow change what he saw. Jaw slack, hands holding the sides of the laptop rigidly, the keen minded man seemed to have short circuited. He could find no words. He could make no sounds. Jackson simply stood still, hands gripping the computer, his blinking eyes transfixed on a black screen.

"It's weird," Maureen Li said. "Mine won't come on, either."

She sat at the other end of the short table, her own laptop in front of her. It was dark, as well, no longer among the living.

"Yours," Vic Jackson started, voice quivering angrily, "is dead because you refused to bring backup batteries. Yours has been dead since we got here...if it wasn't I could use *it* to explore the set up files..."

He squeezed his eyes tightly against the blinking.

"But mine...what could've happened to mine?"

"Maybe your battery died, too."

Her voice was innocently disengaged, as if she were making suggestions she neither cared about nor believed would make a difference. Her face, shadowed in the low light of one flashlight aimed upward toward the ceiling, stared at Jackson blankly.

Victor Jackson rolled his eyes.

"Maureen, I have multiple batteries and I've tried them all. They couldn't all possibly be dead. This is unreal..."

"I wouldn't worry about it so much," she said.

"I want to help the Priests find out all they can," he said sharply.

"Let them do their job. After all, part of our job is confidentiality."

He spun on her, arms tossed upward and dropped by his sides.

"Have you lost your mind? Someone's killing people!"

"Yeah? I hadn't noticed!" she snapped, face twisted sarcastically.

"Oh, you noticed! You just don't seem to care!" he bellowed. "You care more about the contracts and some confidentiality agreement than you do these lives!"

She raised her chin arrogantly.

"One has something to do with me. The other doesn't. Go figure why I'm only concerned with the one impacting me."

He clenched his jaw, anger twisting his handsome face.

"Maureen, if someone kills us all before we get help, there won't be a contract, confidential or not, and there won't be a 'you' to be so selfish!"

"I don't think we have anything to worry about," she said coolly.

"What...do you know something? What do you know, Maureen?" he demanded furiously, slamming his computer closed.

"I know we're not on the list."

"What? What list?" he shouted. Then his eyes widened suddenly and his tone dropped to shock instead of anger as he said, "Maureen, what do you know? What did you do, Maureen?"

"Me?" she shouted. "I don't know what you mean!"

"Did you wreck my laptop?" he railed, pointing wildly.

"No!"

"Did you arrange all this, Maureen?" he howled.

"What? No! Are you crazy? All I meant was that we're not on this hitman's list! He only takes out bad people who are above the law, untouchables, whatever! That ain't me or you, so-"

"Tell me the truth!" he ordered. "Tell me everything, or else!"

"Or else, what?" she snapped, laughing. "Are you the killer? Unless you are, there's not much to fear from you, Victor!"

"You might be surprised," he growled.

Then he stormed out into the corridor, door thrown wide.

She heard him stomping all the way to the stairwell.

“If there's anything surprising about you, Vic, I haven't seen it, yet,” she mumbled, a mirthless grin creasing her face. “But there's hope.”

I did not know what to make of Andreya West's independent streak. I wished she would take more caution but she was a brilliant woman. I had to hope that she had the sense necessary to keep her out of harm's way. Someone had mentioned her genius level intelligence. I hoped some of that fell into the common sense category.

“Hey,” Tayla Barlowe greeted.

She swept back the door to her room and ushered me inside again.

“I barely heard the knock,” she said. “I thought you guys all knocked like it was a raid. What gives?”

“I was trying not to wake Emma,” I said.

“It takes a little somethin' to do that,” she said, gesturing to where Emma slept and slept hard. “Like the fussing crowd. That'll do it.”

“Okay. I'm on my way back downstairs if you're all good. Just checkin' in with you.”

“Good to know. If you're on your way back down it means Andreya was okay. She's a sweet lady, just a little hardheaded.”

Suddenly, the hair I did not have stood on end. I felt as though someone walked across my grave, as my elders used to say. Drawn like a magnet, my face turned toward the overlook. Faintly, barely at all, I heard a click followed by a scuffling sound.

“You know, she's a little-”

I grabbed Barlowe, pulling her close. It shocked her to silence.

I put a finger over my own lips, still not looking at her. My eyes were fixed on the balcony door.

She may have hit me if I had not been holding her so tightly.

“Quiet,” I whispered.

Snidely, she mumbled, “Wow, subtle instructions, since you've pawed all over me, too. Practically makes us family, by the way.”

I scowled at her, noting in a hush, “Nice. Sarcasm.”

“Thanks, Dad,” she whispered. “Most people don't recognize it right off like that.”

“Okay,” I said quietly with a deep breath. “And it keeps coming...”

“What's out there?” she asked softly. “More thunder boomies?”

I could not help giving her that look, the one that chilled some people to their very bones.

“See. The dad look,” she whispered, clearly immune to my glare.

"Hush! I'm going to take a look on the balcony. If anything bad happens, can you get to the lower floors in a flash?" I asked in a whisper.

A louder click. A sharp ping.

"Do bees be? Do flies fly?" she answered quietly, eyes wide.

"If you have to go, don't stop until you get to my wife or James Wyatt," I growled. "I don't know that I trust anyone else."

A sharp clack and the doorknob to the balcony door began to turn.

"Um...that makes three of us..." she breathed.

I caught her by the shoulders and pulled her further aside. Easing around in front of her as she lifted little Emma into her arms, I positioned her in the bathroom and closed the door. Then I took a step backward as I eased my 10mm from its holster, turning cautiously back toward the main room.

There I stood, face to face with the Ghost Revolver, white masked, black garbed phantom of revenge.

For a fleeting, shred of a second, the invisible eyes behind the mask's dark lenses locked with my own. The pause felt like an eternity, for both of us, I was sure. But that was only a feeling, an illusion. The truth was that we both jerked into motion as if set on fire.

I whipped up the 10mm but I was too slow. The Ghost kicked my forearm with a rigid straight kick before I got the gun level. Nerves lit hot in my arm and my hand bucked, opening, going numb. The gun fell free.

Reflex would make most people chase the gun but I knew better. Instead, I pushed for an attack of my own, throwing a hard left hand out to catch the Ghost off guard. The avenger spun about, however. I only caught empty, black coat material with my fist.

A flash of silver glinted in the shadowy clothing. An ancient revolver came out of the black. Urgently, I stabbed out a kick of my own. It struck solidly and the apparition toppled back into the fireplace, crashing over the fireplace bellows, pans, brushes and poker. The gun fell from sight, lost to the assassin, and hit the floor. It skittered underneath the couch.

I ripped my other gun from its holster but the Ghost moved too fast. I felt the full weight of the shadow's form crash into me and it knocked me back, rolling me over a table. I accidentally sent my second gun airborne. I rolled all the way over the table, however, riding the attack's momentum, and it sent me right back to my feet.

I had just reached the floor when the Ghost Revolver pulled that other, silver hand cannon. I lunged forward, sliding across the table, just as the shadow rolled back the hammer. In one slick snatch the gun was mine. The shade kicked out immediately, however, hitting the gun.

The blow spun it from my hand and sent it flying, too.

Instead of going for a weapon, we both accepted that the engagement would be hand to hand. My enemy fired a wild punch, thrown from the back field. I ducked and threw a quick one-two combination of strikes in return, both blocked by the Ghost, who just danced away. I pursued in a lunge and tried a front kick.

Ready for me, the Ghost rolled my leg aside, letting me follow through. I drove forward with weight and momentum and the assassin launched a side handed, knife edge chop for my throat. I managed a counter of my own then, blocking it with my forearm.

I sharply threw my blocking hand backward in a fist. The mask clacked loudly as my knuckles raked over it but there was no real impact. My hand simply grazed the face shield.

The specter spun about with the momentum, however.

To press the advantage, I followed with another kick. Again, the Ghost sidestepped it deftly. Planting that foot, I kicked out with the other, keeping on the offensive. I should have considered my defense.

The nightshade chose not to move away in defense. Instead, the ethereal stalker dropped into a crouch and kicked me in the leg on which I stood. The black boot ground a surgical strike into the side of my left knee...a knee already chronically traumatized in my career.

I slammed straight to the floor, gripping that leg, teeth ground together. The pain made my head spin and I heard my teeth squeak under the pressure from my locked jaw. My senses dulled.

"Aw, c'mon, Dad!" Tayla Barlowe shouted.

The sound of the young mother's voice shocked me back to full awareness. I looked about from the floor and scrambled back to my feet when I saw her at her bathroom door.

She cradled her child close to her chest.

The Ghost rushed me where I crouched, ignoring the Barlowes. In a desperate maneuver, I grappled the Ghost around the waist on approach, lifting and tossing my attacker through the open balcony door. The move collapsed my bad knee in a stabbing pain and I went down again.

Like an actual shadow, the bundle of black long coat, pants and boots rolled all the way to the balcony's banister rails in a shapeless mass.

I was struggling back to my feet, one leg limp, when the Ghost hit the railing. I purposely angled my back toward the young Tayla and put myself between her and the shadow. The Ghost Revolver recovered faster than I did, however, and the black form charged for me immediately.

I twisted at the last possible second as the Revolver kicked out, booted leg shooting out beside me. I spun as hard as I could with only one leg as a support and hit the Revolver in the gut. I put all I could muster into that right uppercut.

The rock solid blow sent the Ghost Revolver tumbling all the way back to the overlook's railing. Balance lost, bearings lost, the Ghost went headlong right between the railing bars.

"And boom goes the dynamite!" Tayla howled, jumping around.

I turned her way by reflex. In the motion I put weight on the twisted knee and I grimaced, nearly going blind with pain. The leg crumbled beneath me and I went straight to the floor again. I tried to get right back up but my right arm, from the elbow to my fingertips, pulsed with every beat of my heart. Numbness, mingled with sharp, grating pain in the joints, disabled that arm and hand completely.

My attacker had been wearing defensive armor.

Tayla Barlowe, Emma snuggled close, dropped to her knees by me and shoved one of my guns into my hand. I winced when I took it. Something popped in my wrist, the hand caught fire and the Colt dangled loosely. I switched it to my left hand and leveled it toward the balcony rail, teeth clenched.

"Just in case," I whispered.

"In case what?" Tayla shouted. "He can fly?"

Thunder clapped in the distance and rolled over the mountainside. Seconds later, when the lightning flared, it lit several new faces.

Sarah broke from Tayla's room, charging onto the overlook, handgun at the ready. Cassandra Clark rushed behind her. A second later came James, Sig Sauer drawn. Shadowing him was Maureen Li.

I leaned over and dropped flat onto my back, just breathing.

"Oh, Mick!" Sarah gasped.

"You okay, Mick?" James asked.

Sarah brought Clark to my side and they crouched by me.

"I was in the hall, just comin' outta Johanna's, when I heard some kinda dull ruckus!" James added. "I practically ran over Maureen, here, wandering down the hall."

"I was looking for Vic!" she snapped.

"Baby, what happened?" Sarah asked me. "Are you okay?"

Barlowe spoke before I could.

"Who, Papa Priest?" she asked with a snort. "He's fine! Won the protective dad award, too!"

"James, Sarah, over the side," I said, grimacing. "Check it out. Revolver took a header."

James rushed for the side of the balcony but Sarah simply watched him, more intent on staying by my side.

"What do you see?" she asked him. "Who is it?"

"We'll know who he is, or was, when they scrape him up off the ground," Tayla said.

"Whoever it was had on body armor," I muttered, grinding my teeth against the pain.

Clark noticed I was clutching at my right forearm and wrist. She took it from me and held it gently.

"Must've had on wings," James said darkly. When Maureen Li rushed the rail for a look of her own, he said, "Ain't nobody down there."

"Huh?" Tayla said.

"There's no one on the ground!" Li replied. "Whoever it was got up-"

"Nobody 'gets up' from that fall," Tayla Barlowe growled. "We know what we saw, what happened."

"James, go after 'em, I'm fine," I urged.

"Mick," James said patiently, "They're gone. By the time I cover three or more levels in a chase, our playmate'll be gone even more."

"Then we chase the trail," Sarah told him. She turned concerned, impassioned eyes back to me. "Are you okay, Mick? Really?"

"Yeah, yeah," I assured. "I'm good."

"We can stay with you," Tayla told me.

"We'll help you up, get you going where you need to be," Cassandra Clark added.

I wanted to say no but they seemed determined, eyes ardently fixed.

"Go ahead," I said. "We'll be along. But see Ms. Li back to her room as you go."

"And she'll *stay* there," Sarah growled at the woman.

"Vic and I were arguing and he stormed out! I was looking-"

"We'll tend to Jackson," James interrupted. "Come on."

Then James and Sarah, escorting Li, set out to pursue a ghost.

"Better take this," Barlowe said, handing me my other 10mm. "You gonna be okay? For real?"

It concerned her that, even with Clark's help, I had only managed to get to a sitting position. We had not even addressed my knee; Clark was still testing the pain in my arm. I had to put one pistol away so I could take the second in my left hand.

"Yeah, yeah, I'm fine," I said. I nodded at her baby, swaddled against her body. "What about Emma? She hasn't made a sound, even with all the shouting and noise. Is that normal for her?"

Tayla Barlowe laughed and dropped the bundle. Inside the wrap was a lamp base, no shade.

"She's fine," she said when Clark and I gasped. She giggled, pointed back to the bathroom and said, "I was in there. You and that maniac started lacing it up so I put all the towels in the tub, made sure she was in a position where she couldn't roll away or get out of the tub, tucked her in the towel pile and closed the bathroom up tight. I grabbed a lamp and wrapped it up and made a fake Emma."

I chuckled in disbelief.

"You should've stayed with your little girl," I said nevertheless.

"No way. I couldn't leave you out here, by yourself. You weren't just fighting for you but fighting for us, too. If you hadn't been able to win, I would've tried to help and I didn't want Emma in danger. Plus, if that freak had gotten by you, I would've rained fake Emma down on his head!" she laughed, patting the oaken lamp.

She impressed me with her courage, her thinking and planning. She was quite the young lady and quite the mamma bear.

"That was a gamble," Clark said.

"That maniac didn't stand a chance," Tayla said in reply. "Emma's new, honorary granddad saw to that."

Then she hugged me.

"And Emma's fine," a woman said from behind us all.

We jerked about as one, eyes wide, breath caught in our throats. My 10mm instantly fixed on the countenance of Andreya West, target seeking with a mind of its own.

West held up her open hands in a halting gesture.

"I checked on Emma on the way through the room," she clarified. "I heard her talking in the bathroom."

I lowered the hand cannon as everyone eased.

"Where were you?" Tayla interrogated, irritated by the woman's sudden arrival.

"Having a nice, long, cool bath," West explained. She tossed her long, wet hair back over her shoulders from where her linen top was wet. "I have yet to even finish my hair."

Tayla shrugged with, "Well, we brought the whole floor, except for Ms. Crimson and her bodyguard guy."

"And no one expected them to respond," Clark said lowly. Then, "Can you walk, Mr. Priest?"

"It's Mick," both Tayla and Andreya West corrected her.

"Are you finished twisting that arm?" I asked.

"No," Clark answered honestly. "But I thought we might get off the deck and inside a room."

She gave me both hands. I took them in my left hand after holstering my other Colt. She pulled me, helping me rise onto one leg. Andreya West helped me, too, while Tayla went to get Emma.

"Is it broken?" West asked Clark.

"The arm or the knee?" she retorted with a smirk.

"Well, the knee, since we're trying to stand him up."

"You want the hopeful or the pessimistic?" Clark asked, observing me hobble about until I steadied.

"Either," West chimed.

"Hopefully, not. I need to get a better look at it."

I had the toe of that foot touching the floor but just lightly, the knee bent, the leg limp.

"It's an old injury and I wear a brace on it," I informed them. "When the Ghost kicked it, the brace gave way and hurt it pretty bad. Hopefully it's just hyper-extended, sprained."

They aided me and I hopped along toward the interior of the room, following the young mother's trail. As we passed through the balcony door, Tayla stopped me, Emma safe in her embrace.

"Thanks, Mr. Priest. Seriously."

"You're welcome. And so's Emma."

She giggled and said, "Mick isn't right, though."

"What?"

"Nah, I can't call you Mick," she said. "Emma's decided you're an honorary Granddad. That makes you my Papa. Honorary, of course."

"Of course," I chuckled.

"And you're pretty cool," she nodded with a big grin. "Emma says."

"Okay."

"So, if you're cool and you're my Papa, too, that makes you Emma's Popsicle. You know, Papa and cool, like a Papa-sicle, Popsicle."

"You're putting a lot of thought into this, aren't you?" West asked.

She giggled.

James Wyatt planned to run the balconies on the western side of the resort. He would take one floor at the time, from the upper to the ground, looking for a sign of passage. Broken windows, open doors.

The pursuit was going to be a grand story and a tale for regaling, especially with the way he was known for elaborating to entertain. He denied it, of course, but the man could add a convincing flourish to a grocery errand that could make it unforgettable.

Nevertheless, there were times he hardly felt like the colorful bard many knew he could be. If he found nothing, it would deflate him, again.

Sarah Priest would race through the interior of the building the same way. Same trajectory, upper floor to the ground.

The efforts seemed fruitless for both of them, at first.

The upper floor balcony and the next one, at first glace, yielded nothing. The first two corridors within the building gave Sarah Priest nothing more.

Was the Ghost Revolver really a ghost? Who could survive a fall like that and get up from it, much less run away and disappear? Leaving no trace? It simply defied explanation...aside from the very hitman's name...

...*Ghost* Revolver.

In any case, James Wyatt and Sarah Priest had agreed to pursue with diligence. That is what they did, meeting the struggle head on.

Cassandra Clark was asked once again to put her knowledge of sports medicine and first aid to use. Mick Priest, stubborn and independent, played it off but the knee needed attention.

She sat down in a desk chair Tayla Barlowe righted for her in the sacked room. Sitting on the battered table, Mick Priest angled his left leg so Clark could get to the knee. Tayla held her daughter close in one arm where she stood by the desk, beside Priest, holding a flashlight.

West stood behind Clark and held another light over the director's shoulder, expression concerned and fervent.

Clark twitched and tossed her long, wavy hair back over her shoulder, out of her face. Both hands worked Priest's knee joint. Moisture glistened over her face and neck but compared little to the bullets Mick Priest felt running over him, beneath his clothes and over his head. The pain was considerable, drawing profuse sweat from him.

"Are you okay?" West asked him after a particularly urgent wince.

"Mr. Priest needs treatment, not a band-aid," Clark said.

"Mick," Tayla and Andreya West said simultaneously.

"Mick," Clark scolded, "you need a doctor, not a sports wrap and not just that hinged brace you've been using. I'm almost positive you've damaged at least the lateral collateral ligament, if not both the lateral and medial-"

"Yep, good ol' sprains in the LCL and the MCL, had those before," he grunted, wincing again.

"No, not just sprains," she said. "If they're sprained it's with grade three sprains, meaning they're torn badly." She pressed her thumb into the inside of the knee joint, causing him to flinch again. "I'd lay money you've got an ACL tear in here, too, not to mention it feels like it's weak enough to dislocate-"

"Done both of those before, too," he said through ground teeth.

"-and you need surgery on it, Mr. Priest. Really. How long are you going to punish this joint?" Cassandra drilled. "That brace is better than nothing but it really isn't enough for much."

"Keeps me hoppin', Ms. Clark," Priest said.

"Hopping. Not running. Barely walking."

"Okay, okay," Tayla said. "Bad knee and all, he still Konged that skull man's jungle."

West could not help but giggle.

"Konged," she echoed.

Clark fired them a sidelong stare. Then she looked back to Priest.

"Regardless of your masterful mat techniques, you need to get this knee fixed, no two ways about it. Stay off of it. No kidding."

"Yep, got it."

Clark looked back at West.

"Would you get us a cold, wet cloth?"

She nodded and left for the bathroom.

Clark stood to her feet and leaned in close to Priest, wiping the sweat from her own neck and brow.

"Okay. Let's see that arm, again."

West quickly returned with the cold cloth, dripping. Clark took it and wiped over Priest's head and neck then left it draped around his neck.

"Ready, Mr. Priest...Mick?" Clark asked. "This may hurt."

Chipper as always, West giggled once the others quieted.

"This is pretty exciting, right?" Andreya West asked, her big, beautiful eyes wide, lovely smile beaming.

Priest chuckled.

"Yeah. Riveting."

Mick Priest had sent a Ghost Revolver reeling and falling from the upper story. The body had never come to rest on the ground below. James Wyatt and Sarah Priest were dead set on tracking the killer's trail, if they could find it. So, one took the balconies, the other, the halls.

James had finished the upper balcony and the next, outside Floor Three, when he stopped. He was simply unwilling to believe there was no trace of the killer or the fall. When he got near the end of Floor Three's balcony, he stopped and turned back, slowly revisiting the long outcropping.

There had to be some sign.

He paused directly below the point where Priest had sent the shadow through the rails, trying to uncover something, anything he could have missed. It was there he finally noticed something off, something worthy of investigation.

Just under the area where the Ghost had fought Mick Priest, a metal, electrical conduit was bent down. It reached out its spindly arm almost all the way to the floor of Floor Three's overlook. Under the yearning angle of metal piping, the concrete and tile floor of Floor Three's balcony bore cracks and chips, minuscule and nearly imperceptible. Stone dust and debris, freshly broken from the surface, littered the space. It looked like something had crashed onto the spot but only if you saw the pointing, metal conduit arm, giving away the secret.

James Wyatt allowed his mind to play the mental video of what he imagined had happened. The Ghost had spun about and slipped between the balcony rails. The specter, about to drop headlong to a grisly death, grabbed onto the small conduit. Thin brackets did not hold and the gunslinger kept falling, seeming to drop all the way down.

Instead, the assassin held onto the conduit and it bent, pulling the killer sideways as it folded toward the building. It dumped the stalker roughly onto the next balcony, one floor below where the fight had started. The impact shattered some tile and mortar but the shadow got up and made an escape into the night and deeper shadow.

James Wyatt looked around. Torn wiring dangled from the place where the conduit used to attach. Any other time, the wires would have been live and could have thrown sparks in the midst of the event. However, with the power out, the action played out subtly. No light show, thrown by raw electricity arcing here and there, gave away the secret. No sounds of crackling power told the story. It was no mystery how he had missed it in the dark on his first pass.

James shifted his eyes to the likely direction the Ghost would have traveled in rushed retreat. The balcony door to Room One of Floor Three called to him. The room inhabited by Rembrandt Lyles.

The path of quickest escape, he thought to himself. *I'd go inside. More hidin' places...if that kid ain't the Revolver, anyway.*

He pulled his gun free and went to Room One's outside door. He stopped, cautious. It was not locked, considering it was not even closed. The door stood ajar by two inches.

James Wyatt brought up the SigSauer .357 at once. He used one foot to sweep the door backward. When the door stopped against the far wall, the hair standing on James Wyatt's neck, the professional defender took his first step into the room.

The posters for an illustrated Revolver glowed in his flashlight.

"Yo, anybody in here better show yourself," he announced calmly, looking for any movement. "I'm James Wyatt, I'm armed and I'm trigger happy. Anybody here?"

Nothing. No answer. No movement. No noise.

Carefully, the defender crept through the room and its bathroom, no one to be found. Nothing jumped out at him as out of place or ransacked, either. The room simply took him along innocently to the interior door, the corridor door, also unlocked.

At the door, James stopped.

Luck smiled on you, Ghost, he thought to himself. *You fell, managed an impossible grab and landed on this floor. Luck ain't even the word for it. You got skills.*

Carefully, he eased the door open and peered into the corridor. He took a very quick glance one way, snapping back inside, then glanced the other way. The hall was uninhabited. James very slowly stepped into the passageway then closed the door behind himself.

"I know how you got away," he mumbled. "I just don't know where."

He holstered the Sig again.

"As for you, Mr. Lyles, where did you get off to?"

Mick Priest put the silver revolvers into a pillow case.

"That's gonna be pretty uncomfortable," Barlowe said.

"Yeah? I'm not laying on them," he said. "Easier than carrying them loosely, though. I need to try to track the Ghost Revolver."

"You already got two people on that," she chimed. "You need-"

"I have to help. I'm going to start with Maureen Li. Right now, I need to get moving," he interrupted.

"Yeah, Papa...about that moving thing..." Tayla said.

The detective stood on one leg, the other cocked, supporting nothing.

"I'm good, Tayla," Mick Priest said.

"Hmmmm," she considered.

He put the foot flat and exerted the tiniest bit of pressure. His hurt knee buckled instantly, squeezing a grunt from him. The rough and tumble detective stiffened the leg and forced the muscles to hold.

"Aaaaaaaannnnd that's known as good?" she asked melodiously.

"Hush," he said.

"There he is. The dad."

"More tending little Emma, less jabbering."

Little Emma said something that closely resembled 'jabbering'.

"We'll walk you down," Tayla tried.

"No," he countered. "You stay right in here, doors locked."

"But-"

"No," he said again. "In this room until one of the good guys comes back for you. Locked up tight. Safe. Get me?"

"Good guys?" she asked, stalling.

"Me, my wife, Sarah, or James Wyatt."

"But what about-" she tried.

He grabbed her face on both sides with gentle hands.

"Tayla, if anyone else tries to come in here, you and Emma get into that bathroom and lock that door, too. One of us will be back just as soon as we can."

"Okay, but you better kiss me and Emma Monkey goodnight on our foreheads if you wanna hang on to your title," she giggled.

So, he did.

Then he hobbled out of the room and limped down the corridor, heading straight for Maureen Li's room.

Mick Priest, no fool and no amateur, had removed himself from all eyes with due intention. He had sent Cassandra Clark with Andreya West as an escort, a 'safety in numbers' kind of thing, though West's room was just across the hall. He instructed them to stay in the room together, even if no longer than for someone else to come back and escort Clark downstairs.

Having succeeded, isolating himself for just a short walk, he stopped into his own room and hid the revolvers, both inside the fireplace. Then, enemy weapons secreted away in their designated wooden case, the detective came back out and limped for Li's chamber.

CHAPTER FOURTEEN

The sky rumbled its disappointment in those it saw below. With flashes of brilliant, scorching light, it revealed all in occasional seconds both born and gone at once. The inhabitants of Shadow Mountain, those unable to succumb to the seduction of sleep, felt their very sins exposed for all to see when the lightning crashed. It was emphatically true when the pursuant thunder, voice of an angry, watching sky, shook the Earth.

Guilty, the judgment was pronounced.

Sarah Priest and James Wyatt had split up to cover more area while chasing a ghost. Both promised themselves they would return quickly to check on Mick Priest and the others with him. They each reminded each other, too, of Mick's last bit of advice.

Remember, somebody still has Grip's gun. The Revolver likely still has more firepower, revolvers or not.

While James Wyatt set off on an expedition down the balcony overlooks, Sarah breezed quickly through Floor Four. In no time, she was satisfied the Revolver was not hiding on Floor Three, either, and she moved on to Floor Two.

She had no sooner stepped off the stairway landing when a door opened up into that hall. The SBI agent whipped up her Smith and Wesson, already in hand. Then she met the figures exiting that room with her light and the business end of her handgun.

Tye Richter, with Helena Makai close by him, halted immediately.

"Agent Priest, it's just us," Tye said.

"Yes, hold your fire," Makai said uncomfortably.

Priest lowered her gun.

"Out of your rooms, again," she said. "I just can't understand."

"We were in the same room, Cassandra's room," Richter explained. "I was waiting with Helena and Gretchen until Cassandra gets back."

"How many times do we have to say it's not safe?" Priest asked.

"This is pretty important," Richter said.

"Yes. Getting off this mountain," Helena Makai said.

Sarah regarded her for a moment, throwing a look Richter's way, too.

Richter said, "That looks an awful lot like suspicion on your face."

"It's okay," Sarah eased. "I'm paid to be suspicious. Continue."

"Mr. Jenkins, trying to find answers on his own, ransacked Cassandra's office," the head server informed.

"Made a mess is what he did," Richter added.

"We're aware," the state agent said.

"He thought there might be something in the contracts for this weekend, with the details about the guests, that could help us find out who was behind everything," Makai tattled.

"Well?" Sarah asked.

"He made a mess," Richter said again.

Priest sighed and rolled her eyes.

"Sorry. Anyway, there was nothin' to find. Cassie could've told him that if he'd asked. So, earlier, we figured we'd clean it up for her. The thing is, when we were cleaning up, we found something else. Something I had forgotten about completely. We found all the original resort maps."

"What maps?"

"Maps of the drives, the road in, the grounds, the historic trails, the riding trails, all of it," Helena said.

Richter then said, "The key point here being the riding trails. The horse riding trails. I know all the rest of that stuff by heart, being the Facilities Director. But some of the horseback trails and historic trails...they were news to this guy."

Makai spoke before Sarah Priest could ask the question.

"We can ride down those trails, into the valley and beyond. We can get everyone out safely."

"We got more than enough horses and tack for everyone and most of our mounts are easy riders," Richter said.

"What about people with no horse sense?" Sarah asked.

"Some of our mounts are trailblazers but most are trained to follow the horse in front of them. No riding skill is really needed, just the desire to hold on."

"Okay. You guys sit on this information. We may just go that way. Until then-"

"Back to the room, got it," Richter said.

Li unlocked the room door for Mick Priest but he had to knock three times. She invited him inside, swinging wide the door.

He panned his light about, despite the ambient light given off by the light Li had on a lamp table. Satisfied they were alone, he closed the door behind himself and set the lock.

Li gestured to a chair, saying, "You could have simply asked if we were the only people here, Mr. Priest."

"Could I?" he asked, sitting down across the coffee table from her. "When it comes to a chance of being murdered, I like to avoid second hand information, assumptions and presumptions. Any one of those can be deadly. By the way, your roommate, Victor...where is he?"

She swallowed a hard gulp of air.

"I've already told you," she said. "He got mad at me and stormed out. Is he on your 'radar' now for suspects? I was hoping you would be trying to find him, not painting him to be a monster."

He met her gaze directly.

"I'm not much for painting. I'm more of a 'written word' type."

She whipped her head around, silken, black hair fanning out beautifully. Her eyes found the writing desk in the room.

"Should I get you a pen and some paper," she asked, staring across the room, "so you can document your accusations?"

"It's early, yet," he allowed with a small, polite smile. "I'm curious, though, how you came to the conclusion that I suspect Mr. Jackson."

"Don't you? You were just asking-"

"I don't believe in luck, Ms. Li, and I don't believe in coincidence. I run on facts and, to get those facts, I have to ask questions. Lots of questions. If one question, like where is Mr. Jackson, could answer all the elements of this mystery, I'd be out of a job."

"Okay. I stand corrected," she said. "What can I do for you?"

"I need you to tell me about Gridlock Publishing, its practices, its people. Anything and everything you believe might help this case."

Priest watched her like a hawk. Every move, every expression, every blink. She never batted an eye, never glanced away nervously. The woman was stalwart and steady.

"I don't know what to say," she said finally.

"You can start with why Victor is angry with you."

She allowed a sad, begrudging smile.

"Is anything amusing?" Priest asked.

"You feel as though that has something to do with Gridlock Publishing and not just a personal squabble?"

"Ms. Li, let's not play games. There's just no time left for it."

Her black eyes focused intently on him.

She replied, "Just what do you mean?"

"Vic already shared with me that he's uncertain about the company and how you guys came into all this. Now, should I be worried about him? Or you? Is it you, not Gridlock, we should suspect of something? Or, if he's helpful, what's he going to tell us? What does he know?"

"Yes, of course, I'm next on the list," she said angrily. "Do you actually think I'm your assassin? How crazy are you people?"

"You were quick to show up when I tossed the Revolver through that railing."

"What did I do? Fly back to my room, change clothes and then make a quick return?" she balked loudly.

He focused on her black eyes.

"Talk to me. Tell me something if you don't like my questions."

"I don't know anything," she groaned. "It's pretty hard to know the truth when nothing's as clear or simple as it seems."

"Truth has a way of showing itself, Ms. Li. The problem is never with the truth. The problem is with mankind. Our perceptions, our understanding, our agendas and our own deceptions."

She said nothing, locking her jaw.

Abruptly, someone pounded on the door.

Maureen Li jumped but Priest simply whipped a Colt from a holster. He angled himself about to see her and the door.

"You get the door, Ms. Li. I'll wait here."

She did as he asked and opened the door to Victor Jackson.

"Come on in, Vic," called Mick Priest, gun at the ready.

Li stepped back as Victor did as Priest instructed.

"Where have you been?" she demanded of the man.

"He and I have been chatting," Sarah Priest said, walking in behind him and closing the door.

Victor Jackson put down a small, black bag under Sarah Priest's light. He quickly pulled an array of battery packs and a cobbled, alligator clip cord from it. He then grabbed up his laptop.

"He's been busy," Sarah noted.

"Wait," Li warned. "What are you...what do you think you're doing? Didn't you hear a thing I said-"

She started forward, as if to physically halt the man. Agent Sarah Priest caught her by the forearm and stopped her still.

"That's enough, Ms. Li," she warned.

"I heard you, Maureen," Victor answered. "I heard you quote protocols, I heard you recite copyrights, confidentiality and I heard you praise company ethics. What I did not hear you do was offer one whit of support to these people when they are trying desperately to save lives!"

"How...where did all this come from?" she demanded.

"You're not the only hardware specialist," he replied. "And that computer conferencing room is just full of hardware, dead to the world. I simply borrowed the guts out of a server backup supply. I can't use the net but I took the power from a backup to bring my laptop back to life."

"For what?" Li shouted. "Just to violate our confidentiality agreements? Just to get us fired?"

"Lady-" Sarah started.

"Shut up, Maureen," Victor barked. "If there's one word in our files that helps these people, they're getting it."

Victor Jackson angled the top of his computer back and went to work on the keyboard. The Priests did not know how many words per minute the man could type but they knew instantly he was a guru on the keys.

"I discharged all those batteries on purpose, Vic!" Li shouted.

"Oh, I figured. And, now, I bring some back to life," he growled.

"I had to protect the company-"

"Shut up, Maureen," Sarah Priest echoed Jackson.

The Priests fixated on the computer, though not to the point that Sarah let Maureen Li go free.

Victor reflected an almost ghastly shade of pale in the softly glowing screen. Displayed in finely tuned detail were all the points of interest necessary for the weekend to take place. Reservations, prices, directions, travel information, pick up and drop off locations and contact information. The set up had not missed a trick.

"This is pretty impressive," Sarah noted, still reading. "You do good work. The world runs on the skill and finesse of the detail people."

Victor said, "I pride myself on my work. Even more so on my Faith. Just like with my family, when I'm at work, I give a hundred percent. However, this detailed rundown of arrangements for this weekend is not my work, I must admit."

"What? Then who put this together?"

"I haven't figured that out," he said with a shake of his head. "That's why I brought it up to Maureen. She said it was handed down through the chain of directors in Gridlock Publishing-"

"It was! It had to be!" she challenged.

"-but I've never known them to do any of our work for us. That's why I sat down to go over everything again."

"So, that's when you said it just came down normal channels for you two?" Priest asked Li.

"Yes! I said we shouldn't worry about it. I certainly wasn't going to look a gift horse in the mouth, you can bet! It was a hand delivered opportunity! The less work, the better!"

"I couldn't ignore it, though, considering what started happening," Victor Jackson said.

"Ms. Li, let's have you go back to sitting on that couch," Mick Priest ordered politely. "Mr. Jackson is going to educate us a little and show us inside Pandora's box."

She sat down, aware of Mick Priest's cautious observation. With a huff and a snide smile, forced, of course, she leaned back in final resignation.

"When Gridlock sues all of you-"

"Hush, honey," Sarah Priest interrupted. "Adults are talking."

"Take us on a tour of Oz, Mr. Wizard," Mick Priest told Jackson.

"Good luck finding a yellow brick road," Li spat.

"At least, we know who plays the wicked witch," Victor grumbled.

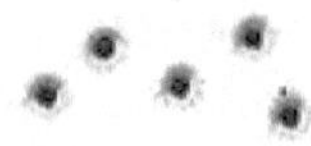

Sarah sat across from me. Her head was not down but her eyes had checked out somewhere around the fourth 'white hat/black hat' explanation and his introduction to 'botnets' and 'rootkits'. I had to admit to myself that I almost nodded off, too, right around learning that a 'RAT' was not a rodent. That was when Sarah got up, stretched her lithe form against her tight clothing and her fatigue-tightened joints, and announced that she was going to make a few rounds.

It was not Jackson's presentation and it was not so much that the topic was dry. Lack of sleep and the sifting away of the night's hourglass sand had more to do with it than anything.

I asked her to escort Clark back to her room if she was going to be about, anyway, and she agreed. She also said she would check on the little mother and her child.

After a time, I had to ask.

"We got anything case-breaking, Vic?"

"I've got quite a bit of data," he said, still crunching away. "I'm pulling a lot out of these packets that were hidden below the surface; there's a lot more info on each of the guests than Gridlock would've had, that's for sure. Personal history stuff, that kinda thing."

"I'm glad Sarah collected you from your scavenger hunt," I said.

He laughed and agreed with, "Yes, I shouldn't have gone off alone but I felt I had to act. To help, if I could. Agent Priest came along just in time to hold a light for me."

"I'm glad you're on it," I said.

Li laughed so boisterously that it bordered on a manic outburst.

"Yeah, I can just bet. It ain't like you could extract it; you wouldn't know the difference between a gigabyte and a bug bite."

Jackson ignored her just like I did.

"So, anything astounding, yet?" I pressed.

"All this deep info is pretty-"

"No, Vic, like any particular thing..."

"Like the Alphabets in black?" Vic Jackson asked with a chortle.

"What?" Maureen Li asked, interest piqued.

"Government boys," Jackson answered, more on reflex than intent.

"CIA, DEA, FBI, ATF," I explained. "Why? Have something you'd like to share?"

She huffed again and folded her arms over her chest.

Vic Jackson stiffened. Something new on the screen caught his eye.

"Mr. Priest, do you see this line? This one right here?" he asked.

I got out of my seat, stretched and hopped to where he was. He pointed to a line of contact information below my name, one with no name attached.

"What's that?" I asked.

"That line falls in the *agent contact*, or alternative contact, category. Like the way Ms. Crimson has a personal appearance agent and Mr. Blackwood has a booking agent. Your agent contact number doesn't have a name listed-"

"I don't have a contact agent," I snapped. "I don't have any agents. Of any kind. I wasn't brought here as a guest, exactly. I was brought here as added security for Johanna Crimson."

He frowned, running his finger to the right, murmuring, "See, here's your personal contact information..."

"Yeah, I get it. But the other?"

He tapped the screen on the asterisk.

"In this file, this indicates preferred method of booking. For you, it's indicating this other contact information. You're in this file as a guest, a writer, and as being agent-notified. There's no identification for the contact but I assumed it was like the others."

I tapped the mystery contact.

"You're saying this was set up for you guys...well, I don't know who sent a writer's invitation out or who that contact is you say received it but I know Gridlock didn't invite me here. James and Crimson did."

"It says here that Gridlock did, it just went to your representative-"

"Vic, I told you, I don't have an agent in any way, shape or form."

"Maybe you should get one," Maureen Li said lowly. "Like a lawyer, when Gridlock finds out you dug into our privileged communications."

"I honestly wish that was important, right now," I said.

James Wyatt tapped on the door to Johanna Crimson's room. Gibson answered the door, his face a long way from cordial.

"Any word on the case?" he greeted very softly.

He was tired, someplace near exhaustion, and it showed.

"Good to see you, too," James remarked.

He then nodded at Crimson's bed. There was an anonymous lump under the covers, the occupant invisible to the room.

Gibson did not back away, nor did he invite the other man inside.

"Kid's asleep. Finally. Tryin' to keep it that way. She needs rest."

"She's gonna suffocate or have a heat stroke," James said wryly.

"It's just a single sheet and she's wearin' nothin' else. Says she has to have a cover to sleep so, everything else had to go." Gibson gave a half shrug, adding, "You gotta do what you need to do."

"Oh...um, yeah," James agreed, clearly dazed by the information.

He stood up on his toes to look over Gibson's shoulder, as if that would somehow let him see beyond the sheet.

"Easy, Ponytail," Gibson said.

James snapped back to himself and looked at Gibson with feigned surprise, eyes huge.

"Gibson, I'm hurt," he said unconvincingly. "I'm a professional, after all. To think that you would believe I was...why, I'm a happily married man. I think of Ms. Crimson, Johanna, as a dear friend, my-"

"You want a prize? I'm completely out of rainbows and unicorns," her armed attache exhaled. "You wanna peep show? Watch another Velvet Edge movie. She's got less on in those than she does, right now. Let's you 'n' me get right to it."

"Oh," James said casually. "No problem. But would you say she has on less in *VE3* than she did in-"

"Aw, come on," Gibson drawled.

"Yeah, back to it," James said. "Here's the thing, Gibson. The SBI doesn't have any news. Mick Priest, however, fought our killer."

"Fought? Where? When? Details, man."

"On the balcony of this floor, the other side, outside the young mom's room."

"So, we got 'im?"

"No. Priest sent the Revolver over the edge."

"So, he's dead?"

"No. I followed the trail-"

"Tell the whole thing," Gibson spat. "I'm getting' tired chasin' you about it, one piece after another."

Then James Wyatt did just that, sharing a quick and precise version of the events, including his current quest to find Remy Lyles.

"Comforting," Gibson growled.

"You 'n' me play things straight, though," James said.

"Yeah."

"We're thorough. Dot our 'i' s, cross our 't' s."

"Yep."

"Solid," James said with a nod. "Show me your torso, Gibson. Your gut, your stomach, your ribs."

Gibson stared at him wordlessly.

"Priest hit our shooter with a massive uppercut to the lower torso. So much force that it shoved 'im back through the balcony rails. I figure I'll ask to see everybody's lower abdomen and ribs 'til I find somebody with a lotta hurt."

"I got no time for-" Gibson started irritably.

"Show him or next he'll be wanting to see mine," Johanna Crimson said, igniting a small flashlight by her bed.

She yawned and her eyes fluttered quite heavily. She rose, sitting up in the bed with her sheet clutched to herself in one hand.

Gibson scowled.

"Wow," James breathed.

Gibson pulled up his shirt and struck his own torso several times.

"No hurt," he said. "And you ain't gettin' a look at Johanna with no shirt."

James looked at Crimson, who winked at him, then back to Gibson.

"Then it's back to the trail for me," James said. "I'll let you know-"

"You do that," Gibson snapped and slammed the door in his face.

"Okay. That's the plan," James said, pretending Gibson was still there, talking with him. "Sounds solid. I'mma get back to it. Dig you up later...you ol' fossil."

James walked away from the room and stalked the rest of the corridor, hawk's eyes raking the very color from the walls. Uncertain of where Rembrandt Lyles hid himself and just as uncertain why, he started making his way back to the little man's room for another look.

On the way by Maureen Li's room, he heard the faintest, telltale resonating of conversation. He had known Mick Priest for decades; he would know his voice, however faint, anytime. The defender stopped and knocked on the door.

It had no sooner swept back when Sarah Priest called out to James from the stairwell.

"Hey," she said, starting the walk for where he was. "Any luck?"

"Sure," he answered. He eyeballed Victor Jackson, the man who had opened the room door for him, adding, "All of it bad."

When she reached them, Sarah Priest joined James and they went into the room. Victor closed the door behind them.

"Okay. What do we know?" Mick Priest started.

James Wyatt shared his experience following the trail of the flying ghost, from the railing to the hallway on the far side of the room held for Rembrandt Lyles.

Sarah Priest told the others about her excursion through the corridors and the interactions she had, including the revelation given by Tye Richter and Helena Makai. A way off the mountain, a way down without a bridge.

Mick Priest filled the others in on what he and Victor Jackson had been discussing and Maureen Li's aversion to helping them, for whatever reasons.

Victor Jackson plugged away at his keyboard the whole time, eyes afire, drilling into the information stored and hidden away. Maureen Li would have likely still pouted, had she not fallen asleep on the couch sometime along the way.

When James yawned and wiped over his face for the third time, seated at a small table with Mick and Sarah Priest, he spoke again.

"Night's bleedin' out," James muttered. "No sleep since Thursday night and we're knockin' on the door of Sunday morning."

"The morning of truth," Sarah noted. "We've got to wrap this all up, get to the end of it all. We have to be close."

"The morning of truth...coming on a day of Truth, a day of worship. I can't help but feel like the end is close," Mick said.

All of them were hot and tired of being hot. Sarah fanned herself, hair tied up atop her head, hot by nature. But Victor Jackson was soaked in sweat, often wiping at his eyes so he could see.

"Thanks to Victor, we now have more knowledge than ever."

"Don't thank me, Mr. Priest," Jackson said from the desk. "Someone embedded this excess information in Gridlock's files, meaning for somebody to find it. There's a reason behind all of this. Somebody's intentionally sharing all of it, banking on one of us pulling it out."

"How?" James asked.

"More to the point, who?" Mick Priest asked.

"A hacker?" Sarah suggested.

Victor shrugged.

"I don't know. Most hackers I've heard of tend to steal information. Compromise databases. Shut systems down. This person provided information, building a database for use, here. They banked on the systems continuing to work..."

"Interesting," Sarah said, nodding at Victor.

"Yeah, considering somebody dropped all the power and the communications. We got two forces operatin' behind the scenes?"

"The Revolver and someone trying to outmaneuver the Revolver?" Mick asked, following the logic of his friend.

"Just good questions, still unanswered," Sarah said.

"Then the three of us talk answers, the ones we got," James said.

"We have three dead," Sarah said flatly. "Two closely linked, one pretty far removed. Two clearly killed with an old world revolver, the other cause of death still unknown."

"Porter looked like a man with a serious cardiac event," Mick Priest said. "Sarah, those empty medicine bottles I found-"

"Lisinopril and Metformin," she said, her sharp memory quick and precise. "Before you ask, yes, I asked Cassandra if she knew what they were for. She doesn't. As she told me, she's an emergency tech at best, not a doctor."

"I wonder if they could kill," Priest said with a sigh. "Who brings empty bottles on vacation? It isn't like he could get them refilled up here. If someone dumped the whole bottles into something like his soda, though, it would explain the empties and maybe-"

"Oh, it'd kill him," Vic Jackson said.

James Wyatt and Mick and Sarah Priest instantly looked at Jackson.

He noticed the sudden attention and shrugged.

"I have family members who take those two drugs," he explained. "Lisinopril lowers blood pressure. Metformin lowers blood sugar, for diabetes. A whole bottle of blood pressure medicine could potentially cause heart failure. A whole bottle of both would definitely cause something terrible."

"Hmmm," James said with a nod.

"Like a stroke," Priest said.

"Like that twisted up face," James said.

"James!" Sarah said in a hush.

Mick Priest shook his head.

"Okay, whatever. We got a missing comic book geek," James growled. "I have a hard time thinkin' he could last any time toe to toe with Mick but I followed the trail of the ghost right through his room and he's nowhere to be found. Seems he's either the Revolver, a new victim or he's on the run, for whatever reason."

"Assumptions," Mick chided. "Like suspicions, presumptions, and accusations. Left unfounded, they're just vapor in the wind."

"Okay, another fact: you got the ghost's revolvers. That ought to slow down the rampage, right?"

"The killer has Grip's 9mm," Sarah reminded James.

"Unless the Ghost Revolver wouldn't work without the pistols," Mick said. "Like a need, a drive. Not just a part of the mythos or the identity but a compulsion, a signature that the killer needs."

"You mean like a serial killer's addiction or a psychopathic tendency? You thinkin' this perp is a bigger nut job than just a loose cannon vigilante?"

Sarah huffed at James.

"Don't you? Mick's got a point; a hitman with morals? High minded justice but hired out for high pay? Something's wired wrong, somehow."

"It's another part of the legend, accruing more weapons in the course of a mission," Victor Jackson said.

"What do you know of the legend, Victor?" Mick asked.

"I've got a background file packet in here on that, too, Mr. Priest," the handsome, white haired man replied.

"Stop that 'Mr. Priest' stuff," Mick said, rising up on his strong leg. He joined the other man at his desk, followed by Sarah and James. "You're on the team. The least you could do is call me Mick."

The man nodded, saying, "Just like those bone handled revolvers, the original vigilante carried a bone handled knife, an Indian...sorry, Mr. Wyatt...*Native American* fighting dagger."

James shook his head and rolled his eyes.

"It's James, Vic," the defender corrected, slapping a hand on the man's shoulder. "And I may as well tell ya, I ain't a fan of political correctness. I'm a firm believer in my mom's teachin' on 'sticks and stones' and I come from a reality where words are just words. People needed to be strong enough to realize that. Our whole nation was stronger when we all realized that."

"About the dagger," Sarah derailed.

"The legend has the Revolver picking up new weapons to use when it's necessary to complete a mission. The dagger was added to the legend's regular arms years after its origin," Vic said.

"Okay. Watch out for Grip's Glock and a knife," James said.

"Here's something else to keep in mind, talking about weapons," Mick Priest revealed. "Searching the rooms, I found out Andreya West has weapons with her."

"Weapons?" Sarah asked.

"Escrima sticks. Genuine. Real deal."

"Escrow sticks?" James asked, confused.

"What sort of sticks?" Victor asked.

"Escrima sticks. They're staves, for fighting," Mick said. "Martial arts of Indonesia and southeast Asia, in general, use them. Like silat, arnis and kali. "

"Gesundheit," James said. "What's she doin' with those?"

"Maybe nothing at all," he said with a shrug. "Just keep it in mind."

"I got a mastery with 'chucks and I'm decent with tonfas but I don't carry 'em around," James said of his nunchaku and police baton training. His face screwed into disbelief as he continued with, "The only weapon I carry around is my piece and I carry it to use it, Mick. You gotta figure she carries those for the same thing."

"Just be aware," Mick said. "No one's been killed here with sticks."

"Yet," James added.

"What else do you have, Vic? I know it's a work in progress."

"I made a spreadsheet and I laid out all I've been able to extrapolate from the file data; who's met whom, who's worked with whom, who's done business with whom-"

"Talkin', talkin', noisy, with whom," James interrupted, his hand working an invisible puppet in the air. "No offense, Vic, but we gotta get to it. Quicker, before we're all dead, killed one by one by the murderer or all at once by boredom."

"Go on, Vic," Sarah said, waving away at James.

"The whole thing's pretty intricate. I don't know if these folks even know it but most've all met, crossed paths or worked with mutual agencies, mutual associates, appeared in towns at the same time...on and on it goes."

"Examples?" Sarah prodded.

"Okay, Johanna Crimson crossed paths with Ricochet Porter," Vic Jackson said in a conspiratorial tone. "Quite a bit. Truth is, she's crossed paths with two-thirds of the guests here, mostly more than just crossed paths. There was real interaction."

"That gets us started," James said.

"The problem is that I can say the same about nearly everyone here! On paper, drawing lines between guests who either knowingly or unknowingly have connections with other guests would make a map that looked like spiderwebs."

Priest tensed his jaw.

"Are there clues about targets?"

"Sure. And motivation. Sins. Crimes. Names of ritzy attorneys-"

"Who's on the chopping block?" Sarah asked tersely.

"All the writers...and publishing...guests," the Gridlock man said. He swallowed hard, brow furrowed. "Okay, I'm a target. Didn't see that coming. Anyway, none of the 'plus ones' and so on are on the hit list, like Sarah, James, and Gibson."

"So, Tayla Barlowe is on the hit list?" Sarah asked pointedly.

"Yes. But not her little girl," Victor added.

"Staff?" Mick Priest asked.

"Some are, some are not," Jackson said.

"Who else on staff is targeted besides Falgrip Bridger?"

"I haven't peeled back enough to find it all but I know Gretchen Clayborne in one of the targets. As far as I can tell, Helena Makai, Cassandra Clark, Tydas Richter and Reginald Jenkins are not."

James Wyatt burst into a mild laughter and shook his head.

"Reginald Jenkins? Did his parents just know he was gonna be a butler, or what?"

"James," Sarah admonished in look and word.

"I did chip out a piece on Crimson, the strangest part of the file on anyone here," Jackson noted. "There's a long thread on the net, detailed in the file, that spins almost out of control on conspiracy theory sites. They say that the real Johanna Crimson died and that the current Johanna Crimson is an impostor, somebody cashin' in on her resemblance."

Priest had an instantaneous flash of the dream...

...she looked the way she had when in her twenties. She was ever so slightly more plush, less defined in her features. Not that she was one iota less alluring currently in her thirties, just a shade different. Before the workout regiment for playing Velvet Edge, before the martial arts training and the stunt training, the Johanna Crimson in her twenties had been softer, more voluptuous...

What was it Crimson had said?

"Everyone changes, Mr. Priest. Some people change into different people altogether."

That was when thunder had crashed violently in the dream.

"Am I here at all?"

"Good question," Mick Priest muttered aloud.

"What?" Victor asked.

"The rumor on the internet, about Crimson. I was wondering if the file happened to suggest that this impostor killed Crimson for her place?" Priest asked. "Would that be her crime, her sin?"

Jackson popped his fingers, noting, "Taking the impostor from opportunist to killer...not that I've found, so far, but I'd put my money on that one. Bringing justice to those out of normal reach. All her money..."

"Untouchable through normal channels," Sarah Priest said.

"She better not be a fake," James said. "I need her checks to go through without any hiccups."

"Was Bridger's transgression listed?" Sarah asked.

"There was a record of why he was here instead of still working as a cop. He was dismissed on 'conduct unbecoming an officer' charges, something that cost him his badge but didn't land him in legal trouble. Looks like he found this place along his way down from police work."

"Anything else?" James asked.

"Sorry, but that's about it. I'm still working it, anyway. I do know that Porter and Mobley were involved in some sexual scandals. Blackmail, rumors of underage prostitution, pandering, nothing proven."

"That's it?" James asked. "I mean, I'm glad you ran outta gas, but that's the whole thing?"

"Right now, that's all. I'm still cracking into the compression."

"Keep at it, Victor, and thank you," Mick said.

"Be extremely careful, too. You lose your laptop, or the progress you've made on the files, we lose an awful lot. As for Li," Sarah started, "you be wary of her. If she tries anything, her *cortafuegos* is mine."

"Language," James admonished Sarah mockingly.

"It means firewall," Mick said.

Reginald Bard Jenkins stood at perfect, statuary attention.

"I cannot see why no one will do as instructed. Agent Priest and her husband only want what is best for us. It would benefit us all if we would just abide by their simple direction until all of this is over."

He rocked from his heels to his toes and back to stillness.

The tall, broad shouldered Staff Director glanced about Cassandra Clark's abode with only his eyes, never moving his head, unwilling to break his rigid composure.

"Well, I'm here, Jenkins. That ought to count for something," the pilot, Gretchen Clayborne, muttered. "Cassie came back with Agent Priest and she was here for a bit. Tye and Helena were out for a while, carrying around a bunch of paper. When they came back, they had Avid with them and Cassie came back, so Tye and Cassie went down to the stables with the papers-"

"What papers?" the handsome staffer asked.

"-and Avid took Helena to the kitchen to go over tomorrow morning's breakfast. And I don't know what the papers were. Don't care, didn't ask, wasn't nosey." She shrugged and added, "And, as for nobody staying where they belong, it seems like they've all decided to wander at will, as long as they use the buddy system. Maybe they figure it's okay to die as long as you do it in pairs."

He took a deep breath, noting her defeated expression.

"Ms. Clayborne-"

Her lower lip quivered and she turned away from him quickly, a hand lifting to her face.

"I'm okay, really," she tried before he could get started. "I'm good."

"Ms. Clayborne...Gretchen," he corrected uncomfortably, "you need to try to sleep. I know it must be difficult but you must try. You need some rest if you want to hold up. You have suffered a terrible-"

A glass rattled from the overlook outside.

"What was that?" Clayborne quipped, eyes big and studious.

Jenkins grabbed up one of the lights from a nearby table. He turned the flashlight about and lit the doors to the balcony.

The young lady strode toward the glass door, passing Jenkins at Clark's desk, but Jenkins caught her arm gently, easing her to a stop.

"Gretchen," he said, sympathy etched in his features.

She stilled, the warmth of his deep voice embracing her raw nerves. Again, she felt a pull inside herself, stronger than before, drawing her toward him. Her lips parted and her eyes drank in the refined gentleman as she edged closer and closer to him.

"You should not be alone," he muttered.

Kind, considerate eyes leaped from her eyes to her soft lips and back.

"I know," she admitted, stepping even closer.

"It isn't safe," he whispered.

"I know."

She put one of her hands on his where he held her arm. She loosed his hand and slowly moved it to her waist. Again, she eased closer.

"Gretchen..."

"I know," she whispered.

The young woman stepped up onto her toes. She met his eyes with both a boldness and a vulnerability. She pulled his arm tightly about her and put her other hand onto one side of his face, leaning so close that each could feel the other's breath caressing their lips.

His breath caught in his throat. His heart pounded. Hers did the same, her body pressing against his.

A scraping sound suddenly raked the outside of the balcony door and the handle clicked, twisting one way then another against its lock.

Both Jenkins and Gretchen spun about toward the door. The young pilot stiffened immediately, infuriated. Her ire was probably roused more from being interrupted in that moment than from someone traipsing up and down the balcony stairs.

"None of you are supposed to be roaming the corridors! Now, you come up the balcony stairs?" Clayborne shouted, rushing for the door.

Jenkins tried to stop her but he was too late to even slow her. She snatched it open angrily. Clark was not at the door, however. Helena Makai was not there. Neither Tye Richter nor the chef waited there.

No, the visitor at the door was death.

Gretchen Clayborne fell back, toppling, as the white skulled figure breached the balcony entry. She hit the floor on her bottom but twisted over to her hands and knees almost as soon as she touched the floor. She slipped and grabbed at the hardwood, doing her best to crawl and scurry away, her mouth wide open. Her voice was lost; fear tore it from her throat. Nothing over a whine escaped.

Death had come to call, lifting gloved hands from inside its black folds. In one hand was a silver, western dagger with a bone handle.

Suddenly, a reflection flared brightly over the silver of the blade. It flashed across the weapon and flooded over the killer, as well. The masked stalker flinched and turned blinded eyes from the source.

"Hold your place!" Jenkins bellowed behind his flashlight. He jumped between Clayborne and the invader, growling, "No more killing, you cur! Run, Gretchen!"

The killer lifted the blade, blinded in the light or no, as the room door opened into the corridor and Clayborne slipped away.

"Just the two of us remain, mongrel," Jenkins spat. "Do your worst."

"I don't want you," the masked invader mewled with a deliberately nondescript hiss. "And you don't want me..."

The killer charged him, swiping with the knife. Jenkins evaded the blade, swinging the big, heavy flashlight at the ghost. The light missed its target, too. Then the assailant barreled into him. The two careened through the open door and into the hallway. Both crashed haplessly into the far corridor wall, destroying a portrait of some great cavalry unit, and went to the floor in a crumpled mess.

The Revolver rolled about, adjusting the dislodged mask. The other hand groped for the ornate, silver dagger, lost in the tumble. Jenkins had dropped the flashlight in the impact, as well. He did not grab for it.

Jenkins, a very formal man, bore the refined etiquette befitting the highborn of old. Regal and distinguished, he was difficult to age with his good looks and charm. Nevertheless, he was, by all means, above fifty years of age. Absolutely none of that completely defined the man who rolled up to his wingtip adorned feet. He ripped off his suit jacket and his white, pressed shirt, buttons scattered to the wind. Considerably taught muscles roped about his chest and his arms, revealed in a v neck undershirt.

The phantom regained solid footing and the lost dagger.

Jenkins moved to a display on the wall. There he snatched down two short swords from their mounts behind a shield.

"Have at thee, fiend," Jenkins growled.

The Revolver, mask realigned, saw the other man arm himself.

"I think you were better off with the torch," the killer hissed, spinning the fighting knife out of one hand to the other.

"I can assure you, my good man, the wall items in this facility are not just décor. All the weaponry is time accurate, combat-ready forged and keen of edge. I-"

A raging clamor erupted in the hall. Out of the stairwell poured Chef Swartzovski, Helena Makai, Tye Richter, Cassandra Clark and Gretchen Clayborne.

"Jenkins!" howled Clayborne.

She ran down the corridor heedlessly with the others behind her. Tye Richter carried a fireplace poker. The chef carried heavy looking pan.

Without another sound, before Jenkins could act, the Ghost Revolver turned and raced back into the room. Jenkins launched into pursuit but the assassin exited onto the overlook. By the time Jenkins reached that, the killer had disappeared.

In the dark, the advantage is yours, phantom, Jenkins thought angrily. *But make no mistake; there will be a reckoning.*

The others invaded the room, looking all about.

"He got away," Jenkins muttered.

"Lucky him," the chef noted, pointing at the swords.

Gretchen pushed herself into an embrace with Jenkins. He hesitated but, after a moment, hugged her in turn. In truth, she was awed at the revelation of his courage. Admiration flooded her.

That sent a shock wave of guilt that hit her like a train. Her boyfriend, Grip Bridger, was dead and there she was, thinking such things...feeling such things...alongside the sadness strangling her.

Quickly, to fill the quiet as much as to inform the group, Jenkins explained what had happened.

"We gotta get to Agent Priest and her husband," Richter said.

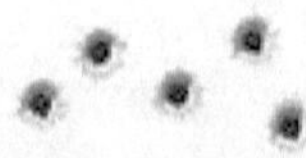

The deep shadows of the night, freed from their nocturnal chains, drifted this way and that across the grounds of H and H Resort. The black garb of the late hour billowed in the wind like leathery wings, clouds in the sky above sifting and splaying moon and starlight. Elements of nothing more than reflection and shade danced on earth to the music of the sky.

Jenkins made me smile despite my mood.

"I'll see that they get there, Mr. Priest," he promised.

He still carried one of the short swords from the hall display and he had taken the shield in trade for the other one. The stalwart knight, I knew he would do his very best.

He and Tye Richter had armed themselves and would be escorting the entire staff to the Dining Hall once again. Not in the morning, not for a breakfast feast. For a gathering, one more time, to plot a possible escape from Shadow Mountain. All would come; Sarah and James would see to that as I played the vanguard.

The wee hours of Sunday morning were pouring through the hourglass. So, I rushed ahead. I wanted to be certain the Dining Hall was secure for our gathering. I wanted to be there first. My hobbled leg and the stiffly wrapped arm, tied in a sling, hindered that but I was resolute.

I wanted time alone to pray, too.

I had been too infrequent with my supplications. I should have been as the Apostle Paul taught, praying without ceasing. Choosing a dedicated mindset, *living prayerfully*, a mental state of mind. Remaining in touch with the One greater than us.

Room secured, adjacent rooms and halls checked, I settled into the Dining Hall. I moved a chair into a corner in view of all the doors and dropped into it. Instantly, a rush of fatigue descended upon me and my eyes blinked heavily. I shook my head, trying to clear the cobwebs, blinking to clear the weariness. Several times, while blinking, I struggled to clear my sight while my vision became increasingly grainy, blurred. I finally let my eyes close for just a moment.

I prayed. While the sky outside sang an angry song, the clouds crying tears for the dead, I was praying. And not only for the case. I prayed intently on behalf of all of us.

In the darkness, too, I wrestled with the guilt of violence, of the killing in my own past. I was hunting a vigilante, someone who sought justice on their own terms and by their own definitions. It touched on the hypocritical, except for the fact that I was licensed by the state. That brought me little solace when I thought back on some of my own exploits. I had never set out to shoot people. I had not wanted to kill. But I had done both. Like King David, I bore bloody hands.

Actions in moments of crisis, defending the innocent, bringing the guilty to justice...so many times they came with a lingering cost.

My prayers reminded me, however, that God is a God of infinite mercy, renewed each day with the morning. I knew He forgave when we sincerely asked and chose to do our best to turn from our wickedness. I knew His grace covered my many sins and that is where I found solace.

Not in my own judgment. Not in my own will.

King David was a man of many sins and mistakes, himself, and was still called 'a man after God's own heart' in the Bible. Studying that, it first seems confusing. When put into perspective, however, it easily becomes clear. King David was a man after God's own heart not because of his weaknesses, failures and sins. It was because he always, every single time, came back to God in humble regret and a genuine desire to do better. Asking forgiveness. Asking a blessing on his path to righteousness. He was not only willing to change but desired the change wholeheartedly. His history illustrated repentance and his story gave the rest of us hope.

I knew that I was not a murderer. I was not a killer. I would always do my best to avoid striking others down. I found great comfort there in my relationship with Almighty God, the God of second chances.

Porter had been killed. Mobley had been killed. Bridger had been killed. The situation felt like grains of fine sand slipping from my closed fists. What was I placed there by God to do if the killing went on unabashed around me? I knew God had a plan for my presence but I struggled to see it.

Then I remembered also that Christians walk by Faith, not by sight. I might not be able to see my path or my plan but I knew God had one for me. I had to trust that, though some things were clearly not meant for me to change, I was needed for something within the plan. Like the disciples in the garden, I needed to watch and pray.

Father God Almighty, Lord Jesus, show me the way, I asked.

It dawned on me then that the dream ushering in the whole experience had not even been about the resort gathering. It had been about Johanna Crimson alone. I had dreamed about her the way she was when she had been much younger. When her form was more supple and less trained. When she still bore the birthmark.

My eyes popped open.

CHAPTER FIFTEEN

When my sight cleared, the lights were different.

Something had changed.

Suddenly, the hallway lighting, the emergency backups, went black. The minuscule radiance from the night's sky, formerly casting a weak glow through the stable stalls into the corridors, blinked out. It was as if all the stars had died at once, the moon stolen away by the night itself. Darkness as thick and pervasive as pitch inked the lobby in black and, for a moment, I was blind. It was far darker than storm darkness. It was far darker than night; it was as dark as night*mare*.

Just as quickly, it changed again. Starting off faint and growing into a considerable, indigo ambiance, a new light ignited from beyond the reach and purview of man. The eerie glow spilled from some other place, some other time. Its colored illumination cast odd, bluish hues throughout the space and created even stranger shadows.

My body shivered at the sight of the weird light and more so at the feeling of a presence.

She sashayed into view as if a creature purely nocturnal, as if born of the bluish glow of the heavens. Her flowing, lithe shape materialized slowly as she approached. A low cut, gossamer dress, spun from thigh length, ivory dream webbing, added to her weightless look as she drifted, perhaps floated, toward me. It was as if the room were some underwater kingdom, as if she were a siren from the deep.

I realized then we were not in the lobby but one of the guest rooms.

"Mr. Priest," her voice drew me. "Trouble sleeping? Not that you tried, of course."

Full, plum lips pulled at the corners, a playful tug at work on them. Her pixie face, as beautiful as an angel, tilted slightly, high cheeks and pointed chin building the classic heart shape. Bright, glowing green eyes boldly sought my own, pushing, pressing into them, trying to see inside me.

Flame red, ethereal hair floated about her and a lock of wavy crimson broke our stare.

"Johanna Crimson?" I asked, my thoughts racing. "Are you Johanna Crimson?"

I knew the woman by sight, or I thought I did. I had recently met her, the famed actress. Johanna Crimson was in the room and I had neither heard nor seen her arrival.

Her sly smile curled thick lips as she tamed her mask of hair.

"What is it about a name? What really is the difference? There isn't one, if I'm neither Johanna Crimson nor anyone else...not anymore..."

She ran a fingernail horizontally across her chin and the beauty mark there.

The Crimson I had met bore no such birthmark on her chin.

You're not her or she's not you...you're not the same, I thought to myself.

At least, I thought I was only musing to myself. It was odd because she giggled and nibbled at her fingernail, staring into me, as if she had heard every word.

She looked the way she had when in her twenties. She was ever so slightly more plush, less defined in her features. Not that she was one iota less alluring currently in her thirties, just a shade different. Before the workout regiment for playing Velvet Edge, before the martial arts training and the stunt training, the Johanna Crimson in her twenties had been softer, more voluptuous.

"Everyone changes, Mr. Priest," she answered my thoughts as if she could hear them. "Some people change into different people altogether."

Thunder crashed violently and shook the foundations of the house. The rumble had not even faded before she threw both arms out to her sides and, as if she controlled them, the two doors to the balcony blew open, deadbolts exploding into pieces, wooden doors raining shrapnel. A raging wind ripped through them and into the room, overturning tables and blowing away bed covers. The sound, a deafening rush, almost hid her words.

"Am I here at all?" she called, barely audible to me. "Am *I* here...or is another?"

She arched her neck backward as her blood red hair masked her completely.

The color of the nocturnal glow darkened to a deeper, more ominous violet. The new hue seemed to envelope her and, incredibly, it lifted her up higher from the floor. She shook where she hovered, suspended in the storm.

"Where am I?" she howled, the voice of a whirlwind.

I had both hands up before my face, trying to see into the gale, trying to peer beyond the the rage of a tempest.

"Who...am...I?" she roared and thunder shook the earth.

"You tell me!" I shouted into the wind. "Name yourself!"

"Name?" she cried. "I...am..."

"Forgotten!" another voice bellowed.

I tried to turn about but could not, my body paralyzed, shaking.

Low, graveled and malicious, the words continued from behind me.

"Now leave her in the past and dance with me!"

Hands grabbed my shoulders in a vise-like grip. They not only held the power of iron but burned me, as if newly pulled from the forge. They spun me around as the burn smoked my shirt and seared my skin.

"How 'bout a kiss, lover?" the presence growled, the voice a vibrato nightmare resonating an echo upon itself.

I yanked and pulled but could not free myself, the touch burning and the fear suffocating me. A wretched perversion of Kimber Mobley, far taller than Mobley had been, leaned close, eyes blood red. Split skin cracked and flaked across the twisted countenance, hair gone from a lumpy scalp of lesions and burns. Her breath smelled of decay and burning flesh. I gagged and twisted about, trying to breathe.

"Not shy, are you, mate?" she gurgled.

A greenish bile bubbled from her lips.

"In the name of Jesus, the name above all names," I howled, causing the thing to flinch, "I rebuke you! Back away!"

Immediately, the presence released me and recoiled as if struck. The dark thing could not resist stepping back. Its jaw unhinged impossibly, however, opening to several times the size it should have been. Some wicked flame, laced with a green fluid, spewed forth at me, igniting the air as it came.

That is when the bluish glow present with Johanna Crimson flooded over me, encapsulating me before the flame hit. Meeting the fire half way, the light and the fire warred in the gap, surging one way and another, pushing and pulling, the light singing and the heat sizzling.

"In the name of Jesus Christ, Son of Almighty God," I roared, the putrid presence reeling, "I command you, be gone!"

The flame sputtered and faltered and the light touched the presence. It screamed through the most bone chilling sound I had ever heard. It railed against me in words, sounds and indecipherable noise. The form bowed and crouched as if under an invisible weight it could not maintain, crying out in desperate hatred. It stepped backward all the way to the far wall and the deeper shadows there, growing shorter with each move. One leg, first, then the other started melting into the shadows.

The evil thing dissolved slowly, disappearing into darkness and screaming all the way. Then an audible, simple 'pop' sounded and echoed in the room and it was gone. A knot in my gut as hard as stone still squeezed my interior, sickening me. I had faced the vile remnants of the supernatural on past occasions, reflections of the dead stolen by evil forces, but it was never easy, nor was it something to which anyone could become accustomed.

Stilling in the moment, I faced the woman resembling Johanna Crimson. The young apparition wore a dress out of antiquity, a Civil War era design. The lace and fabric clung to her then flowed outward at the waist. The blue illumination shone from outside the windows before which she stood, casting her shape as a silhouette in nightshade. I could not see her features anymore, even when she lifted her face toward me and spoke.

"Thank you," she said, her voice soft, velvet tone upon the air. "The light I bear with me could not have held that vile creature at bay forever."

"Don't thank me," I said, my voice echoing in the distance between us. "I called on God. He saved us."

"Truth," she said emphatically. "I do not thank you for rescuing us. I thank you for calling upon God, the only hope we had. I thank you for doing the right thing."

Her shadowy visage evaded my sight. I could only make out a flash of her eyes from time to time and then only briefly.

"You don't seem shocked by...anything," I muttered.

"I'm dead, Mr. Priest. I've crossed. There are no more surprises."

"The dead I encounter, those God allows to speak with me, oftentimes don't understand where they are. When they are. Not even that they're dead." I rubbed my still burning shoulders, adding, "They sure wouldn't stand in the face of that...thing."

"God allowed me here, Mr. Priest. I am not without some ability. I am not helpless in this state...or any other. However, the travel between what was and what is and what shall ever be can, at times, lend distortion and confusion. Traversing the span is difficult. Everything was not perfectly clear, even to me, until you called upon God. Then the fugue was stripped away completely. By natural order, I would war with any demon. By God's clarity, the two of us, together, prevailed."

A demon. Not Kimber Mobley. Not the woman she had been. A stolen image of her. Sent to slow me, to derail me, to destroy me.

"But you're not an angel, you're Johanna Crimson?" I clarified.

"You know I'm not an angel," she said patiently. "You know His Word. The Scriptures. Man is of mankind, angels are of their kind. Man does not become angelkind in death. Nor does he become that wretched kind. In death, however, some of mankind does not pass into paradise but into the other. There they are often mimicked, their likenesses stolen."

I nodded, with, "I understand. But, if you're Johanna Crimson..."

She took a few steps closer and her face lit with a bluish-white hue. She was dressed in the 1800s costume in which I had first seen her. It was an outfit from her first major movie role, *A Gunman's Prayer.*

"The woman you know is no more Johanna Crimson than I was."

I stared at her trademarked, playful smirk, the way it was before it was heralded as sexy.

"I honestly don't understand that," I said. "What are you saying?"

"My name is...was...Kelli. Not Johanna. Not Crimson," she said with a flourish of her dress and a spin in the shadows. "Nothing so dramatic, so striking or vivid. Just Kelli."

"Kelli," I heard myself say.

"I was happy when I was Kelli," she said thoughtfully. "But my big break required a new mantle, a new name. So was born Johanna Crimson, starlet. Now there is a new Johanna Crimson."

"Am I here to rescue her?"

"She is in danger," Kelli confirmed, her voice an airy, velvet tone in the night air. "But it is not the woman you know as Johanna Crimson you must rescue. You must rescue her protector; he stands to lose far more than she does."

"Wait," I slowed her. "She's in danger but I need to rescue Gibson?"

"She is in danger, as are all who are targeted on this mountain. There is evil being worked here and evil brings danger and death. But you must rescue Mark Gibson...from himself."

"I don't-"

"Many here are in mortal peril, their lives at stake. Gibson is in danger of losing himself to his own passions, his own desires. Losing his very...self."

"Someone is killing people. One at the time. I need to know-"

"You already know there is a killer here. You already know there will be death. Repercussions. Consequences from humanity having free will. I am not chosen to know the murderer's identity. You are not chosen to hold the *mortal* fates of all men in your hands. You have been chosen, however, to move on behalf of justice, to the best of your human ability, and to touch the *immortal* fate of a man in dire need. He is precariously balanced between being lost forever...and seeing the Light."

"Gibson?"

"Mark Gibson will be torn apart from within if you cannot stop him. It will be his soul that is lost to him. This will be his point of no return."

"First, rescue him? Now, stop him?" I said.

"Sometimes...those are the same thing."

The room filled with a fog, a cool mist. The low cloud bank built so quickly it seemed to be pumped into the room. Reflected throughout it was the indigo glow, the blue shade.

"What does Gibson have to do with Crimson's fate? With you?"

"Nothing. And everything." She smiled genuinely, saying, "My name was Kelli...Kelli Gibson."

I literally gasped and spat, "He's your father?"

She nodded.

"But the other woman, Johanna Crimson, she somehow took your place? And your father protects her? He has to know she isn't you. He has to know something happened to his daughter-"

"He knows, Mr. Priest," she said.

"What is he doing? What is he-"

"Like anyone, his sins are his to reveal, his confessions his own to disclose, as is right. What I can say is that he needs you."

"Me?" I asked. "What makes me-"

"Mr. Priest, you have faced loss and found grace and love on the other side. You returned to your place, in God. Mark Gibson's torment is nearly complete; if someone does not step in before this encounter on this mountain is over, he will be lost forever."

The fog had thickened and risen, walling us away from each other. The color made it difficult to see her clearly.

"Kelli Gibson?" I called.

"Good night, Mr. Priest," her disembodied voice haunted the night.

Then my eyes popped open and I was again in the Dining Hall.

Jenkins walked into the room at that moment and passed me on the way to the Kitchen. Refined, sophisticated, even in an undershirt, slacks and a medieval shield.

"No meetings without something for the taste buds," he said. "My formal training would drive me insane, Mr. Priest."

"Oh, sure," I said absently. "Would haunt me, too."

Seconds later, the rest of the staff came through the room, followed by the remainder of the people on the mountain.

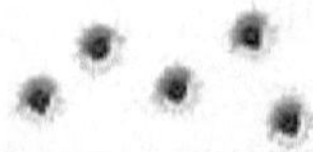

Everyone sat in the one room, the Dining Hall, with a couple of exceptions. Jenkins stayed in motion, back and forth to the Kitchen with Helena Makai. Chef Swartzovski stayed in the Kitchen, plying his trade.

Rembrandt 'Remy' Lyles was still missing. Hiding. Hurt or dead. The verdict was still out. The others had searched, of course, the hunt spearheaded by James Wyatt. Still, the man was absent.

Flashlights stood erect around the room, light reflecting from the shiny ceiling and the walls all around. It added to the yellowed ambiance offered by the flickering candles.

Sarah Priest stood, hands on her hips, blocking the doorway to the eastern corridor. James Wyatt guarded the western passage, arms folded.

Mick Priest had turned a chair backward and sat on it, leaning forward against the framework. He had placed it in the doorway to the south, the Conference Room.

Everyone else sat inside the room, resting in the chairs and leaning on the tables. All were quiet and doing their best to relax. No one was really relaxed, however. Between exhaustion, terror and the unknown, most were doing good to avoid pure panic...providing they could remain awake.

Marcus Gibson was having trouble with neither.

"I'm about ten seconds from goin' off on everybody," he said loudly, pointing around the room. "I blame this bunch for everything else that happens. I told all of you about Lyles and now he's the only one unaccounted for; he's the Revolver, sure as I breathe, or he hired the Revolver and got taken out to keep it hushed-"

Sarah Priest said. "That's a good plan. Keep it hushed. Now take a seat, please. We have matters to discuss...calmly."

Gibson did not sit down. He stayed on his feet behind Johanna Crimson's seat, face defiant.

"If I have to tell you again, Mr. Gibson," Sarah warned slowly, "you will be unable to stand and you will have to sit. Are we clear?"

He considered a challenge. Then he saw her husband stand up, over his chair, in the southern doorway. His eyes caught B'Rone Matwahali fold his arms across his broad chest. James Wyatt, in the corner of his peripheral vision, slid his hand inside his coat.

Gibson tipped his head and pulled out a chair, dropping into it.

"Wine?" Jenkins asked the group, putting a last dish on a table.

"Bad call," Gibson said. "We need to keep our senses."

"Oh, of course," Jenkins allowed. "What was I thinking? A sip of wine and we would all fall into drunken debauchery."

"You know what, Skippy?" Gibson barked, pointing a finger.

"Me. I'll take some wine. A lot of wine," Johanna Crimson said. She braced a hand against her brow and held her glass in the air with the other. "Wine, please. Now. Thank you."

Jenkins tended her glass and followed up by moving to Clark.

The others skipped the wine but James Wyatt filled a napkin with rolls and spreads and began eating, standing at his passage post.

"I don't like this," Kess Melkin bemoaned. Again.

"You said that already," Andreya West muttered.

"Well, I'm sayin' it some more," Melkin sniped.

"Don't start again," James Wyatt said. "We just got ya'll quiet."

"Amen," Tayla Barlowe said, jostling little Emma and checking to be certain the little girl was still asleep.

"Maybe, if we knew what it was we were-"

"We're here to discuss a way off the mountain," Sarah Priest said, interrupting Paul Blackwood. "Among other things."

The room fell silent again with the exception of a tiny, adorable snore from little Emma.

"Tell us, by all means. Let's get off this mountain," said Maureen Li.

"In due time," Mick Priest stalled. "First things first. You don't wanna take an assassin down the mountain, do you?"

"Is there an option?" Cassandra Clark eventually broke the silence.

The room's inhabitants turned as one to look at Mick Priest.

"The killer could surrender now," he said lowly.

Nearly everyone looked around in surprise. It was as if they expected others to acquiesce, to stand and confess, no arms twisted, no weapons employed.

It did not happen.

No one made a sound except the sleeping child, little Emma Barlowe. Everyone looked about, though, seeking out the shadowed eyes in the room.

Thunder sang outside and it seemed to prompt Gibson to speak.

"That's just stupid, Priest," he said.

Silence was the initial rebuttal from the room.

"And why is that, Gibson?" Mick Priest asked.

"The only person who ain't here is Lyles; I think we can safely say he's our Revolver and, as we can see, he won't be goin' with us if he ain't here."

Several other voices chimed in with agreement.

"Oh, well, makes sense," Priest allowed almost sarcastically. "If you believe he's the Revolver. Which not even you believed...until this."

Murmurs, gasps and disdain.

"What are you on about, Priest?" Paul Blackwood demanded. "Who else could it be?"

B'Rone Matwahali said, "The bloke's an international killer! I heard o' him on some of me own operations! The *very* best! It could be anybody; he's just that good!"

Priest gestured at him with an open hand, as if presenting him to the group, and said, "Ladies and gentlemen, my point made for me."

Questions, debate.

Gibson said, "You're draggin' this out like a slow dance at the prom. Wastin' time, rattlin' on when the talkin' is done, already."

"Plain talk, then," Priest said. "See, Gridlock Publishing got this nice little file. Well, huge file...okay, more than one file...anyway, my friend, Victor, has been combing through it for us."

"Gridlock got a file," Tye Richter repeated.

"On what?" Helena Makai mused aloud.

"All of us. Everybody. Even the Revolver," James Wyatt said. "Your strengths, accomplishments, weaknesses, crimes...and sins....the reasons you might be a target and the ways you might be the Revolver."

"Fat lotta good that does any of-" Gibson barked.

"It's informative," Priest interrupted. "Gives us a peek behind everyone's mask. And, make no mistake, a lotta people wear masks. They don't have to be bone masks. Really lets you see how possibilities shape up...Vic?"

"B'Rone Matwahali. Military, paramilitary, freelance tracker, hunter, survivalist, marksman, blade specialist, adept pilot, professional adventurer. Demolitions expert. Quite the physical specimen. Television host, entrepreneur, about to become a writer, if you can land a publisher. You'd make an efficient Revolver."

"And, if I ain't, why would I be targeted? Brought here?"

"You're wanted on two continents for poaching and participating in insurrections. So far, your notoriety and fame have kept you free."

Silence rang loud and clear.

"We gonna do round robin and share everybody's personal stuff?"

Priest shook his head at Gibson.

"No. I'm simply going to say that all of you have formidable skills, some obvious and some private, that make you a potential Revolver. All of you, also, have something in your history that could or would paint a target on your back for the one and only Ghost Revolver, in person."

"This makes no sense," Melkin said. "Who'd get info on all of us and the Ghost Revolver and send it to a publisher?"

"Who else? Lyles!" Gibson said.

A cackling of debate erupted but Sarah Priest met it head on.

"Quiet, people. Listen," she warned.

"Remy Lyles is absent and that's suspicious," Priest said. "And, like what Gibson said, it fits pretty well. He was selling the idea for a graphic novel series of comics, based on the legend of the Ghost Revolver, to Gridlock. But, in itself, it doesn't mean he was the Revolver. It means, unless I miss my guess, he planted that file in the data systems over at Gridlock and got all of you brought to this retreat. He arranged this...and that would mean he hired the Revolver to get one of you, too."

"How would that artsy-"

"Elementary, right, Priest?" Andreya West chirped with a smile.

"Yeah," he said, "it's pretty elementary. Vic?"

"Lyles has two degrees. One from the Atlanta Art Institute, the obvious one. Another is from MIT. Computer programming and design."

"That comic book store crustacean?" Johanna Crimson exhaled.

"He's after Johanna, ain't he? I knew it! I tried to tell you-"

"Dude, shut up," James barked. "Stop interrupting and listen."

"All of you are likely targets," Priest continued. "Lyles, or whoever, drew the Revolver here to get at least one of you in particular, maybe Crimson, maybe not. I know he has history with more than her. Perhaps an unrequited love."

Gretchen Clayborne looked around, flustered.

"But, by pulling so many of you fairly influential people, he built a puzzle of targets. The Revolver can run wild and take all of you down and no one would know who funded the hit on any one of you."

"No one would seem to have more motive than another," Gibson said. "A handful of survivors, unspecified target, unknown moneybag..."

"It's brilliant," Andreya West muttered, one of the few times her smile waned. "In a sadistic, manipulative way."

"And just the kind of thing, if the Revolver was manipulated into coming here, too, that could get Lyles killed. Bankroll or not."

The crowd nodded along with Sarah Priest, most having lost their voices. Again, tomb quiet. Again, the storm outside was the only voice.

At last, after long, uncomfortable moments, it was Chef Swartzovski who broke the oppressive silence.

"Only on a writers' weekend. I still remember that last time, when those horror writers got so wired on caffeine and-"

"Chef," Director Clark said, waving away his reminiscence.

Priest continued with, "Now, I don't feel like I have to say this...but here it is. Someone in this room killed Mobley. Grip. And I'm pretty sure they killed Porter. He wasn't shot but there are drugs and poisons that could've caused his death. I found empty pill bottles in his room. Vic?"

Victor Jackson nodded.

"Absolutely. And some natural stuff could-"

"Yeah, 'cause everybody knows about that sorta stuff," said Melkin wryly. "I mean, I'm a chemist in my off time."

"No," Victor corrected her, "but you did date a chemist. He was later arrested and charged with drugging underage boys-"

"I didn't know nothin' about that!" she howled.

The space erupted with the siren song of a little girl.

"Thanks," Tayla Barlowe called sarcastically.

"See what we've done?" Priest asked the crowd.

"Please, excuse us," Tayla Barlowe chimed with a false sweetness, looking at Melkin. "Let me get baby Emma back to sleep!"

Mick gestured for her to go to his wife, saying, "Of course, Tayla."

The young woman took her child away from the group, mumbling about 'throat punches', and into the hall behind Sarah Priest. Sarah realigned her stance so she could see the Barlowe girls and the room, as well.

"Well, I don't know about the rest of you, but I'm curious! Who else could whip up a special dish to poison Porter? I mean, I could; I have a minor degree in chemistry! But who else?" Andreya gabbed.

Several people remarked under their breath about her misplaced glee.

"Paul Blackwood, for one," Victor answered. "One of his previous books revolved around herbal remedies, and maladies, and the history of baking with them. He was also accused of poisoning a former, live in girlfriend who tried to take everything he owned through a law suit. Nothing has actually been proven, however."

"And some of you know people who could've taught you about poisons. Like belladonna. People like Brenda Lynn Wright, wouldn't you say, Gretchen?"

"Knowin' her might paint a bullseye on my back but it would do it double for Remy. Everybody already thinks he's nuts," Clayborne said.

"Sounds like what some of 'em think of Blackwood," James said.

"Ya know what, ya daft bloke? We're all scared enough! You wanna flop your gob, how 'bout telling us how to get offa this nightmare mountain!" Blackwood shouted, his courage surging again, his face blood red. "All this talkin' is just a buncha codswallop! It means nothin' to us, we just wanna go!"

"Wrong," Mick Priest replied, his voice so low it was not much more than a guttural noise. "It means you stay really still. Nobody flinch. Twitch. Jerk. If you do..."

He shook his gun with his good hand. He then nodded to his wife and his friend, James Wyatt.

"...*we* might think you're dangerous..."

The crowd followed his look and saw that Sarah and James, too, already held their guns at the ready.

"I've had enough of this!" Paul Blackwood said, abruptly coming to his feet. "What're ya gonna do, shoot me?"

Both of the Priests leveled a gun on him instantly and he froze.

By reflex, Gibson's hand shot inside his jacket for his weapon. He stopped still, however, without drawing it free of the holster. James Wyatt aimed his gun at the fellow bodyguard and spoke.

"Whoa, there, Quick Draw," James said to Gibson. "Keep it in the saddle."

Gibson opened his hands and lifted them back into view then slowly put them down.

"And you, Galloping Gourmet," James said to Blackwood, "sit your pot back down."

The Brit did as he was told...very carefully.

James and the Priests slowly lowered their weapons, even if they did not put them away.

Then the crowd began to bite at each other with talks of which of them deserved to live. Which ones were just so much dead weight, which ones would most likely kill. As if any of them knew best.

"Then what do we do?" Kess Melkin spat at Priest. "What was our big escape plan? If we can't identify the killer, if it ain't comic book boy? What do we do, now?"

"We can send you down the mountain in groups. We'll scatter the armed defenders through all the groups so that every group has a protector. It's a gamble that the Revolver, if he's one of you, won't be able to finish the mission here. It would mean, should the Revolver act in the small group, the defender would engage our killer, one on one, and the smaller group would mean less people endangered in the crossfire."

Mumbling ran the gauntlet with its old friends, fright and cursing. It did not stop Priest who was, as James Wyatt often said, on a roll.

"You're not unhappy, yet, people," he said. "Wait 'til we tell you how we're gonna travel. How do ya'll feel about mountain horseback riding at daybreak?"

Outrage. Shouting. Yelling. Then threats.

Mick Priest, for a time, did not care. He scoured the faces for a hint of honest reactions. Guilt. Shame. Fear.

"Well, split us up and send me on out," Kess Melkin spat finally. "If I've earned me some hate, sorry, but who cares? Send me out!"

"Jolly well right," B'Rone Matwahali added. "Send me, too! I'm finished with this circus!"

The earlier manner of chaos returned. A boom of thunderous voices all argued over each other.

"Enough!" Mick Priest railed at them. "That's enough!"

The room silenced again.

"Yes, listen to Mr. Priest. There's more. Okay. Start it, then," Andreya West chimed at him, smiling.

Her chipper tone was surprising, if not disturbing.

"Start what?" Li asked skittishly.

Everyone else asked it, too, with raised eyebrows and pensive stares.

"Not you," West said. "*Detective* Mikhael Priest."

Mick Priest sighed.

No one else actually 'got it'.

"Oh, good grief! Have none of you ever read anything but your own writing?" West exploded in disappointment. "Haven't you at least watched television and movies?"

Several had open mouths, nearly offering answers, but she continued unabashedly in her thought.

"From Agatha Christie's *Poirot* and *Marple* to the *Chan* novels by Earl Biggers and *The Father Brown Mysteries* by G.K. Chesterton, what's something they all shared? Not to even mention every film and television detective they ever inspired, from Peter Falk in *Columbo* to Dick Van Dyke in *Diagnosis Murder*! There's always that one, closing scene that wraps up the mystery!"

"And some people call me crazy," Melkin said.

"It's a moment, not necessarily the very end of the work but the end of the mystery, where questions are answered and all the secrets are revealed! The detective, or whatever the main character is, most often a professional or an amateur sleuth, has figured out the identity of the culprit by then. The protagonist has gathered up the players involved and proceeds to unveil the unknown for everyone else, exposing all the details. This is the wrap up, right, Priest? Let's get it started!"

Priest raised just his left eyebrow, waiting for her to take a breath.

Others regarded her with disbelief. Her tone, in the midst of murder, still bordered on glee.

"And the 'happy lunatic' award goes to..." Melkin muttered with a grimace.

"Thanks for the nomination," West chirped almost immediately. Her smile openly masked her real emotions when she cut back with, "I'll give you the same consideration when there's a 'hillbilly harem girl' award."

Melkin wanted to say something but Mark Gibson took the floor.

"Well, Priest, is the lady right? Is this it? You got all the answers?"

Priest shrugged, saying, "Nope."

What? quite a few voices demanded.

"Nope," Priest reiterated. "I hate to disappoint all of you...especially you..." he said to Andreya West, eyebrows lifted high.

"No?" Paul Blackwood asked.

"What does that mean, exactly?" Johanna Crimson demanded.

"*No,*" Priest clarified with no explanation attempted.

"Whaddaya mean, no?" Melkin demanded, looking back at West as if the woman had lied.

"You gotta share what ya know, mate," Matwahali declared.

"Nope."

"Mr. Priest, what is this, some kind of joke?" Jenkins shouted.

The room swarmed with warring voices.

Mick Priest waited for the din to wane then spoke again.

"I don't think I can play the scene from Ms. West's favorite mysteries. Right now, I have my suspicions. I don't have proof positive. I'd rather spend my energy trying to get the rest of you safely home."

Disbelief ran rampant throughout the room.

"We'll go ahead with the Director's plan. We'll split up into three groups," he said, raising his voice.

It makes no sense! We're more vulnerable divided! It serves no purpose! The killer will still be with us! This'll get us killed!

"Each group will have an armed defender. Sarah, James or me."

"Why would we go along with this?" Blackwood bellowed.

"Right now, it's the only game in town. You gotta better plan, share it. Now," Agent Sarah Priest answered.

Silence, even from the gourmet groaner.

"That's what I figured," Sarah Priest said.

"Cassandra will break us up and assign each group a member of staff familiar with the horse trails or their signage, markings," Mick Priest said. "We'll form our small groups and wait for her to brief us."

Everyone looked at the Resort Director.

"Brief?" she asked Mick Priest.

"Yeah. You know your horses and tack best. Help us get the most amiable mounts and most comfortable gear. We're going down mountain horse trails into a valley; you need to assign leads and helpers for those who've never touched a horse. Look at it this way: it might get us all so distracted that the killer forgets to kill anyone else."

"Mr. Priest, I don't think I'm-"

"Lady, you're the director of this place. Start directing."

CHAPTER SIXTEEN

Everyone wanted off the mountain. Everyone wanted answers. Everyone wanted to survive. Mick Priest had no qualms about holding firmly to the plan.

This is the way, he insisted.

The dim emergency lighting gave just enough glow to see how to do what needed to be done. The heavier rain and clouds drowned out the moon and stars so there was no help filtering in from the outside stall windows. Nightshade crept about thickly in the stalls and the halls. Flashlights added to the available light, a beam here and a glow there, enhancing the overall vision. Still, it was dark and the sun was nowhere near its next conquest.

Every time someone looked up from the tasks at hand they found Mick Priest watching and waiting. The light was just enough to find him there, in the shadows, his eyes hidden by the dark. Everyone who found him watching knew he saw everything; something uncanny about Mikhael Priest resonated with nearly every person there.

"I've ridden," Gretchen Clayborne said to Cassandra Clark. She moved quickly in the low light, cinching her own saddle band. "I'll ride in the front, if that's what you need."

"It'll help," Clark said. "We've put you on one of the leader horses. The other horses in your group will follow it. If you've ridden and you can simply stay saddled you'll lead your group easily."

"What group are you with?" Clayborne asked.

"That group," the director said, pointing to another stall area.

Gretchen looked that way and saw James Wyatt. He stood, arms folded across his chest, as Tye Richter saddled a horse for him.

"At least you and Tye will be in the same group," the pilot said. "He really thinks a lot of you, Cassie. It must be nice to know someone cares the way he does."

"Yes, and I think the world of him."

Clark wanted to say something kind about Grip Bridger but she feared striking such an intimate chord with Gretchen. To distract her at that time might endanger her and those she was going to help.

Gretchen felt the charge in the air. She heard all that was not said.

"It's okay, Cassie," she said. "I know."

Several stalls away, there was discontent.

"I don't like it," Mark Gibson told Priest for the hundredth time.

"Duly noted," Priest said, looking down the corridor. "Again."

Priest and Gibson stood in a clump of people, their own little group, as they finished tacking up.

"I should be with Johanna."

"James will be with her the whole time," Priest restated.

The two men were both experienced horsemen. They had their mounts ready before anyone else, leaving them time to meander, watch and talk. Priest had abandoned the arm sling already, unwilling to be hampered by it any longer.

"I just don't leave her-"

"Gibson, she's a stated target," Priest said. "I grouped her with James, someone I know, and some of the people here I know are not the Ghost Revolver."

"I thought Clark made the groups-"

"Nope. See, I may not know who the Revolver is, for certain, but I do know some who are definitely not the Revolver. I grouped Johanna with them. Now, relax. Keep your head straight. I might need you."

Priest felt torn about Gibson but he believed the ghost of Kelli Gibson. That meant something, whatever it was, threatened Gibson's heart. It meant Priest wanted the man close to him as the case was ending.

"What do you need from me?"

"James will protect Crimson and the young mother and child in one group, the safe group. You know I wouldn't risk the life of a child. Sarah will keep an eye on the other group. I added you to my group because I wanted some backup the others won't expect. I put some people I suspect into our group; I just might need that back up."

Gibson seemed to chew it over for a moment then, huffing, he propped his hands on his hips.

"So, you don't know me well enough to trust me to be the protector of one of the groups but you trust me enough to back you up?"

"Yep."

"Willin' to make the tough calls and take the chances, huh?"

"Yep."

He laughed, saying, "I knew you were solid, Priest."

Priest watched the other man's blue eyes. They seemed genuine. Yet, behind them someplace, locked away, there was a mystery, a pain held in check by precarious, smothering silence.

Gibson reviewed their little group.

"So, which of these folks made the list of-"

"I don't want to influence your perspective. I don't want to make you distrust anyone or trust anyone. I want you to use your eyes while I use mine."

"You're in luck. I don't trust nobody."

Priest looked at him directly, his face stark and sobering.

"Now you know who you need to watch. Everybody."

Gibson nodded and the two men shook hands.

Mick Priest had watched both of the other teams when they left on the cusp of morning. Each took a different trail and started from a different point on the property, slightly separated by timing, too.

The detective thought back just a short time. He had extended a hand toward the lovely Sarah Priest, his love. She took it with her own. She watched and prayed with him, a prayer for protection, a prayer for guidance. A prayer for justice.

He had kissed his wife before she left with her group, refuting her claims that it should be her responsibility to manage the last, 'loaded' group, full of possible Revolvers. He had chosen that task for himself, charged by the spirit of a young woman to rescue Mark Gibson from himself.

It had to be. I had to be on the last ride, he thought to himself.

His little team was upset that no staff member had been assigned to their group, however. It was not left unsaid, either.

How do we get down the mountain? one demanded.

Another said, *This is nuts!*

Then, *We won't get killed by a killer, we'll die in the woods!*

Priest sat straight in his saddle, somewhat distanced from the rest of his group, ignoring their complaints and their questions. He busied himself with considering the words of his own mind.

The last ride. Was it some modern western, destined to end in a dramatic firefight? Was it a reflection on some last chance for Mark Gibson to redeem himself in the eyes of Kelli Gibson? Was it some recognition that, if he failed to bring Gibson to his own side and conflict exploded on the trail, the ride really could be the last Priest would have?

He wondered if death rode the trail ahead, long in the saddle and eager for blood.

Sweat ran down into his collar from his shaven head. The cold rivulet trickled down his spine and gave him a chill. Shaking it off, he wiped over his head again and slid his hand over his pants.

At least it stopped raining.

He looked away from the group, studying the skyline.

Dawn approached. The mountain silhouettes still wore midnight blues and blacks but the sky crept back from the pitch black of night. A smear of indigo, awash with striking purples and the first hints of a lavender morn, splayed across the horizon. The colors took inspiration from the coming dawn, the birth of a new day, the resurgence of a hope previously hidden in deep shadow. The very creation echoed the will of the Father. God's mercies are renewed with every morning. Gloom and despair have to flee or simply dissolve in the light of a new chance at mercy, grace...and hope.

"Priest," Maureen Li called meekly. "Are we ready?"

Priest waited for a moment before answering. Then, when he did so, his voice rumbled lowly.

"You in a hurry, Maureen?"

"Well, no," she muttered.

"I am," Mark Gibson said. "I need to catch up to Johanna."

Priest angled his head and eyes back to the group.

"We aren't going to catch up. That's the idea, Gibson."

"I remember," the older man said. "I still don't like it."

"May as well get used to it, mate," Paul Blackwood complained. "He and his wife, they've been runnin' all this since the jump off."

Maureen Li breathed a hushed curse in Chinese.

Blackwood said, "But I'm with Gibson. Let's get down this mountain before anyone snaps and starts thinning us out."

"What a lovely thought," the curvaceous Andreya West said, pulling her long hair up into a ponytail.

She wiped at the sweat running over her, sticking her clothes to her, as the heat tried to smother them below the newly rising sun.

Mick Priest had an odd smile on his face.

"A couple of more minutes," he said.

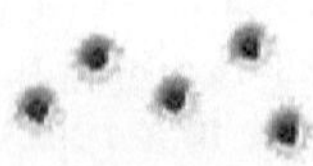

I held them there until the dawn had come and the sun rose completely. It brought a steamy, unrelenting heat worse than before.

Everyone was at least damp in their attire. Most of them already had their garb glued to them in a thick sheen of pure sweat.

All five of us were as antsy as we were hot. The horses picked up on it. The tension. The static in the air. The steeds nickered and sidestepped and paced back and forth. The day was upon us, long awaited, and a moment of reckoning came with it.

"How 'bout it, Priest?" Blackwood asked abrasively.

I had forced them to wait a full fifteen minutes in silence while I stared at the sky. I had picked the rose garden as a waiting place where we could watch the birth of the morning and the onset of the day, allowing the group to spread out quite a bit. It was a place where our mounts could smell and snuffle and, yes, nibble at the flowers.

"I don't think they're allowed to do that," Andreya West giggled.

"I always have been a bad influence," I said with a sigh.

Most importantly, the garden was also on the opposite side of the resort building from the horse trails. That ensured that we had no idea which ways the other two groups had taken.

My horse turned at the slightest lead of my reign, an old veteran of trail rides. I would have gambled on the Palomino's ability to know what I wanted before I even led him into it. Old Gordon Lightfoot, or so the name on his halter read, had been around the block a time or two. When he brought me about to face the others straight on, before I even asked it of him, I spoke.

"Paul, I have a confession to make," I said calmly.

"Ready to admit you have no idea who's the Revolver and who isn't?" Li demanded in his stead.

"Let the man talk," Gibson said. "Go ahead, Priest. I think we know what's comin' out. Somebody's 'bout to get exposed."

"Well, he couldn't think all of us are these Revolver types," Andreya West said flatly. "I'm in this group. I know I'm not...he doesn't think...oh, good grief. Am I a suspect, Mr. Priest?" she asked, oddly happy and bubbly at the thought.

Gibson could not stifle his chuckle any more than Paul Blackwood could bridle his tongue.

"Why not? If the rest of us are, why not you?" Blackwood said, turning to me again. "Now, how 'bout it?"

"I'm not going to lead you down the mountain 'til we talk this out," I said, a wry grin on my face. "One of you, and you know who you are, might start killing those of us who aren't involved. In a shooting, someone might accidentally hit one of these fine horses and that isn't acceptable. Worse yet, you might just shoot me in the back and leave me up here. No...everybody step down off your horse and let's talk. Right here. Right now. A new morning, a new sunrise, a last chance at honesty."

They were too stupefied to speak before I swept a leg out of the stirrup and slipped to the ground. I flinched on the bad knee but I kept Gordon's reigns in my hand and kept one hand free, just in case. I was careful not to eyeball the saddlebags, however. I had hidden the Ghost Revolver's guns and gun case within them.

"Priest, I ain't havin' any more of this nonsense!" Blackwood exploded. "Now you get up in that saddle and take us down the mountain! You're the only one in our group that's seen the trail maps and the others are way ahead-"

"And out of reach," I said, my smile infuriating. "Nice and safe."

Blackwood, irate, snatched about in his saddle, trying to free his feet from the stirrups. Gibson was laughing at the British baker as he dismounted his own steed. Li leaped like a cat, pouncing down upon her feet. Andreya West dismounted gracefully, carefully, watching us all. A second later, as West crouched, twisting at a boot and adjusting it, Paul Blackwood crashed down from his horse into the mulch.

I shook my head, putting my hands on my hips.

"Priest!" the man howled as he tore himself to his feet, mulch all over him and leaves in his hair. "That's it! I've had it with you!"

"If I put you on the ground you won't get back up that easily. You sure you wanna ride this train?" I asked, my smile waning.

"I think I do!" he challenged loudly. "I wanna knock ya around 'til ya tell us who ya suspect! Let's get it over with!"

"I'm suspicious of all of you, in one way or another."

"You do suspect all of us?" Andreya West chirped merrily. "Even if I'm a suspect, I'm glad I actually get to be included. Imagine not making enough of an impression to either be suspicious or an active ally!"

"You're a loon!" Blackwood barked.

We had all dismounted, by intent or by happenstance, in a wide expanse. Between some of us stood underbrush and the flora of the garden. As I watched the body language on hand, I was silently grateful for the widened space between us and the slight camouflage.

"Just a buncha tripe!" Blackwood shouted. "Priest, get us off this mountain!"

We all faced each other, looking from eyes to eyes, waiting.

In one smooth, quick motion, West suddenly reached into her knee high boots and pulled out her two escrima sticks.

"Just in case," she said to me with a nod. "You never know."

"Well, you're not wrong," I agreed. "Just like all of you. This little group of people fits into a specific, special category. You're not here because I'm sure about you, one way or another," I admitted. "You're here because I'm not."

"Do you ever stop talking?" Li asked me.

"The longer we talk the farther everyone else gets," I said.

"And if you're wrong? About any of us?" Li insisted. "A killer is in one of the other groups!"

"Do tell," Blackwood said flatly.

I chuckled, saying, "You know, Paul, you'll find this interesting. Jenkins pulled me aside. He told me that the Revolver said something interesting when they fought. He told Jenkins he would be better off with the torch instead of the short sword. See, Jenkins had been holding a flashlight-"

Gibson huffed and shook his head.

Andreya West literally jumped up and down.

"Torch! The British term for a flashlight! Ha!"

"That doesn't mean..."

"You may as well drop it, Blackwood," Gibson said with a laugh. "It's done. Priest's onto you. It's over."

"No, Gibson, I have to say, it doesn't sit right with me," I corrected.

All of them, particularly Gibson and Blackwood, stared my way with wide eyes and mouths agape.

"A professional who takes the time to mask his accent, since Jenkins said the speech was American, wouldn't slip up with a dialect mistake like using 'torch' for 'flashlight'."

"No, that dog really don't hunt," Gibson allowed.

"It seems more like someone purposely using a phrase to throw suspicion onto someone else," I added.

I eyeballed them all, watching for any tells as I lifted my guns free of their holsters, holding them by my sides.

"I'm expecting that someone anytime now..."

"Priest, don't keep waggin' those things around," Gibson said. "You got two and I got one and somebody's got that dagger-"

"And I have one," a man said. "The fact is...I lost the dagger."

Abandoning his cover, the last shadow of the night strode into the open, as grim as could be in the daylight. Black overcoat, listless in the air, still bearing the moisture of the rain, the figure stopped outside our circle of contention. A black glove held a 9mm Glock aimed at me.

The other hand stripped back an ill-fitting, black and white, bone face mask.

"Lyles," Gibson growled lowly.

With surprising speed, Gibson drew his gun and brought it level. Lyles whipped his weapon around at him and gave me a chance to move.

I jerked my Colts up level to cover the whole crowd.

"Now, hold it, hold it," Gibson urged.

"Who do you think you are, Lyles?" howled Li.

"*Los conocedor*, woman," the little man whined. His eyes darkened as he squinted her way, snarling. "Remember that."

She shook her head, confused.

"Judge," Andreya West informed her.

I was about to speak when Gibson interrupted me.

"So, you're the judge, now?" he challenged the last shadow. "And here I thought that was the real Revolver and you were just the recruiter."

"I don't want to shoot anyone," I said lowly, "but I will. Put down the guns."

"Is he talkin' to us?" Lyles asked Gibson.

"I guess the daft peeper can't count," Blackwood said nervously. "I can't see where anybody has an upper hand."

I growled, "I'm not counting bodies or guns. God has never left my side and He hasn't on this mountain, either. He's even sent others to give me insight. I've been ahead of the curve."

They were at a loss, confused. I could see it in their eyes, the blindness of the unbelieving.

"This looks like a little stand off, to me," Remy Lyles said with a grin of his own. "I'm gonna have to pencil this into an issue when I get my graphic series running."

"You really are insane," Li snapped. "And to think I-"

Gibson said, "Hold it, people. If this is our last ride, let's do it right. Let's play the movie scene Andreya wanted back in the resort."

"Yay!" West chirped and clapped her hands.

I stared at her, truly wondering if she was insane.

"Okay, you start, old man," Remy Lyles said with a sneer. "Age before...before anything else."

"Whatever, ya brat," Gibson sniped. "All of you, listen. For my own reasons, I decided to do somethin' a while back. About people, about this world, all of it. I had to get the scales of justice set right..."

Blackwood openly cursed and challenged him.

"You started all this? Caused all this? Ya broke down creaker!"

"Shut up!" Lyles exploded. "Let the old man ramble."

Andreya West subtly cut her eyes to me and I responded with mine.

We goin' sideways, Priest? I imagined her asking.

We're already there, I would have told her.

"I was taught a moral code, ethics," Gibson said. "I was trained in honor, duty and loyalty. Our world's abandoned all that. Leaders, law enforcement, entertainment and common people, from the mansions to the streets. Crime, hate, perversion..." he trailed, blue eyes truly pained. "Workin' inside the boundaries ain't fixin' what's wrong. Good hands are always tied up by somethin'. So, I decided to fund an operation, an operative, who could set things right. Colorin' outside the lines. Exactin' justice without cripplin' red tape slowin' 'em down..."

"Man takes forever," Lyles spat. "He hired the Ghost Revolver to work some justice for him!"

"You?" Li asked Lyles with shock. She shook her head with, "I thought you just researched-"

"What?" Gibson barked. "No, not him! I hired the real Revolver!"

"Idiot!" Blackwood screamed. "What're you thinkin', old man? What've ya done?"

"It's simple," Gibson mewled and the air became electric. "No more gettin' away with murder for the rich and powerful...like you...I should put you down, myself..."

I wondered for a moment if he would open up a firefight right there, particularly when almost everyone took a few paces backward.

"Easy, Gibson, think this through," I calmed.

"He's crazy! All the things they've brought at me, in the press and the media and even by that family? All false!" Blackwood swore.

"Whatever, bakin' man!" Lyles shouted. "I did my research and-"

"Lyles does research. Sits in his basement, in the dark, on his computer, diggin' into stuff. Findin' dirt on people and sellin' it back to 'em. That's how he got tied up with Ms. Li, ain't it, darlin'?"

"I resent that!" Li barked at Gibson.

"Me, too! You make me sound like some typical blackmailer! I'm an artist, too!" Remy said angrily. "I get proof on the untouchables and I make them pay, to teach them a lesson! If I use the money to further art, that's up to me!"

"Enough," Gibson said, disgusted. "I'd heard of the Revolver. In our circles, who hadn't, right, Priest? I started lookin' 'cause I wanted the best. Let's just say that this contact led me here and that one led me there until somebody pointed me to Lyles. Said he could get anything on anybody. That would be my source of information. Turned out, Remy boy said he could contact the Revolver usin' the net and keep everybody anonymous. Him, me, the Revolver. Nobody would know anybody."

"Are you saying the two of you don't even know who the Ghost Revolver really is?" Andreya West asked directly, disbelievingly.

"Nope. And don't want to," Lyles said. "Knowing secrets like that one is hazardous to one's health. I didn't even know the Revolver existed until Gibson came to me about it."

"Wait a minute," West demanded. "If neither of you are..."

"Naw, we ain't the Revolver, how many times have we gotta say it? I wanted to hire the gun and Remy made the contacts!" Gibson bellowed. Then, looking back at Lyles, "And you came up with an idea of using the Revolver in a comic book, ya nut! Just stupid!"

I trembled a bit with my weak arm and the 10mm dipped just a bit. I tightened the arm again and made sure the gun was steady.

"So, for the kiddies playing along at home-" I started.

"The man had some justice he wanted dispensed!" Lyles shouted. "He came to me, told me to make an offer to the Revolver and there's been a lot the last few years! Man spends a lotta Johanna Crimson's money, lemme tell you!"

"I earn it, at least!" Gibson yelled. "Not you and your publishing pals! Tryin' ta blackmail me 'n' Johanna, too!"

"There never was a conflict over a comic character, was there?" I asked pointedly. "Gibson, you headed up a counter movement against Lyles and his little blackmail operation-"

"You're finally on the right track!" the impatient Lyles said.

"And, Lyles, you put a hit on Johanna Crimson, a little payback for her and Gibson not paying you," I said.

"Hey, Gibson taught me about the very best assassin in the world, with the legend dating back a couple of centuries! Why not turn the killer around on them?"

"Boy encountered a problem, though," Gibson said. "Revolver's got a code, a moral rule. No innocents. That's why Remy lodged false lawsuits against us. We had to look untouchable, look like we were runnin' hard on little people."

"You lied to an assassin...about the why and how of the target...and what the situation really was?" Andreya West asked, aghast. "Did you *want* to get killed?"

"I want no part of this," Li said flatly. "Lyles, your contract is effectively retracted. We're not touching this character-"

"That'll depend on who gets off the mountain alive," Lyles growled.

"You sicced the Ghost on a buncha big wigs and high rollers," Paul Blackwood told Gibson. Then, to Lyles, "And you played the contact man? Passin' notes in class?"

"Where you been, Cockney?" Lyles barked. "Yes, for the tenth time. What's so hard to-"

"Then neither of you know the Revolver," West added. "Like I was asking, if that's the case, who's the Revolver?"

"Not my problem," Lyles said, wagging the gun around. "Soon, I'll be off this mountain. And, Li, one way or another, that series will get published..."

"Where'd you get the costume, Lyles?" West asked.

"It's a promotional advance from Gridlock," he said proudly.

"For the record," Maureen Li shouted, "I allowed Lyles access to our databases to set all this up but only as a promotional operation! I knew he was at odds with Crimson and RC Comics but I had no idea he would use the opportunity to kill!"

Lyles laughed boisterously.

"You loved this idea, as long as you were able to peek into that file I gave you and get enough secrets to run your blackmail operation for years! You didn't know everything but, then again, I ain't killed nobody, yet," he said.

Everyone stilled.

"Where'd you get Grip's gun?" I pressed.

"I found it, Priest," the young scarecrow replied to me. "Wish I'd found it before I fought ol' man Jenkins! I had found the knife, first, and had that run in with Jenkins. I was just out to scare some of you, keep the Ghost thing going. After that, though, somebody put this Glock in my room and stole that dagger! Nice trade, if you ask me, even if I didn't understand why!"

"Nice trade?" Gibson guffawed. "Nice set up!"

"Anyway," Remy Lyles said, "I don't know who the Revolver was or is but they were taking too long! You and lady Priest and the Indian were gaining too much traction."

"Native American!" Maureen Li corrected by sheer reflex, her public relations degree showing. "You are *so* low class, Lyles!"

Time itself seemed to slip into slow motion, nearly grinding to a halt. When he turned toward Li, Remy Lyles let his weapon lead off for the first time. It betrayed him, belied his random movement pattern. It revealed his change. His destination. Intent. A little man playing dress up, brushing up against killers and conspirators, suddenly decided he was a major player, too. In a snap reaction to her insult, Remy Lyles chose to murder her right then and there.

It began there, that very second, with the world stalling on its axis. Li tried to get her hands up in front of her as Lyles brought the 9mm to full extension, still in slow motion.

My vision instantly went wide, taking in the whole scene as I thrust myself backward. I still did not know who could be trusted. For me, in any case, we were too close for comfort. I leveled both Colts on Lyles as I toppled backward into the underbrush, my bad knee folding on me.

In that second, Lyles squeezed off a single shot from the Glock, aimed for Maureen Li. Li screeched and whipped around, falling into a nearby bush.

Gibson jerked to one side, the veteran combatant anticipating the move. He twisted backward into the underbrush, ducking away, as did Paul Blackwood and Andreya West.

Before I even hit the mulch on my back, I had fired three shots into Rembrandt Lyles, his body jumping and twitching. Like the ghost I had fought on the overlook, however, Lyles had on body armor.

The horses reared and bolted, all but my friend, Gordon Lightfoot. He simply wandered away as the others panicked, running about in our midst before taking off completely.

One of them careened into Gibson and knocked the man down; I could not see him but I heard him cursing. Another leaped over me. I covered up and drew myself into a ball, trying not to be trampled.

Paul Blackwood scrambled and escaped deeper into the nearby rose garden, head down, hands and feet digging into the mulch.

West reappeared with the speed and grace of a gazelle, running and sliding to a stop on the ground by Maureen Li. West grabbed her up roughly, extracting a scream from the bleeding Li, and tugged her out of sight.

Lyles, to my shock, never fully reemerged from the bushes. He was groaning loudly with every inch he moved, his free arm wrapped around his torso, as he fled the arena, crouched low in the foliage.

I popped off two more rounds, one from each hand. One shot punched into his black vest again, in the back of his shoulder, spinning him to the right. He did not fall, however, and kept running for the resort building proper.

Though I could not see him, I heard Gibson squeeze off two rounds and curse Lyles. He missed him both times, killing roses in bloom in his stead. Then I heard Gibson rustle about in the shrubbery as he set off in pursuit.

I pushed up to my feet, feeling the sting of my injuries. I kept one of my Colts extended but one dangled at the end of my wounded arm. I staggered on my weak leg, turning about to each direction.

Lyles was gone. Gibson was gone. And Blackwood had been gone from the onset.

"Li! West!" I shouted.

"I've got Li's wound wrapped with a belt!" West called, stepping into the open.

"Is it bad?" I asked, watching all around us.

"I'm not a doctor! I did my best!" she snapped. "Now go after Lyles and Gibson! You've got to end this here, Priest!"

I knew she was right. And logic suggested there was little to no choice in all of it. Only Blackwood would remain a loose end.

Following their trail, a chaos of scattered mulch, trampled roses and more, was easy enough. I had to hope West and Li would be alright on their own. My leg popped and bucked but, with the tracking, I had it easy. I followed it with no more difficulty than if I were traipsing down a city sidewalk. The path took me to the resort lobby, the very entrance outside which Grip Bridger had been killed and I pressed inside.

My mind whirled. If Lyles was telling the truth and had not killed Bridger, who had? Who was the Revolver? The well trained individual from that balcony had not been Remy Lyles. I simply could not imagine it. And to have blown up the bridge over Nightshade Pass? Who was-

Suddenly, the sound of thunder clapped in the lobby space, booming twice and sending me scurrying for cover. My distraction had nearly cost me the game...permanently. The thunder was the explosive 'crack' bellowing from the stolen Glock.

I dropped flat behind an ornate reception area and display, head down. Lyles and the 9mm spat wads of lead at me but missed, smacking the wall near me and shattering a wall sconce.

"Stand still!" the man howled.

The lobby's twin, spiral stairwells, one on the east and one on the west, rose to a mutual landing. From there a single staircase carried on to other floors. Around the second floor landing stood a guard wall about waist high and Lyles had been crouching behind it, hidden. He had whipped out of hiding just long enough to target me, leaving cover for only seconds.

I was blessed; the young man was an unrealistically bad shot. He rained at least seven more shots at me, hitting everyplace but close.

"May as well quit, *mate*," Lyles called in a bad British accent. "I'm on high ground. You budge and *ol' Bob's your uncle*, I put you down."

I opened my mouth to reply but Mark Gibson spoke first.

"Nice! Now you remember the accent with your Brit phrases," he said sarcastically. "Of course, you couldn't remember it with ol' Jenkins, could ya? Calling a flashlight a torch and forgetting an accent..."

Gibson's voice echoed from the entry to the eastern corridor. I was closer to the west, pinned down behind the reception structure.

"Old man, Johanna Crimson's still a target and the Revolver is still loose!" Lyles called. "Since I'm gonna finish you here, my accents are the least of your boss lady's worries!"

"Who is the Revolver?" Gibson asked. "You tell me I might kill you quick. If you don't...well..."

"Gibson, don't do this," I shouted. "Your heart isn't this black! We take this guy down the moral way, the legal way, together!"

Remy cackled with laughter.

"Well, we know somebody's optimistic," he said sardonically.

"Should I just leave you two to finish each other?" I asked. "It sounds like neither of you plans to let the other get out of town alive. A real white hat versus black hat, hero on villain showdown. Of course, it's all in the perspective..."

"Mick, I like you, son," Gibson called. "You an' James take justice seriously. I got no fight with you."

"He knows what you've done," the younger man barked. "He's not letting you or me or the real Revolver just walk off this mountain!"

Gibson's gun belched light and fire three times. The flashes and reflections flared from the corridor with each shot. Wood and plaster cracked and splintered along the banister wall of the landing center. It rained down onto the marble flooring in white powder and wooden debris. Lyles popped off a couple of random shots in return.

Lyles was laughing and Gibson was cursing. I waited silently, a gun for each of them, peeking from my vantage point and watching both directions.

Then, after Gibson fell silent for a moment, he called to me again.

"Priest, if they manage to drop me, get by me, save Johanna."

"What's her part in this?" I asked.

"She ain't got one," Gibson said. "She's the most innocent-"

"She still doesn't even know! She bankrolls the biggest assassination op in the world and doesn't have a clue!" Lyles howled and laughed.

Gibson said, "She makes massive money. I use it to pay for blood."

"Priest?" another voice called.

It was Andreya West and her voice echoed from the western corridor, the one nearest me and farthest from Gibson.

Another angle, I growled to myself. *I hate geometry.*

I heard the distinct clicking and clacking of someone changing the magazine in a semi-auto just before Lyles let go with several shots meant for West. The doorjamb on that corridor opening popped and spat wood splinters.

Great, I thought. *He's got Grip's reloads, too.*

Gibson whipped into the open and fired off several shots. I lifted and fired once with each hand and blew chunks out of Remy's rail cover. Remy Lyles unleashed a small burst at me, too, peppering the wall between me and Gibson.

"Like an old cowboy shootout," Gibson said loudly and chuckled. "Funny. It's how it started way back when. Way before all our times but here we are, livin' it."

I did not blink. I waited, looking from one gun nest to the other.

"Doesn't have to end this way," I said flatly.

Unexpectedly, Rembrandt Lyles popped into the open and broke into a run across the ground floor, gun leveled in our direction. The artist and video game veteran had apparently slithered down the spiral staircase on our side of the marbled room, hiding behind the railed wall, creeping on his belly. He fired repetitious rounds in a reckless charge and scattered lead around wildly.

I heard Gibson's Sig Sauer bark twice just before I rose up from behind my cover. Frozen in place, Remy stared in Gibson's direction, aiming, waiting. He was determined to hit Gibson the next time he rounded the corridor entry. That left Remy Lyles completely unready for me.

My wounded arm was too tired to lift and too shaky to hold. I lifted the other and trained the Colt on the young man. I popped off a calm, patient shot and punched a hole in his shoulder. Blood plumed from the wound, well outside the protection of the tactical vest, and spun him around backward, stopping him cold. He held on desperately to the Glock, though, the weapon secured in his opposite hand, and I called out a sharp warning.

"Remy, stop! Now!"

Like a maddened, rabid animal, he howled and lifted that 9mm again, meaning to kill me. My finger immediately tensed on the trigger.

Suddenly, Gibson squeezed off a couple of rounds from his corridor entry, walking into the lobby as he did so. The young man jerked this way and that and fired off several rounds of his own into the air, aimed at nothing. Between his shots and Gibson's it sounded like there were even more shooters in the chamber, echoes ringing from every direction.

I was about to add another of my own to the cacophony when bright red blood misted the air and the artist went down flat. The 9mm fell lifelessly to the hard floor with him, as still as he was.

When Gibson turned my way with his smoking weapon, he found me ready. My good hand's gun was trained on him, waiting. The gun's bore stared like a watching eye, seeing all, covering all.

"Well, Priest," he said with a grunt. "We gonna finish it...cowboy style? I sure hate to. I...wasn't kiddin' when I said I was fond of ya."

I noticed his wince and the gasps in his speech. The hand he clamped to the right side of his gut, painted in scarlet, seeped with blood where it ran between his fingers. His light blazer, cotton ranch shirt and his khakis were reddening quickly.

"He hit you," I said, more thinking out loud than talking.

"Yep. Super Mario shot through several mags...since all this started. Had to get lucky sometime." He gave a half shrug with, "I've had...a lot worse...'course I had a medic in the unit, too."

I said, "We gonna put these guns down?"

Gibson let his gun hand lower, gesturing to the far hall with his head. He then tucked away his Sig Sauer and clamped both hands on his side.

"Check on West," he said. "Ain't no point in lookin' the boy over. I could've sworn I...went for the shoulder o' that gun hand...but I must be shaky from the bleedin'. Boy ain't getting' up with that headache."

"Are you-"

"Go, Priest," Gibson urged, easing down to the floor. "I ain't runnin' off anyplace. Gonna sit down for a minute, though."

I holstered my Colts and limped around the corner.

Andreya West had hidden within a door's alcove.

"Priest?" she asked, relieved.

I noticed the thick smell of gunpowder even as far as her hallway. There had been a lot of shooting.

"Yeah," I answered her. "Gibson's down. I think Lyles is dead. We need to get help and get Gibson's bleeding stopped."

"I'll check on Lyles," she said as she pulled off the belt sash that fastened about her top. "You take this and tie off Gibson's wound-"

"It'll probably take both of us," I said, waving her onward as I started back. "He's gushing and-"

"Hmmmm, no," she said and shook her head emphatically.

I paused for a second.

"C'mon, West!"

"Um, heh, I don't think so. Mmm, nope. Not going to work."

"What's your problem?" I pushed.

"Germs, Priest! I can't play in open wounds and blood and tissue-"

"What?"

"I'm a germaphobe, *Detective*, do some research!" she cried.

"West, you have to-"

"Not going to. Not. Nope, not."

"I thought you were hard core," I taunted.

She ground her teeth together and snarled at me, one of the first times I had ever seen her seem anything but happy.

"I...am..."

"Good, come on!"

She nodded finally and I turned in a whirlwind and hobbled my way back to Gibson. I ripped off my shirt on the way and wiped my sweating head and face then tore it into multiple pieces.

"What're you doin', Priest? A striptease?" he coughed.

"Gibson, quiet down."

"Oh, that's so gross!" West railed at me. "Did you really just wipe your sweat on the fabric you'll use for bandages?"

I glanced at her, rolled my eyes and turned back to Gibson.

"You gonna let me wrap that wound with my nasty shirt?"

"I'm a Marine, Priest," he said, a gleam in his eyes. He fell back to one elbow and sighed. "I don't scare easy. Do what you gotta do."

The sticky, red truth of it was still running between his fingers. Time was running out faster than his crimson lifeflow.

"West, get that belt ready," I called, glancing over my shoulder.

I moved his shirt and blood ran everywhere. I pinched the big hole closed and it took my whole hand to do it. Gibson grimaced but made no sound whatsoever. Andreya West made all the noise necessary, 'icking' and 'ewwing' for us all. I pressed the shirt parts against the well of blood, checking for depth. It was the worst abdominal shot I had seen close up. I pressed the shirt material deeper and squeezed the flesh closed.

"You tryin' to make me yell, Priest?" he asked through gritted teeth.

"Hold this in place. Stay still and don't do anything stupid."

He dug his fingers into his own flesh and squeezed with both hands.

"Andreya, belt him up," I ordered.

She took a deep breath and moved in on the man.

"The boy," he muttered and swore bitterly. "Got lucky with that...three round burst, Priest. That little 9mm didn't make this tunnel in me...three rounds to the same...general spot did. Early on. Been bleedin' a while now. I think what we got here is...an exercise in futility."

"Hang in there," I said.

"I'm gonna get some help," West said, stepping back from Gibson and gasping for air. "I'll be back. I did all I could; stay with him and I'll go for help."

She turned and ran like a flash for the outside.

I said, "Hey, West! Where you goin' for help?"

"West is better off runnin'," Gibson said. "I'll die anyway; don't make her stay here and puke on me, too."

"Take it easy," I said.

His face was stricken when he said, "Listen to me! I ain't got long..."

"Just relax. You ain't dead, yet," I prodded.

"Can't outrun it this time. Man my age? Livin' violent all this time? The Bible's true. I lived by the sword. Gonna die by it. I'm pretty sure it blew through my kidney."

"You don't know that," I said.

"I seen more action than you've seen days and more 'n my share of dead and dyin', too. I know three wadcutters through my kidney would've cut all the blood vessels goin' to it...and the bleedin' ain't gonna stop. You can quit callin' that girl...unless she's a surgeon with a go bag in her pocket. I'm finished."

"Gibson?" I muttered, pausing there with him. "You can't just quit."

His blood was everywhere and his face had bleached pale.

"Aw, don't get all sentimental. The pain is one thing, the dyin' another, but a grown man cryin' is too hard for me to handle," he said with a grunt and a wince.

"Save your breath, Gibson," I warned.

"Besides, I'm still a Marine. We don't quit. Don't mean we can't read the writin' on the wall, though."

"Gibson, we got it tied off-"

"I'm not our killer but I footed the bill for a lotta hits, Priest. Keep in mind, though, I never targeted a soul who didn't deserve it. I just wanted justice..."

"True justice would mean we all deserve it," I said. "We're all guilty of something, Gibson. Who are we to set the price of retribution?"

His brow furrowed as he said, "Once you start passin' judgment on the rest of the world it gets easier and easier...easier to forget your own crimes, your own sins...now, you listen to me-"

"No, you listen," I urged him. I exhaled in exasperation then said, "Listen to Kelli, Gibson, and what she told me."

His lips trembled and his eyes grew wide.

He muttered, "What do you know about that name?"

"I know about Kelli Gibson. She was your daughter."

He locked his jaw and squeezed closed his eyes against an onslaught of emotion. The dams he had erected to withstand his loss had no fortification against the sudden breach. The abrupt confrontation with all he had felt and barricaded deep within himself burst through to the surface. The floodgates washed away entirely.

"Where did you hear that name?" he demanded in the howl of a wounded animal. Spit ran from his lips as they twisted and he began crying. "How could you know? Oh...that file...that deep file Remy planted in that publisher's computer..."

"No, Gibson," I corrected. "That's not it. The file on you didn't know your secret. Lyles didn't know that secret."

"Then how, Priest?" he roared, wracked with pain both emotional and physical.

"I'll tell you. It's up to you to believe me."

Then I told him quickly about the vision and the dreams, sharing what his child had said.

"My name is...was...Kelli. Not Johanna. Not Crimson. Nothing so dramatic, so memorable. So...striking or vivid. Just Kelli. I was happy when I was Kelli. But my big break required a new mantle, a new name. So was born Johanna Crimson, starlet."

"Who is Johanna Crimson? Is she in danger?" I had responded.

"She is in danger. But it is not the woman you know as Johanna Crimson you must rescue. You must rescue her protector; he stands to lose far more than she does."

"She's in danger but I need to rescue Gibson?" I had asked.

"She is in danger, marked for death by the Ghost Revolver. But you must rescue Mark Gibson...from himself. Crimson is in mortal peril, her life at stake. Gibson is in danger of losing himself to his own passions, his own desires. Losing his very...self. Know this...Mark Gibson will be torn apart from within if you cannot save him. This will be his point of no return, his doomsday...unless you stop it. Stop him."

"First, rescue him? Now, stop him?" I had said.

"Sometimes...those are the same things. You see, my name is Kelli. Kelli Gibson."

"He's your father?" I had asked.

"Yes."

"But the other woman, Johanna Crimson, she somehow took your place? And your father protects her? He has to know she isn't you. He has to know something happened to his daughter-"

"He knows, Mr. Priest."

"What is he doing?" I had asked.

"Like anyone, his sins are his to reveal, his confessions his own to disclose, as is right. What I can say is that he needs you."

"Me? What makes me-"

"Mr. Priest, you have faced loss and found grace and love on the other side. His torment is nearly complete; if someone does not step in before this encounter on this mountain is over, he will be lost forever."

Then I hurriedly told him my story, from Tamara's death to my mental break and denial. From my realization of reality to the vision of our loving Savior, Jesus Christ, reminding me that life goes on and is still worth living. I told him just how much we are truly loved, even in the trying times. Especially in the trying times. I told him most fervently about forgiveness and redemption.

Even for men with blood on their hands.

He wept, broken. In a voice strained with emotion and pain, one cracking with personal torment, he told me bits of his story.

He was the devoted husband of a woman who had died young. The proud father of a young woman who made it as a star. The ragged, avenging specter, shattered inside, hunting the stalker who murdered that daughter. And he was the man who had killed that stalker...slowly.

He continued walking that dark path afterward. Revenge had not satiated his blood lust. Vengeance had not quelled the screaming need for retribution, as suddenly the need was for retribution for others. Any others, as long as it gave the man an excuse to exact more revenge.

Not wearing the shadows, becoming the driven vigilante who forged a murderous undertaking himself. Instead, he started using excess money from accounts he controlled to hire out 'justice' and, more to the point, vengeance. Gibson used money to buy the services of an assassin with a reputation built on history and legends, smoke and mirrors...and death.

Behind tears and anguish, feeling and questioning his own actions for the first time in years, a broken man admitted his rage, his violence, his wrath and his fury. He wrestled with it and, in the end, acknowledged the cancerous decay in his heart and soul. The emptiness. The poison. They were all eating away at him and he wondered if he had actually died already and his body had just refused to stop.

He admitted, too, putting another young woman into Kelli's place...as Johanna Crimson, world famous starlet.

"Kelli," he sobbed, wracked with agony of the heart.

At least he feels again, I thought. *It's a start, Lord...*

"Gibson, let go of it all. You don't have to confess anything to me. Kelli, your daughter, came to me because God loves you. Don't you see? He wanted to save your soul from the final fall! He allowed Kelli to come to me, Gibson. He knew I would come here! Now, come to Kelli. Come back to your faith. Come back to God."

A lot of men would have refused to believe the miraculous, the supernatural. Mark Gibson was too smart to deny it. I could see it in his tears and it radiated from his eyes. But, though I could see his burgeoning faith, I saw fear. Desperate fear.

"Priest, I've gone too far..." he cried. "You just don't understand...the killing...the murders..."

His eyes fluttered. When they opened steadily again, they seemed distant, glassy. He looked to be lapsing in coherence.

"Gibson, it's a simple thing, so simple! Ask forgiveness. Offer your heart to Him. Ask Him to save you and take you home to Heaven. And mean it. Really mean it."

"...too far...Priest..."

"Not as long as you have a single breath left!" I yelled at him. "It's not about what you've done! It's about who He is! And it's never about who you are! It's about what He's done for you!"

"But you don't know–"

"Come on," I said and started praying with him.

Dear Father God, please forgive me for all my sins. Make me new. I want to be yours. I accept your Son, Jesus, as Lord and I accept your gift of eternal life, given through His sacrifice. Please have mercy on me and take me to Heaven to live with you there.

I watched as he mouthed the words as I spoke, even as he was running out of air and out of time. He finished with, "...Heaven..."

I took a deep, grateful breath.

"And mean it, Gibson. I do believe you mean it."

A stillness fell over him. I thought he was gone for a moment. Then he moved his eyes, concentrating on the distance. It seemed like the pain was gone. Thoughtfully, he smiled then hoarsely mumbled one last thing.

"There. Comin' this way...it's Kelli..." he murmured and squinted, "...and...there's a Lion with her..."

He fell still again. I reached out and closed his eyes then dropped back, sitting down completely on the marble tiles. I wiped over my face and smeared my own tears.

The Son dried up my sadness almost instantly, however, and I began to smile for Gibson. Then I began to praise God.

Old Gordon Lightfoot was gone.

He was the only horse that had not run off, spooked by the gunshots. Nevertheless, when I went back outside, he was gone, too.

Paul Blackwood, the British baker, had still not returned. I wondered if the man had run all the way down the mountain. Then I wondered if he was really guilty of the things in that file.

Then I wondered if he could be the Revolver.

Andreya West had taken off someplace for help. Had she taken Gordon and made a run for one of the trails?

Then I wondered if she could be the Revolver.

I shook my head. I was too tired for more questions. There were plenty of unanswered questions, already.

Maureen Li was linked to Remy Lyles in a blackmail racket and the two were getting money from Gibson to keep his secret, the fact that he was paying the computer guru, Lyles, to arrange hits to be carried out by the Ghost Revolver. Gibson was transferring him money for the Revolver, then money for blackmail. It was something Lyles and Gibson claimed Johanna Crimson, the money maker, did not even realize.

Was that true?

I rushed to where Li had fallen after being shot then followed the drag trail. West had pulled her to safety and hidden her in the bushes from Remy Lyles. She had also wrapped her wound.

It had done little good. The shot to the neck, a lucky one by the amateur Lyles, had finished Li in a short time of massive bleeding.

Li had probably been blackmailing the whole guest list in one way or another; whether she was complicit in luring them all to a meet with the Revolver would likely never be known.

If Lyles was an organizer and Gibson a pocketbook, who was the Ghost Revolver? Everything kept coming back to that main question. Who was the Ghost Revolver?

Still, a man's soul had been pulled back from eternal loss and that was a victory snatched from the very jaws of evil, in any case. Gibson had been a part of a dark operation but there had been light in him, a remnant. I wondered what the rest of his secret was. Neither he nor the ghost of Kelli Gibson had seen fit to tell me. I wondered if I would ever know.

I checked around outside for a while, wondering if the Revolver would make an appearance. It did not happen. I found newer footprints embedded in those made during our conflict and I gave time to curiosity, following their trail. Blood tainted them, painting the footprints in red. They led me to another track.

Horses' hoof prints outside, in the mulch, leading off for the trails. Old Gordon and a rider. A mystery rider. The Revolver?

I had imagined it all ending differently. I had pictured myself throwing the Revolver over my mount, Gordon, like a saddlebag. The image was another throwback to the cowboy and bounty hunter era like the legend of the Revolver, itself, and the standoff in the roses.

That ending was not to be. Instead, I was left to wait for a rescue team, sent by whichever guests made it down the mountain first. Left to wait for them...and think.

I thought again of the explosives and the destruction of the bridge. Since Lyles was not the Revolver and Lyles wanted the computers and the files in play for the weekend, it stood to reason that the Revolver had indeed been the culprit behind the fireworks. It returned my thinking to the identity of the Revolver anew, with the perspective that the individual would have to be proficient with explosives and the one most often out and about...alone.

A most likely loner...

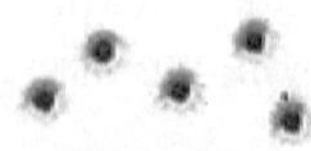

The Brit ran for his very life, heedless and without caution. The heat of the day thickened the very air he sucked down while trying to keep up his pace, burning his lungs all the hotter. Blackwood was a sturdy man, muscular. He was not, however, a long distance runner. Far more adept at defending himself, his actions testified to his fear; he had fled, afraid. He had just as determinedly become one with the wind.

The group was about to explode into violence, gunfire and murder. That was his cue to race away, ducking through the gardens and foliage. That took him on a path through the open grasses of the grounds and beyond, rushing with all he could manage.

He hit the fence that served as the boundary without ever slowing. A leap and a struggled scaling took him over the top of it and dropped him recklessly into the woods just beyond it. The forest treeline accepted him with open arms and he raced into them, disappearing into the greens and browns, begging sanctuary.

For a time, as he blindly pressed through bush and vine, limb and leaf, each one left a bit of itself on him or took a bit of him in payment for passage. He felt it was worth the strain. With each passing moment, he just knew he was making good his escape from a certain doom.

After a time, however, he slowed to a stop, finally unable to keep running. He had made all the time and distance he could manage, making a world of noise along the way, too. He did not figure it mattered; there was no one to hear him.

The baker drooped over forward, hands braced on his burning thighs, arms taught and trembling. He kept an eye open on his surroundings when he could lift his head but that was fleeting and sporadic, at best.

"No one pronounces judgment on me," he gasped, "no one."

His breathing was ragged and desperate as he took another long look around himself. When he felt completely alone, he relaxed.

"I'll get this 'Revolver' after this. I'll end this American 'legend'," he babbled aloud angrily. "The legend, the detective, the SBI, the bodyguard, all of 'em. I'll teach 'em all or I'm not-"

"Paul Blackwood," a voice said nearby.

The Brit spun about just in time to take an incredibly brutal blow to the temple from a slender staff. Blood sprayed from his head as he fell straight down into the leaves and straw on the forest bed. He did not move after that.

A few yards away, Gordon Lightfoot nickered impatiently.

"Don't be so impetuous, boy," the Ghost Revolver said to him. "I have to wipe my staff down. I would've used one of the 'judges' but that kind of noise...it was best to forego tradition this once, wouldn't you say?"

Then, after cleaning the weapon, the Revolver mounted up again.

"Now, ride again, like our grandfathers before us! Ride!"

I had been pondering it a long time, replaying the weekend in my head time and again, when the whipping sound reached my ears.

Coming into view was a helicopter, chopping the wind in its approach. *Whup whup whup* it chanted, vocalizing promises of rescue. A North Carolina Forestry Service logo glinted on its green sides in the blazing sunshine.

I waved at the slowly descending bird.

No way somebody made it down to the nearest town, I thought to myself. *Not enough time's passed. No, this is something else.*

The chopper lit on the grass and Forestry Officers bailed free. A passenger leaned from a side bay door, looking this way and that.

Out jumped Andreya West, tying her hair up in a knot.

Something else entirely, I thought.

CHAPTER SEVENTEEN

At the chosen rendezvous, an equestrian friendly hotel with horse and tack stalls, two men stopped by the hitching posts. Nearby were secured the reins of horses from the resort, Horse and Heraldry, reins emblazoned with gold lettering.

The little place was a lot smaller than the world class resort and seemed to think a lot less of itself but, showy or not, it was a quaint, charming locale.

The two men turned, pointed across the property to a crowded parking lot and walked away. One of them spoke into a radio.

Mick Priest slid one of his 10mm Colts back into a holster. He let the glass sliding door's curtain in his ground floor room close again.

Sarah Priest, smelling of fresh melon after a long, hot shower, embraced her husband lovingly from behind. She squeezed him and pressed her face into his muscular back.

"You can relax," she fussed. "It's over. The State Police are all over this place and all over H and H, up the mountain, too. They're like bees around a bumped hive."

"I saw some county folks, too. I guess the state called in the locals to be nice."

"Nope," she said. "I did."

"I think you miss being a local LEO," Priest said with a soft smile.

"There's a lot of Deputy Sheriff in this State Agent," she admitted.

"Who gets the case?" he asked her. "Home team or the locals?"

Sarah Melindez-Priest, Special Agent of the North Carolina State Bureau of Investigation, wandered over to the queen bed and sat down in her towel. Where the locals were concerned, she had held them all at bay. Informative, helpful and decisive, she nevertheless told them the data on hand was hers to give to the SBI and they would not concede jurisdictional restriction.

She had already made the call to her superior, Eric Lockner, and he was on the way with a response team. One mention of the internationally known Ghost Revolver and Lockner had called the FBI, in turn. He suspected the feds might even bring in Interpol but Sarah considered that way above her pay grade.

She said with a sigh, "If I had given everything over to a county department that doesn't even have a CSU division, can you imagine Eric's head not exploding?"

"I get it," he said.

At least she had given them leave to interview the survivors.

All were staying at the little inn, except for Paul Blackwood. The baker had not yet emerged from the forest. With every passing moment, there was concern he never would.

Supervisory Special Agent Eric Lockner would be setting up a post in a medical facility in Swannanoa immediately upon his touching down, waiting and hoping for the British baker to be found.

"Is that a big place?" Sarah asked Mick.

Some of the paramedics, after checking out the refugees, had worn the location designation. Sarah Priest had retained the information, the queen of details.

Mick chuckled.

"Oh, yeah, quite cosmopolitan," he said with amusement.

It was a fairly small town.

The air conditioning in their room blew for all its worth. Mick Priest had dropped the dial to fifty degrees, the lowest setting it wore stamped and inked. He relished the cool, comfortable for the first time in days. Sarah shivered but Mick was fully dressed after his shower.

"You leaving, now?" she asked.

"Yeah. I don't wanna leave things to the staties or the county crew. Not where Crimson is concerned. I wanna tie things up. Finish it. For Gibson...and for Kelli Gibson."

"I can imagine," she said sweetly.

Mick had given her the facts since his arrival.

"You're a good man, Mick Priest."

"I try, Sarah."

"I know that, too, Lover."

After a deep, grateful kiss, he walked out of the room. He instantly frowned at the wave of heat and wiped over his head by reflex.

"That look is familiar," a woman said from his left, farther down the main hall. "Don't you have another face, Mick Priest?"

He cut his eyes that way first then leaned his head with a slight turn.

"No, I'm boring," he said. "What you see is what you get..."

Andreya West smiled knowingly with, "I sense questions."

"I'm glad you're on top of the game. I can't seem to keep up."

They locked eyes in a fierce but silent engagement for a few tense moments. Then both of them seemed to soften at the same time, unable to pierce the other's veil, to peer through the windows to the other's soul.

"I think you spend most of your time ahead, Mick Priest, not just keeping up," she said finally.

"And I think there's more to you than most realize," he countered.

"A lady needs a little mystery about her. Keeps her interesting."

"Like the mystery of why you ran off? With my horse, no less. I know you said you wanted to get help as quickly as you could-"

"That's right," she said with that trademarked, chipper smile.

"-and you-"

"-knew Gibson was beyond my help. And Li was...gone."

"I appreciate your help, I do. But I wonder, you know?" he pressed.

"Oh, don't we all?" she giggled. "What do you wonder about?"

"You. And my horse. Well, my saddlebags, anyway. Losing the two silver revolvers, having them 'fall out' on the way down into the valley...and I had taken such care to secure them."

"Weapons of a ghost killer got lost, disappearing forever...it seems appropriate. For a legend."

Priest said, "Would be quite a coincidence."

"Wouldn't it?"

"But I don't believe in coincidence."

"You know, one of the county detectives said the same thing, Mr. Priest. Is the 'no coincidence' thing a cop mentality?"

He took a long moment before answering.

"Among others," he said candidly.

"Like suspicion? Guilt by association? When you realized I'd ridden off, you thought I was involved."

"You are a woman of mystery," he said.

"And the fact that I rode to a Forestry Station to get you help all the faster, instead of riding for a town? How did that strike you?" she asked pointedly.

"With surprise."

"And the fact that I returned to help with the Forestry Officers instead of going on to town? How do you meet those facts?"

"With gratitude and more surprise."

"You are most welcome," she said graciously.

"And with questions."

"It really is like one of those novels," she giggled again.

"Uncanny."

"I am a woman of mystery, as we've established," she said.

"Yeah. Like how you managed to simply 'run across' a Forestry Station on a mountain you've never explored."

"Have I mentioned how lucky I am?" she asked with that grin.

He chuckled, wiping the sweat from his head, again.

"Are you linked to the Revolver?" he threw out suddenly.

The detective was trying to hit her flatfooted, to take her off guard.

"I'm a lot of things," she quipped. Her cool demeanor never faltered. "I'm half American Indian. I have multiple degrees and mastery in everything from history and linguistics to chemistry and Cuban dance. I'm a writer, a professor, a speaker of multiple languages, a germaphobe, a vegan, a game nerd, a ballet enthusiast-"

"A Kali martial artist," he interrupted.

"Actually, I train in Silat, not Kali," she said with a shrug. "Besides, a girl's got to keep in shape."

"There's so much more to you than meets the eye," he said again.

She let the smile go. She did not giggle. There hid no mirth in her usually jovial eyes. When she stepped close to him, locking eyes with him again, her veil was once again flat, impenetrable.

"And you're always a step ahead, despite the circumstances. There's something about you, too, Mick Priest. It defies an easy description...or understanding. The way you just seem to 'know' things, to 'sense' things. I suspect you wouldn't share it all with me no matter how much I ask. So, let's leave it there. Both of us have our secrets."

He met the defiant gaze with his own green eyed fire.

"A guy has to have a little mystery about him."

"And there you go." She curtsied, saying, "*Touché, mon ami.*"

"I still wonder," he said frankly.

She turned and walked off down the hallway, laughing lightly.

"You'll have all you need for a new novel," she chirped. "Let that be your keepsake from all this and your consolation prize."

"That's not what worries me, Andreya," he called to her.

"Stop worrying so much, Mr. Priest. It's going to give you gray hair."

He ran a hand over his smoothly shaven head as West disappeared around a corner in the corridor.

"Funny," he muttered absently.

Sarah Priest stepped out of their room, dressed and dry.

"Did I hear Andreya out here?" she asked.

"Yeah."

"She really stuck her neck out, ya know?"

"Yeah."

"Andreya was a big help. I like her."

"Well...yeah."

"She would be great for Eric," Sarah Priest decided.

He said nothing that time, staring blankly down the hallway.

"D. Eric Lockner, SSA. She said she hates the name Eric but, hey, that's what the D is for. Dennis. Maybe she'd be good with a Dennis. I know she sounded excited about a Supervisory Special Agent with the SBI. He's really interested in brainy types and her looks won't hurt, either. He's got a ruggedly chiseled look, he's tall and athletic...hello, can you think of anyone better for Andreya West? And she's way too mature and stable for guys her age, so she told me. She gets disappointed in most of the guys she-"

"Sarah," he said with a quick turn of his head, "where did all this come from?"

"Okay, what's wrong, Mick?" she asked him.

He nodded with, "Something...but I have no idea what it is."

"Did she get the last word, Mick Priest?" Sarah teased, a smirk flirting with her lips.

"No," he said, a little too quickly. He ran a hand over his head, thinking about the gray hair remark. "Well, maybe. But that's not it."

"Some of the ladies and I were talking, that's all," Sarah continued. "Nerves are still raw, Mick. I'm a good listener and talking helps."

"Yeah."

Sarah sighed and rambled in Spanish. Then, "Well, it helps some people."

She went back into the room.

"Yeah," Priest muttered.

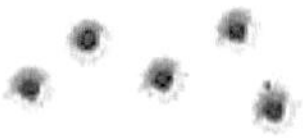

James Wyatt folded his lean arms across his chest. He wore a brown, leather bracer on his left forearm, etched with raging bears. Face emotionless, he put his back to the room door in the hallway and stood as a strong and silent sentinel. Dark, almost black eyes watched and saw everything.

"Hey, James. I see you had a shower. Maybe you should grab sleep while you can. I'll sit with Johanna," I promised.

He sighed and put his hands into his pockets.

"Time for the talk?" he asked, knowing what was coming.

I had given him a run down on what had happened and what had been said up on the mountain before Gibson died. He knew what was coming. He realized it was needed to finish things, to end it.

"Yep," I said simply.

He dropped his head, shook it then gestured to the door.

"I'm gonna wait out here," he said.

I opened the door, slipped inside the room and closed it again. The room was dark, the shades drawn. Crimson sat on one of the beds, the covers piled in disarray and covering her legs. She lay against a bank of pillows, propped up, her hair a wet bird's nest. Her face, makeup free, was puffed and reddened with crying. She actively surrendered tears from swollen eyes.

She wore a Bugs Bunny t shirt.

"What's up, Doc?" I asked softly. I pointed to the shirt, adding, "I love Bugs. Next to Charlie Brown, Snoopy and Scooby Doo, he's my favorite."

She sniffed.

"I believe the Charlie Brown part," she said, looking down at her shirt. "You're both follicle free."

I gave her a sad, soft smile when she glanced up at me with only her eyes. She returned a half shrug for my smile.

"Kidding, of course," she said, downtrodden.

"It's true," I said, gesturing to a chair at a small table. "May I?"

"I'm sorry. Of course," she allowed, returning her eyes to her shirt.

She sniffed again and rubbed her nose with a tissue.

"Johanna, I want to-"

"Mr. Priest, Marcus Gibson was my world. I don't expect you to understand but he kept me...sane...not just safe. Hollywood and the industry are illusions, on the best days. Most days they're nightmarish lies. Gibson was everything the fame machine isn't."

I waited.

Quivering, she drew a deep breath and added, "Now, he's unmasked as the Ghost Revolver's bankroll...and I'm adrift. I'm dealing as best I can but I can't promise anything anymore. What is it you want to talk about?"

"Gibson. The Revolver. What happened. Listen, I know it seems impossible, unbelievable," I said, leaning over and bracing my arms on my legs. "These things take time to soak in."

"Hardly."

I honestly did not see that coming.

"Excuse me?" I asked.

"Mark Gibson was the closest thing to a father, to a parent, I ever had," she said, voice tight. "I knew him better than anyone else alive and, if I'm honest, I suppose I knew this sort of thing could happen."

"What exactly?"

"Revenge, Mr. Priest. Rage. I thought he was constantly tempted with the idea of 'justice' but holding it back, staving off the need. I thought I helped with that. Now that I see he had been embracing it all along, I feel foolish for not seeing it clearly."

I watched her closely as she wiped at the tears.

"I'm at a loss," I admitted. "You didn't know he was using your money to pay a killer for hire but you suspected he was capable of it?"

She huffed, shaking her head. Drops of water fell from the tips of her long hair.

"Let me explain."

So, she did.

Her name was not really Johanna Crimson.

There was no Johanna Crimson, in reality. She was an ethereal entity, an idea, an image...an illusion, no more corporeal than the faceless Ghost Revolver.

The young woman who had renamed herself that had originally been Kelli Gibson. Kelli Gibson, daughter of United States Marine and government operative, Mark Gibson, had reinvented herself in her acting career and bestowed the moniker upon herself.

She made Johanna Crimson a household name, too, all the while never forgetting her real self. She even took her best friend from middle and high school, Tabitha Grey, along with her into fame and stardom. Gibson gave Grey a position handling a lot of her press and appointments and day to day needs. She always kept her close, once her best friend, always her best friend.

As children, they had been nearly inseparable. Mark Gibson had been like a father to his daughter's best friend, too, an orphan living with a single aunt she could barely stand. The girls were more like sisters and people often commented on their natural resemblance to each other, which was not exactly natural since they were not, in reality, related.

As adults, just as inseparable, just as close, the two managed a seriously impressive amount of money. They excelled in business acquisition and management, investments and holdings and the like, all spawning from the mass success of Johanna Crimson. Kelli even fronted the capital to set her father up with his own security and protection company, three floor office building, fifty man staff and company cars included.

Then, as the family had its own security firm, she used them herself.

Gibson and team got the detail of a lifetime. Kelli Gibson, as Johanna Crimson, handpicked a protection team from their company. She chose her own candidates instead of her father's recommendations, however, but all was well. After all, they had to suit the movie star lifestyle. They had to have the 'look' and no one knew it better than Johanna Crimson.

Darkness would befall them, nonetheless. One of the detail, obsessed with her and intent on having her at any cost, lost his tenuous grip on reality. He killed Kelli Gibson, in her role as Johanna Crimson, in a hotel room in Greece.

No one ever heard a thing.

Mark Gibson, in a twist that would forever haunt him, had come to Greece with the entourage, taking a bit of a holiday from work. He was only rooms away when she was so brutally slain.

Afterward, Gibson pulled his most loyal men and women, former military like himself, aside. He pulled Tabitha Grey aside, too. He told them that there were too many charities, too many foundations and too many good programs depending on the fortune made by 'the entity' of Johanna Crimson. His daughter, Kelli, was dead and there was nothing he could do about that. That did not mean that 'Johanna Crimson' had to die. He swore them to secrecy and asked Tabby to become Johanna Crimson...for the 'greater good' of their work.

Tabby agreed to become Crimson, leaving very little behind, in her opinion, and gaining the world. Gaining, in particular, a father she loved as if he were her own blood. And she knew he loved her, too. It was an easy decision for her.

Local authorities were told Tabitha Grey had been killed by a murderer. A member of Johanna Crimson's own protection detail. That was a lie. Kelli Gibson, as 'Johanna Crimson', had been killed.

They were told that the obsessed man, crazed, had fled. That much was true. He was never destined to meet the police, however. He would be found later, at another hotel, having killed himself. That could have equally been truth or a lie; she always wondered if somehow Gibson had caught up to him.

Gibson was ravaged by the loss, raw and angry. The young woman loved Gibson but she had no doubt in her that his love for his child and his rage could have pushed him beyond normal limits.

Whatever the case, time passed. With a little cosmetic touch up, a boost here and reduction there, Tabby's stark resemblance to the famed Crimson became identical. Gibson took over as her full time protector and advisor, helping her find the right avenues to use the fortune to good effect. Of course, she wondered over some of the monetary decisions and the discrepancies she found from time to time but he was the *real* Johanna Crimson's father. How could she ask...anything?

There was always *that* talk, too, and the way it made her feel. He would say there should be better ways to deal with evil people. Courts and warrants and laws only worked so well. There should be organizations like the upstart posses back in the old west. Dedicated to putting down the guilty, righting wrongs, enforcing justice, not laws. She did not like it but she thought it was just talk, murmurings and stirrings from the broken heart of a scarred father.

She had finally been able to forsake the worries when the illustrious Ghost Revolver had targeted her. Gibson finally condemned the idea of vigilantism...or so she thought. He was so upset when the threats started but all of that had been a simple perspective, she supposed. It was okay for him to propose assassination on people he felt deserved it but far be it for anyone to target her with it.

When faced with the facts, she could not blind herself any longer. She could also find nothing in herself to condemn the man, more a father to her than anyone she had known. It simply was what it was and there was nothing she could do to change it or make it an easier pill to swallow.

For his part, Priest told her about Gibson's spiritual awakening and decisions before he died. She was terribly happy about that and had cried unabashedly. There was a large place inside the young woman where Faith still lived, whether she actively practiced hers or not. She knew the Truth and it was louder than ever before.

Also, in Priest's turn, he told her the whole truth; he was not sure what to say about her using the Crimson identity. He told her he really did not feel like it was his place to judge. She had been invited in by Kelli long ago and Mark loved her. What other justification should she have? He told her that he would not reveal the dual identity of Johanna Crimson, the Velvet Edge. What she chose to do with or without her mask would be up to her.

Before he left her, he was careful to remind her just how much the man had truly loved her. It was what finally broke her again.

Priest simply held her while she gently wept.

On his way out, Priest had asked to pray with her. She had gladly accepted.

"I can't think there's a better option," James Wyatt told me outside the room.

"We all wear blinders where loved ones are concerned, at least sometimes," I said.

"I'm gonna hang with Johanna...well, Tabby...oh, whoever she is this week. I'm gonna keep it to myself that you filled me in, let her tell me herself, if she wants to. I'm her only hired gun left and she's still famous. There's more nuts out there than just the Revolver."

I nodded.

"You think he'll still come for her?" James asked.

"I don't," I said honestly. "The Revolver was on that mountain with us. We have to figure our gunhand knows whatever we know, more or less. He got played by a vindictive Remy Lyles."

"Yeah. Where you off to? Your feet look restless," James asked.

"I'm going over to that med center to talk with Eric Lockner. I wanna know if Blackwood has turned up."

"Tell Special Eric I said what's up," James said.

I checked my phone for the time.

"Will do. He should be there by now."

He turned back for Crimson's door and I turned away but he called me back, suddenly.

"Hey, man, by the way," he stalled.

"Somethin' on your mind, James?"

"What do you think the chances are of Blackwood actually bein' our ghost? I mean, it's possible, right? And with him runnin' off, kinda likely."

"Yeah...maybe."

"Okay, who's your pick, then?" he asked.

The dining room at the small Rustic Inn and Suites was nothing like the glamorous Dining Hall at Horse and Heraldry Resort. It held a lot of qualities similar to local coffee shops and sit-in bookstores. It was quaint, simple, traditional. In a word, homey.

"Like the pubs back home," B'Rone Matwahali decided aloud.

"I've never seen England," Kess Melkin said, her eyes soft, genuine.

The two sat together at a little, round table with flowers and a lamp between them.

"You really should," he replied, his eyes not flirty but sincere.

"I'd like that," she said with a smile.

"Me, too," Gretchen Clayborne said from her perch at the diner-style counter. "We should all go. Together. After all, what could happen? There's no thinkable way anything bad could happen to this same group, twice over. What're the odds, right?"

"One does not tempt fate with such a possibility," Jenkins said. "I mean no slight, of course, but I have seen my fill of this particular gathering of people."

Gretchen looked at him curiously.

"With exceptions...such as yourself," the tall man clarified.

He stood near Gretchen, not sitting on his stool but simply propping against it. Near him stood Tye Richter, leaned against the counter, sipping at his fourth cup of black coffee.

"Yeah. Ya'll seen the *Die Hard* movies? Everywhere that guy goes breaks down into chaos."

"Those are movies; to be sure you realize the difference," Andreya West said.

"Terrible things happen. That's no movie, it's a fact of life," Cassandra Clark said, sitting at the counter just beyond Richter. "But we can't let them paint the rest of our lives. It doesn't mean we stop living."

"All you can do is *Be Still and Know*," Tayla Barlowe agreed.

She bounced little Emma on her lap, making happy faces for her.

"Ya'll ever wonder what sins got us all on the list?" Kess Melkin asked.

"I wouldn't think on it," Andreya West said thoughtfully, fairly subdued in comparison to her normal, giddy composure.

"Why? Ignorance is bliss? Better to not know if it's still coming?"

West shook her head and frowned at Victor Jackson.

"No, not at all," she said. "But the Revolver is supposedly a consummate professional, right?"

Jackson nodded.

"So, the legend goes."

"To be sure, one to do independent research and investigation, anyway. If any of us are truly guilty, we would've already been 'hit' this weekend. I think those of us here are innocent of whatever charges were on that little file of yours."

"If I wasn't so exhausted I'd be indignant and defend Grip, West," Gretchen Clayborne growled. "Maybe...if I still believed he was as innocent of things as he claimed. I look back, now, though, and I wonder."

She sighed and leaned over against the broad chest of Jenkins. He put an arm around her and squeezed.

"What all was in that file, Vic?" Melkin asked.

"I'm sorry. I'm not about to further any of the claims in that file. Not unless they're proven to me."

"Or unless she makes you," Tye Richter said.

He thumbed over his shoulder at the front picture window.

Sarah Melindez-Priest looked on from outside the glass. She was on her phone, keeping her conversation to herself.

"Yeah, Eric, I'm still on the premises," she said, wiping perspiration from her brow. "I'm melting but I'm still here."

The agent listened to Supervisory Special Agent D. Eric Lockner, giving a lengthy reply from the other end.

"Well, yeah," she answered him after a few seconds. "Mick's already on the way."

He offered more input and she listened patiently. She focused through the plate glass window, staring at no one particular person.

"I hope you can find a way to help, too. At least, for these folks, it's all over," she muttered.

Andreya West noticed Sarah Priest looking at them from outside. She lifted her glass to the agent and offered a smile.

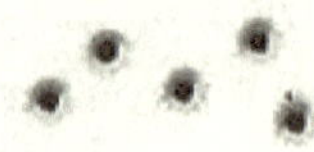

It was crowded.

It was, after all, the only medical outpost available for a long way.

A Highway Trooper, a member of the state police, had been kind enough to ferry me there. He had been heading that way anyway, so I was told. He even escorted me inside, too, as proper in protocol as he was in uniform and dress code. I could see my face in his shined badge and polished, patent leather ops boots.

"Thanks, again, Trooper Ritt," I said, reading his nameplate.

"You're welcome," he said with a succinct nod.

Two suits started our way, one from the nearest room door and one from the nurse's station. He nodded to them before she turned to go.

"Agent Barry Steppowitz, this is Mick Priest," the taller, thinner state agent introduced. "Mick, this is Agent Steppowitz. Everybody around the agency calls him Steppo."

"Eric, it's good to see you," I greeted the speaker.

He offered a hand and I shook it heartily. I knew him pretty well and my fondness for him was not feigned. The lean, hawk-eyed agent was my wife's supervisor but he had become a good friend, too.

"Mick, same here," Lockner replied.

Then Steppo and I shook hands. The difference was night and day. His handshake was soft and timid where Eric's was bold and strong. Their physical demeanor was much the same way. Lockner was tall and fit, a runner, with a predator's movements. Steppo was pudgy, round shouldered and plodding when he moved. He had a great many freckles and his sun bleached hair poked here and there in need of a trim. Lockner wore his trademarked 'close cut' on his coal black shock of hair. Time had finally installed a little silver in the ebony, however.

"Steppo's our electronic forensics guy for this case," Lockner explained.

"I'm glad to be aboard," the other agent said, more to Lockner than to me. "In North Carolina, the SBI cyber-ops lead the war on child predators, first and foremost. Our Computer Crimes Unit runs proactive undercover investigations in our own right and we lend help to law enforcement agencies all over North Carolina, and around the world, for that matter. We bring the computer forensic expertise to all kinds of investigations and we head up the response for cyber-tipline referrals."

"And you print the best pamphlets," I said, totally deadpan, unable to resist the urge.

Steppo looked at Lockner, the SSA trying to swallow down a burst of laughter. The data specialist still did not understand my humor when Lockner intervened.

"Mick, Steppo's fiercely proud of our divisions and our work," he explained but raised his eyebrows high just for me.

Intense and sensitive, his expression whispered.

"Hey, you don't have to sell the SBI to me," I covered. "My wife's a proud agent."

"As for Maureen Li's coded laptop and the files, we got it all," Steppo announced. "I could give you a brief depiction of-"

I bet you couldn't, I thought about the 'brief' part.

Luckily, Lockner made the save with an interruption.

"Mick had the files open before we got here," he reminded him. "He asked Victor Jackson to do it; you remember."

"Oh, of course," Steppowitz allowed and nodded at me, though arrogantly. "And I'm sure the information, incomplete as it was, may have helped. However, we're running a drillfire on the portion of the files that held the secrets and sins this Jackson character encoded before-"

"We haven't extracted any more than Jackson left us," Lockner deflated him. "Mick, I was hoping you might convince Mr. Jackson to open it up for us instead of leaving us to break it open."

"I doubt he could have done anything that can stop us when we get going," Steppo bragged, popping his fat fingers.

"Right, unless he programmed it to do a nuclear wipe if it's tampered with," Lockner retorted.

"Eric, I know we wanna get the Revolver. I know, like me, you probably think there's information in the file that will help with that. But there's a lotta dirt and private matters tucked away in there that don't involve the Revolver. Plowing through everyone's personal pasts-"

"Has to be done," Steppo insisted.

"Hey, calm down," I snapped, too sleepy to catch myself. "How much coffee have you had, anyway?"

"Mick, I'm sorry," Lockner started.

"How did he know about the coffee?" Steppo asked Lockner.

"What I was gonna say was that plowing through everyone's personal info should be done with a lotta care and with an assurance of confidentiality," I said. "It may be necessary, not just for catching our gunhand but for catching some other criminals previously untouchable. However, the other privacy factors need to be protected at all costs."

"Privacy is overrated," Steppowitz said. "No one should feel allotted any level of privacy, whatsoever. In fact-"

"Steppo, go stick your head in that pot of coffee," Lockner ordered.

He said it with the flat, deadpan delivery I would have used.

The other agent wandered away, considering whether or not he really had to put his head into the pot at the nurse's station, I was sure.

"Mick, we'll be as professional as possible," Lockner told me. "But the information is going to be golden, I suspect. For instance, we extracted the name of another contact Lyles worked with to get info out there to the Ghost Revolver and some others. A hacker calling himself, or herself, the Scribe. This Scribe kept their stuff posted on the mercenary sites and the hiring pages, all like that. Dirty dog, that one."

"The more tips we learn like that, the more we can use," I said.

"Exactly. And I've got an appointment later today with some Feds rolling out of their Charlotte field offices. If I get the information open before they get involved, I can make sure it's respectfully used for the right reasons. When they take it over, I won't have that purview."

"I know, Eric. Let me talk to Vic. He's a stand up guy. Speaking of control, how did you land lead on this? All the way out here?"

"One of my agents was involved, endangered. It's agency courtesy, so far, anyway. The SBI SSA for this region gave me the green light."

"Here's to family having your back," I said, "so far."

He finally laughed a little before I asked a question.

"Any news on Paul Blackwood?"

He shook his head.

"None. It's like he simply disappeared."

"City boy from London, lost in North Carolina mountains? If he doesn't turn up..."

"Movie of the week," he said.

"I wish Telly Savales wasn't dead," I offered thoughtfully. "He'd make a great me."

Lockner chuckled and we shook hands, again.

While telling the story later, Mick Priest reminded the entire crowd back at the little hotel that Paul Blackwood might still be alive. Time would tell and there was no need to anticipate the worst.

No one there mourned him very much. In essence, at first glance, it really seemed that no one cared. Perhaps they were all just tired or worn. Maybe they had endured all the negativity they could undertake for a time. Whatever the case, nightfall brought no fear, no dread to them. Darkness veiled the little hotel and the surroundings but the lights fought it back well enough. The power did not fail. The air conditioning blew and cooled well. The horrors of the Ghost Revolver and its weekend slowly, reluctantly began to edge into the past, to vaporize into memory. As far as the participants were concerned, no one was going to focus on it. They had survived and made it beyond the weekend; it was over. The crowd seemed bold, comparatively speaking.

Of course, the place was still crawling with state police and the county Sheriff's Deputies.

At an outside pool, the survivors gathered with refreshments and an unreal kinship. The trauma and the fear had cast a bond between them. It felt to most that they had known each other for years, as if they knew each other closely, intimately. Their time together was at an end; even in their newfound calm, a melancholy regret lingered.

For some more than others.

Most of the survivors sat around the pool and lounged but Kess Melkin was never one to shy away from a chance to strip down in public. She had pried on her bikini and enticed B'Rone Matwahali to join her in the water.

Tayla Barlowe also got into the pool. Little Emma would have it no other way. They played at the shallow end where Sarah Priest sat, chatting with them. Johanna Crimson sat near them at the shallows, only her feet in the water. No one knew what to say to Crimson about Gibson but that was okay with her. She did not know what to say in response if anyone worked up the courage to ask about him.

James Wyatt watched over them from a short distance. He sat with Andreya West and the watchful SSA Eric Lockner. Lockner had brought Mick Priest back from the medical center.

Andreya took a liking to Lockner instantly, as Sarah had predicted.

"Supervisory Special Agent D. Eric Lockner," West said again, tossing her hair back, "tell us about how this will play out for all of us. Will there be a lot of witness testimony? A lot of court?"

James rolled his eyes.

"Will you stop saying his whole title and name like that?"

"She's fine," Lockner said dismissively.

Attention from a woman like West was not chafing him, in the least.

"I happen to like his name. I like the initial. It gives such formality, a regal sound to things."

"It stands for Dennis," James Wyatt said with a frown. "What's regal about it? No offense, Lockner."

"None taken," he said.

"I like Dennis," she said.

"That much is clear," James said, wryly twisting his smile.

"I meant the name," she answered.

"Oh, that too?" James asked.

"To answer your questions," Lockner derailed, "there will be official statements, affidavits and electronic statements taken. I don't know how many of you will be called to testify, to what you would testify or to how much. I wouldn't expect a lot of you to be tied up too long with the process unless you directly saw some of the actions and interactions."

"So, you got no clue," James said with a laugh.

"The way I said it sounded a far cry more impressive," Lockner said, almost smiling.

"Gibson wasn't the Revolver," Priest said. "Neither was Lyles. And neither was his blackmail partner, Li. They were all just associated. Now, they're all dead. Paul Blackwood's still missing. With three weekend victims dead, no one else wounded and no one else suspected, I don't really see what any of us can testify to, Eric."

Andreya West turned her big eyes to Priest's own.

"We're proceeding with caution. We won't take chances with their lives," Lockner said, nodding at the group. "The search is still on for Blackwood and we're still hoping for the best."

"Good to know," Priest said. He did not look away from West's stare. "I'm thinking of joining the search tomorrow. Who knows? We might even find the lost revolvers."

"I'd call that a miracle," Lockner continued.

"I don't think it so unlikely," West said with a tilt of her head.

"I might tag along," James Wyatt said.

"The more eyes the better," the SBI agent agreed.

Priest nodded.

"If they find Blackwood I hope he has some answers," West said. "If he could give us some insight it would be nice."

"Any insight he offers would likely reflect on his own guilt or innocence. The crimes, the 'sins' in the file...they make some strong allegations," Lockner said.

"I wish I'd checked everybody for bruises on the ribs, like I planned," James said. "I told Gibson I was gonna but it never played out. I'd like to know if baker man was black and blue."

"The Ghost Revolver had on tactical armor," Priest reminded them.

"Oh, well. If he's guilty of anything else and he ain't our masked man, I bet we never see him again," James said.

"Not surprising," West chimed. She shrugged, again challenging Mick Priest's eyes, saying, "That is the reputation, isn't it? No innocents, no quick decisions, only strike the really despicable...and no mistakes."

"Oh, there was a mistake this time," Priest said with an odd little smile of his own. "The Revolver crossed me; I won't likely forget."

"I'm sure the ghost won't, either," West said. "You may remember each time your bad knee flares up but the Revolver is bound to feel your presence along the rib cage for quite a while...body armor or not."

The stare down, the fierce glare.

In that moment, Priest saw a tiny nick on Andreya West's right hand.

It could have been anything, especially after she had been scurrying about in the garden. So, why did his mind immediately whisper at him?

Slide bite.

Had they never checked her hands when they checked the others? He was too tired to grapple with it. At least, for the time at hand. It would wait one more day.

"If you'll excuse me," Mick Priest said then.

"You out, Mick?" James asked.

"I have an ongoing vacation I'm missing," Priest informed.

As he stood up, wincing with the pain, he pointed to the shallow end of the pool. Sarah Priest, Tayla and Emma Barlowe and Johanna Crimson were there, waving to him.

"So, it's over?" Andreya asked before he walked away.

The question had been openly posed to the table but, somehow, he knew she was asking him, specifically. What was she really asking?

Water splashed and a woman's voice howled. In the pool, Melkin and Matwahali played like teenagers. At a table sat Gretchen and Jenkins, not close in their chairs but eyes locked and hands touching, going slow.

Cassandra Clark leaned against Tye Richter under a gently flapping canopy.

Let it go, Priest told himself, drawing a breath. *One night. Give it one night. You don't know anything for sure, anyway.*

"I'd say, at least for tonight, it's over," Priest said.

Lockner did smile then and lifted his glass of tea.

"To its final ending," he said and West giggled.

Priest left the table and went straight to his lovely wife. There he started to play with Tayla Barlowe's little girl.

James saw the look Andreya West gave Eric Lockner and he huffed.

"If ya'll think I'm gettin' up and leavin' to give you time to get to know each other, forget it," he told Lockner. "I'm just gonna sit right here. I'll mind my business, be respectful. I'll even be quiet. But I ain't leavin'. Ain't losin' my seat. I don't mind bein' as quiet as a third wheel but I ain't a flat and I don't need changin', so third wheel I am. I mean, I know how to be quiet when I need to..."

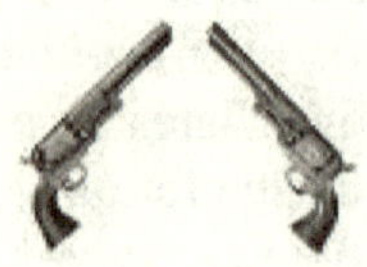

It was over for a lot more than just one night, as it turned out. A couple of months passed without an incident resembling any Ghost Revolver operation.

The Revolver is holstered, James would go on to say, bragging.

It still haunted me. It was incomplete. It was not over.

We found Paul Blackwood, however. The man had been run down and killed in the woods, running for his life. Bludgeoned to death.

He was not the Ghost Revolver.

Then there was West, in and of herself. I always felt like I had only been seeing a photograph of her, never seeing *into* her, like I did most people. One of the gifts of a good investigator is seeing more than what individuals wanted to reveal. Andreya West seemed invulnerable to it. I felt unable to penetrate the woman's veneer.

Sarah giggled over it at one point, however. Apparently, West had said the same of me. The woman had become a regular guest in our home, dating our friend, Eric Lockner, and she had gotten comfortable with Sarah.

What is it with you and her, anyway? Sarah had asked.

She told me I seemed to be in surveillance mode when she was around, watching her, not visiting with her. She told me my conversation leaned toward interviewing or interrogation, not chitchat.

I don't chitchat, I always said and just left it at that.

Eric Lockner had been able to answer one of my questions, however.

There had been confusion over my listing in the secret file and in the guest file. As Victor and I had gone over with James, I had been invited into the weekend by James Wyatt. I was never invited as a writer.

Yet, in the files, I was listed as an invited guest with a contact agent, no less. I was listed as an invited guest and I was listed as a target of the Ghost Revolver, with egregious 'sins' for which I had to pay.

Lockner's tech team had uncovered the link. Rembrandt Lyles had sent that write up to Gridlock Publishing, as we all knew. He had listed me with the other guests and put his own contact information in as my agent. Maureen Li had never tried to contact me, however. She had apparently looked at my body of work and thought I was not big enough to invite and not big enough to blackmail, either. Lockner told me it was literally happenstance that I was invited by James Wyatt instead, on a working weekend, not a writers' retreat.

Of course, I knew there was no happenstance. I was right where God wanted me to be, doing His work. He saw to that.

As for my 'sins' and the way Remy Lyles was put onto me, that connection was simple and a ghost from my own past, so to speak. Lyles was getting in close with Brenda Lynn Wright, a former member of a corrupt, influential women's organization known as the Belladonnai Violettes. They were a group not unfamiliar with vigilantism, either. Sarah and I had been key in stopping and exposing the group.

For her input and support, Wright had told Lyles to set me up for a fall. Put the Ghost Revolver on my trail, like the others, with lies. He had done his best but failed. Brenda Lynn Wright and some of my other old playmates from the evil ladies only organization would be going right back to prison after more conspiracy charges.

I would have to drive to Wilmington and pay them all a visit. I wanted them to know I was still alive and I know. I know about it all.

Tayla Barlowe kept in touch, true to her word. She was serious about adopting us as parents and as Emma's honorary grandparents. We loved it as much as they did and we promised them that if and when the Revolver ever came around again, if they were on the naughty list, the killer would have to go through us.

Our famous friend, the implacable Velvet Edge, Ms. Johanna Crimson, kept in touch, too. She kept James as her head of security and his business boomed like never before. I was happy for them both; James deserved to be big time and Crimson, Ms. Tabby Grey, deserved a good friend, confidant, and protector.

Just like that, the summer rage had passed. Soon enough, fall came upon North Carolina. The cool wind of seasonal change brought on thoughts of change in general.

Only God is eternally the same. All other things change. It is the natural order of the world and everything in it.

I put my free flowing, black pen to paper and scribbled down a few notes. I wondered about how to start yet another story. A story about redemption and the love God has for everyone.

After all, is any other story worth telling?

Even at our worst, Jesus Christ loved us and came and died for us, taking on our sins and our shame and setting us free...if we can just accept the gift. Freedom. Eternal life. Forgiveness. Love.

I had to tell that story again, this time through the lens of a man who knew it well; Mark Gibson.

I was going to tell Gibson's story, detailing his painful road through hate, vengeance and murder, all the way back to the loving Savior and the always forgiving, ever waiting Father God. But what words to start it off? What way would be best to set the stage for a man who died from an old style, cowboy shootout in our modern times?

Again, I put pen to paper as Sarah walked up behind me where I sat and slid her arms around my neck.

"Stop thinking so hard," she whispered. "Let it flow. Let it tell itself. All legendary stories do."

I smiled softly. Legendary.

"Fire's goin' out. Gonna get cold. Better get up some wood."

The little man fidgeted nervously. He stepped from one dusty boot to another, wringing gloved hands. In the flickering light of the campfire, his eyes were hard to see though he turned them skyward. The agitated individual watched the full moon as if he were watching a clock.

"Clinton, that's the third time you done said that," another man said.

Flat on his back on a wool bedroll, head propped up on a downed limb and covered by his hat, he gestured for the first man, Clinton, to go away.

"You wanna go pick up sticks, go. But quit yer yammerin' 'bout it."

"Yeah, yeah, I guess," Clinton said. "I just...ya know, we got that posse ridin' after us...it's got me all worried. My hair's standin' up like an ornery ol' cat's."

"Oh, no foolin'?" the resting cowboy said. His sarcasm was as disdainful as his expression beneath the dusty hat. "Never woulda knowed it."

"Easy, Kent," a third man warned. "A little worry keeps ya livin'. Go on, get that wood, Clinton. An' you get first watch. Stay awake with your fire."

He sat with his back to a rocky formation, hat pulled down to cover his eyes. The man was difficult to see, even in the firelight, dressed in all black. His bone handled, silver revolvers glinted brightly enough, however, as he cleaned them, readying them for reloading...

THE END

I hope this tale has both entertained and inspired. For those wondering
where our detective's cases could lead from here, fear not.
As one adventure comes to a close another is already brewing. Keep a
lookout for the next 'Mick Priest' novel,

Trail of the Priest .

Until then, enjoy and God bless you.

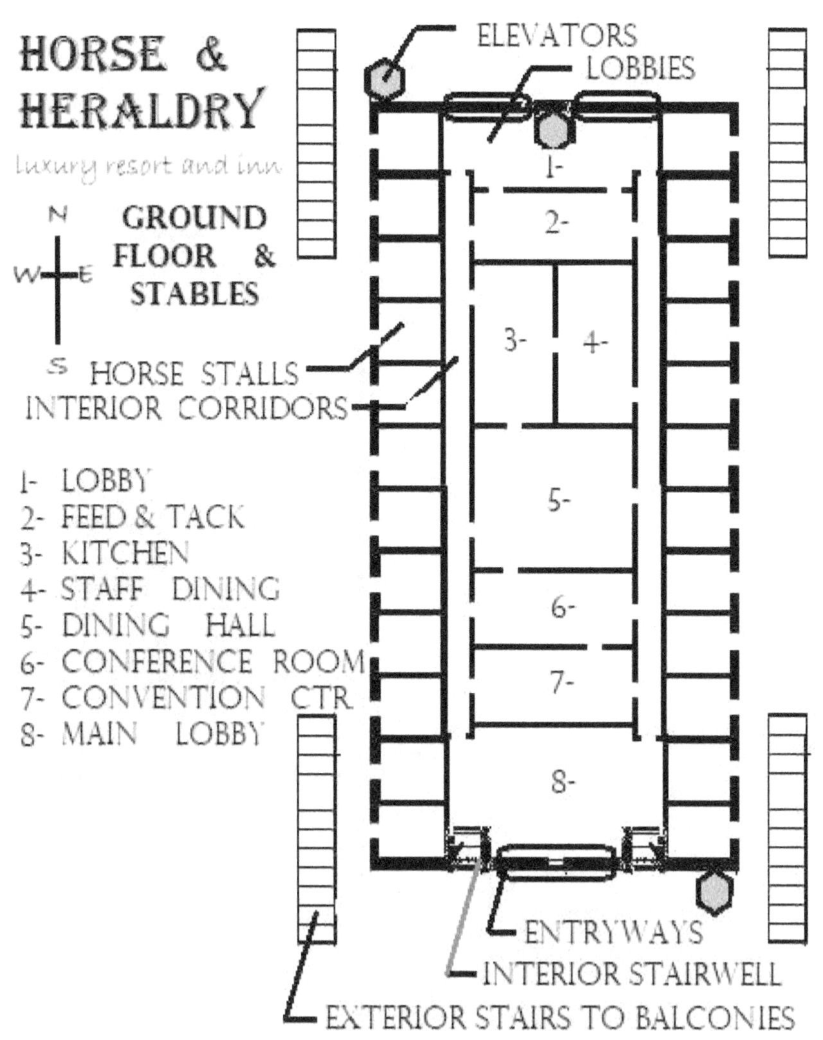

GROUND FLOOR

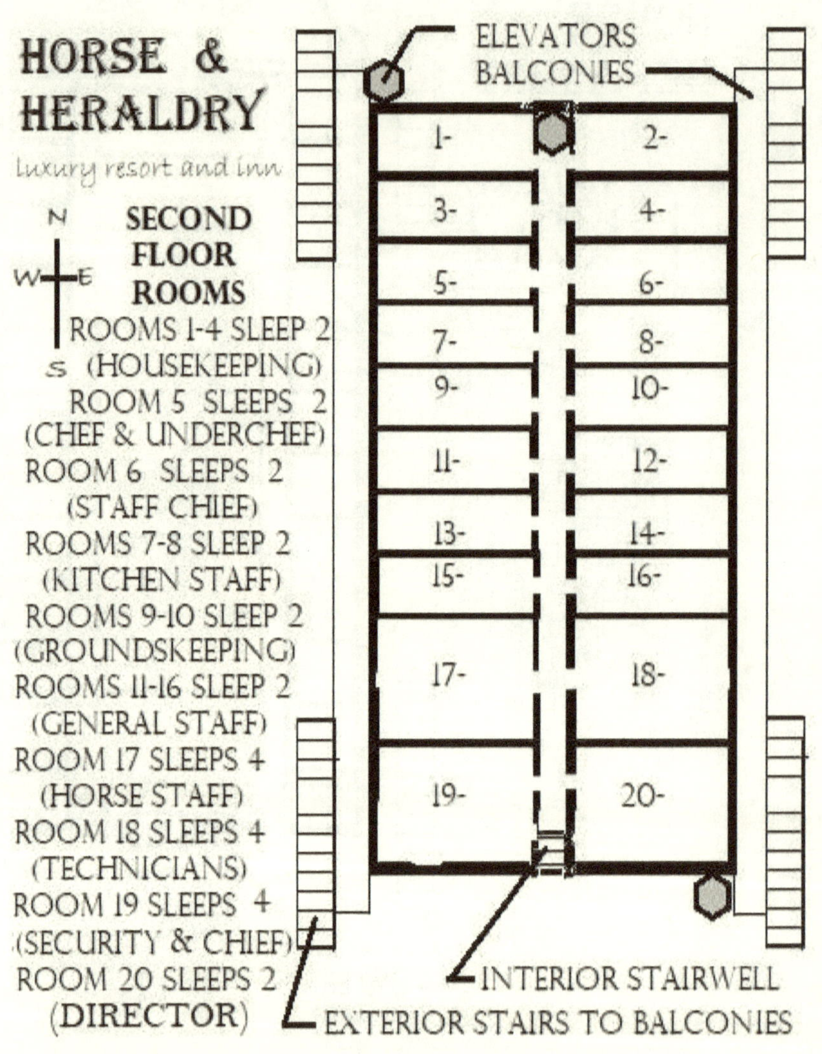

SECOND FLOOR

HORSE & HERALDRY
luxury resort and inn
N
W E
S
THIRD FLOOR ROOMS
1- Rembrandt Lyles
2- Kimber Mobley
3-
4- R.C. Porter
5-
6- Paul Blackwood
7-
8- B'Rone Matwahali
9-
10-
11- Kesley Melkin
ELEVATORS
BALCONIES
1
2
4
6
8
11
INTERIOR STAIRWELL
EXTERIOR STAIRS TO BALCONIES

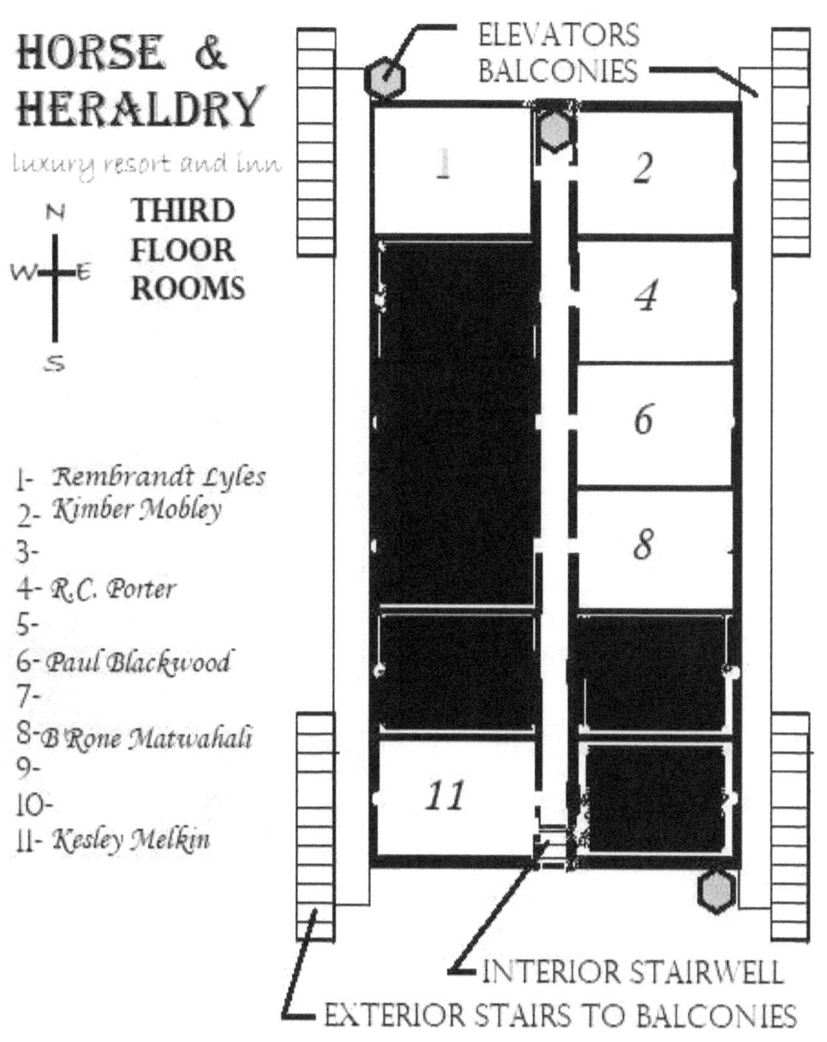

THIRD FLOOR

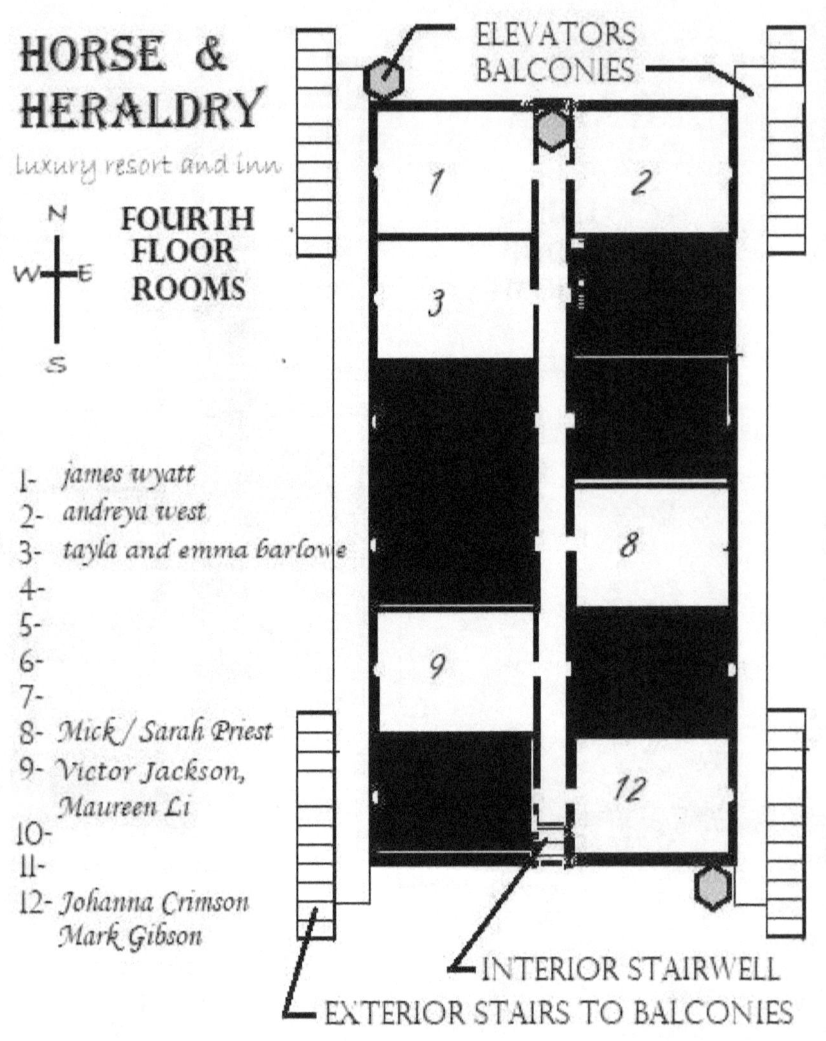

FOURTH FLOOR

www.ingramcontent.com/pod-product-compliance
Lightning Source LLC
Chambersburg PA
CBHW021057110726
47900CB00007B/1920